ENDORSEMENTS

A sweet western romance novel set in South Texas, 1880. I enjoyed the sassy and competent Maggie Gallagher who cares for two orphan children, relations of hers. The complication when Alex Lancaster is found wounded and with a memory loss pulls two strong-willed but likeable characters together. Struggles with witchcraft and intrigues combine with believable relationship conflicts. They must deal with suspicion and mistrust issues when secret, unhappy pasts clash. Good pacing of development of relationships. Appreciated the surprise twist.

— JANET CHESTER BLY, AUTHOR AND CO-AUTHOR OF 32 FICTION AND NONFICTION BOOKS

Molly Noble Bull produces another western novel that is so authentic I felt as if I were there in South Texas. I've been there a number of times, and she has the setting perfect. I loved the characters who tugged at my heartstrings throughout the story, and I kept turning pages to find out how it would all end.

— LENA NELSON DOOLEY, AWARD-WINNING, BEST-SELLING AUTHOR OF OVER 30 BOOKS

This book is dedicated to Charlie, Bret, Burt, Bren, Jana, Linda,
Angela, Bethanny, Dillard,
Hailey, Bryson, Grant and Grace, Carmen, Noe, Kathleen, and Kathi.
But to God give the glory.

And Laban had two daughters:
the name of the elder was Leah, and the name of the younger was
Rachel.

Genesis 29:16, KJV

MOLLY NOBLE BULL

2016
First Place
TEXAS
ASSOCIATION OF AUTHORS
Christian
Western

Scrivenings
PRESS
Quench your thirst for story.
www.ScriveningsPress.com

Published by Scrivenings Press LLC
15 Lucky Lane
Morrilton, Arkansas 72110
https://ScriveningsPress.com

Edited by Kathi Macias

Printed in the United States of America

2nd Edition

Note: This book was originally published in 2015 and is being republished as is.

Paperback ISBN 978-1-64917-100-9

eBook ISBN 978-1-64917-101-6

Library of Congress Control Number: 2021933310

Cover by www.bookmarketinggraphics.com.

All scriptures are taken from the KING JAMES VERSION (KJV): KING JAMES VERSION, public domain.

All characters are fictional, and any resemblance to real people, either factional or historical, is purely coincidental.

Published in association with Joyce Hart, agent, Hartline Literary Agency

AWARDS

When the Cowboy Rides Away won the 2016 Texas Association of Authors contest in the Christian western category.

In the same year, *When the Cowboy Rides Away* also placed in the Will Rogers Medallion Award in the Inspirational Western Fiction category.

1

Southern Texas
Early May 1880

S omebody was coming.

Maggie Gallagher slowed her sorrel mare. A small dust cloud hung over the north pasture like a puff of smoke. As she continued to eye the trail of sand and dust, it grew larger.

She glanced back at her younger sister. "Hurry up, Sarah. A rider's headed this way. See if you can get ole Short Legs to trot."

The little red-haired girl covered a yawn with the back of her hand. "I said I was coming."

"Well, can you get that pony of yours to move a little faster? We need to go on out to the cemetery, leave our flowers, and rush right home. A caller will probably be waiting for us at the house when we get back."

The main house was over a mile from the ranch cemetery and a mere twenty miles from the Gulf of Mexico—and it was almost always windy there. In fact wind and South Texas were like many married couples—together, but sometimes fighting.

The morning breeze felt cool on Maggie's face, but that wouldn't last long. By noon the temperature could reach 100 degrees. Her aunt often said that South Texas was the only spot on earth where the wind could be hot, even in the shade.

She loosened the bow under her chin and pushed back her blue-flowered bonnet. She might as well sit back in the saddle and enjoy herself. It was obvious Sarah was in no hurry.

Maggie thought about the dust cloud she'd seen. She wasn't expecting visitors. But since company appeared to be on the way, she hoped it was Roger. He'd said he might ride into town. On the way back to his place, he often stopped by the Gallagher Ranch to leave Maggie the mail he picked up for her, and she was hoping for a letter from Aunt Violet.

HE'D WATERED his horse in a creek with only a trickle of water in it and crossed a bridge. Now, Alex Lancaster guided his black stallion through thick brush, leaving a trail of dust and sand behind. He had to find Dee. Until he did, nothing else mattered.

But his horse needed rest. The animal wouldn't hold up much longer without it, and he'd pushed him relentlessly since he rode north from the border, stopping at creeks and lakes when he found them, sleeping and then moving on again.

Now he wasn't sure exactly where he was. The entry gate said Ranch Headquarters, One Mile, but it didn't include the name of the ranch.

He thought the ranch he was searching for was at least fifty or so miles north of here, but as long as he was in the area, he might as well stop and check. At the least he could water his horse again, and maybe the ranch owner would give him directions.

Alex could barely see the outline of a two-story house in the distance, but that was enough to keep him moving forward. He would talk to the folks at the headquarters, cool off for a while, and then head out and keep going until he found her.

But would she let him explain what happened? Would Dee be able to forgive him?

Alex blinked, sucking in his breath. Would he ever forgive himself?

MAGGIE LOOKED BACK. Sarah kicked her pony with the heels of her black boots, and the paint horse broke into a light trot. At ten Sarah Ann Gallagher was eleven years younger than Maggie. Yet she still wasn't as comfortable on a horse as Maggie had been at six, nor was she as handy in the kitchen.

Maggie glanced at the clump of spring flowers clutched in Sarah's hand. The bouquet looked slightly wilted despite the colorful blossoms. "Sarah, don't drop your flowers."

"I won't."

"Good. We'll need them if we expect to put some on each of the graves."

Turning her attention from Sarah, Maggie saw that the dust cloud was bigger now. She squinted for a better look. Was she imagining things, or was that a rider on a black horse? Roger didn't own a black horse as far as she knew. Whoever was coming sure wasn't him.

ALEX WISHED he'd bought a straw hat before heading north; his felt one made his head feel even hotter. Sweat poured down his forehead. He pulled out a white cloth and wiped his face and neck, but it wasn't so easy to wipe away memories of what happened in Brownsville, Texas.

He could still see Dee in her white wedding dress and veil,

standing beside him in front of God, Pastor Garza, and a few other people. The joy he felt at Dee's cottage in Brownsville on their wedding day would have lasted a lifetime if the pastor had been a real one instead of a wolf in sheep's clothing. Joe Garza was no more a man of God than Alex was a millionaire.

Alex knew that common-law marriages were legal in Texas because of the lack of preachers on the frontier, so in the eyes of the law, Alex and Dee were married. But Dee would never be satisfied with anything less than a Christian marriage; neither would Alex.

Alex was no lawman, but he'd thought he was a good judge of character—until Garza robbed a bank in Brownsville the day after the wedding. That was when Alex learned the truth about Joe Garza. Alex got so riled up when he discovered that Joe only pretended to be a minister, the bank robbery was the last straw in the hat. Alex had to go after him—lawman or not—and bring the crook to justice.

Alex's jaws firmed just thinking about it. He'd trusted the man and encouraged Dee to trust him. But plainly their marriage wasn't legal in the true sense. Once he realized that, he'd followed the fake preacher-turned-outlaw across the Rio Grande River. Unknown to Garza, Alex hid in the brush while Garza buried the money. Later, after Alex reburied it, he searched the streets of the Mexican village for Garza. But he didn't find him until that night when the outlaw came out of a cantina.

Alex rubbed the small scar on his chin as he recalled that fateful night.

Lively music had blared from inside the Cantina. A soft glow came from the lamps that lined the front of the white structure. Garza, in ragged trousers and wearing a wide sombrero, held a bottle in one hand. He'd stumbled around, no doubt from too much whiskey. Then he turned, saw Alex, and threw the bottle at him. Alex ducked, and Garza pulled a knife from his belt. A fight followed. Alex's nose was bloodied, but he avoided the knife except for a small cut on his chin.

The next thing Alex knew, he and Garza were incarcerated. Alex was thankful they were put in different cells and later in different prisons; otherwise, one or both of them might not have survived three years in a Mexican jail.

Alex had wanted to write to Dee while he was in prison, to explain everything and let her know he intended to return to her. But he wasn't allowed to write Dee so much as one letter. Inmates in Mexican jails had no rights, not even American prisoners who were innocent. Now more than ever he had to find Dee and make amends.

Alex squinted straight ahead. The house was a little closer now but still some distance away. It stood on a rise and looked shiny-white in the blinding Texas sun. He wanted it to be Dee's home, but it wasn't, not this far south. In any case, Alex sensed that he had another problem. Someone was watching him.

He gazed around and didn't see anybody. Still, he felt that somebody was out there. He knew ranchers didn't take kindly to strangers on their land; whoever owned the white house wouldn't either. He could get shot for trespassing, especially after nosing around that cabin.

Alex entered a plowed field. A feeling of foreboding shot through him. He pulled back slightly on his reins and looked over his shoulder. Had he seen something he shouldn't have when he rode over and took a look at the wire fence and then the cabin? Was he being followed now? Or was he just spooked from spending three long years behind bars?

———

THE BLACK HORSE and rider Maggie saw earlier seemed to vanish in a burst of cutting wind that whipped the sandy soil all around them. Blinded for a moment, Maggie wiped her eyes and brushed away grains of the whitish sand sticking to her lips. As she opened her mouth to remind Sarah not to hold the stems so tightly, a gunshot reverberated off to their left.

Both horses shied. Sarah grabbed her saddle horn to keep from falling off.

"What was...what was that?" Sarah asked in a shaky voice.

Maggie jerked around in the saddle, gazing off in the direction from which the rifle blast came. Dust hovered just above the brush-line.

"Don't worry." Maggie tried to feign a calm response. "I'm sure it's nothing to worry about."

She wouldn't tell her little sister they might have plenty to worry about. The shot came from the same direction as the dust cloud. If somebody was shooting on Gallagher land, Maggie wanted to know about it. It appeared the gun was fired from the other side of a group of small trees.

One of their ranch hands plowed that part of the ranch yesterday, but Maggie didn't know who might be there now. The trees obstructed her view.

"It's probably one of our cowboys shooting at a rattlesnake or something," Maggie said after a long pause.

She couldn't share with her little sister that the gunman couldn't be any of their ranch hands. With the exception of an elderly cowboy they called Big Lupe, all their men were working cattle on a different part of the ranch now.

The dust cloud moved away at a rapid speed.

"What's happening?" Sarah demanded in an unsteady voice.

"Don't worry. Everything's going to be fine."

Maggie was tempted to grab hold of the reins Sarah held and lope back to the house, pulling her sister and the pony behind her. But someone could be hurt out there and in need of help. She couldn't leave without knowing.

"Why don't you stay here?" Maggie suggested. "I'll ride over there and see what's going on."

Sarah's eyes widened and her face paled. "Please don't! Do you expect me to stay here all alone?"

"I thought you could for a minute while—"

Sarah shook her head. "No! Take me with you."

Maggie took a deep breath and released it. "All right, but stay behind me."

They hadn't traveled more than fifty feet through the tall grass when Sarah trotted Short Legs up beside her.

"Maggie," she whispered, "do you really think somebody shot a rattlesnake out there?"

Maggie hesitated then decided to speak the truth. "No, I don't. And don't you make a sound."

Sarah whimpered, but Maggie didn't have time to stop and comfort her.

They skirted the trees; then Maggie saw something, though she wasn't sure what. A dark object lay in the plowed field beyond the tall grass. It looked too big to be a coyote or a newborn calf.

"What is it?" Sarah whispered.

"I don't know yet."

The moment she said it, Maggie knew that what she saw was a man in dark-colored clothes.

Sarah gasped as if she came to the same realization. "Is he dead?"

"I'm not sure."

Maggie's heart pounded so loud she imagined Sarah could hear it. She knew better than to become involved in unknown situations, especially with her little sister at her side. Hadn't her late parents warned her time and again about something like this? But as a Christian she couldn't leave a wounded man out there in the open. Without attention the poor stranger could die.

Maggie dismounted slowly, handing her reins to Sarah. "You stay right here. And don't try to follow me over there when I'm

7

not looking, hear?"

Sarah nodded.

Maggie's hands shook so much she had difficulty unhooking her small quirt from her saddle horn. If only she'd thought to bring a rifle.

Taking control, she gripped the thin leather whip firmly. She'd only planned to be away from the ranch house for a short time, and her late father's pistol and rifle were heavy and burdensome. She'd left them behind. She would never leave the house unarmed again.

The braided leather quirt wasn't much, but it was the only weapon she had. She felt slightly more confident and crept forward then glanced back at her sister.

"If anything bad happens," Maggie said, "I mean real bad, I want you to hightail it back to the house and ring the bell. Promise?"

"I promise."

"I'm counting on you, Sarah Ann."

Terror rose in Maggie's throat at the thought of what she might find if she moved any closer. After what happened that day five years earlier, approaching any man she didn't know tied her insides in knots. And there was no way of knowing if this man was dead or alive—or dangerous.

Oh, she could play the part of a secure person; her role in life demanded it. She was responsible for rearing Sarah and Jon Anthony, her late sister's child. But inside where no one could see, Maggie was soft like melted butter.

She needed to lean on her faith and pray. Somehow, simply knowing that God had promised to be with her always gave her the courage to continue.

Maggie turned back toward the man on the ground and started walking toward him again. Her heart slammed against her ribs with each step. Out of the corner of her eye, she combed the pasture for any strange movements that might indicate a gunman lurking in the area.

A flock of doves fed on the ground nearby. She took another step, and they scattered. Maggie jumped as if she hadn't expected it to happen. The rustle and white flash of their wings when they soared upward startled her a second time. She looked around cautiously before going on.

Blood. Maggie gasped, digesting the situation. The sight of blood always made her queasy, and the man's left shoulder was almost covered with it.

2

The wind caught the stranger's hat. Maggie watched it fly through the air as if invisible hands had grabbed it and wouldn't let go. At last the dark-colored Stetson caught on the branch of a tree at the edge of the clearing, dangling in a way that added to the unsettled feeling in the middle of her stomach.

She forced herself to look back at the cowboy. Blood oozed from his shoulder and upper arm and from a big cut on his head. The man wore a brown shirt, dark brown trousers, and cowboy boots. As far as she could tell, he might already be dead.

Maggie wanted to turn around and walk away, but her moral upbringing wouldn't let her. She forced her attention to the unmoving man.

He lay in the middle of the plowed field, his face turned to one side and caked with dirt. Steeling herself, she bent down and searched for a pulse. She found one, but it was weak.

The large bump on the back of his head might have been caused by the plow. It was right next to him, partially buried in deep sand along with two other pieces of farm equipment. Whatever had happened, it was obvious she needed to do something to stop his bleeding before his weak pulse gave out altogether.

Her white blouse wasn't dirty, but she had put it on before daylight. She needed clean cloth for bandages. She lifted her riding skirt. Her divided petticoat would have to do. She ripped white fabric from the hem and bandaged his shoulder and head wounds as best she could.

Maggie expected to see a horse in the plowed field. She didn't, but horse tracks caught her attention. The stranger must have been riding a horse when he entered the field. But where was the animal now?

She imagined his horse might have bucked at the sound of a gunshot. Deep hoof prints marked a small area nearby. The man must have fought to control his horse until his wounds got the best of him. Without a rider's skill in restraining animals, the horse no doubt raced off somewhere, leaving the injured man behind.

She studied his wounds again. The bullet hit his left shoulder, and he must have hit his head on the sharp edge of the plow. Neither of these facts explained who shot him.

Somebody was still out there, probably on foot and walking a horse. Who could it be? And why did he or she shoot this man? Maggie paused to consider, but the questions themselves sent a stab of fear straight to her heart.

The wounded cowboy could be an outlaw. The possibility sent a shiver down her spine. Still, as a human being he deserved medical attention. In fact he needed to see a doctor, but in his condition he might not survive a trip all the way to town in the back of a wagon.

Maggie intended to help the stranger if she possibly could. At the same time she wanted to make sure her little sister was safe.

"Come here, Sarah."

The child sat on her pony. She didn't move.

"I said, get over here, Sarah. Right now."

Slowly Sarah nudged her pony forward, pulling Maggie's mare behind her, but she didn't dismount. Her cheeks were colorless, and her shoulders shook. The flowers tumbled to the ground.

"Is he still...alive?" Sarah asked.

"So far."

Before she died, their mother had taught Maggie some basic nursing skills, but she didn't feel prepared for the task ahead. She'd applied the bandages in an attempt to stop the bleeding, and she prayed she'd done it right. There was nothing else she could do where they were; she needed to get him home.

"Listen to me very carefully, Sarah, because I want you away from here. Now ride as fast as you can back to the house, and as soon as you get there, ring the bell."

She frowned. "Real loud, or...?"

"Loud." Maggie hooked her reins to the limb of a tree, reminding herself that Sarah was still a child. "The men won't hear the bell because all of them are out in cow-camp except Big Lupe." Maggie did her best to speak calmly and gently. "But their wives and families will hear the bell if you ring it hard enough. Tell them what happened here, and they'll come running." She paused so Sarah could absorb her words. "Any questions?"

"I guess not."

"Then get going."

Maggie turned to check the man's bandages and thanked God when she discovered the blood had stopped flowing. She stood and pulled her blouse loose from the waistband of her skirt. She wiped her hands on the long shirttail hem and let out another deep breath. When she glanced back to check on her sister, she realized Sarah still hadn't moved.

"I thought I told you to go."

Sarah sat like a stone statue astride her pony. The frozen

look in her eyes reminded Maggie of a rabbit an instant before being struck by a rattlesnake. Maggie started to insist that Sarah go on then remembered a few more instructions she'd forgotten.

"When the ranch families get up to the house and you've told them what happened here, tell them to get the wagon."

"Which wagon?"

"The only one that's there, for heaven's sake." Normally patient, Maggie rolled her eyes upward and shook her head. "The other wagon is out in cow-camp with the men."

"I forgot."

"Well pay attention now because this is real important. I want you to tell the folks back at ranch headquarters to hitch up the mules to the wagon and drive out here as fast as they can. Bring blankets, sheets for bandages, Mama's medicine kit, and… and a gun and plenty of bullets." Maggie studied the quiver in her little sister's lower lip. "Can you remember all that?"

Sarah nodded slowly, though her expression was anything but confident.

Maggie unhooked her reins from the tree. "Now get off that pony of yours and ride my horse. She's faster."

Sarah's eyes went wide again. "But I've never gone that far on horseback by myself before, and—"

"Then today you'll do it for the first time. This man could die if you don't."

Maggie hated putting such pressure on a ten-year-old, but she had to do something to get Sarah to move.

She reached up and took the pony's reins out of her sister's hands. "If you really want a full-size horse like you've been begging for, you'll get off that pony and ride mine." She slipped the narrow strips of leather over Short Leg's head and held them. "Come down, Sarah. Now."

The child did as she was told. When Sarah had mounted the sorrel and taken hold of the reins, Maggie handed her the quirt.

"Take this, and use it."

Sarah frowned.

"My mare will run if you make her. So get going, and don't look back."

Sarah's green eyes radiated fear. Yet she pulled the mare's head around in the direction of the house as if she'd done it a million times.

Maggie had coasted on a sudden burst of energy since hearing the gunshot. Her sister's riding success seemed to dissolve that energy. She tied the pony to a bush nearby and sat down by the cowboy. Her heavy breathing came more from the uncertainty of the situation than exhaustion.

She looked back at the injured man. When she saw no change in him, she diverted her gaze toward her sister. Sarah was galloping the mare back to the house, surrounded by a thick cloud of dust and blowing sand.

At least Sarah got away from here.

The cowboy lay on his stomach, looking lean and about Roger's age. A gun belt circled his waist. She felt a little better when she saw his gun still in the holster.

From what little she knew of gunshot wounds, he'd been shot in the back of his shoulder. The bullet must have gone all the way through and out the front. Obviously, he'd lost a lot of blood, and he still wasn't moving. But since he was breathing, maybe he had a chance.

It could be quite a while before the wagon arrived. Until then there was nothing more she could do for him.

She couldn't help but notice his slim body, and his legs were long like a young colt. Under all the blood and dirt, his skin looked dark probably from the Texas sun. Then she noticed something else. A bit of white paper protruded from the back pocket of his trousers.

Maggie reached down and pulled out a weathered envelope.

The printing looked dim. At first she declared it unreadable but finally managed to make out the faded script.

The letter was addressed to a Mr. Alexander P. Lancaster in care of Juan Villa, Vasite, Mexico. Maggie wondered if the cowboy was Mr. Lancaster and why he lived in a small Mexican village like Vasite. Maggie had visited Vasite once with her father when he went there to buy horses. At the time she was about nine years old. She remembered the ranch owner had a son perhaps eight or ten years older than Maggie. She recalled vividly the smell of burning firewood in the kitchen hearth and the desolate surroundings just beyond the grounds of the big ranch house.

She shoved away the memory to concentrate on the envelope she held in her hands. Printed in small letters in the upper left-hand corner was another name and address: Mrs. Willard Parson, 211 Elm Street, San Antonio, Texas.

Maggie wasn't accustomed to reading mail addressed to someone else, but she needed to learn the cowboy's identity. He certainly wasn't talking, and he could have a family somewhere. She convinced herself it was in his best interest that she learn all she could, so she opened the letter. A three-year-old date was printed in one corner of the page: February 15, 1877. She began to read.

Dear Alex,

You may be surprised to hear from me again so soon, but you did not answer my last letter. I am glad you are enjoying living and working for Mr. Villa on his ranch in Mexico, but I cannot help but be concerned about you. After all, you are my only brother, and I am anxious to learn what happened with Dee. I would also like to hear about your trips to Brownsville. I have always wanted to visit there. Maybe now I can. My husband sends his regards. Did I mention that I am in the family way? In September Will and I are looking forward to the birth of your first niece or nephew. Write when you can.

Love,

Ruth

Maggie gazed off toward the pasture, not really seeing anything. Her mind was too caught up with thinking about Brownsville, for it was there her late sister, Sadie, had lived and taught school before she died. Maggie had always loved Sadie and still did. She'd tried not to judge her, but it hadn't been easy.

The repercussions of what happened in Brownsville would be with Maggie and her family for the rest of their lives. She needed to put her grief out to pasture and concentrate on helping the injured man, but sometimes the past pounced on her when she least expected it.

Maggie started to put the letter back in the cowboy's pocket then decided against it. The thought of reading and keeping somebody else's letter went against her moral code even when she had a good reason for doing it; it was like peeking into a window while the curtains were only partly drawn. Still she sensed it might be important to hang on to it. And at least now she knew where the stranger came from and the name and address of his sister.

Or did she? How could Maggie be sure the wounded man was Alexander Lancaster? Just because the cowboy had a letter with that name printed on it didn't mean a thing.

The thought bothered her as she glanced down at the injured man again. He hadn't moved; he looked so still and helpless. A lump formed in her throat. If this man was the Mr. Lancaster mentioned in the letter, he had kinfolk in San Antonio who cared about him. It was her duty to let them know he'd been shot.

Her gaze settled on the blood again. A wave of what her mother had called a "weak spell" swept over her. She couldn't give in to it. She had too much to do.

A shooting hadn't turned up on the Gallagher Ranch in years, and Roger had said the sheriff went on a fishing trip and wouldn't be back for a week or more. What a time for the sheriff to be miles away.

She closed her eyes and bowed her head. If she'd ever needed to pray, it was now. When she finished she opened her eyes.

Maggie stiffened, sensing someone watching. She'd been so caught up in nursing the man, worrying about Sarah, and then praying, she hadn't had time to think much about her own safety. The person who took a shot at the stranger could be waiting for the opportunity to strike again.

Maggie pulled his gun from the scabbard. Then she stood, scanning the area. Nothing moved for miles but the wind in the grass and the branches of a few scrubby trees.

3

The wagon finally appeared on the horizon. The sun had climbed halfway up the sky, and heat filtered through the clouds like a warm blanket. Perspiration trickled down the back of Maggie's neck. The injured man's Stetson must have blown off its perch, but she found it in the weeds nearby. She still hadn't seen his horse.

On her hands and knees, Maggie hovered over the stranger again, using his hat to fan away the gnats and flies swarming about his head. If he wasn't Alexander P. Lancaster, it might be a while before she learned his true identity, but for the present she'd call him Alex. She had a cousin named Alex and was always fond of the name.

She squinted back toward the ranch and could barely make out the team of mules pulling the wagon. As it moved closer she noticed Lupe Salinas' gray beard as he drove the mules down the ruts they called a road. Concha, his wife, sat beside him. Two other women from the ranch squatted in the back of the wagon. Maggie was glad the three women had come along to help. Without them and their knowledge of nursing, caring for this man might be difficult if not impossible for Maggie to handle.

Once at the house Maggie, Lupe, and the other women carried Alex to the downstairs bedroom that had belonged to Maggie's late parents. After placing him on the bed, the women washed and dressed his wounds and put a compress on his head. Maggie sent Sarah to relieve her maid, Elena, and to bathe their two-year-old nephew, Jon Anthony.

When Maggie turned and glanced toward the bed, the women were gathered around the stranger. She assumed they had removed the cowboy's tattered clothes and were bathing him. Blushing she shut her eyes and turned away.

"You must go now, *Señorita*," Concha Salinas said in broken English, "until we finish washing the *Señor*."

"Will he…recover?" Maggie asked.

"If there is no poison in him, he should live. The hole, she is clean, and the bullet, he went through his shoulder and out the other side. But the *Señor* is in the sleep of death. And I am not sure he will ever wake up."

Maggie winced. "Ever?"

Concha nodded then went back to supervising the man's bath. Maggie moved toward the door but had no intentions of leaving. If Alex lived, she'd be partly responsible for nursing him back to health, and she needed to learn a lot more than she knew now in order to do it.

The women huddled around the bed, blocking her view. Maggie leaned against the back wall to catch her breath and wait.

When they finished the Mexican women walked over and stood by the windows. Petra and Juana whispered in Spanish.

Even from across the room, Maggie could see they had dressed him in one of her papa's old blue shirts. She moved closer to the bed for a better look. Instead of giving off the odors of sweat and blood, his skin now had the clean, fresh smell of lye soap mixed with Hooper's Ointment and other medicines she couldn't identify.

Her heart skipped a beat. A man with a face that handsome didn't come along every day, not in these parts. Maggie had her back to the other women in the room, and she intended to keep it that way. The last thing she wanted was to let them see her reaction.

His brown curly hair shone in the sunlight coming in from the open window, looking damp to the touch and as thick as Maggie's. His cheekbones were high and well-defined, and he had a square jawline, punctuated by a cleft chin. Since his eyes were closed, she couldn't tell their color, but his lashes were long and black.

Maggie knew he would be tall and broad-shouldered because of the way he filled up the wagon, but she never expected him to be so young looking. She did her best to assume a bland, unreadable expression and turned back around.

The younger women watched her, amusement gleaming in their brown eyes; almost immediately their smiles turned to laughter. Petra and Juana sang silly songs in Spanish about women who liked good-looking men and told jokes that were only funny in the Spanish language. Maggie found that once translated into English, all the humor in their stories vanished, but she'd always enjoyed hearing them—until now.

She glanced down at the wooden floor. Obviously her facial expressions were readable after all. Looking up again she noticed Concha standing apart from the other women.

Concha clapped her hands. "Enough." She motioned for everyone to be silent. "The *Señor* needs rest."

Petra and Juana stopped talking.

Maggie wasn't surprised. Everybody respected Concha and followed her orders because she was the oldest woman on the Gallagher Ranch.

The old woman started to walk off. Then she whipped

around, focusing her black gaze on Maggie. "If this man lives, it will be because the Lord doesn't want him to die, no?"

Maggie nodded. "Yes, that's true."

"Then I think Jesus must have sent you this man, *Señorita*, to be your husband."

"Husband?"

"*Sí*. May you have a long and happy life together, and may he give you many sons and daughters."

Sons and daughters? On hearing that statement Maggie figured her face must have turned as red as Sarah Ann's hair. But she couldn't think about that now. She needed to go out and see how Sarah had managed with the baby.

Elena poked her head in the door. Two-year-old Jon Anthony slept in her arms. Sarah Ann peeped around from behind Elena.

"Show me the wounded man," Elena demanded in Spanish.

Maggie swallowed before answering. "Of course, Elena. And will you please remember to talk to me in English in front of Sarah from now on? A South Texas ranch-child like Sarah needs to feel comfortable in both languages, and she's been speaking mostly Spanish lately."

Elena moved forward. The hard look in her eyes indicated she might resent Maggie's request, though she said nothing.

Maggie stepped to one side to make room for her. "And Elena, I'll want you to do most of the nursing for this man."

Elena grimaced, handing the sleeping child to Maggie. Then she moved over to the bed and peered down at Alex. For an instant Maggie thought she saw a hint of recognition in Elena's dark eyes, as if she actually knew the injured stranger. Then her expression went blank, and she whirled around and started for the door.

"I want you to stay, Elena," Maggie said. "The other women have to leave soon to cook for their families. I'll need your help in here."

Elena looked over her shoulder. "What about the baby? Who will take care of Jon Anthony when he wakes up?"

"Sarah Ann can take care of him."

The servant turned, aiming an icy glare at Maggie. "I will not work in here."

"Excuse me?" Maggie was stunned. Elena hadn't refused to follow an order since Jon Anthony was ten days old—the day Elena put lighted candles all around the child's baby bed. When Maggie ordered her to remove them, she wouldn't—until Maggie insisted. Elena had confessed she learned this strange practice from her father who was a *curandero*, a sort of witchdoctor. Now, as they stared at one another across the room where the stranger lay, Maggie wanted to know why Elena was behaving so strangely.

"I will not take care of this man." Elena glanced at Jon Anthony. "My job is to take care of this motherless child." The look she sent Maggie was filled with anger. "When I first come here, *Señorita*, you say I clean the house, help with the other chores, and take care of Sadie's baby boy, no?"

"Yes, but—"

"I no hired to take care of sick people," Elena said in broken English. "I will not do it. Get someone else to help you in here."

"There isn't anybody else. All the other women have husbands and children to take care of."

Elena shook her head. "I will not do it, *Señorita*. You do it."

Maggie couldn't believe what she'd just heard. Elena was often difficult, even stubborn, but never quite *this* stubborn.

If her mother were alive, she would fire Elena on the spot, but Maggie didn't have that option. Even a little help from a servant was better than no help at all.

Elena marched out the door, leaving Jon Anthony in Maggie's arms. She kissed the sleeping toddler on his forehead, trying to pretend Elena's outburst didn't matter.

The other three women left before the afternoon heat rose

with the climbing sun. Concha promised to return the next day and clean the man's wounds. Until then, Maggie was on her own.

"Sarah." Maggie forced a smile. "As you can see, the baby is still sleeping. Sit with the cowboy for me and hold Jon Anthony, will you? I need to change clothes and fix dinner. When we finish eating you can play with Jon for a while and then put him down for his afternoon nap."

"Do I have to?"

Maggie's smile dissolved into a frown. "You know the answer to that. And you'll sleep in Jon Anthony's room tonight."

"Where will you sleep?"

"On a cot in here."

"In here?" Sarah looked dumbfounded. "You're gonna sleep in the room with a man?"

"I most certainly am."

"What would Mama have said if she were…alive?"

"If Mama was still alive, I wouldn't have to do it. But she isn't, and somebody has to take care of this poor man."

Sarah opened her mouth as if she planned to say something. No words came out.

"Hurry up now, Sarah," Maggie said, "and do what I told you. I have a lot of work to finish before sundown, and you have to help me." As an afterthought Maggie wiggled her nose at her little sister in hopes of making her laugh. It was a sort of game the two sisters had played since Sarah was three.

Sarah neither wiggled her upturned nose nor smiled.

Maggie tried again. "I want to thank you for doing what you did today, Sarah Ann. Riding off like that for the first time was a brave thing to do. I'm very proud of you. Papa would have been proud too."

Sarah's grin surfaced then, and her green eyes sparkled. "Do you really think so?"

"I know so."

With Jon Anthony in her arms, Sarah sat down in the rocker by Alex's bed and started rocking.

Maggie smiled. Her little sister was not immune to flattery. And Sarah *was* brave—at least on that day. Maggie meant every word she'd said.

That night the moon was full. Maggie sat in the chair by the wounded man's bed, reading several chapters from a mystery novel that had belonged to her late father. It was about a family who lived in a castle in England. Then she read a chapter from the Bible like she always did every night. She wondered if she would be able to sleep.

By midnight the moon was a yellow ball in the middle of the sky. It was almost as bright outside as it was inside before Maggie blew out the lamp. From her cot under the double windows, she could see the bed and the man who slept on it.

Slowly she unbraided her blonde hair and let it fall about her shoulders. Her hair was long enough for Maggie to sit on, with shorter strands curling around her face. She rested her head on the feather pillow and tried to relax.

Her papa had always liked long hair. He'd often said the glitter and shine in Maggie's golden locks gave the stars something to worry about. Yet she'd almost forgotten her nightly ritual—100 strokes. She rolled over on her side and reached for a hairbrush on the chest of drawers nearby. But she didn't pick it up.

A white candle in a metal candleholder caught her attention, reminding her again of the time Elena surrounded Jon Anthony's bed with lighted candles—and of the fact that Elena's late father was a witchdoctor. In Mexico he was called a curandero, and when Elena first came to the ranch, she followed some of the ceremonies she had learned from him. However once Maggie insisted Elena put those strange practices behind her, she did. At least, Maggie thought she did. Elena had even studied the Bible with Maggie and Sarah a few times. Still Maggie wondered. Was Elena really free of the curandero curse?

Maggie remembered that on the day two years ago, when she saw for the first time what the curanderos do, she was in the hallway and the baby was crying. They never kept a woodstove anywhere near the hallway, yet it felt strangely warm for December.

All at once the smell of smoke caused Maggie to stop in her tracks. It was so strong she could almost taste it, and for a moment she couldn't stop coughing.

She'd prayed the smoke and hot air weren't coming from the baby's room. Then she'd closed her eyes, trembling as another thought formed in her mind.

The house is on fire.

She raced to the open doorway, praying as she went. Fiery lights so blinded her that for a moment she was unable to see the infant's crib. She covered her mouth with her hands. *He's only ten days old!* She hurried inside.

Scores of lighted candles circled the baby's bed. The heat in the room was tremendous. But how did candles get in here?

The baby screamed. She dashed forward, her eyes on the bed. Then she sent up a quick prayer of thanks. Her precious nephew was at least a foot from the flames.

Jon Anthony's baby bottle fell out of the crib, landing on the floor. She glanced down. Another step and the skirt of her blue dress could have caught fire.

Maggie looked around for something she could use to smother the flames. Her gaze found her housekeeper, seated in a chair in the corner. "What is the matter with you, Elena? Get over here and help me put out these candles."

Elena didn't move.

"Are you asleep?" Maggie said in Spanish.

She longed to speak to the servant and the ranch cowboys in English, but Elena didn't know English then. In fact nobody on the Gallagher Ranch spoke much English since the deaths, not even Sarah.

"Wake up, Elena, and help me." Maggie reached for the quilt on the top shelf. "You get the other one and do as I am doing."

"Do not put out the candles, *Señorita*," Elena finally said in Spanish. "They will keep the evil spirits away."

"What are you talking about?" Maggie replied. "Get up and help me."

Quickly Maggie extinguished the candles. When the last one was out, she cuddled the crying child in her arms as she realized Elena still wasn't helping, though she was out of the chair and standing a few feet from it.

"I'm going to sit in this chair you are so fond of now and hold Jon Anthony until he stops crying," she informed Elena. "And I want you to clean up this mess in here. Then we will talk about why you put lighted candles just inches from the baby's bed."

Elena stood there for a moment, glaring at Maggie. At last she folded up the scorched quilt and put it back on the shelf.

"And throw away all those candles," Maggie added.

"No." Elena whirled around. "They are mine. I will not throw the candles away."

"Oh, yes you will if you want to keep working for me. You could have set the house on fire with those candles. I want them away from here now."

"I brought the candles with me from Mexico, and they are very dear to me." Elena continued to glower at Maggie. "They belonged to my father. He used them when he healed people."

"Healed people? The curandero?"

"Si."

Maggie would have fired Elena instantly if the servant wasn't such a hard worker, but she needed someone to help with the children. Elena was new to the Gallagher Ranch and didn't know the rules, so Maggie decided to give her another chance.

"Do you promise never to light those candles again as long as you live here?"

"Si."

"All right then, but leave the candles. I'll put them away. If I decide to let you go, I'll give them to you then."

"Thank you, *Señorita*."

Maggie noticed something small and white under the crib, something that shouldn't be there. "Bring me that thing under the bed, Elena. I want to see it."

Elena stared at her again. Maggie wondered if the servant was going to refuse another request. Then Elena got down on her hands and knees and retrieved the object.

"What is it?" Maggie asked.

"An egg."

"How would an egg get under the baby's crib?"

"I put it there."

Maggie frowned. "Why?"

"The baby's forehead felt hot. I think he had a fever. I put the egg under his bed to make the fever go away."

"That must be something else you learned from your father." Maggie took a deep breath to steady the pounding pressure in her head. "We are a Christian family, Elena. We don't believe in witchcraft. I won't allow such nonsense in this house. If I decide to keep you on here, you must forget what you learned from the curanderos and never practice such evil on this ranch again. Do you understand?"

Elena had looked away, but she turned back and nodded. Maggie still wasn't sure she really meant it.

Ranger, Maggie's hound dog, barked, bringing her back to the present. She glanced at Alex, and he moved his good arm.

Instantly alerted she sat straight up in bed. In the novel she was reading the dead man moved his arm in the same way. But of course he'd only pretended to be dead. Was Alex Lancaster awake now, feigning sleep for unknown reasons?

The book was on the table by his bed. Had she allowed a made-up story to cloud her judgment?

Still, if he opened his eyes as the man in the story did and turned his head to stare at her, at the least she would finally know whether he was sleeping or playing possum. If need be, she would stay awake all night in order to find out.

During the next long hour, she sat waiting to see what Alex might do. Her mind conjured up all sorts of reasons not to trust him.

Who was this man, really and truly? He could be anyone. He could be an outlaw. Why else would someone want to shoot him? Maggie forced herself not to dwell on such thoughts.

Alex Lancaster moved again.

Her heart pounded so hard she thought she could feel it through her heavy cotton dress. Concha had placed the cowboy's pistol and holster in the trunk at the foot of his bed along with the other items she found in his pockets.

Should she get the gun while she had the chance? Or had she substituted imagination for common sense? A man with injuries as serious as Mr. Lancaster's couldn't actually harm her, could he?

Maggie moved to the trunk on tiptoes and removed the pistol. It felt cold to the touch. It didn't make her feel invincible, but she felt a lot better with it in her hand.

Somehow she'd managed to retrieve it without making a sound. She thanked God for His help in making that possible and started to cock it...then stopped. If she cocked the pistol, she would make a noise, maybe loud enough to wake up the man. Still she clutched it firmly in both hands.

"Better safe than sorry," her papa always said.

The man's breathing sounded normal. He snored once or twice. Slowly Maggie began to relax but not enough to risk falling asleep. Still grasping the gun she sat down at one end of the cot with her back to the wall.

"Dee," he whispered between partly closed lips. "Where are you?"

Maggie tensed. Could this be the Dee mentioned in the letter? What if Alex thought Maggie was Dee and he hated the woman? She positioned her forefinger on the trigger.

He groaned, and she saw that his injured shoulder pressed hard against the mattress. He turned over on his right side and went back to sleep. The pistol grew heavy in her hands.

After a minute or two, she allowed the gun to drop to her side. Later she slipped it under the cot. Her eyelids drooped, and the desire to sleep engulfed her. For a moment the room grew quiet except for the *tick, tock, tick* of the old clock on the wall beside the bed.

Outside night sounds both soothed and haunted her. The wind had changed to the north. Shivering Maggie got up to close the shutters attached to the north window. As she hooked the latch, unpleasant barnyard odors drifted over from the milking pens. Maggie wrinkled her nose then went back to the cot and sat down.

Crickets chirped. A locust called. In the distance coyotes yipped and yelped. A chilly wind played and whispered among the live oaks, while Ranger howled back at them all.

She thought Alex slept soundly enough for someone in his condition, but she wouldn't close her eyes until her doubts disappeared.

None of this would have fazed her late sister, Sadie. Why, Sadie could listen to scary stories by the hour without one goose-bump popping out. But Maggie was made from a different mold.

She stretched her legs. She told herself she shouldn't fall asleep, but what could be wrong with resting her head on the pillow for a minute?

Slowly her eyes closed.

THEY FLUTTERED OPEN AGAIN. It had to be morning because sunshine streamed in the east window. She blinked and sat up then glanced at the bed.

The man was awake, watching her...with the bluest eyes she'd ever seen. Maggie felt trapped, but her fear subsided a little when she noted the gentleness in his hooded gaze.

"Are you an angel?" he asked with a heavy Southern drawl.

"A what?"

"Are you my guardian angel?"

Guardian angel? She eyed the cowboy warily. He looked a little woozy, which might explain why he'd asked such an odd question. His voice sounded weak and non-threatening, but his question baffled her. She wasn't quite sure how to reply.

At last she said, "No, I'm not an angel."

"You're not?"

She shook her head. "No."

He sighed. "Then I reckon I better explain."

She waited, wondering what he would say.

"When I first woke up, I saw you sleeping there in your long white apron over your blue dress and your yellow hair all spread out around you, and I figured you must be my guardian angel." He watched her a moment. "So if you're not, who are you?"

She raised her eyebrows. "Who are you?" she shot right back.

"Well, I'm..." He angled his head to one side. Briefly he fixed his gaze on the wall near the foot of his bed. A strange blank expression appeared on his face, like Sarah's writing slate when nothing was written on it. "You know, ma'am, I couldn't answer that question if my life depended on it."

4

M aggie watched Alex from a cot near his bed. Had he really lost his memory? She'd never known anyone who had. Should she reveal the name Alex Lancaster and other facts mentioned in the letter? She paused, giving herself time to think. The mystery novel she was reading warned against it.

In the book a woman lost her memory, and the case sounded a lot like the cowboy's. Maggie concluded it could be dangerous for Alex to learn too much too soon. If only she could talk to Doc Smyth to make sure the doctor agreed with the advice given in the book.

"Do you remember anything at all?" she asked.

He shook his head.

"Oh. Well, I'm sure your memory will return very soon."

Maggie considered telling him about the story she'd read but decided against that too. She should probably consult a real doctor before giving him any information.

She studied the bandage on his head. "Are you in pain?"

"My head hurts a little."

Alex looked weak and helpless, despite his tall, well-muscled frame. One arm hung limply over the side of the bed. He seemed to struggle to lift his head and was likely dizzy too. But if he was paralyzed with fear and worry, as she'd be if the situation were reversed and she lay in that bed, he hid it well.

Maggie gazed at the small bucket they used as a chamber pot. Concha had set it on the floor to the left of his bed. She should let him know it was there and what it was for, but the thought of actually telling him something of such a personal nature caused her face to warm with embarrassment.

His eyelids slowly closed. Alex needed to go back to sleep, but she hoped he'd be able to answer a few questions first.

"Do you know what happened to your horse?"

"Frankly, ma'am, I don't know whether or not I own a horse."

Of course he wouldn't know. If he didn't know his own name, how would he know anything else? Why had she asked such a ridiculous question?

Alex moved his left arm and flinched. "What happened to me?"

"Somebody shot you—hit your shoulder from behind and it came out the other side."

"Well, I'll be." Alex waited a moment before saying more. "Know who did it?"

Maggie shook her head.

He winced again and sent her a pleading half-smile. "You wouldn't happen to have anything for pain, would you? 'Cause if you do I'd be obliged if you'd fetch me some."

"We keep a bottle of laudanum in the kitchen. I'll go and get it." Maggie felt a blush coming on and turned her back to him. "And there's a bucket on the floor next to your bed in case you... in case you need it."

"Oh, yes. I see it now. Thank you."

Maggie learned Christian values from her parents. Since their death propriety had become even more important. An unmarried woman with two children to raise couldn't be too careful.

She looked down, trying to press out a few of the wrinkles from the shirt of her white apron. The style and thick fabric of her blue dress and apron reflected her modest taste and nature, but the garments really looked wrinkled. And why wouldn't they? She'd slept in them all night.

She wished she were wearing something fresh. Maybe she should iron something. She felt her cheeks warm again. Ironing would give Alex more time to do whatever he needed to do with the bucket.

"I have a few things to attend to," she said without looking at him. "I'll leave you alone now. But I'll be back in ten minutes or so with the medicine."

"I'd appreciate it."

She needed to attend to her morning chores once she got Alex settled. Still she was hours behind schedule, and this was the first morning in years she wasn't up and ready for the day by 5:00 a.m.

Maggie left the room, returning ten minutes later with the painkiller. She'd changed into a green-print blouse and a green skirt under a fresh apron. Alex was sleeping again. She placed the medicine bottle and the spoon on the lamp table by his bed and studied him for a moment to make sure he was still breathing.

She felt ashamed and embarrassed by what she'd thought and assumed about him on the previous night. At the time the poor man lay unconscious, yet she'd falsely accused him of numerous crimes in her heart with no proof he'd committed any of them.

The memory loss couldn't be easy. Maggie wondered what she might be feeling under those circumstances. Being shot was bad enough, but to wake up in a strange house and not remember your own name had to be awful.

She drifted to one of the windows and looked out. Whoever shot Alex Lancaster was still out there somewhere. Who could it be, and why would someone want to do that?

The folks she knew who swam the Rio Grande in order to find work in Texas were humble, honest people. She'd never known any workers from south of the border who owned a rifle. Maggie gulped. From experience she knew that bad people were out there and that they were capable of anything.

She didn't want to recall the unpleasant incident again. It had played out inside her head more often than she liked to remember. If there was a way to make those bad memories disappear, she hadn't yet found it.

Five years ago spring had arrived in early March. She remembered the scene vividly—the flowers, the green grass, the birds chirping in the trees, the scent of clean country air. Yet she didn't want to remember.

She dipped her dusting cloth in the can of bees wax. If she kept busy these disturbing thoughts might go away. Maggie rubbed the brownish mixture on the rounded back of the chair by Alex's bed.

But on the morning it happened, she'd had the urge to pick wild flowers and managed to convince Ana Salinas, Concha's youngest child, to pick some too.

Maggie was told a thousand times never to stray far from the main house, but patches of Bluebonnets and other spring flowers in various pastel colors covered the south pasture behind the ranch house. It would be fun if she and Ana got on their horses and rode out there.

They'd worn sunbonnets that day and carried straw baskets to put the flowers in. Maggie had placed a sharp knife for cutting stems in the big center pocket of her white apron. Her mother had warned that bandits sometimes came across the border to rob, steal, and even kill. But she had dismissed the warning, telling herself, *That was then—when*

Mama was a girl. Texas is safe now. Bandits aren't crossing the border anymore.

The air was cooler than normal that morning as they walked their horses through the corral gate. Ana had giggled and joked, obviously as excited and ready for an adventure as Maggie.

The prettiest flowers dotted a field about a mile from the house. Maggie hadn't planned to travel that far, but she felt justified because the Bluebonnets and Indian Pinks had never looked lovelier.

"Let's stop and cut our flowers now," Maggie had said in Spanish. "We won't find flowers any better than these."

The girls let their horses roam free and graze while they gathered their bouquets. Ana chose a spot near the edge of the brush, but Maggie stayed right where she was, wishing the flowers smelled as good as they looked. But they were almost completely odorless.

She was about to reach for a blue blossom when a man, maybe from across the border in Mexico, emerged from the brush. A chill coursed thought her, locking out her next breath. Before Maggie could make a sound, the man grabbed Ana from behind, placing a brown hand over her mouth.

Maggie froze, too frightened to scream. When her bay horse trotted up beside her, all Maggie could think about was mounting and riding out as fast as possible.

The man threw Ana to the ground. She screamed, and her horse ran into the brush. Even Maggie's horse shied, but she managed to seize the reins. The bay lifted his front legs and plowed them into the sand. Trembling, Maggie swung into the saddle. She didn't know what she should do next, but she knew she had to do something.

The man glanced at her then peered down at Ana. Maggie couldn't see the look on his face, but she imagined him leering at her friend, like a bobcat sizing up its prey.

Maggie's heart contracted as she guided her horse into a

slow walk. Fear of the unknown mixed with rage squeezed her insides. She clutched the knife in the pocket of her apron to make sure it was still there.

Maggie moved toward the man slowly instead of racing away as she so wanted to do. He must have known she was coming, but he was focused on Ana.

When she was near enough to reach out and touch him, Maggie gripped the knife and yelled with all her strength, "Get up, Ana! Get on my horse. Now!"

The man jerked around and glared at Maggie. The hard yet mocking expression on his face was all she saw. Maggie lunged for him, slashing him any way she could. A deep cut startled her. She'd sliced him from just to the side of his right eye almost to his chin. The man fell back, moaning and covering his bleeding face with both hands.

Maggie helped her friend up in the saddle behind her. "Hold on, Ana. We're going home."

The man reached for Maggie's reins, but the blood running down his face must have hampered his vision. He missed the reins, clutching air instead.

God is good, Maggie thought, kicking the bay as hard as she could. As they raced out of the clearing, she glanced back.

The man had pulled a rag from his pocket and was wiping his face. Maggie turned back and hunched over the saddle as they sped through the underbrush. But she hadn't felt truly safe until she saw the big white house at the top of the rise.

Alex moaned and turned over in the bed, forcing Maggie's mind to return to the present. Sometime during the remembering she'd dropped the dusting cloth. Instead of reaching down to pick it up, she gripped the post at the head of Alex's bed with both hands. She shook her head, willing the memories away.

5

She and Ana got away, and some would say the man got what he deserved for attacking them. The cuts to his face must have left scars, but there wasn't time to consider longtime outcomes and repercussions. She'd simply retaliated, using the knife to prevent a greater possible wrong.

The girls were physically unscathed, and she thanked and praised the Lord for that blessing. But what happened in the clearing would remain with them, perhaps forever. Maggie had only seen the man briefly, yet his voice and physical appearance were etched in her mind.

He'd worn a dirty white shirt, tied at the waist, and his nose looked as if it had been broken. He had black hair and eyes, a dark complexion, and as he turned, the scent of garlic and rotting teeth had drifted up to her. Later, when she and Ana were riding away, he'd cursed them in Spanish in a raspy voice she would never forget.

Maggie thought she'd put the past behind her. Yet somehow what happened while picking those flowers had eventually melded with Sadie's tragedy, the death of her parents, and every other unhappy event in her life. Being alone with Alex in the field while she waited for the wagon had triggered that same helpless feeling Maggie encountered in the pasture five years earlier.

She glanced at the cowboy then reached down and grabbed the dusting cloth. It was time to get back to work. Like any other human being, Alex deserved the best care she could give him, no matter what he might have done in the past.

Though his southern drawl sounded pleasing to her ears, he didn't talk like a Texan. Alex was probably from the Deep South. Maggie had never been to that area of the country, but two of her uncles had died in Atlanta during the War Between the States. Someday maybe Alex would be able to tell her about some of the places he lived before coming here. To hear him speak with that warm drawl of his and listen to what he had to say would be almost as exciting as actually being there.

JOE GARZA EMERGED from the Rio Grande River, walking barefoot onto the muddy bank on the Texas side. He'd tucked leather sandals into the pockets of his aged trousers, and he was eager to put them on. Sticker-burrs and prickly-pear thorns hid in the underbrush, not to mention rattlesnakes and irate farmers and ranchers with guns.

Had he really been in a Mexican prison only three years? It seemed longer. Joe was a tough *hombre*, at least in his mind. He'd fought other prisoners just to stay alive. Still the prison guards kept asking him why a man as short and thin as Joe got into fights in the first place.

It was true that Joe was skinny and small-boned, and eating hardly more than tortillas and water for three years hadn't made him any bigger. Nobody knew about the weak spots underneath his rough exterior, and that suited Joe just fine.

He wondered how he should react when he finally saw Alex again. Acting tough didn't work with Alex Lancaster, but Joe knew how to appear scrawny and powerless if he needed to in order to reach a goal. He'd done it dozens of times. He simply let his weak side out and hid the tough hombre.

He pulled out his sandals, dropping them on the damp ground. He wished for a cloth so he could dry off his wet feet, but what did it matter? His shoes were water-logged too. In fact he didn't have so much as a dry inch on his entire body. Recent rains flooded the river. Even his black hair was soaked, and drops of river-water rolled down his face and shoulders.

Quickly he slid his toes into his leather sandals and headed for cover before someone noticed him.

Joe swam the Rio Grande many times in the last ten years, even wading across during a drought. The *gringos* would call him a wetback. But after doing his time in a Mexican jail, he was a free man. He could have walked across the bridge from Matamoras, Mexico, to Brownsville, yet he chose to swim the river. The fewer people who knew he was heading back to Texas and trailing Alex Lancaster, the better.

Joe ducked his head before stepping into the underbrush beyond the river. The trees were small and grew close together. Shadows, scrubby trees, and brush were all he could see. Still he knew of a ranch not far from the border, and that kept him going. Tio worked on that ranch, and though he wasn't Joe's uncle as his nickname indicated, Tio was a childhood friend from Mexico. Joe would be safe there.

He'd tried to think what he would say when he got to the shack where Tio, his wife, and their eight children lived, what lies he would tell them this time. But all he could think about was finding Alex Lancaster and then the money.

A line of small houses where the ranch cowboys lived loomed ahead. Tio lived in the one on the far left, and the last time he swam the river, Joe stayed there.

If it were nighttime, a light would be shining from an oil lamp near the window, but it was mid-afternoon. Yet he knew someone was there because smoke billowed from a metal tube mounted on the tin roof.

As soon as Joe knocked on the door, Tio welcomed him into his home. However, by gringo standards the dwelling was more of a shack. The last time Joe visited Tio's house, Joe stole money from the sugar bowl. But Tio never believed Joe did it. Tio never believed anything bad about anyone. He was an easy man to fool.

It was a hot day, and in addition the hot wind that blew through the open windows, the wood-burning cook-stove inside made the house scorching. Even the dirt floor was likely warm. But at least Tio's wife gave him a cup of coffee, leftover tortillas, and a blanket he could spread on the floor that night. And Tio might have information Joe would need for his plan to work.

The next morning Joe got up before the chickens. He and Tio headed for the holding pens where the ranch horses were kept. Joe would need a horse, and he sure didn't intend to buy one. He eyed the horses from a shed near the pens. They looked old and bony, but even an old worn-out horse was better than no horse at all.

Tio told him exactly where the horses were held and how to find the saddle room. He'd also taught him word-for-word what to say to his boss to make sure Joe was hired on as a ranch cowboy. But Joe only pretended an interest in a ranch job so Tio would show him around. He wanted to find Alex Lancaster and get back the money Joe stole from the bank. Once he got his hands on the money, Joe wouldn't need a job. As the gringos would say, "He would be plenty rich."

IN HER ROOM a few minutes later, Maggie ran a comb through her hair and went out to check on Sarah and the baby. Despite Elena's stubborn attitude Maggie intended to give her a list of duties for the day.

Normally Maggie rang the bell at a little after five and gave the men their daily orders, but today that wasn't necessary. The cowboys were trapping cattle, preparing for the annual spring roundup, and they camped each night in another part of the ranch.

By nine o'clock, Maggie had prepared and served breakfast and soaked most of the breakfast dishes in a big metal pan near the stove. She was pumping fresh water from the hand-pump into a blue china pitcher when her sister put down her fork.

"Maggie, where are you going with our best china pitcher?"

"To take the cowboy some water. And would you please talk to me in English?"

"Oh, all right." Sarah still gazed at Maggie. "Can I go see the cowboy, too?"

"Absolutely not. I want you to correct those arithmetic problems you missed. Then you have to do the next page in your book. Hear?"

Sarah nodded. Then she sighed loud enough to be heard out in the hallway.

Maggie shook her head. Sometimes she wondered if she was capable of raising two children alone.

Her room waited at the head of the stairs, and the downstairs hallway leading to Alex's room was long and dark. She hurried down the hall, wishing she had a small bell so Alex could ring it when he needed something. Maggie doubted she'd be able to hear if he called out and she was in the kitchen. The only bell they had was the big one just off the back porch that they used to call the ranch hands.

Maggie opened the bedroom door and saw Alex sleeping.

She put down the pitcher and the cup, went to her mother's desk by the window, and removed a pen and ten or so sheets of writing paper. She couldn't afford to spend the entire day at his side but hated not to be there when he woke up. Until then she'd catch up on her letter-writing.

How many times was she told that a true rancher didn't go to town unless he or she had a good reason? Her late parents seldom made the trip except to buy medicine, supplies, and gunpowder, or to pay a visit to the doctor.

For a while after Maggie dedicated her life to God, she drove into Bayview to attend church as often as she could. But after her late sister blackened the family name, she stopped attending. Some of the town folks persisted in gossiping about what happened to Sadie, and all that hateful talk couldn't be good for Sarah and Jon Anthony.

Besides writing to Aunt Violet, she would send a letter in care of the address in Mexico that was printed on the envelope. She would write to Alex's sister in San Antonio, and she would also write to the sheriff in Bayview. She'd known the sheriff all her life and would feel better if he knew about the shooting. When she finished her letter-writing, she planned to send Big Lupe into town to mail the letters and fetch the doctor for Alex.

ALEX WOKE up shortly before noon, looking somewhat improved. His eyes showed clarity and focus, and his movements and coordination seemed better too.

Maggie smiled for his benefit, though in the last twenty-four hours she'd developed a bad case of nerves. Being around any man she didn't know made her uncomfortable, and Alex's injuries multiplied the problem. What if he died under her care? True, the injury to his shoulder would no doubt heal quickly, but head wounds could be another matter entirely.

Maggie wouldn't let herself think about it. She would feign a cheerful voice to go with the smile, no matter what. "Hope you are feeling better, sir."

"I'm all right."

"Your laudanum is on the table next to you there if you need it."

"My what?"

"Laudanum. You wanted something for the pain."

"Oh, yes, thanks." He gazed at Maggie. "You know, you never did tell me your name. I don't know what to call you."

"I'm Miss Gallagher, the one who found you yesterday."

"Yesterday?"

Maggie nodded. "Today's Friday."

"And the month?"

"May."

"Thank you." He moved his left arm and frowned. "I think I'd like that laudanum now."

"Of course." She rose from her chair and swept across the room. "I put some laudanum in a small medicine bottle and mixed it with a bit of wine. Expect a bitter taste." She poured the liquid into a spoon. "Open your mouth."

He did as she requested, took the medicine, and swallowed. "Thank you, Miss...Miss..."

"Gallagher," she reminded him with a smile. "Would you like some water?"

"That would be mighty kind."

She lifted his head so he could drink. His dark hair felt soft, curling around her fingers. "Don't try to drink too much at a time. Just take a sip or two and wait."

He drank and paused as she instructed, but then continued to drink until he consumed the entire cup of cool water.

"You know," he said, "you really are an angel of mercy."

Maggie felt a frown coming on. To her way of thinking, his comment sounded inappropriate, and she wouldn't allow Alex or any other man to think she was a loose woman. Maggie straightened her back. She put the cup on a shelf by his bed next to the blue pitcher.

"Would you like something to eat?" Her voice sounded kinder than she felt.

He nodded. "I am kinda hungry."

"I'll have my sister bring you a tray."

A hint of a smile curved his lips. "Is your sister as pretty as you are?"

Her eyes widened at his remark. "My sister's name is Sarah, and she's ten years old."

His smile disappeared. "I've offended you, haven't I? Please accept my humble apology."

Maggie stood there gazing at him. She'd never met anyone quite like Alex and didn't know what to make of him. At last she nodded. Maybe his forward-sounding remarks were merely his way of covering the anxiety and confusion he probably felt—flat on his back and in a strange house. If her papa were alive and in the stranger's situation, she knew he'd try to hide his vulnerability at all costs.

She would give Alex the benefit of the doubt and forget it— this time. But if there were a next time, she would send him to town, even if it meant a rough ride in the back of a wagon.

Maggie bit her lower lip. "I should go now."

She almost tacked the word *Alex* at the end of her sentence, yet she'd promised herself she wouldn't call him by his first name except in her deepest and most private thoughts. Not only had the book she read warned against saying too much to a person in his condition, it wouldn't be proper to call a perfect stranger by his given name.

"I have to finish cleaning up the kitchen," she added. "But I'll look in on you again later."

She'd almost reached the door when she remembered the whistle Concha found in the cowboy's pocket. Why hadn't she thought of it sooner? He could use it if he needed to call her. She whirled back around, and her dark green skirt ballooned out around her.

The smile he sent her in response looked warm and friendly and full of life. She had to force herself not to grin back.

Maggie marched over to the trunk, retrieved the small wooden whistle, and placed it in the palm of his hand. "Blow this if you need something."

He fingered the whistle as if in deep thought. "Where did you get this?"

"From that trunk there. Why?"

"I don't know. It just seems familiar somehow. Reckon I had one like this once?"

"Do you think this means your memory is starting to return?"

"I sure hope so. I'd hate to end up in the loony house for the rest of my life."

Loony house? She chuckled under her breath. Her father had used that very term to describe children who laughed or told jokes at the table, and it had always conjured up mental pictures of a house filled with children, rolling on the floor and laughing.

"Young women are expected to have good morals and be serious-minded," her papa had said. "Only silly young girls giggle all the time."

When she faced Alex again, his eyes twinkled back at her in a way that made her think he wanted to tease the living daylights out of her. Then his expression became more apologetic. Maybe he was sorry for being so unseemly earlier.

Her late sister, Sadie, often said that some men were wolves in sheep's clothing. Was Alex a wolf in wolves' clothing?

Their gazes connected again, but Maggie glanced away. After a moment she looked back. He rolled the whistle between his thumb and forefinger, studying her every move.

"How can I ever repay you for all you've done for me? I figure you saved my life yesterday."

She stood in the doorway with her hand on the latch, wondering how to reply. He sounded truly grateful and so tender and kind she wanted to cry. Yet only a moment before, he'd seemed completely different.

A little-boy-lost look came over his face. She felt protective toward him but couldn't give in to such thoughts and feelings. With a ranch and a house to manage as well as Sarah and little Jon Anthony to look after, she simply didn't have that option.

"I'll have Sarah come in later and read to you." She'd tried to sound soft and melodious, rationalizing that a sick person deserved that no matter what he or she might have done in the past. "My sister does her school work here at home and needs practice reading the Bible out loud."

"Is she the ten-year-old?"

Maggie nodded.

Amusement replaced the tenderness in his blue eyes. "I'm beholden to you, ma'am, and I'll be happy to help your little sister out, as a favor to you. Do y'all look alike—you and your little sister?"

"Actually, I thought Sarah would be doing you a favor." Maggie put her left hand on her hip. "And if you really want to know, we look nothing alike. I'm like my mother's side of the family, and with Sarah's red hair, she looks like Papa's side."

Why did she keep changing her opinions of this man? Why, there were more sides to him than one of Jon Anthony's toy blocks of wood. If she ever saw all the sides at once, her mind would likely explode like an overripe melon. Yet with all those sides to his personality, she still loved the sound of that southern accent of his.

Texans used *y'all* too. She'd always thought of it as the plural for the word *you*, but when he said it, he made her almost wish she wasn't mad at him most of the time.

And bless his heart, he looks so helpless—all spread out in the middle of that bed.

She looked closely at Alex again, and he grinned back at her. Why, he wasn't helpless or weak, not at all. He was possibly as strong as a full-grown bull. Having a bump on his head and being shot hadn't slowed him down a bit.

The sudden realization caused her unwarranted sympathy to turn to instant irritation. Was he trying to take advantage of a young woman and two children living alone?

Still staring at Alex, Maggie blew away a blond curl that had fallen across her forehead. "Well, I never," she muttered then spun around and headed for the kitchen.

ALEX HEARD the metallic bangs of pots and pans. He pictured Miss Gallagher's honey-brown eyes flashing as she puttered around the kitchen, dropping utensils and clattering dishes. Obviously her spirit matched her beauty and charm, yet he sensed a sensitive side to her nature that had to be in conflict with all that fire.

Earlier he'd watched her from under his lashes. He'd awakened when she first came in but had pretended to be asleep in order to observe her without having to stop and explain himself. The young woman he'd called his guardian angel had seemed upset about something, but even when she glided quickly around the room, he liked the way she moved.

She'd floated on the balls of slender feet, dusting things while clearly preoccupied. Maybe angels lived on a higher plane than the rest of the world and felt energized when they helped people or engaged in some kind of task.

He loved the look of her soft ivory skin when a blush colored it peachy-pink, and he liked the way her nose turned up even when her wide mouth didn't. He was sure he'd never met a golden-haired lady that was anything like her. That much passion was usually reserved for redheads.

Alex tensed. What did he know about redheads and golden-haired ladies? The thought had to come from someplace, but he had no idea where.

6

Alex closed his eyes, hoping for a short nap. After a moment the image of a pretty young woman with auburn hair appeared before him. He wasn't certain if he was awake or asleep, but the woman's face intrigued him. As he opened his eyes, the letter *D* flashed into his mind. He didn't know what the *D* meant or why he remembered it, but when he pondered the auburn-haired lady still more, a feeling of deep sadness filled his heart. Alex wanted the vision to continue so he could understand it, yet it faded quickly and did not return.

Who was the young woman with all that reddish-brown hair? Could the *D* be the first letter of a woman's name—his wife's perhaps? Somehow he didn't think so. Too much pain was associated with the letter. If he were to guess, he'd say that he lost whoever the *D* represented, perhaps to another man.

He'd felt disoriented and out of focus since he first woke up. The fact that he'd lost his memory hadn't improved his situation. Did he have enemies who wanted him dead? If so they could return to finish the job, and Miss Gallagher and her little sister might get caught in the crossfire. He could not allow that to happen. Alex resolved to leave the Gallagher ranch as soon as he could muster the strength to crawl out of bed. Of course, Miss Gallagher would insist that he stay even longer if he let her know how weak and helpless he felt. He would have to keep his physical condition a secret.

He thought then about how upset she became when he teased her. Maybe he'd overdone it. The last thing he wanted was to hurt the kindhearted lady who'd saved his life.

The door to Alex's room opened with a creak. He looked toward the sound with anticipation, hoping to see Miss Gallagher again. A young girl with enormous green eyes stood in the doorway, holding a wooden bed tray. The joy he'd felt an instant before faded along with his smile.

The child continued to stand there, staring at him like a judge in a court of law about to pronounce a stiff sentence. He had to admit she was a cute little thing with all those freckles across her nose.

After the burst of memory he'd had earlier regarding the letter *D* and the redhead, it seemed ironic that the child had long carrot-colored braids. Still her reddish pigtails were nothing like the wavy, dark-auburn locks of the young woman in his vision.

"Maggie Sue said I had to bring you this," the child said with a slight accent.

"Who's Maggie Sue?"

"My big sister."

Alex grinned. So that was her name. Maggie was probably a nickname—for Margaret or Margaret Susan, maybe.

But why had the child spoken with a Spanish accent when her older sister hadn't? And where had he learned to identify different kinds of accents?

Alex glanced back at the child. "You must be Sarah Gallagher. Please come in."Sarah studied him carefully as if putting his face to memory, and she didn't move an inch or let down her guard.

"Is that my food you've got there?" he asked.

She nodded. "Yes."

He'd tried to sound as warm and friendly as possible, but she still hadn't moved.

"Something smells mighty tasty. What kind of soup is that?"

"Chicken."

"I don't suppose you could bring the tray over here and set it down on the table by my bed, could you?"

She nodded but still didn't step forward.

"Well, Sarah, I sure am hungry. And I don't rightly know if I can hold out 'til supper, empty as I am right now. Would you kindly bring me that tray?"

The girl hesitated then started toward him at last.

"Thank you," he said.

She set the tray on the small table. Milk sloshed over the side of the pitcher, spilling onto the floor. Sarah bent down and mopped up the mess with a white napkin, but her eyes remained focused on Alex.

He supposed she'd thrown up a barrier against him because he was a stranger, but he wished that weren't the case. He needed as many friends as he could get, and he wanted Sarah to be one of them.

Alex tried to sit up. A blinding pain in his head put a stop to it.

"You're not supposed to sit up." Sarah put a small hand on his chest and attempted to push him back against the pillow. "Concha said you're supposed to lie flat on your back for two more days."

"Who's Concha?"

"The smartest woman on this ranch."

"Are we on a ranch?"

"Of course we are, silly. Where else would we be?" She paused, and her forehead wrinkled like a teacher examining a naughty child. "You sure don't know much, do you?"

He chuckled under his breath. "No, I don't reckon I do."

"But you sure do have pretty hair. So now I'll have to touch it —if you don't mind that is."

"I don't mind at all. But why do you think you have to touch my hair?"

"Elena says a baby will be cursed if you say it's cute and don't touch the baby's head after you say it or even think it. I don't want you to be cursed in case it also means strange cowboys with curly hair like yours."

"Do you think I'm strange?"

"A little, I guess."

He laughed. "Well, I sure don't want to get cursed, so go on and touch my head."

As she reached out and touched the top of his head, he thought of another question. "By the way, who is Elena?"

"She takes care of Jon Anthony. He's my little cousin."

"And are all these people related to the smartest woman on the ranch?"

"Elena and Jon Anthony aren't. But most of the smart people around here are."

"I see." His laugh became a contented smile, and he relaxed against the pillow.

Something thick and bulky was tucked inside the front pocket of the child's apron, and she smelled of rosewater. Earlier that same fragrance had radiated from Maggie's slender form. He wished Maggie would hurry up and come back to his room. He would have used that whistle she gave him to call her if her little sister hadn't arrived when she did.

"I guess a pretty girl like Maggie has a lot of young men courting her," Alex said.

"Maybe. Roger Dawson comes over here all the time, and he's always trying to hold her hand."

"Who's he?"

"A neighbor." She tossed her head. "His family owns a ranch

on the other side of the creek. His house is back a ways." Sarah dipped the spoon in the bowl full of soup.

"And he's sweet on Maggie, huh?"

"I guess so." She guided the spoon to his lips. "Will you please open your mouth?"

Alex had a lot more questions, and the idea of being fed didn't appeal to him. But since he could hardly rebuke a child, he did as she asked.

Sarah turned the spoon a little to one side and poked it in his mouth. A dribble of the warm liquid trailed down his chin and onto his neck. It felt slick on his skin. Maybe it was sticky too. The spoon clattered to the floor.

"Oh, I'm sorry, mister. I dropped the spoon." She reached down and retrieved it.

"That's all right. Don't worry yourself about it."

Alex struggled to keep from laughing out loud when Sarah wiped the soup from his face and chin with the same napkin she used to mop up the spill. Then she dried the spoon with that same cloth before dipping the spoon back in the soup like nothing unusual had happened.

"Will you open your mouth again, please?" she asked.

The next spoonful found its target. He tried not to think about the dirty cloth. The soup tasted salty but was really quite good. He wondered if Maggie had prepared it.

"How come you talk funny?" Sarah asked.

"I didn't know I did."

"It's not so much what you say; it's the way you say things." She cocked her head to one side. "You sure don't sound like anybody from around here."

"Where's here?"

"Texas." She frowned. "What part of Texas are you from anyway?"

Alex smiled. "You ask too many questions."

He failed to add that he couldn't remember where he came

from or much of anything else. But he'd learned some interesting particulars from the child, things he planned to consider later.

As soon as he finished eating his soup, Sarah reached in the big pocket of her white apron and pulled out a small Bible. "Maggie said you wanted me to read to you."

"She did, did she?"

Maybe Maggie expected him to get upset or turn the child away. He would do neither. "Do you like to read the Bible, Sarah?"

"I might if I understood it." Her eyes widened. "Would you help me with the words I don't know, Mr. Cowboy? Maggie always asks me questions on what I read each day, and sometimes I don't know the answers."

"I'll try my best to explain the words you don't understand, but I can't promise I'll be of much help. Is that all right with you?"

She nodded, flipping to a page marked with a blue ribbon. "I'll start with chapter one of the Gospel of John." She cleared her throat. "'In the beginning was the Word, and the Word was with God, and the Word was God.'"

Alex had no idea who John was, but as soon as she started reading, he felt the words were written for him alone, and he was sure he'd heard them before. It was almost as if the author of the Bible knew him personally, knew everything about him and exactly what he needed to hear. Even in Sarah's little voice, the message captured his full attention.

Sarah finished reading, and she hadn't needed his help with any of the words. She started to put the Bible back in her pocket.

"No, please. Don't put your book away. I would like to borrow it...if I can."

"You want to read the Bible?"

"If you don't think Maggie would mind."

"She wouldn't mind. She'd be glad. Besides, Maggie has another Bible in her room." Sarah handed the Bible to Alex. "But it's not just a book, sir. Some folks call it The Good Book. We call it the Holy Bible."

"I think I'll call it the Holy Bible too." Alex hesitated. "I guess Maggie must read the Bible pretty regular."

Sarah nodded. "She reads it every day, word for word. She makes me read the Bible every day too." Sarah slanted her head to one side and gazed up at Alex. "Do cowboys like you read the Bible?"

"I can't speak for everybody. But from now on I plan to read it as often as I can."

After Sarah left, Alex read the Bible until his eyes grew tired. Then he went to sleep. When he woke up again, two pairs of black eyes studied him. He flinched and hurt his shoulder.

"Lie still, *Señor*," the old woman said with a Spanish accent. "I am Concha, and the boy, he is my grandson, Little Lupe. We are here to help you."

Little Lupe looked to be about ten or eleven. Alex tried to shake the boy's hand, but Concha prevented it. Then she attempted to remove Alex's shirt.

Alex recoiled, a wave of embarrassment sweeping over him. He reached for the covers and pulled them up to his neck.

"You must hold still, *Señor*," the woman warned. "You could hurt yourself. You will let us help you, no?"

He considered saying *no,* but he was helpless in his present condition and needed assistance. At last he said, "Yes."

They bathed him then changed the bandages and dressed him in an oversized blue cotton shirt exactly like the one he'd been wearing. The process took at least twenty minutes. In all that time the woman and boy spoke in Spanish as if Alex didn't exist. He didn't let on that he understood every word they said and that he'd gained privileged information he might not have heard otherwise. Alex was pleased to learn that he understood the Spanish language because it told a little about his background and about himself.

"I am leaving now, *Señor*," the old woman said when she finished. "My grandson, he will stay and help you."

"Thank you." Alex turned toward the child. "You speak English, boy?"

Little Lupe grinned from ear to ear. "*Si, Señor*. I speaky the English good."

Alex soon learned that Concha was indeed the smart woman Sarah told him about, and that Little Lupe hoped to be a cowboy someday like his grandfather, Big Lupe. Things were going to be easier with the boy around to help him, but Alex missed Maggie and wondered where she was.

MAGGIE STEPPED INTO THE KITCHEN, gripping the handle of the empty wash bucket. She'd fed the chickens and hung wet clothes on the line outside. She released a deep breath. Now what chore had she intended to attack next?

The piercing sound of a whistle echoed through the house, and Maggie jerked to attention. Was the cowboy in danger? She raced down the hall to Alex's room. The door was open, so she barged right in.

"Well, Maggie Sue." The edges of his teasing eyes crinkled with merriment. "It's good to see you again."

"How do you know my name?"

"Sarah told me. Or was it Little Lupe? Guess my memory isn't what it should be today."

"It's not your memory I'm worried about; it's your attitude."

Still holding the bucket with one hand, Maggie moved closer to the bed and put her other hand on her hip.

"Maybe wherever you came from men act the way you do. But around here men show more respect for their womenfolk."

"I didn't aim to show you disrespect, ma'am. I respect you for sure. I was having a little fun, that's all. Don't you people joke with one another in your family?"

"We do." Unconsciously she drummed a soft metallic beat on the side of the bucket. "But not the way you do it."

He sent her a searching gaze. "Why are you always so nervous around me?"

She took a deep breath, willing herself to be calm. "I'm sorry. Guess I'm just tired."

"Overworked more likely, and I reckon it's my fault. Not only did I heap extra work on you, but I've been teasing you besides. I need to get out of this bed and out of your way here." He tried to sit up.

She gently pushed him back down. "It's not you. I have a lot on my mind."

His gaze turned tender. "My mama always said I was a good listener. So why don't you tell me what's ailing you before it gets too big to handle? Sometimes it helps to put what's bothering you on somebody else."

"You just mentioned your mother." She put down the wash bucket, moving closer to the bed. "Does this mean your memory has returned?"

"Not yet, but it's slowly getting there."

She hadn't expected his contagious grin to cause a smile to form on her lips.

"Sometimes things I didn't think I knew just pop out," he went on. "For example, I didn't know my mama said I was a good listener until I up and said it. In fact until that instant, I didn't know for sure that I had a mama."

Maggie could have stayed there and talked to Alex for the rest of the day. She guessed that was a sign she was lonelier than she thought. She needed to have someone to talk to, someone other than Sarah, Concha, Elena, Roger, and little Jon Anthony.

She hadn't been to town in months, but after Alex hinted

that his memory was beginning to return, she didn't want to destroy his good news by saying anything negative. Maggie felt dejected since Sadie disgraced the family name, but she would never share something as personal as that with a stranger.

"You'll be meeting my nephew, Jon Anthony, in a few minutes," Maggie said. "Jon is my late sister's child, and…" Her throat tightened with emotion. "…and I thought you should know that both my parents died of a fever almost three years ago."

"Your sister and your parents too?"

She bit her lower lip. "Yes."

"I'm so sorry."

Maggie swallowed. "Thank you."

"Sounds like you've had your share of sadness."

She couldn't speak for a moment. It often happened when she discussed her losses. She was anxious to change the subject.

"I discovered a letter in your pocket the morning I found you." She knew the moment she said it that she shouldn't have, but it was too late to take back her words.

"What did it say?"

"I wish I hadn't brought this up in the first place because… Well, I hadn't planned to tell you about the letter—at least not yet."

"Why not?" The pleading expression in his eyes begged for answers. "Please, Maggie, read me that letter."

"I shouldn't." She released a deep sigh. "But I suppose I will." She pulled the letter from the center pocket of her apron. "The letter was from a Mrs. Ruth Parson from San Antonio and addressed to her brother, Alexander P. Lancaster. She called him Alex. Ever heard of either of those names?"

He shook his head. The hopeful expression on his face disappeared.

Maggie moved down to the foot of his bed to read the letter. "I've been praying that in time, you'll remember everything."

She tried to make her voice sound as positive and friendly as possible. "Who knows? Maybe when you hear me read the letter, you'll remember something."

After she finished reading, their gazes intersected again. A wave of disappointment shone in his eyes, but she saw something else too. Had something in Ruth's letter surprised Alex or given him a new problem—as if he didn't already have enough worries?

Despite all she'd said to the contrary, she thought he was probably an honorable man. Still she knew little about him.

He could be married. Hadn't he called out a name during the night that sounded as if it belonged to a woman?

"Who's Dee?" she asked.

His startled expression suggested that he hadn't expected her to bring up that subject.

"You mentioned the name Dee before you came to yourself." Maggie eyed Alex slowly. "That name was also mentioned in the letter."

"I know." Alex paused before continuing. "When I think of that name, all I feel is deep pain and regret."

"I'm so sorry."

Neither of them spoke for a moment. Maggie wondered what he was thinking.

"We both probably had our share of unhappiness," he said at last. "I can't even remember mine. But I'm not going to let it ruin the rest of my life."

Neither was Maggie, but she didn't feel like expressing that thought to a man she hardly knew. She'd already told him more about her private life than a proper young woman should.

She stood by the big double bed, one hand on the bedpost. Alex appeared worried about something. Maggie wondered if he was thinking about Dee. She was considering what she might say next when her sister came in, leading Jon Anthony by the hand.

"Well, Sarah, you finally got here." Maggie set the wash

bucket by the bedroom door, turned to the two-year-old, and put out her hands in order to take Jon Anthony in her arms. "And how's my little bag of trouble?"

"Is this the little boy you were telling me about?" Alex asked in that slow drawl of his.

"Yes." Maggie reached down, picked up the child, and cuddled him. "He's my nephew, Jon Anthony."

"*Our* nephew," Sarah corrected, surveying the room. Her glance settled on Alex. "Where's Little Lupe?"

"He went outside a while ago. I had a little job I wanted him to do for me. Should be back before too long."

"Can we go out and play when Lupe gets back?" Sarah asked Maggie.

Maggie nodded, but she was looking at Alex. "Stay close to the house, Sarah."

"I will." Sarah hurried to the door. "I'll wait for him outside."

Jon Anthony had jumped down to the floor. Maggie barely noticed until she heard him pull out a drawer. She started across the floor toward the child. "Now what are you into, little man?"

The child raced around the room, getting into mischief at every turn. For a moment Maggie stood still, thinking how cute Jon Anthony was and how Sadie would have loved to see her son at that moment.

Jon Anthony opened another small drawer, pulled out one of Maggie's mother's old aprons, and dragged it behind him. Before Maggie had time to say a word, the child began fiddling with the whistle by Alex's bed.

Maggie grabbed his chubby hands and held them. "Don't meddle, Jon. It isn't nice." She took the whistle away from him, lifting it out of his reach.

Jon Anthony cried and tried to get it back. "Mine!" he shouted. "Give me."

"No, no, Jon."

"Let him have the whistle." Alex's deep voice sounded kind. "He can't hurt it, can he?"

"No, but he could try to swallow it."

"I hadn't thought of that." Alex sent her what she perceived as an appreciative smile. "You're good with children. You should have some of your own someday."

Maggie shrugged, more from embarrassment than anything else. "Not much chance of that." She put the whistle on a high shelf. "Don't let me forget to give that back before I leave."

"You're staying then?"

"I suppose we can stay a little while."

She lifted the child off the floor in one swoop and set him in the empty wash bucket. Jon Anthony laughed, banging the metal handle against the side of the bucket as if there were no place he would rather be. Maggie reached down, tousled his brown curls, and sat down in the rocker.

"He sure is a cute little fellah," Alex said. "Does his father, Mr. Anthony, live around here?"

Maggie swallowed. "Jon Anthony is an orphan."

"Oh, I'm sorry."

She turned the conversation in another, less personal direction and answered some of his questions about the local area and the ranch. Jon Anthony had toppled the wash bucket and was crawling around on the floor before she finally told Alex they had to go—though going in to prepare the evening meal in no way erased Alex from her mind.

There has to be a way to help him remember his identity. She also hoped he would soon recall the name of the shooter. But she had no idea how to make those wishes come true.

———

ALEX STARED at the ceiling long after Maggie and Jon Anthony left his room. Was he the Alex mentioned in the letter?

He couldn't remember his past, but somehow he knew he'd never put much faith in doctors. Yet he found himself almost wishing the doctor Maggie mentioned would hurry up and come. If he was as smart as Maggie claimed, maybe the doctor could explain why disconnected thoughts and unexplained memories kept swirling around inside his brain and help him find the answers to all his questions.

Someone had tried to kill him and might still be out there, waiting for the chance to try again. How could he possibly learn who that person or persons might be when he was so weak he couldn't get out of bed? He hated the thought of putting Maggie and her loved ones in danger. Yet he knew he wasn't strong enough to simply walk away.

Concha said he should stay flat on his back for two more days. All right then. In two days he would get out of bed and leave.

Before that could happen, he developed a bad ailment—coughing, sneezing, fever, and chest congestion. Alex found it difficult to breathe. Added to his wounds, the illness doubled his recovery time.

Five days later his fever broke. Six days after that Alex's breathing was full and deep, and the wheezing was finally gone. He was still weak as a half-drowned kitten but tired of being cooped up. He felt he should be out solving his problems instead of wasting time in bed.

"Dr. Smyth is off somewhere, fishing with the sheriff," Maggie had told him.

But Alex had never really wanted a doctor in the first place. He just wanted to get up and get moving. With Little Lupe's help Alex discovered he could walk as far as the privy, but he wasn't yet strong enough to ride away.

The boy had the afternoon off, and Maggie had said Alex needed some sun. She invited him to go out on the patio with her and visit a while. Alex agreed.

Maggie came into Alex's room at 4:00 p.m., looking dainty and very appealing in a yellow dress that showed off her slender silhouette to its best advantage. Alex sat up in bed and shifted around until his legs touched the polished pine floor.

Maggie handed him her papa's slippers and a brown robe and waited while he fumbled, trying to put them on. With one arm in a sling, it wasn't easy. He managed to get his right arm in the sleeve of the robe and drape the rest over his left shoulder before struggling to get up.

Obviously trying to allow him the privacy he needed to complete his task, Maggie stood with her back toward him until she finally asked, "How are you feeling?"

Alex shrugged, and a sharp pain shot through his shoulder. "Can't complain."

She turned toward him. "I don't believe you. You're hurting —right this minute."

He grinned. "I should have known you're not the kind of lady to be taken in by play-acting."

Alex was only a few feet from the French doors. He took a step and waited before taking another. She moved ahead of him and opened both doors. He took another step. "Thank you, ma'am. Concha said my wounds are healing nicely. I just had a little setback caused by my nose and chest ailments."

"I just want to make sure you're safe and comfortable is all," she said. "And that means seeing a doctor. By now Dr. Smyth has likely returned from his fishing trip. It's been over three weeks since you came here. I think we should drive into town so you can see the doctor."

I don't need a doctor; I need to ride out of here. He ground his teeth together so he wouldn't have to say anything.

The seating arrangements on the red brick patio consisted of three chairs painted white and a small table. Maggie indicated the chair nearest the French doors. "Is this chair all right?"

"Perfect."

Slowly he lowered himself into it. Pain engulfed him, causing all other thoughts to leave him for a moment.

"You're hurting," she said. "I know you are." Maggie sat down in an identical chair across from his. "Is there anything I can get you?"

"No, but thanks for asking."

He tried to focus on the well-tended back yard. Flowerbeds edged the fence leading to the pasture beyond. A large oak shaded the west end of the grassy area, and a rope-swing with a wooden seat hung from one of its branches, blowing to and fro in a brisk wind.

A dark-haired stranger was in the garden, pulling up vegetables and putting them in a wicker basket.

"Who's that woman?" Alex asked. "Haven't seen her around here before."

"That's Elena. She works in the house and takes care of Jon Anthony."

"Oh, yes. Sarah told me about Elena, but this is the first time I've actually seen her. And that Jon Anthony is some boy." Alex grinned. "You must be real proud."

Maggie smiled. "I am."

Maggie's gaze melded with his, and his grin slowly faded when he thought about the fact that Jon Anthony was an orphan. Poor child. Somehow Alex knew he'd lost loved ones too. If only he remembered their names.

"It's too bad about the little boy's parents. What happened to 'em?"

"His mother died in childbirth," she finally said.

"How unfortunate. And the boy's father? You said Jon was an orphan."

Maggie shifted to a new position in her chair. "If you don't mind, I'd rather not talk about that right now."

"I should never have asked so many personal questions in the first place."

"That's all right. I welcome your questions—most of them anyway."

Sarah trotted her pony in the pasture nearby. Maggie leaned forward as if she had a sudden interest in her little sister's horseback riding skills.

"You need to get that girl a bigger horse," Alex said. "Her legs are almost touching the ground."

"I know. In fact Sarah would be in heaven right now if she knew that Ole Lupe is breaking a two-year-old out behind the barn for her."

"Now who did you say Lupe was?"

"He's Concha's husband."

Alex released an exaggerated sigh. "Then he has my deepest sympathy."

Maggie chuckled. "You'd like Concha if you got to know her."

"Well, I will say this for the woman: she really knows how to change a bandage and make it hurt real bad."

Maggie laughed. Then he did too.

Slowly the laughter vanished, and the moment became more intense. Alex centered his full attention on her lips, wishing he had the nerve to kiss her.

She blushed and looked away.

Men likely showered her with those kinds of wishes, but she didn't appear to want it—at least from him. She didn't seem to want to talk about her late sister either.

Maggie was a good woman. From all he'd seen so far, she was kind and a good mother to her nephew and little sister. If she would allow it, he wanted to help her in any way he could. But until she opened up more, he doubted that was possible.

JOE GARZA SHIVERED, watching as a strong east wind blew the rain sideways. He turned up the collar of his worn brown shirt against the dampness and cold.

He left the possibility of a ranch job behind and stole a horse from Tio's boss. Tio didn't know about the horse yet, and Joe hadn't bothered to tell him he was leaving.

Joe looked up at the rain, cursing it. His clothes were soaked, plastered to his skin. He longed for a dry place to wait out the storm. He kicked his bony excuse for a horse; the animal barely moved. Joe kicked him again; the horse moved but not much faster.

At least he was out of that rat-hole of a Mexican prison, but he was no closer to finding Alex Lancaster or the money he stole from the bank. Joe peered down the muddy trail ahead.

Alex and Dee were instrumental in helping Joe get the job at the bank in the first place. He'd told them he was a young pastor without a church and he needed a good job until he found a ministry. He'd sounded convincing too. As a child he'd learned to read and write in both Spanish and English at a school set up by the nuns of his village. He also knew how to talk like a gringo despite his Mexican heritage.

Church-people were easy to fool. Alex and Dee believed every lie he told them, including that he was an ordained minister with the right to legally join them in Holy Matrimony.

He'd served as their pastor for several months before Joe performed the wedding ceremony in Dee's home, and he'd also worked as a janitor at the bank, biding time until he could pull off the bank robbery. He chose the morning after the wedding when Alex, Dee, and their wedding guests were less likely to come into the bank. Joe had taken the day off too, or so the bank president thought.

He'd dressed as a cowboy that morning, with a red bandana over his mouth. Joe marched into the bank with a six-shooter in his hand as if he robbed banks every day, and after pushing the other customers out of his way, he'd stepped up to the teller's window.

"Give me all your money," he'd said in a loud voice.

The teller handed him the money, and nobody said a word. He didn't know that Alex had come to the bank ahead of him to pick up cash for the honeymoon or that he was standing in the teller line with several others. As Joe headed for the door, a hand reached over and pulled off his bandana. Joe flinched at the look of surprise mixed with seething anger in Alex's eyes.

Joe could have killed Alex then and there—and many times since then wished he had. But at the time all he cared about was the money. He shot his pistol in the air a couple of times and raced out the door. His horse was hitched to the post outside. He jumped on him and headed for the river, the small leather bag of money tucked under his shirt. How could he have known that Alex would follow him into Mexico, see where he hid the money, and take it?

When he finally got out of jail, Joe had expected to find Alex and Dee, as well as the money, in Brownsville. Joe hadn't found either of them, but he knew where to find his sister. Joe would go there first and rest up, see what she might know.

He'd track Alex down sooner or later. When he did Joe would get the money back, and Alex would die.

Joe Garza kicked his horse with the heels of his sandals, coaxing the animal into a trot. The bay gelding jerked its head around as if it intended to bite Joe. Joe's jaw tightened, and he kicked the horse again. The animal moved forward but slower than ever.

Joe continued to kick the horse, harder and harder. For a moment the animal refused to move at all. Then he sort of leaped forward. Joe grabbed the saddle-horn. The horse took another step and tripped. Joe heard a crack, and the horse fell to its knees. If Joe hadn't stretched his legs away from the saddle at the last instant, they would have been crushed under the weight of the animal's body.

Joe hopped off. He attempted to get the horse to its feet again, cursing in Spanish with every breath. But the animal wouldn't move. Joe finally had to face the fact that the horse's leg was broken.

He pulled out the knife he'd stolen from Tio. The bay horse didn't deserve to live anyway. Now he'd have to walk the rest of the way if he hoped to find Alex Lancaster.

8

As they sat watching Sarah ride her pony, Maggie wondered if Alex was going to say anything more. Maybe she should.

She leaned forward, and her lawn chair creaked. "I noticed dark clouds coming up from the south. Maybe it's going to rain. We can always use it."

Alex nodded. He was still watching Sarah—at least she thought he was.

"When will your sister's horse be ready?" he asked.

"By mid-July, I hope." She studied him from under her lashes. "It's a surprise birthday present from Jon Anthony and me. Sarah's been begging for a full-size horse for ages, but I want the horse well trained before I give it to her."

"She wants a big horse that bad, does she?"

"There's nothing Sarah wants more."

Maggie realized she was doing most of the talking. It was time for Alex to add to the conversation. She waited, and silence reigned again.

When she couldn't stand the lack of conversation a moment longer, Maggie sneaked a glance at Alex. He was watching

Elena, not Sarah. Elena had finished her gardening and was standing by the yard gate, holding her basket and glaring at Alex.

"That woman is very strange," he said. "She acts like she hates me, and I don't ever remember seeing her before. Is she all right in the head?"

"Of course. Why?"

Alex shrugged, wincing a bit as he lifted his wounded shoulder. "She just keeps staring, like she's trying to put a curse on me or something."

Maggie's muted laugh sounded flat to her ears. "It's funny you should say that. Elena's from Mexico originally, and she said her father was a curandero. I guess maybe her ways are a little different from ours because of that."

"Curandero," he repeated. "I don't know how I know this, but that's sort of like being a witch doctor, isn't it?"

Maggie nodded. "And I've been praying for Elena, hoping sooner or later she will find the Lord and give up her superstitious beliefs."

"I gather, then, you're a Christian."

"I am."

"I figured that out the day Sarah came and read to me from the Bible."

"You're reading the Bible I left for you then?"

"Yes." He looked at Elena again as if to change the topic of conversation.

Should she invite Alex to the Friday night worship service she and Sarah had in their home each week as she wanted to do? Or was she rushing things?

Elena sent Alex an especially frosty glare. Then she went around the corner of the house and out of sight.

He rolled his eyes. "See what I mean? Elena definitely doesn't like me."

"She can be a little strange."

"But why? I don't even know the woman." He glanced at Maggie. "Tell me more about Elena and this curandero business."

"Well, she came here with my sister. My parents had died of a fever, and Sadie was about to have a baby. My sister wanted her baby to be born here on the ranch. Elena didn't speak a word of English back then, and I hardly knew her when Sadie died in childbirth. Elena was very devoted to my sister and insisted I let her take care of the baby, Jon Anthony. So I did.

"Then one day I found lighted candles all around Jon Anthony's crib and an egg under it. That was when I learned Elena was practicing some of the things she learned from her curandero father."

"So why didn't you fire her?"

"I almost did. But I have to be honest. Part of the reason I let her stay was because she is such a good worker, and I really needed help. Within a short period of time, I had lost my sister and both my parents. I suddenly had the complete responsibility of running a house, a large cattle ranch, and two children to raise. I needed all the help I could get."

"And then?"

"I prayed. Elena promised never to practice the curandero way again, and I believed her. I took away all those candles she had and hid them, and she didn't seem to mind at all. Best of all she hasn't done anything strange like that since then, and every now and then she attends the home Bible study Sarah and I have on Friday nights."

Maggie hoped Alex would ask her to tell him more about the Bible study. Instead he said, "I want to hear more about this curandero thing. It sounds interesting."

Maggie smiled. God worked in mysterious ways. Maybe they could have a Bible study after all—right here, right now.

She cleared her throat. "The Bible teaches us how to live here on earth and how to prepare for heaven. It also teaches us a lot about our Lord—our God. We are to repent of our sins, be baptized, and pray in the name of Jesus, and from reading the Bible we learn what God likes and what He doesn't like. One of the things He really doesn't like is idolatry."

Alex grinned. "He doesn't like adultery either, does He?"

Maggie's face felt warm all at once. "No, He most certainly does not. But as to *idolatry*, the Bible teaches that God doesn't want us to combine our worship of Him with the worship of false gods. The Lord hates that. He wants us to be separate and faithful to Him only. In my opinion the life and practice of the curandero beliefs combines the two. Many have altars set up in their homes with Bibles and pictures of Jesus on them, as well as objects connected with curandero witchcraft. When they're sick, they visit the local curandero instead of getting down on their knees before the Lord. However, on Sunday morning some go to church and try never to miss."

"Where in the Bible does it say that believers shouldn't mix the two?" Alex asked. "I'd like to read it for myself."

"It's in the Old Testament, where the children of Israel made the golden calf—Exodus 32. The Israelites had just left Egypt where they were slaves, and the Lord had Moses lead them out of slavery and into freedom. God had showed them many miracles along the way, yet they turned and worshipped a golden calf they had made with their own hands, calling what they did the 'worship of God Almighty.' They combined the worship of the Lord with the worship of false gods, just like the curanderos do, and if you read that passage of the Scriptures, you'll see God was definitely not pleased."

"Interesting. I'll read that tonight. And thank you again for loaning me that Bible." He cleared his throat. "When I woke up the day after I was shot, I didn't remember anything. I didn't even remember my own name—still don't. I didn't remember ever going to church or reading the Bible either. But when

Sarah read to me from the Bible that day, I suddenly realized the words were familiar; I'd read them before. It was like coming home or something. I think I must have prayed a lot and studied the Bible before I came here, and if little Sarah hadn't read to me from the Bible that day, I might never have found what I lost."

Alex smiled. Then he stretched out both arms in front of him—or tried to until his wound stopped him. Slowly the smile faded, and he grimaced, grabbing his left shoulder.

He's hurting, Maggie thought. *His shoulder where he got shot could be getting worse, and the poor man has lost his memory besides. He might even be having headaches because of hitting his head when he fell.*

"Why don't I get Lupe to hitch up the wagon? He could drive you into town so you'd be there when Doc Smyth gets back?" She bit her bottom lip. "As I said earlier, he might already be back."

"No need for that." He sent her a dismissive glance and gazed off toward the pasture again. "I'm doing fine—just sore from the wounds and weak from the fever and coughing."

He was wearing the white sling she'd fashioned for him from one of Sarah's outgrown petticoats. He nursed the injured shoulder, rubbing it occasionally with his other hand as if it really hurt.

Regardless of what he'd just said, it was apparent to Maggie that Alex was *not* doing fine. Though he'd insisted he wouldn't see a doctor, she wasn't about to give up.

"I know you're a lot better," she said, "but I still think you need to let a doctor have a look at you, hear?"

He shook his head without turning toward her.

Anyone who knew what happened to Alex would agree with her conclusions. She imagined he also agreed but was too stubborn to admit it. She considered trying again but decided to wait and mention the visit to the doctor at a time when he was likely to be more receptive. Besides there was another matter she wanted to bring up, and it couldn't wait.

"Lupe found a horse and saddle this morning when he was out checking fences," Maggie said. "I think they belong to you."

Alex turned and gave her his full attention. "Really? Why?"

"Your initials, APL, were etched on the saddle. If you are who I think you are, the initials confirm it, and that pretty much rules out Mexican bandits as being the ones who shot you."

"Sure 'nuf?" he said, his tone casual though Maggie suspected he was actually quite interested. "Why?"

"Bandits would have taken the horse and the saddle and especially the...the rest of your gear." She hesitated, not wanting to say too much too soon.

"When can I see the horse?"

"In a few days, when you're strong enough to walk out to the stable."

"I'm plenty strong enough right now."

Maggie shook her head. "Oh, no you don't! Not in your condition."

His mouth tightened. "You might as well show me the way 'cause if you don't, I'll just find it on my own."

At that moment there wasn't a question in her mind that he meant what he said. If there was one thing they had in common, it was stubborn determination. She sighed. "Oh, all right. We'll do it your way this time. But don't think I'll be giving in to you very often."

His slow grin warmed her heart. "I wouldn't expect you to give in," he said. "That's part of your charm."

Alex leaned forward in his lawn chair like he planned to get up. Maggie saw the pain etched in his eyes, and a wave of empathy swept over her.

Before he'd straightened to a standing position, he stopped and then sat back down.

"Are you all right?" Maggie asked. "You look pale."

"I'm fine." He tried to get up again, and this time he succeeded. "And I fully intend to take a look at that horse, but I best go inside and change before you try to talk me out of it."

He started to walk off then turned back and faced her. "You're still going to show me that horse barn, aren't you?"

"I said I would, didn't I? Are you sure you're up to it?"

"Sure I am."

"Well, then, I'll sit right here in this lawn chair until you're ready to go."

Alex turned around and made his way inside, letting the door slam behind him.

The air was hot and muggy on the patio as she waited for Alex, and a fly landed on her arm. She swatted it away, but it returned. Then it buzzed about her face.

Maggie got up, hoping the fly wouldn't follow, and walked around the corner of the house. Crossing her arms over her chest, she gazed out at the southern pasture. Dark clouds banked the sky; if a rainstorm came up from the border, it would likely arrive by nightfall.

She'd been praying for rain, and her papa always said it was good to pray to God for earthly needs. He also said something else that she would never forget: "As important as it is to ask the Lord for rain, Maggie, it's also important to thank Him when the rain comes. Some people forget to do that."

Maggie closed her eyes. After she prayed she went back to the patio and sat down. Her thoughts returned to Alex.

He would change into the shirt and trousers he wore on the day she found him. She'd mended all the rips and torn places in the material, but the clothes still looked far from new, and Alex was almost helpless with that injured shoulder of his. Maggie knew she should go in and help him change, but Alex was stubborn. He probably wouldn't want a woman's help.

Besides it wouldn't be proper for an unmarried girl to help a man dress. Mama always said that only a lady of the night would do something like that. Yet she knew part of her reluctance stemmed from the fact that his mere presence reminded her that he was a man and she was a woman.

When he opened the French doors and came out, his good arm was in the long sleeve of his brown shirt. The arm with the sling was inside the shirt. Only the bottom three buttons were buttoned. In his physical condition she didn't know how he managed even that simple task.

Maggie considered leaving the patio immediately, but Alex needed help. Anyone in his condition would. She couldn't just leave him standing there. She should have gone down to Lupe's house earlier and asked Little Lupe to help Alex dress. If she had this would never have happened.

"Come on out," she heard herself say, "and I'll finish buttoning your shirt."

"You?" He gave her a double-take then shook his head. "Naw, that's not necessary."

"Why not?" She faked an air of confidence she didn't feel. "I'm perfectly capable. I button up Jon Anthony's shirts every day."

His mouth turned up at the edges, and he moved toward her. Had she persuaded him so easily?

She tensed, wondering if she'd lost her mind. His smile and those blue eyes would charm the feathers off a wild duck, but that was just a minor part of her problem. He was starting to dominate her thoughts and dreams.

She shook inside as she twisted the first button into the buttonhole of his brown shirt. She didn't remember doing the rest of them. Was it possible she completed the job with her eyes closed?

But somehow with Alex pretending didn't work. He was too close and far too manly to block from her mind, and she was far too aware of him.

She finished the last button and took a step back.

Maggie wanted to glance away, but eventually she'd have to look at Alex again. When she did, would she be blushing?

It took a moment to recover from being near him. Did Alex take pleasure in the fact that she was obviously nervous around him? She should never have buttoned his shirt. If anyone found out, her reputation would be ruined. Did he think less of her now? Did she think less of herself?

Well, it would never happen again. She lifted her chin then nodded in the general direction of the horse barn.

"Shall we go?" she asked.

He nodded and offered her his good arm.

Maggie pretended she hadn't seen his arm and moved ahead of him. But oh how she wanted to look back.

9

A lex was becoming suspicious. Maggie wouldn't take his arm and allow him to escort her to the horse barn, but she had stopped several times along the way. She said it was because she hoped to make him aware of various points of interest at ranch headquarters. But he knew she did it to make him rest. He sent her a hard look on purpose.

She appeared to ignore his hard look and pointed to a cabin painted white with a porch across the front. "The bunkhouse is over there. It's where the single cowboys live."

"I kind of figured that...since it's a bunkhouse."

"Here we call it the camp house. The barn is over there," she said, "straight ahead."

The big red barn was open at both ends. Alex went and stood in the doorway. The scent of fresh hay would make going inside a pleasure were it not for the other not-so-pleasing odors. The stalls were on one side of the barn, and a line of doors marked the opposite wall. He glanced up. A hayloft hovered over whatever was behind those doors.

A sorrel mare caught his attention. "Nice looking mare you've got here."

"Thank you," Maggie said, nodding to her left. "Your horse is over there."

"If he really is mine," he mumbled.

Alex ambled over to the corner of the barn, stopping in front of the last stall. The black stallion stood with his head poking over the wooden gate. Alex had no memory of the animal and didn't think the horse remembered him either. Somehow he knew that saddle horses often showed some kind of recognition when the owner approached, and a big physical reaction if the animal had been abused. Since the black stallion showed no reaction at all, Alex concluded that if the animal was indeed his, he hadn't owned it for long or hadn't seen it in a long time.

Alex stroked the horse's nose and gave it another brief pat on the head. Suddenly the horse turned toward the mares and nickered. Alex glanced back at Maggie.

"If I were you I wouldn't put a stud in here with all these mares, Miss Gallagher. You're asking for trouble."

"All our mares have already been bred."

Alex delivered a slow smile. "For a young woman you know a lot about horses."

"You know a lot too—for a man."

He laughed. "Men are supposed to know...certain things."

"So are women."

Was his teasing beginning to amuse her? He hoped her half-smile meant she enjoyed being in his company.

———

MAGGIE STUDIED the sorrel mare to keep from looking at Alex. She'd felt common and slightly earthy when she buttoned his shirt, and that bothered her. Not only that but she'd broken her own rule: she'd accidentally touched his bare chest.

The incident with Alex totally confused her. No man had

ever made her feel the way he did. Certainly Roger hadn't. She knew better than to get too close to Alex again.

He still studied the black stallion.

"Mr. Lancaster."

He turned in Maggie's direction.

"I want to show you the saddle." She opened the door to one of the storage rooms on the wall opposite the stalls. "Lupe put all the gear in here."

A saddle with a rope tied to the back of it straddled a sawhorse. A Mexican saddle blanket and a pair of chaps were draped across a dusty-looking table, but no reins or bridle. Alex touched the weathered leather seat of the saddle and ran his fingers across the torn wool blanket.

"The saddle's pretty scratched up," he said, "and the blanket isn't in very good condition either. Where are the bridle and reins?"

"They were broken beyond repair, so Lupe threw them away. The bit was missing too."

He nodded. "I see." He traced the initials on the back of the saddle, peering at the saddlebags. "Have you checked these?"

"Lupe did."

Alex opened one of the bags with his good hand and pulled out a white shirt. He put down the shirt, opened the other saddlebag, and scooped up a handful of coins and paper money.

She saw the look of surprise pass over his face. "That's thirty dollars you've got there, Mr. Lancaster. What did you do before you got shot? Rob a bank or something?"

"If I knew what I did before I came here, I'd be a happy man right now." He looked at the money in his hand. "Unless you have some objection and since you referred to this as mine, I'll just keep the money until we find the rightful owner." He grabbed the rope. "Guess I'll keep this too. I could make a bridle out of it." He paused. "Are you all right with that?"

She shrugged. "Of course. Everything is likely yours anyway."

He gazed at her for a moment. "Do you really think I'm a thief?"

"Frankly I don't know what I think about you yet. I'll let you know when I do." She went over and stood in the doorway. "But I must say, you sure claimed that money mighty quick."

He looked puzzled and shook his head. "As I said, if we find out it's not mine, I'll gladly turn it over to the rightful owner." Alex folded up the shirt, put it back in the bag. He looped the rope over his good shoulder, folding the bags over his arm.

Maggie felt bad about her last comment, and he really did look as if he could use some help. She knew she should have helped him regardless of the fact that he was probably too proud to ask for it.

When Alex grabbed the saddle horn, she decided it was time to speak up. "If you're thinking of slinging that saddle over your shoulder and carrying it back to your room in the ranch house like some kind of caveman, think again," she said. "Until we find out for sure who owns that saddle, it belongs to me. So the saddle stays right here in the barn. It's heavy and burdensome. It would be impossible for you to carry the saddle all the way to the house without hurting your bad shoulder."

Alex removed his hand from the saddle horn. "What about the chaps? Do we leave them here too?"

"Yes, for now. We can always pick them up later. And by the way, we don't use the word *chaps* around here. The leather pants the men put over their regular trousers are called leggings."

"You're the boss-lady," Alex said with a teasing tone.

She wondered if he'd ever taken orders from a woman before, as he sure seemed a bit prickly about it. But at least she was learning more about him, even if it wasn't much.

Maggie went outside, and he followed her. She shut the door and slipped the wooden board they used for a latch back down in the slot. She'd no sooner finished than Sarah came running up behind them.

"A rider's coming," she announced in Spanish.

"Can you tell who it is?" Maggie asked.

"Roger, I think." Panting, Sarah shifted her sixty pounds from one leg to the other. "It looks like his gray horse."

"Lupe said Roger might come by," Maggie said, translating their conversation into English for Alex's sake.

ALEX BLINKED. An uneasy feeling had formed in the pit of his stomach. He understood every Spanish word the two females said and didn't like deceiving Maggie by pretending he hadn't. A lot of new information rolled around inside his brain, but he didn't feel like discussing any of his thoughts and feelings until he knew more.

His current concern was the fact that he was sick to his stomach and slightly dizzy. He also had a headache, and his shoulder felt like liquid fire. If he moved another foot, he was liable to fall on his face.

I can do this, he told himself. Alex was determined to keep up with Maggie and Sarah all the way to the main gate on the north end of the big corral, despite his labored breathing.

I can do this. Where had he first heard those words? Another memory surfaced. He was in church with his mother and sister, and the preacher was delivering a sermon.

"Don't say,' I can do this or I can do that. It's prideful. Give the Lord credit for your accomplishments. Instead say, 'I can do all things through Christ who strengthens me.'"

Was he prideful? He'd need time to think about it.

"Feeling all right?" Maggie asked, cutting into his reflections.

He gritted his teeth. "Couldn't be better."

"I don't believe you." Maggie watched him a moment longer and turned to Sarah.

The child stood by the big wooden gate. "Can I swing on the gate until Roger gets here? Please, Maggie."

"You certainly may not. That gate has to last us a long time."

"Why don't you go ahead and let her play on the gate, ma'am? Looks like fun to me."

"Pretty please," Sarah begged.

Maggie hesitated. "Oh, all right. I guess you can play on the gate this one time."

Alex was glad for Sarah. But all he could think about was his pride and his painful shoulder. The fire in his shoulder was getting hotter by the minute. Even the weight of the saddlebag hurt. If he didn't put it down immediately, he would likely let go with a loud holler.

He dropped the saddlebag in the middle of the corral. Then he moved his shoulder up and down as he walked toward the gate, hoping to get the circulation in his arm going again. His bad shoulder always hurt, but he wasn't about to say anything about it.

"Your shoulder hurts," Maggie said. When he didn't reply, she said, "I thought so."

He liked Maggie—a lot. If he were a local or planning to stay around for a while, he would gentle her as a horseman gentles a young colt, but he didn't want to lie by telling her he was going to stay when he wasn't. He wouldn't say anything.

Sarah had already climbed up on the gate and was in the process of riding it back. The gate hit the big fencepost with a bang. Sarah held on, giggling as it banged again and again like a kind of echo.

He heard the tinkle of Maggie's laughter. Turning toward her he had the pleasure of seeing as well as hearing her laugh.

"I'll bet you rode the gate just like that when you were Sarah's age," he said. "Didn't you, ma'am?"

Maggie nodded. "How'd you guess?"

"Saw it in your eyes just now."

Maggie fluffed strands of her blonde hair that escaped the tight bun on the back of her head as she gazed off toward the approaching rider.

"How long have you known this Dawson fellah?" Alex asked.

She shrugged. "I don't know. All my life, I guess."

"What's he like?"

"I never really thought about it. But he's...he's nice...in his way."

Roger was close. He'd reach them at any moment. Alex had no idea what to expect.

"Jump down off the gate now, Sarah," Maggie said, "and hold it open for Roger."

Maggie turned back to Alex. "Folks around here don't go to town much. And when they do go, they do favors for one another, like bringing them their mail."

"Mighty neighborly, I'd say. Do you think this Roger fellah is bringing your mail today?"

"I hope so. I've been expecting a letter from my aunt."

Roger trotted his gray horse through the gate, tipping his hat to Maggie and Sarah. But his friendly expression turned sour when he saw Alex. The muscles around his mouth hardened.

"You're the one Lupe told me about, aren't you?"

Alex shrugged with his good shoulder and tried to smile.

"And why the sling?" Roger asked. "Get in a fight or something?"

"I'll explain about him later, Roger," Maggie said. "Now come on up to the house. I'm fixing to make a fresh pot of coffee."

Roger sent Alex a cold look. Then he jerked his horse around, looking down at Sarah.

"Want a ride up to the house, little one?" Roger asked.

Sarah grinned. "Sure."

Roger lifted Sarah up with one hand and put her in the

saddle in front of him. Alex retrieved the saddlebag and trudged back to the house behind the gray horse and the thin, lanky cowboy who rode him.

The deep white sand would be hard to trudge through even if he were feeling strong and healthy. In Alex's weakened condition, it was torture. Yet if he hinted that he was tired, Maggie would have him back in bed and flat on his back before he knew it.

Alex needed to thank Maggie for all her help and tell her he planned to leave in a day or two. He would tell her as soon as Roger left—if he made it all the way to the house without falling on his face.

Alex stumbled but caught himself in time. At the rate things were going, he might fall on his face after all.

10

Maggie led the way into the kitchen of the ranch house. Roger handed her the mail and sat down beside her at the big table. Alex stood in the doorway, watching Maggie sift through the stack of letters. His wounds were healing, but he shouldn't have carried the rope and saddlebag this soon after having such a high fever. He wished he were in the room at the end of the hall and resting in the middle of that lumpy bed instead of standing there gawking.

"Aren't you going to sit down, Mr. Lancaster?" Maggie asked.

Alex put his gear down on the floor by the door and took a chair across from them.

Maggie fixed her eyes on Alex as a slow smile warmed her face. "Congratulations. From the way you marched from the gate to the house through all that thick sand, you must be in good physical condition."

Before Alex could come up with a response, Roger interrupted, speaking directly to Maggie. "Get any important mail?"

Maggie glanced at Roger and then back down at her mail. "I finally got that letter I was hoping for from my aunt in Brownsville. I also got several other letters."

Alex wondered if she'd gotten a letter from his sister in San Antonio. According to Maggie he arrived at the ranch over three weeks ago. Yet Maggie hadn't mentioned a letter, and he didn't plan to bring up the topic in front of Roger. He'd just met the man, but already he didn't trust him. The less Roger knew about Alex, the better.

Roger moved his chair closer to Maggie's, placing an arm on the back of her chair. "Is Miss Violet still teaching school?"

"No, she retired last year. I thought I told you." Maggie inched her chair away from Roger's then stood up. "I almost forgot about the coffee."

Maggie went to the table below the hand pump and began making coffee. Alex didn't like the fact that Roger was watching her. Ogling was a better word for what Roger was doing as Maggie moved around the room. Alex thought Roger would probably like to do a lot more than look. And each time Roger's gaze strayed from Maggie to Alex, his eyes burned with obvious hatred.

Alex wondered if Roger saw Alex as a threat or competition for Maggie's affection. He couldn't know Alex intended to move on in a few days, and Alex could hardly fault Roger for being jealous. He was having shades of that emotion himself. Maggie set cups of hot coffee on the table in front of the men and poured her sister a glass of milk.

"Go out and play now, Sarah," Maggie said. "I'll call you when supper's ready."

Sarah grinned her thank you and went out to drink the milk.

Maggie sat back down and turned to Roger. "I found Mr. Lancaster shot and bleeding here on the ranch a couple of weeks ago. He's recovering from his injuries and from a fever and a bad cough. He also seems to have lost his memory. I'm hoping it will return soon." She went on to tell Roger everything else that had occurred since he stopped by the last time.

By the time she finished, Roger was glaring at Alex again. "So you got shot and then lost your memory, huh?"

Alex nodded.

"Sounds fishy to me. What kind of trouble are you in, boy?"

"None that I can remember."

Roger sneered. "As they say, ain't that convenient?" Roger blasted him with a look so hostile Alex wanted to duck. "Did you get robbed, mister, or do just have a lot of enemies?"

Alex shrugged. "I'm afraid I don't know."

"Mr. Lancaster, are you telling me you don't know why you got shot?" He shook his head. "I just don't believe that. There has to be a reason."

Alex studied the man, trying to keep his temper under control and not say something he would regret. Roger had thin lips, a big hooknose and a space between his front teeth; but he was also tall and well built. Silly young women might describe him as ruggedly handsome.

When Alex still didn't answer, Roger turned his attention back to Maggie, who had once again risen from the table. Alex wondered if her actions were an effort to turn the subject. It seemed to work, as Roger was once again ogling her as she moved around the kitchen.

Alex's anger had dissipated, replaced by overwhelming weariness. He could scarcely keep his eyes open. Every muscle in his body begged for rest, and he wished for a swallow of Maggie's pain medicine. At the same time he had no intentions of leaving Maggie alone with a man like Roger Dawson, even for a moment.

In a simple, blue-print dress, Maggie glided over to what Alex supposed was the pantry, opened the door and took out some potatoes. With a knife in one hand and a bowl full of potatoes in the other, she returned to the table.

"Well, Roger," she said, a bit too brightly in Alex's opinion. He watched as she dug the knife into the outer surface of a potato, peeling the vegetable carefully, as if it were the most important job on earth. "What's the news from town?"

Roger pulled his upper lip down over his front teeth and grinned. "Mighty glad you asked that question 'cause that reminds me of something."

"What's that?"

"There's a Founder's Day Celebration in town in a week or so. Starts on Saturday morning and goes on 'til late that night. This will be a big shindig—a barbecue, a parade, maybe even have a marching band. I was hoping you'd come."

Sarah was standing on the back porch, drinking her milk. Upon hearing Roger's words, she raced back inside, the door slamming behind her. "What's this about a shindig?"

Roger smiled at the girl. "I'm inviting you and Maggie to the doings over in Bayview, that's what it's about. Folks will be coming from as far away as Nueces and Corpus Christi."

Before Sarah could respond Maggie said, "You know I don't like to be around a lot of people, Roger. I especially dislike fancy parties. So I'll have to say no to your kind invitation. Besides we'd have to leave by Friday morning, drive all day and stay the night in order to be there in time Saturday morning."

"Oh, that reminds me," Roger said in a way that suggested he was unaware of Maggie's lack of interest. "Mama made me promise I'd invite you to stay with us at our Sunday house for the whole weekend."

"Oh, can we, Maggie?" Sarah's eyes sparkled as she set her empty glass down on the table and wiped her white milk-mustache with the back of her hand. "It sounds like so much fun!"

"The Dawsons were kind to invite us," Maggie said. "And though it would be nice to go to church on Sunday, I can't waste an entire weekend in town like that."

Sarah's lips turned down as if she were about to cry. "Please, Maggie, let's go, just this once. I haven't seen Noma Elaine or any of my other friends in months."

"Well..." Maggie paused as if considering what she was about to say. "If our cousin Jim Caldwell takes over when the current pastor in Bayview retires, like he said he was going to, you'll have plenty of chances to see your friends then." She glanced at Alex. "If things go as planned, Sarah will be living with Pastor Jim Caldwell and his wife, Elizabeth, when school starts next year. It's time she attended a regular school anyway." She looked back at her little sister. "Would you like that, Sarah Ann, living in town and going to school with your friends?"

"I guess so. But can we still go to the shindig in town?"

None of this was any of Alex's business, as he planned to be miles away from the Gallagher Ranch by then. And yet he somehow knew that most children liked shindigs. If he hadn't noted a change in Maggie's facial expression from opposition to acceptance, meaning that she might now consider going, he would have spoken up on Sarah's behalf.

"Oh, all right." Maggie shook her head and shrugged. "I guess we can go."

Sarah squealed with delight and clapped her hands, and Alex couldn't help but be pleased for her. It would no doubt be good for Maggie and Sarah to drive into town and socialize more, but Alex couldn't help but wish it didn't include Roger Dawson. If he could spare the time, he'd go along with them in order to protect them.

Alex leaned back in his chair, wondering if he should delay leaving until after the shindig. He looked at Maggie. "I've been thinking about what you said, ma'am, about me paying a visit to

Doc Smyth and all. The more I think about it, the more I think you're right. Maybe I should ride into town with you when you go for the big shindig."

Maggie looked surprised. "You mean you're willing to go see the doctor?"

"If I won't be putting you out in any way."

She smiled. "Of course you won't. We'd love to have you drive into town with us." She glanced at Roger. "And I'm sure Roger's mother will insist you stay at their Sunday house, won't she, Roger?"

Alex watched the emotions play over Roger's face as he made an obvious attempt to bring them under control. At last he nodded and said, "Of course. My mother wouldn't have it any other way."

"Then it's settled," Maggie said. "We shall all go into town together."

"I appreciate this, ma'am," Alex said. "I really do."

The hateful expression on Roger's face focused on Alex, but it softened when he turned to gaze at Maggie. "I'm glad you're coming," he said, "and I'm putting in my bid right now to escort you to all the events."

Before Maggie could reply to what was more of an order than an invitation, Roger changed the subject as he glared back at Alex. "So you've been living in the camp house since you arrived with the other single men. Right, boy?"

Alex stiffened. *Here it comes.*

"Guess it gets pretty lonely," Roger went on, "with the other men away from the camp house from before sunrise 'til suppertime. Bet you got hungry with nothing but beans and tortillas to eat—and you too sick to cook something for yourself."

"I've been cooking his meals," Maggie explained. "Sarah takes him his meals and his medicine. Concha looks in on him too, and Little Lupe stays for most of each day to run and fetch for him."

Maggie glared at Sarah as if to say, "Keep your mouth shut, Sarah." It wouldn't be good if Roger knew Alex was still staying in the ranch house with Maggie and the children. He needed to make Maggie's lie come true by moving to what Maggie called the camp house where the other single men lived—and as soon possible. A good reputation was important, especially to a woman. With all the help and care Maggie gave him since he got shot, he wouldn't return that kindness by ruining her good name.

Maggie smiled, patting Roger on the arm. "Roger here is my best friend, Mr. Lancaster. He and his sweet mother are the best folks I know. We've always thought so. When you get to know them, I know you'll agree."

Roger got up out of his chair and glared at Alex. "Guess I best be going."

"Oh, I was hoping you'd stay while longer," Maggie protested. "You just got here."

"Wish I could too, Maggie, but I have things to do. I sure appreciate your hospitality though." He'd been looking at Maggie, but Roger turned and sent Alex a smile loaded with sarcasm. "I think I'll stop by your camp house on my way home and get me some ranch bread. I never could pass on a piece of hot *pan* straight from a black-iron skillet."

Roger left then, and Maggie gathered up her letters and began reading them.

Alex hadn't missed Roger's plan to visit the camp house where Alex was said to be staying. If Maggie had hoped to keep the truth from Roger, it would soon be out.

He needed to move out of the main house at once, but he was too tired from the little walking he'd done that day to consider doing it now. He would go to his room to rest up, and then tomorrow right after breakfast, he would move into the camp house.

He got up and glanced toward the door, but Maggie's voice interrupted his thoughts.

"Mr. Lancaster."

Alex looked back.

She held up one of the letters. "You need to read this. It's from your sister. She must have written right back after getting my letter." The edges of her mouth turned up in a smile that warmed his insides. "Go into the parlor. There's a good light in there."

Alex had no reason to believe he had a sister, but it wouldn't hurt to read the letter. He settled onto a rocking chair near a small table, moving the kerosene lamp as close to the rocker as he could get it, and opened the letter.

Dear Miss Gallagher,

Thank you for writing. I have not heard from my brother in over three years, and the man you found on your ranch does sound like Alex. I am sending you a photograph of Alex in order to make sure.

The woman in the picture is our mother, Mrs. Hannah Fowler. The man is our stepfather, George Fowler. The boy is Alex, and the young girl is me, Ruth Lancaster Parson. I do not know Dee's last name or anything about her. All Alex ever said was that she was a beautiful lady and he looked forward to seeing her again.

Alex was born on January 5, 1854, near Abbeville, South Carolina, and I was born in Abbeville two years later. Our papa was Alexander Paul Lancaster. Papa died in battle at Antietam in 1862 during the War Between the States. Later Mama remarried. We moved to Texas in 1866. The picture I am sending was taken at the farm where we lived north of Austin. Alex was fourteen years old then.

Please send back the picture when you have finished with it because it is the only copy I have, and tell Alex he has a nephew, Paul Lancaster Parson. Pauley is two and a half years old, and Will and I are expecting another child. I hope to hear from you again soon, Miss

Gallagher, and if your Alex is my brother, please ask him to write to me.

Regards, Mrs. Ruth Parson

Alex studied the young man and the other people in the photograph. None of them seemed familiar, but unless he had a twin brother, he was most definitely the young man in the picture.

He held the photo up to the light for a better look. Sadness captured him. A kind of loneliness covered the boy in the photo like a dark blanket, and Alex sensed the family was not a happy one.

He saw a barn in the background with a wagon parked in front, but no reflections came with it. Still staring at the photograph, he noted the young girl had long, dark pigtails that hung below her waist. The man and woman were frozen-faced, looking hard and as set in their ways, as did Alex. Only the young girl with the pigtails had a hint of a smile on her face. He supposed all photographs were like that, but he couldn't help wondering why the boy in the picture—why he—appeared to be so miserable.

He'd hoped that seeing the picture and reading Ruth's letter would revive his memory but tried not to become discouraged when it didn't. He would simply write to Ruth Parson and ask her some questions she hadn't covered in the letter. He was especially interested in learning if Ruth remembered anything else about the woman he called Dee.

MAGGIE SMILED when Alex entered the kitchen the next morning. "Mr. Lancaster, how are you feeling today?"

"Can't complain, especially when I smell coffee and fresh biscuits." His perky comments contrasted with the slow and perhaps painful way he moved when he sat down at the table. "Where are Sarah and Jon Anthony?" he asked.

"They ate early and went out to play for a while," she explained. "And thanks for asking. Sarah and I need to ride over to the ranch graveyard and put flowers on all the graves. I thought we'd go in the wagon this time, and we'd love to have you join us."

"I'd planned to move into the bunkhouse right after breakfast."

"You can do both. We won't be leaving until around three this afternoon. Sarah has her school lessons of a morning, and I have my chores. But by mid-afternoon we like to do something special. The graveyard is less than two miles from here, and the area around the graveyard is kind of pretty—or it is to us, with the oaks and wild olive trees nearby and all. I thought I'd pack a picnic supper. We could eat there before driving back. What do you think? Will you go with us?"

He shouldn't go, and he knew it. The men would see him riding off with Maggie and Sarah, giving them something to talk about. But after all Maggie had done for him, he could hardly say no.

"I'd enjoy that. But do you think it's wise?" He paused, waiting her to reply. When she didn't he continued. "You didn't want Roger to know I've been living here in the house, and the men will see us together if I go with you and Sarah. Wouldn't it be best if I didn't go?"

"I could use the help," she countered. "It rained last night. The wagon can be contrary driving through all that heavy sand especially when it's wet. That's why we usually go on horseback. And I wouldn't expect you to do any pushing if we get stuck, or any heavy lifting." She smiled as if to confirm her words then continued.

"The reason we're going in the wagon this time is because I have some flowers I want to transplant. It's kind of late in the year for that, but I thought I'd give it a try. And the men won't think it's strange, you going with us. I always take a hand or two along when we go in the wagon."

He nodded. "All right, although in my condition I won't be much help. But if that's what you want, I'm looking forward to it."

11

A porch painted white stretched across the front of the bunkhouse. Alex reached out and touched the top of Little Lupe's head before going inside to steady himself and show his fondness for the boy. His shoulder throbbed, and he was still weak from the fever. He needed rest, but with a burlap bag full of clothes tucked under his good arm that seemed unlikely.

His belongings consisted of a blue work-shirt that had belonged to Maggie's father, the shirt he found in the saddlebag, the clothes he wore on the day he arrived at the ranch, the rope he picked up in the barn, and the blue shirt and tan trousers he had on that had also belonged to Maggie's late father. Maggie gave him a bedroll and an extra blanket, but he doubted he'd need the blanket as hot as it was. Little Lupe had already dropped off his bedroll and now brought the blanket.

Fortunately for Alex the boy would be working for him during the daylight hours. At night Little Lupe would stay in his own home beyond the barn with Big Lupe and Concha. In Alex's opinion it wouldn't do for a child to sleep in the room with all those grown men.

Alex and Little Lupe went in through the entry door leading to the camp kitchen. Big Lupe stood in front of an open fireplace. A fire crackled and popped in the table-level hearth. The heat coming from it was scorching. Alex took a step back, dropping the heavy sack by the door.

As the camp cook, Lupe was baking bread in a Dutch oven as black as his Spanish eyes, and the scent of the bread made Alex's mouth water. Camp bread reminded him of a giant pancake, and when it was still warm from the hearth, there was nothing in the world that tasted better. Alex smiled—another memory.

"Give me bread, Grandfather," Little Lupe said in Spanish.

"Not now, boy. You must wait. The *pan* is not ready to eat yet." The old man gazed at Alex. "Can I help you, *Señor?*"

"I will be moving into the camp house here today. Can you tell me which of the cots I can use? I wouldn't want to take another man's bed."

"The men sleep in the big room, right through that door." He indicated a doorway beside the long table and a line of wooden benches. "The cot nearest the kitchen, she is vacant," Lupe said in broken English. "She is *always* vacant. Nobody wants to sleep there. The corner is hot. No windows are near the cot, no breeze."

"I'll take it," Alex said.

"*Si, Señor.*"

"Come on, Little Lupe." Alex grinned at the child, nudging his shoulder. "I need you to help me spread out my bedroll. When we're done maybe that camp bread will be ready. I'd sure like a slice or two myself. Then you can go out and play for a while. I won't need you again until morning."

The first thing that caught Alex's eye when he entered the long rectangular room where the cowboys slept was a deer mount nailed to the wall over the cot in the corner—his cot, he supposed. The mount was a white-tailed deer. The head was well formed, and the buck was a ten-pointer.

Windows on both the east and west sides of the room gave somewhat of a cross-breeze, and he counted seven cots under the row of windows—eight counting his. But Alex's cot didn't have a window over the small cast-iron headboard. It backed up to the west wall next to the back door, and Big Lupe was right. It was probably the hottest cot in the camp house.

In the corner beside his bed, he saw a small table with an oil lamp on it. The back door was located on the other side of his cot, and even with the door open all the way, the heat inside the room seemed to be building. All the while the eyes on the deer-mount above his bed kept watching him as if the stuffed head were still alive.

He could be thankful for one thing. The other cots were about two feet apart, but the door gave Alex a space of about three feet between his cot and the next one, providing him with more privacy than the other cowboys had.

Alex stretched out on the cot after Little Lupe left, but it was much too hot to sleep. Sweat poured out of him. Alex felt as if the entire cot were perched up on that sizzling hearth in the kitchen. Even so it was good to be lying down with his boots off.

He'd hooked his black Stetson on one of the points of the deer's antlers, and Alex put his head on the small pillow attached to the bedroll. He would clean up a bit before he went to the cemetery with Maggie and Sarah, but for now he would rest.

MAGGIE LEFT by the back kitchen door at three o'clock that afternoon, carrying a wicker picnic basket. Sarah was close behind her. Big Lupe had hitched up the wagon and left it in the corral outside the fenced-off yard. The flowers for the graves were in a wooden box in the bed of the wagon, along with a shovel, seeds for planting, and buckets of fresh water.

The weights on the chain connected to the yard gate jingled when Maggie opened it and jingled again when it closed behind her. Big Lupe stood beside the wagon, patting one of the mules, and Alex sat in the wagon, on the driver's side. Neither of the men made a sound.

Maggie's hands twisted into fists at her sides. Who did Alex think he was, taking her rightful place behind the reins? And if he thought she was going to let him drive the wagon in his weakened condition, he was wrong. *Besides, it's my wagon.*

Alex smiled at her and waved. Lupe probably smiled too, but she was watching Alex.

He wore the same dark-colored trousers, black boots, and hat he wore when she found him, and the long-sleeved white shirt from the saddlebag. The shirt was partly unbuttoned down the front, and his white collar blew in a gentle breeze.

Maybe she should wait until she'd greeted Alex properly before chastising him for sitting where he didn't belong. He looked as handsome as ever, but as she grew closer, the dark circles that ringed his eyes caused her to wonder if he felt as well as he claimed.

She shook Lupe's hand, thanking him for having the wagon ready on time, and then she gazed up at Alex. "I see you shaved since morning and put on clean clothes."

"I try to do that at least once a month." He didn't smile, but his blue eyes sparkled with amusement. "Summer or winter."

She laughed as Lupe helped her up onto the wagon. She still planned to scold Alex, but apparently he had a talent for making her laugh even when she didn't feel like doing so.

After Lupe lifted Sarah up into the bed of the wagon, Maggie grabbed the reins. "Move over, Mr. Lancaster. I'll be driving this wagon."

He moved in order to make room for her.

When she moved a blonde curl fell across her forehead. Maggie sent it flying with a toss of her head. "Driving this wagon has been my job since our parents died. Oh, and how are you feeling? Were you able to get any rest at the camp house?"

"I stretched out for a while."

She cracked the whip. The team of mules moved forward at a slow pace. Maggie noticed when Alex looked to her side of the wagon and watched her for a moment, grinning.

"I've never seen a woman drive a grown man," he said. "Never that I know of."

"How wonderful. You're remembering things." She cracked the whip again, and the mules moved a little faster. "Then are you saying I shouldn't be driving this wagon?"

"Widows, old maids, and married women with children likely drive wagons. I just can't remember ever seeing a woman drive when men were available."

"You can't remember a lot of things, Mr. Lancaster."

He laughed. "You're right about that."

Her face warmed. "I'm sorry. I didn't mean…"

"I know."

"Still, times are changing." She smiled. "This is 1880. Soon you'll be seeing women drive men everywhere."

"That'll be the day." Alex chuckled then looked down the ruts ahead. "You better slow down, ma'am. I see a big bump a-coming."

"Don't you think I know that? I drive this way all the time."

The left wheel hit the bump, making the left side of the wagon higher than the right. Maggie slid over next to Alex. She might have slid right off the wagon seat if Alex hadn't been there to stop her.

"That was fun," Sarah shouted from the back of the wagon. "Can we do it again?"

"No, Sarah, we can't," Maggie answered. "Now check to see if the buckets and the flowers are all right."

"All right, I will," she said in Spanish.

Maggie hesitated. "Well, are they?"

"The flowers are all pushed over on one side. But the buckets look just fine."

"What about the water *in* the buckets?" Maggie asked.

"Some sloshed over the side," Sarah reported, "but not much."

"Good. And speak English, Sarah. Mr. Lancaster doesn't know Spanish, and it isn't polite to speak in another language in front of people. Now tell him you're sorry."

"I'm sorry, Mr. Lancaster."

"That's better," Maggie said. "And we're almost there. In the meantime I want you to see if you can get those flowers to stand up straight like they're supposed to."

"Yes, Maggie."

The ranch cemetery was centered in a nest of live oak trees. Some called the entire pasture the *Monte Negra,* a Spanish term for Black Forest. Maggie stopped the wagon, jumping down before Alex could come around and help her. Some of her white-faced cattle grazed in the tall grass. The oaks were just ahead.

"We'll leave the flowers in the wagon for now," Maggie said. "I want to show Mr. Lancaster the graves first." She headed toward a small opening in the trees. "We can come back and get everything later. I want to try and transplant some of the flowers. I've also brought seeds and buckets of water. I just hope we can get something to grow."

Maggie assumed Alex was trailing her, but she didn't look back to make sure. Sarah ran ahead.

The breeze picked up, and the force of the wind almost flattened the grass under her feet. The trees had dark trunks no thicker than the width of a rolling pen, and the branches were thin and twisted. Even the dark green leaves looked old and lifeless, yet they fluttered almost happily in a brisk breeze. The roots of some of the trees were exposed like ebony snakes about to attack, and the trees grew so close together it was impossible to go to the actual gravesites except on foot.

"Nobody knows how old the oaks are," she explained when Alex finally caught up with her, "or how long they've been there. And the few trees we have aren't reproducing, as far as I can tell. But it's nice to be among trees of any kind in this part of Texas."

"It's shady here," Alex put in. "That's always nice. But the trees sure grow close to one another. Good thing we're all three skinny. I don't see how a man with a belly as big as Lupe's could reach the place where the graves are."

"He cut a path to the cemetery." Maggie nodded as if to confirm it. "But you can't see it unless you go all the way around to the other side of the trees."

Alex gazed at the gravesite. Vertical planks stood like soldiers around it. As Alex grew closer he could see the fence was held together with nails and bailing wire. Stunted flowering trees with black trunks were planted on each side of the entry gate, leading to the actual graves, and large white flowers and dark green leaves dotted what Maggie called her "wild olive trees." Alex untied the rope-latch and opened the wooden gate. Then he stood back so Maggie and Sarah could enter first.

Most of the graves were unmarked, but wooden crosses marked a few. Yet all the grave mounds were covered with something shiny that caught the sun's rays. He wanted to ask what the shiny stuff was, but when he turned back to Maggie, she was standing in front of an actual headstone in the center of the fenced area. She motioned for Alex and Sarah to join her.

"This is where our family is buried, Mr. Lancaster." She paused, giving him time to read the inscription: *Here lies Henry Gallagher, his beloved wife, Mary, and five of their seven children— Hank, George, Peter, Matthew, and Sadie.*

"I had no idea you lost so many members of your family,"

Alex said in a tone filled with empathy. "All four of your brothers, too. May I express my deepest regrets?"

Maggie nodded. "Thank you. But the boys all died in infancy. Sarah and I didn't even know them. Only our older sister, Sadie, lived to adulthood."

"And she was Jon Anthony's mother?"

"Yes."

Alex wanted to dig deeper, find out more about Sadie, but Maggie still didn't seem to want to talk about her older sister. Did a mystery surround Sadie's life and early death?

"By the way, where is Jon Anthony?" Alex asked after a long pause. "I miss seeing him."

"Elena is keeping him."

Maggie was looking down at the graves, and if the moisture at the edges of her eyes was an indication, she was about to cry, so Alex didn't say anything more. Sarah pulled a tiny rag doll with yellow yarn hair from the pocket of her white apron. The doll looked to be about five inches long, and when Sarah sat down on one of the graves as if she planned to play there, Maggie's forehead wrinkled.

"Sarah," Maggie called. "Get up off that grave this minute. You know we honor the dead here."

The child got up, dusting off the back of her blue dress with one hand and holding tightly to the doll with the other.

After the outburst the hint of tears in Maggie eyes disappeared. Alex felt it was the right time to ask his next question.

"Miss Gallagher, I was wondering about all the shiny things on the mounds. What are broken pieces of colored glass doing on the graves?"

"Thank you for asking." She smiled up at him with a sweet expression, warming Alex's heart. "You see, the ranch-hands can't afford to buy headstones, and wooden crosses don't last long. So they collect pretty pieces of glass they find in the trash heap and put them on the graves. Sometimes the sun and wind slowly change the color of the glass from clear to green or deep purple." She gazed down at the gray-granite headstone. "We never had a headstone for our family either. But after Mama and Papa died and then Sadie, I sold the third wagon and bought this stone. We didn't really need three wagons. Two is plenty. I'm glad people in future generations will know the names of those buried here."

He already knew how careful Maggie was with her spending, and he wondered if she felt guilty for buying the stone. It wouldn't hurt to say something that might make her feel better about it.

"I think you did just the right thing, Miss Gallagher. As you said, two wagons are plenty for a ranch this size."

"Do you really think so?"

"Yes, I do."

They stood there a moment longer, studying the graves. Then they went back to the wagon and got to work, planting flowers. Later Maggie found a wide space between the trees that was just outside the fenced area, and she spread out a tablecloth and the contents of the wicker basket. They had a picnic supper of fried chicken and biscuits.

After supper stories of Maggie's childhood on the ranch kept Alex amused but wishing he had memories he could share as well. When Maggie told about a time when she and Sadie played hide-and-seek in the hayloft, she paused once as if she couldn't find the words to go on.

"I'm sorry," she said at last. "For a moment I couldn't think of the English word for pitchfork. I was going to say that I almost fell on one, but didn't."

He started to say that he was glad she didn't, that falling on a pitchfork would have hurt. But that would have been inappropriate and downright silly. To make a joke of what could have been a serious accident had a sickening ring to it. Instead he merely looked at her, hoping his concern for her safety showed in his eyes.

"Maybe you guessed," Maggie went on, "that we often speak Spanish in our home. It's sort of a tradition among many of the ranch families of South Texas that Anglo children are taught Spanish before English. Maids who help in the house as well as the ranch cowboys speak Spanish, and it's important that we know the language in order to run a ranch as well as to just get along. Many of the wealthy families around here hire nannies from Mexico to care for their children from infancy. Our parents never did that, but we spoke Spanish as often as English around the dinner table. I think Sarah is more comfortable speaking Spanish than English. I have to constantly remind her, or she would speak Spanish all the time. Obviously it's important that she know both languages."

A tinge of guilt haunted Alex on hearing her revelations. He knew Spanish too, and it was time he owned up to it.

"I still can't remember much about my past, ma'am. But I've learned things about myself that I need to tell you about."

"What's that?"

"I know Spanish. I haven't tried to speak it yet, but I understand everything anyone says in that language. I should have told you sooner." His laugh sounded forced even to his ears. "Maybe I couldn't find the English words to explain it."

He'd meant his last statement as a joke, but his words sounded as flat as Big Lupe's camp bread.

"I'm glad you told us," Maggie said after what seemed like a long time. "But I wish I'd known sooner. My translations must have sounded ridiculous."

"Never," he said. "You've been nothing but kind since I woke up that morning in your parents' bed."

"Thank you for saying that." She glanced at Sarah who was combing her doll's hair with her forefinger. "My sister and I are grateful we found you when we did. I hadn't planned to ride out that day, but something told me we needed to go to the cemetery and leave flowers on the graves. I'd prayed earlier that morning, and I think it was God who prompted me to go right to you."

"I've been reading that Bible you let me borrow," he said, "and I think it was, too."

Alex still had questions that needed to be answered, but for now he would listen and let Maggie do the talking. He'd heard somewhere that women needed time each day to sit and talk. He wanted to give her that. Then he wondered when and where he'd heard such a notion.

His memories and his reasoning powers were improving. He just wished those abilities would improve a little faster.

———

MAGGIE PACKED the leftovers in the wicker picnic basket and had planned to put it back in the wagon, but Alex insisted she keep it right there on the ground between them. "I might want another biscuit or two before we go back to the house," he said.

She'd laughed, and now she couldn't stop looking at him as he ate his fourth biscuit.

Maggie had to admit to herself that she enjoyed his company, though at times he still made her nervous. Her mother would have said that until she met Alex she'd never been around a man who made her feel like a woman. Maybe that was true, but she still wasn't sure how she felt about it.

She had to face the fact that she was fond of Alex Lancaster and that her feelings for him were growing stronger with each passing day. Each time he told her he would be leaving soon, she died a little inside and wanted to demand that he stay. But she was afraid that might send him packing for sure.

"I'll give you a penny if you'll tell me what you were thinking about," Alex said, breaking into her reflections. "If I had a penny to give you and knew it was mine, that is."

Maggie's smile served as her initial reply. "The day is ending. See that golden glow in the eastern sky? There's something sad about dusk. When I was a child, this time of day always made me think about the end of the world...what it would be like."

"And now? What does it make you think of now?"

"That night is coming, and we'd better start back."

Maggie got up, and Alex followed. She felt guilty about not sharing the real thoughts running through her mind, but what she'd said made for nice closing words to end the picnic.

Alex helped her fold up the tablecloth. Then she lit the oil lamp Lupe had attached to the front of the wagon. It was dark by the time Alex put a sleeping Sarah on a pallet in back.

"I'd like you to drive now," Maggie said.

She didn't add that he seemed to know a lot about horses and cattle and that she needed a foreman—had needed one since her father died. Maybe she would offer him the job when the time was right. Alex made her feel safe, and she needed that with two children to bring up on her own.

A hooting sound in the underbrush, followed by the rush of flapping wings, caught Maggie by surprise. She jerked around in her seat just as a ghostly white owl with a monkey face erupted from the bushes. It flew off into the shadows.

"Are you all right?" Alex asked.

She nodded. "Yes."

And for the first time in years, she felt that she truly was.

12

Five days later and shortly before sundown, Alex sat in the wagon beside Maggie, gazing at faint dots of light in the distance. "Is that Bayville?"

"Bayview," she corrected.

Alex grinned, and humor mixed with joy sent his heart soaring. He still had minor aches and pains, but he was a lot stronger now than on the day Maggie showed him the horse barn. But he'd stretched the truth a bit in order to convince her he was well enough to drive the wagon all the way to town. He tired easily, and he'd driven the team of mules since early morning. Alex was bone-tired, though he'd rather take a whipping than say anything about it.

Briefly he turned in order to check on those seated in the bed of the wagon. Elena was holding Jon Anthony, and Sarah sat beside her on the patchwork quilt.

Elena hardly said two words to him since he arrived at the ranch, but she'd sent him plenty of evil stares that said more about her thoughts and feelings than words ever could. Alex couldn't help wondering if she had truly walked away from witchcraft or if curandero practices still ruled her life.

He'd expected Elena to put up a fuss when Maggie asked her to go to town with them, and Maggie said that at first Elena refused to go. Then a few days later, Elena agreed to go and to abide by all of Maggie's rules, as if she actually looked forward to driving into town and looking after the children.

Alex thought Elena's sudden change seemed strange if not unlikely. He didn't trust the woman, and he thought Elena was hiding something. He just didn't know what it could be.

Maggie wanted to leave for town the day after he agreed to go, claiming Alex needed a doctor right away, but he'd insisted they wait. He wasn't eager to make the long, hard journey, and if they left too soon, Sarah might miss the celebration going on in town.

Roger stated that a cowboy who fit Alex's description had visited the seaside village of Bayview. Apparently Alex spent a night at the local hotel the night before he rode out to the Gallagher ranch. However he had no memory of the event.

Alex gazed off at miles and miles of grassy flatlands. Though he hadn't seen or heard anything suspicious since they left ranch headquarters, he wanted to make sure they weren't being followed.

The temperature was over ninety degrees by mid-morning, and it hadn't cooled much since then. Even in the shade the stiff, humid breeze off the Gulf felt warm.

He pulled his hat down lower on his forehead to keep what was left of the sun off his face. He'd needed a straw hat, and Maggie gave him one.

The black straw version looked something like a Stetson and had belonged to Maggie's father. Alex felt honored that she wanted him to have it. Still it was as hot as blazes. As an afterthought he gave his hat an extra tug for good measure. Earlier the wind blew his hat right off his head, and he'd stopped the team in order to chase after it. His shoulder still hurt some, and he'd rather not have to stop like that again.

It rained on the previous night; so on top of the hot, humid temperature, the road was a muddy mess. And though the sun was low in the western sky, and it was getting hotter by the minute, dark clouds gathered off the Gulf of Mexico.

"Is it always this hot and windy?" he asked.

"No." The edges of Maggie's mouth curled upward. "Sometimes it's worse."

He grinned. "You doing all right?"

"I guess I'm making it—considering."

"Considering what?"

"Considering I had to help push the wagon out of the mud twice, and now my dress is all dirty."

"I sure wouldn't have had that happen for anything, ma'am, if I'd had the power to prevent it."

Her nod contained a hint of a smile.

"I saw those dark clouds last night," Alex went on, "but never figured it would rain that much between the ranch and town. Bet some places got close to four inches."

"Or more."

He nodded. "Or more." Holding the reins in his right hand, he briefly lifted his left arm and adjusted his sling with the tip of his forefinger. "Sure sorry about that pretty dress of yours. How 'bout your shoes?" He glanced down at her muddy shoes and shook his head.

"I don't mind," she insisted. "Really."

Judging from the tense expression on her face, she did mind, regardless of what she said to the contrary, but he decided he wouldn't question her about it.

"It is hot back here," Elena said from the bed of the wagon. "What will we do if it starts raining?"

"If you're hot find something to fan yourself with," Alex replied. "And if it starts raining, climb under the tan blanket. It's made out of tent material and folded up back there somewhere."

Elena hadn't stopped complaining since they left the ranch.

Alex simply tried to stop listening. His horse was tied to the back of the wagon. He gazed beyond the folks in the back of the wagon to check on the animal.

The black stud appeared fit enough. He'd managed to keep up with the wagon without much of a lather, but Alex was glad they'd be in Bayview before the stallion gave out completely.

MAGGIE SQUINTED at the half-dozen or so two-story buildings just ahead. Bayview wasn't a big town, but it was growing. Then she looked up at a darkening sky and held out one hand, palm up.

"Feel any rain yet?" Alex asked.

"Not yet, but it's coming. I can smell it."

"Me too."

Maggie tossed back her long braid and fingered the bow of her cotton bonnet. Since the day Alex first asked if she was an angel, their friendship had slowly grown. Now she felt almost as comfortable teasing him as she felt teasing Sarah.

"Mr. Lancaster, did I ever mention that you have dimples when you smile?" She laughed. "Just like a girl!"

He joined in her laughter. "No, I don't think you did. Do I really look like a girl to you?" His eyes lit with anticipation, waiting for her answer.

She appraised him for a moment. "Maybe," she said, "when the light's just right."

"Maybe?" He wadded up a piece of writing paper he'd jotted some notes on and threw it at her. "Take that."

"And this." She laughed, tossing it right back.

The ball of paper hit his reining hand and bounced off. It was captured by a gust of southeast wind. The crumpled paper flew to the ground, rolling and rolling across the pasture and out of sight.

"I guess that about ends the war, doesn't it, Miss Maggie?"

"It ends a battle. We'll have to wait and see who wins the war."

He laughed again.

Alex made her feel all warm and bubbly, but she forced herself to look away before he noticed. Theirs was a strange relationship, she decided. She wanted to move closer to Alex, but each time she did, she recalled what happened to Sadie. Then she found herself backing away from him faster than when she'd moved toward him.

The situation was hopeless. In order to focus her mind on happier thoughts, she gazed out at her surroundings.

Sheet lighting flashed above the horizon; thunder boomed in the distance.

"Hope the rain doesn't spoil the barbecue tomorrow," she said, still studying the sky.

"I thought you said parades and barbecues were a waste of time."

"I did, but I'd hate to disappoint Sarah."

AT SUNDOWN ALEX looked down at a pair of ruts the ranchers and town-folks called a road. In spite of what she'd said to the contrary, Alex thought Maggie looked forward to the doings in town as much as Sarah did. He saw excitement sparkling in those big brown eyes of hers when she talked about the coming event. A smile probably danced in his eyes too.

Alex coaxed the team of mules down the main street of Bayview and slowed the wagon in front of the general store. Branleys' Mercantile was already closed, but The Happy Redfish across the street was open and all lit up.

Spanish music blared from inside. Two drunks stood in front of the building, drinking from large mugs and laughing.

Sarah stood up in the back of the wagon and pointed to the two old men. "Look at them. Aren't they funny-looking?"

Maggie turned around in her seat. "Hush, Sarah. They'll hear you. And sit down!"

Alex cracked the whip, and the wagon jerked forward. Sarah sat down suddenly and hard.

"Sorry, Miss Sarah," Alex said. "You all right?" He glanced back at the child.

Sarah rubbed the part of her body that no doubt hurt the most.

"You deserved to get bumped, Sarah," Maggie said. "You know better than to stand up in the back of a moving wagon."

The wagon continued on by the cafe/saloon; then Alex turned left. Maggie had said the Dawson Sunday house was out of town on the road to Corpus Christi. He was eager to get everybody settled and safe before total darkness swallowed them, but he wasn't looking forward to seeing Roger again...or to meeting his mother.

Maggie glanced to the right then her left. He smiled to himself. She'd talked about scary stories her older sister told her when they were children, and he figured she was listening for suspicious sounds in the shadows. She'd also told Alex she didn't think his attacker was a thief, leaving murderer as a possibility.

But why would someone shoot him from behind...unless it was for money? Yet the money was still in the saddlebag when Big Lupe found the black horse. It didn't make sense.

Obviously the person or persons who took a shot at Alex knew him well enough to want to kill him. He had to face the fact that until the gunman was found and arrested, they were all in danger.

"We need to let Sheriff Ethridge know what happened to you, Mr. Lancaster," Maggie said, interrupting his thoughts, "while we're here in town."

"I intend to." Alex pointed to the eastern sky in hopes of changing the subject. "Will you just look at that sunset? Beautiful, isn't it?"

"Yes, it is." But she wasn't looking at the gold-colored sky. She was looking at him. "You have a nice profile, Mr. Lancaster."

"Thank you."

"No need to thank me. I'm just stating a fact."

Maggie looked away and smiled. "My father had a nice profile. Mama said all the young ladies of her day thought so, and I'm sure you'll be the main topic of conversation among the unmarried ladies of Bayview on Founders Day."

"Is that all you wanted to say, ma'am?" Alex asked.

"No. Please remind me to mail my letters while we're in town this weekend. I'm pretty forgetful sometimes."

"I'm forgetful too." He turned her way briefly and chuckled under his breath. "In fact I have a real bad case of it."

"I...I'm sorry. I didn't mean..."

"I know you didn't. I reckon I was teasing you some, in hopes of getting a rise out of you. You see, I like your smile, ma'am. It means you have a merry heart. I heard somewhere that a merry heart is good for what ails you."

"A verse something like that is in the Bible."

He rubbed a spot behind his right ear. "I really like reading the Bible now. Reckon I'm a preacher or something, ma'am, and don't know it yet?"

"I wouldn't bet on it."

He cocked his head to one side. "Anyways, I'll sure be glad to remind you about those letters you need to mail—if I remember. 'Cause I have one I plan to mail to that Mrs. Parson in San Antonio."

MAGGIE GLANCED down the road ahead. She'd written to Mrs. Parson and to her "old maid" aunt, but she hadn't mentioned Alex or the shooting to Aunt Violet, who tended to jump to conclusions. If she knew Maggie let a man, wounded or otherwise, move into the spare bedroom, she'd be on the next northbound stage out of Brownsville.

The faint sound of modern music tinkling from a piano somewhere caused Maggie to glance up. Alex slowed the mules and pulled them to a stop.

She must have been dreaming because she hadn't realized they were even close to the Sunday house, much less practically at the front door. The big two-story house on the bay was painted white, and lamps lit up the long front porch. The salty air was shaded in a variety of odors including the faint scent of fish, and three fancy carriages were parked out front.

Alex tied up the reins and glanced over at Maggie. "Looks like a party is going on. Did you know about this?"

Maggie shook her head. "No, but Roger's mother has lots of parties."

"I'm not dressed right for something like this."

Maggie looked down at her soiled dress and shoes. "Neither am I. But don't worry; you look just fine. I'm sure Miss Lucy will give us time to change before supper."

Alex jumped down and went around to her side of the wagon as if he intended to help her down. He raised his good arm. "May I help you down, ma'am?"

"Thank you for the kind offer, Mr. Lancaster, but I climbed up in the wagon all by myself, and I can climb down the same way. I'm sure Sarah and Jon Anthony would appreciate your help, but I'm fine."

Maggie took hold of the back of the seat and started to jump down.

"So you intend to try this?" he asked. "People inside the house could be watching."

She wished she hadn't forgotten the wooden ladder she usually brought along for occasions like this. For all she knew the people inside the house really could be standing at the windows, looking out.

Elena jumped off the back of the wagon, her skirt billowing out around her. Maggie blushed. A flash of Elena's white bloomers had burst into view like a white flag in the moonlight.

Alex cleared his throat, looking away from the back of the wagon. "May I help you down, Miss Sarah?"

"Sure you can." Sarah giggled, and he swung her to the ground with his good arm.

Alex lifted Jon Anthony down next and grinned back at Maggie. "Changed your mind?"

She hesitated. He crossed his right arm over his sling and waited.

Maggie knew she was being childish, planning to get down on her own. What if her bloomers showed as Elena's had? But if she backed out now, she would look like a silly young girl in his eyes. Alex stood perfectly still, smiling as if he enjoyed her dilemma.

"Would you mind turning your back to me, please?" she asked.

He laughed and did as she requested.

As soon as he turned around, a man and woman stepped out onto the wide front porch of the Dawson house. Mr. and Mrs. Branley waved. Maggie waved back. With the two of them watching and possibly Alex as well, jumping down like a wild woman was out of the question.

"I changed my mind," she said. "Would you please help me down, sir?"

Alex turned back around and chuckled again. "I'd consider it an honor."

"Then stop laughing and get it over with."

He reached out and wrapped his right arm around her

slender waist. In spite of all her efforts to appear indifferent to him, she feared he already knew she thought more of him than a decent young lady should. But she hoped she didn't seem as nervous as she had at first.

Alex lifted her to the ground as if she were weightless. He set her on the gravel path in front of the house and offered her his arm.

"Shall we go inside?" he asked.

"Of course," she answered, ignoring his arm.

Maggie's cheeks felt warm as she moved ahead of him. Maybe he wouldn't notice that she was blushing.

The couple on the porch had either gone back inside or moved around to the other side of the house, and Maggie was glad. The less people knew about this romantic nonsense with Alex, the better. If it continued she could end up with a reputation as bad as her sister Sadie's.

13

M aggie ran the soles of her muddy shoes over the metal scraper next to the door. Roger's mother would have a fit if somebody dared track mud on her polished hardwood floors, and Maggie had already warned everybody from the Gallagher Ranch not to break that rule.

"I guess this is an odd question," Alex said from somewhere behind her, "but how did the Sunday house get its name?"

"I thought I told you, but apparently not." She stepped back so Alex could scrape his boots. "Ranchers around here live miles from any town, and that means miles from the nearest church. Some people build small houses they can camp in on weekends so they can attend church services. The Dawsons built a really big house. They call it the Sunday house, and Miss Lucy, Roger's mother, lives here all year long. Only Roger lives at their ranch."

Alex nodded. "I see."

Elena and the children were already scraping their shoes when Maggie knocked on the door. As she waited for someone to answer, she took in once more the white Southern-style house with its pillars and wide porch. "Isn't this place lovely?"

"Overpowering might be a better word." Alex let out a low

whistle. "Somebody around here must be plenty rich. Who built it? Roger or his mother?"

Roger's father had it built shortly before he died," Maggie said.

"When was that?"

"When Roger was fifteen."

Maggie would have said more, but Roger's gray-haired mother opened the front door. Maggie introduced Miss Lucy to Alex. At first she didn't appear to be as eager to have him in her home as Maggie had hoped. But Miss Lucy recovered quickly and became the perfect hostess again, bubbling and smiling all over the place.

While Miss Lucy got acquainted with Alex, retelling a long story about the house Maggie had heard a hundred times, Maggie surveyed as much of the Sunday house as she could see from the entry hall. Miss Lucy loved to redecorate, and there was always something new and beautiful to see.

The entry often held a subtle scent of fresh flowers, and that evening was no exception. Maggie stepped forward slightly in order to study the huge vases of yellow roses that banked both sides of the front door. She was admiring the thick coat of bees' wax on the railing of the stairway and the way it made the wood shine like honey-glass while Miss Lucy told Alex another juicy story. Maggie smiled. Miss Lucy was a mess all right—but a lovable one. But Maggie couldn't help but wonder what Alex was thinking.

Mrs. Lucy Dawson always insisted she didn't like gossip or idle talk of any kind, but she never missed the opportunity to tell the latest news. Oh, Lucy had her faults all right, and so did Roger, but Maggie would always love them because they were practically the only ones in the area who didn't turn against the entire Gallagher family after Sadie's scandal became known.

Roger even offered to marry Maggie as soon as all the talk started, and he'd never stopped asking. Maggie's loyalty to him and his mother would continue no matter what, but she would never agree to marry Roger merely to prove they were still friends.

Miss Lucy turned then and was about to escort them up the stairs when a house-maid wearing a white apron interrupted.

"*Señora*," the maid said in broken English, "may I talk to you, please?"

"Can't it wait, Maria?" Miss Lucy asked.

"No, *Señora*."

"Oh, well, all right then." Miss Lucy shrugged apologetically. "Please excuse me. I'll be back as soon as I possibly can."

"Of course," Maggie said.

Maggie and Alex still stood just inside the entry hall. Elena and the children had come in soon after they did, and Jon Anthony looked tired. Maggie nodded in the direction of a long wooden bench near the door leading to the library. Elena led the children over there to wait.

"As I said," Alex whispered, "this house is real nice and all, but it sure looks expensive. Seems like a waste of good money to me."

Maggie nodded. "I've always enjoyed being here though."

She motioned toward the open archway. "As you probably guessed, Miss Lucy has a passion for entertaining."

"Maybe Party House might be a better name for this place than Sunday house," he suggested. "And it's so big."

"Seven bedrooms."

"Roger must be from a large family."

"No," Maggie said. "Since his father died there's just Roger and his mother."

"Then why all the bedrooms?"

"Miss Lucy likes big houses, and she loves to remodel this one."

Alex nodded, glancing around the entry hall.

Maggie's papa would never have wasted money on a second

home, especially one that wasn't truly necessary. She'd always thought the Dawson house was probably a lot more costly than their ranching interests justified, but she'd never voiced that thought to anyone.

A door opened to their right, and Miss Lucy rushed toward them. "Forgive me for being so long. We had minor problems in the kitchen, but everything is straightened out now." She indicated the stairway. "Just follow me up, and I'll show you to your rooms."

Maggie motioned for Elena and the children to follow, and they trailed Miss Lucy to the winding staircase.

At the foot of the stairs, Maggie hesitated long enough to catch a brief glimpse beyond the archway. The parlor was well lighted, she noticed. The furnishings inside were as tasteful and as expensive-looking as ever—a flash of blue brocade here and navy velvet curtains there. A settee was added since her last visit, in blue and ivory print.

Four people stood with their backs to her, talking. Maggie raised the hem of her mud-splattered blue dress and started up the flight of stairs.

"Maggie," Miss Lucy said as she continued up the stairs, "you and Sarah will be in the big room in the east wing, the one with a view of the bay. It has a connecting door, of course, and I'll put Elena and Jon Anthony in there." Miss Lucy paused briefly and glanced back at Maggie. "Is that all right with you, hon?"

"Oh, yes, ma'am. It most certainly is."

"Will Noma Elaine be here tonight?" Sarah put in.

Miss Lucy lifted her chin. Her smile had a condescending edge. "Her parents will be, dear, but not Noma Elaine. You'll see her tomorrow at the barbecue."

The older woman turned to Alex. The warmth Maggie noticed earlier in Miss Lucy's face suddenly disappeared. "You can have the small bedroom on the lower level, sir, across from the butler's room."

The butler's room? Maggie was speechless. Why had Miss Lucy turned on Alex like this? By lower level she must mean the basement. And where was the butler? She certainly hadn't seen him.

She would have a word with Miss Lucy on this matter at her earliest opportunity, but now wasn't the time. Maggie smiled in Alex's direction, hoping to lift his spirits, and headed for the bedroom she was assigned.

As she was closing the door, she heard Alex tell Miss Lucy that he would need to see about his horse and the mules before he went all the way down to his bedroom.

Maggie opened the connecting door and looked toward the smaller bedroom. "Sarah, Miss Lucy will want you and Jon Anthony to have your supper in here with Elena tonight. I 'spect she'll be sending up a supper tray before too long, so don't go downstairs and start bothering the help."

"Where will you eat?" Sarah asked in Spanish.

"At the supper party downstairs, I imagine." Maggie looked down at the mud-spots on the front of her dress and let go with a sigh that didn't begin to describe how exasperated she felt. "Guess I'll have to change first. And for heaven sakes, Sarah, don't talk Spanish all weekend like you did the last time we were here."

"I won't."

"Well, I should hope not. Mama would turn over in her grave if you did something strange like that in public again."

"Would she really?" Sarah asked.

"I don't know. Just make sure you don't forget. I need to change my clothes."

Maggie took a sponge bath in front of a white porcelain bowl and changed into the gold-colored evening gown edged in gold lace that Aunt Violet sent as a birthday gift. The dress was designed in the latest fashion and soft to the touch. As she put it on for the very first time, Maggie hummed the Spanish tune the young women sang the day she found Alex.

Then she pinched both her cheeks and hurried downstairs to the parlor. The Dawsons and their guests were still gathered there, but Alex hadn't joined them yet.

———————

MAGGIE SETTLED onto the stylish settee that she'd noticed earlier. Roger was across the room talking to his lawyer. But where was Alex?

A few minutes later two cigar-smoking elderly gentlemen joined her there on the settee—Mr. J.B. Abbott on her right and Mr. Percy Cline on her left. The men were discussing who might buy the Blevin place. Apparently Roger wanted to buy it but didn't have the cash to close the deal.

The portly Mr. Abbot cleared his throat. "I heard that what little of the Dawson money they have left comes from Miss Lucy's side of the family. Roger's late father was nothing but an outright drunk and lazy as the day is long."

"Roger's following in his father's footsteps, if you ask me." Mr. Cline took a puff from his cigar and blew it out, making a gray halo in the air.

Maggie coughed, wiping away the smoke as best she could. She didn't want to hear such talk about her lifelong friends even though she'd smelled whiskey on Roger's breath when she first came in. She wanted to get up and move to another part of the big room, but the two men had scooted forward on the settee. Their knees angled toward each other and were almost touching. It would be physically impossible for Maggie to squeeze between them without making a spectacle of herself. She vowed not to listen to anything else they said, though she knew that would be impossible.

"Mr. Blevin said that if Roger really wants the land, he needs a down payment." Mr. Abbot leaned still closer to skinny-legged Mr. Cline. "Blevin said he's willing to take the Sunday house as a down payment. Otherwise, he's selling his ranch to old man McGregor and those sons of his."

"Is that a fact?" Mr. Cline chuckled. "Serves Roger right. I heard-tell that one of the McGregor sons is a cowboy and the other is a preacher or soon will be. Can you beat that?"

"A preacher? That *is* funny." Mr. Abbot laughed, shaking the entire settee and causing Maggie even more discomfort. "I heard McGregor is interested in buying the Sunday house too. And he's got the money."

"Over Miss Lucy's dead body."

"You're right. But the land the Sunday house sits on is right across the fence-line from the Blevin ranch. If McGregor gets to buy the Blevin place, he'll want the Sunday house too."

"Then Roger has got to come up with the money. How long does he have?"

"Not long. And McGregor has cash. Maybe it's already too late for Roger."

"It's *never* too late for Roger," Mr. Cline insisted. "I wager Roger will get the money somehow. He always does. Now let's go in to dinner. I'm starved."

Mr. Cline put his lighted cigar next to Mr. Abbot's in the small bowl that centered the table in front of them and turned, gazing back at Maggie as if he suddenly realized she was still sitting there.

"Miss Gallagher, will you do me the honor of allowing me to take you in to dinner?"

"Thank you kindly, sir." She coughed again. "But you...you go on. I think I'll just sit here a while longer."

"Of course."

Maggie pulled a white lace handkerchief from the tiny evening purse that dangled from her wrist. After coughing for the umpteenth time, she wiped her watery eyes with the handkerchief. All at once she noticed Roger standing before her.

He grabbed her arm. "Come, my dear. It's time I took you in to eat."

As they walked under the archway leading to the huge dining room, Maggie studied the long rectangular table with its white lace cloth, spotless white china, and silver place settings. She counted six chairs on one side, six on the other. Roger would sit at the head of the table. His mother was already seated at the foot. Maggie would be expected to sit in the vacant chair to Roger's right, and there were no more vacant chairs.

"Roger," she said, "where is Mr. Lancaster going to sit?"

Roger looked off as if he hadn't heard her question. Then he turned his back on Maggie. Leaning forward he began talking to his lawyer again, now seated at the table to his left.

She didn't know why Roger never answered her question, but obviously somebody made a mistake. Miss Lucy would never be so unkind as to leave Alex off her guest list. He was a visitor in her home, notwithstanding the fact he was sleeping in the basement.

Her curiosity ballooned during the meal. Where was Alex? She needed to find out.

After they finished eating, the entire group moved back into the parlor. Maggie excused herself.

"Are you ill?" Roger asked.

"No, I just need to leave the party for a moment. I'll be back."

"All right then."

Roger's smile never reached his eyes, and it held mocking overtones as if he thought she planned to go out back to the privy. It wasn't true, but what if it was? Was it Roger's business if she chose to leave the room?

To anyone who saw her, Maggie was merely exploring the mansion, a house she'd visited many times. She even took a short tour of the basement, but she was unable to find Alex.

A light rain pattered on the windowpanes by the time she finally located him. Alex sat in a straight-backed chair in the kitchen, eating his supper alone, and somehow, he looked rested —as if being in town was just the tonic he needed. She took the chair across from his.

"Why didn't you join the rest of the guests at supper" she asked.

"I wasn't invited."

"What?"

"I probably wasn't on the guest list," he said.

"Miss Lucy isn't like that, sir. It must have been a terrible mistake. I intend to discuss this with her as soon as I can and see she makes amends. The fact you're sleeping in the basement is bad enough, but this is beyond acceptable and then some."

Alex shook his head. "There was no mistake. And don't make amends on my account. A maid came to my door a while ago and showed me the way down here. Then she served me a plate of leftovers."

"Miss Lucy wouldn't let one of her guests eat warmed-over food, especially in the kitchen. The maid must have misunderstood."

"I'm not complaining." Alex reached for a slice of lemon on the side of his plate. He squeezed out the juice with his thumb and forefinger, spreading the liquid over his fish. "The food is very good, and the kitchen's fine with me. I didn't want to go to Miss Lucy's fancy party anyway." He dug his fork into a piece of the baked fish. "Best redfish I ever flopped a lip on."

"Redfish have scales," she said.

"I know."

"But catfish don't. And we also had catfish for supper. "

"So what's your point? Are you teaching me a lesson on fishing, or practicing up for when you teach Sarah her next school lesson?"

"I just thought you might find it interesting." She tossed back her curls. "I read in the Old Testament that the Jews were allowed to eat fish with scales, but not fish without them. Do you know why?"

Alex grinned, showing his dimples. "No, but I have a feeling you're going to tell me."

Maggie's cheeks warmed and her heart raced as she considered how very handsome this cowboy really was. But she did her best to ignore it. "Well, catfish and other scavengers eat garbage they find at the bottom of the sea, and catfish don't have scales. I think God was trying to tell the Jews not to have anything to do with nasty things like dirty talk and dirty deeds."

"You're talking about sin."

"Yes," she said, "I guess I am."

"Interesting." Alex reached his hand across the table and guided his fork right to her mouth. The aroma of fresh fish broiled in butter and spices drifted over to her.

"Just try a mouthful of this," he said, "and see how you like it."

"I've already eaten." But her mouth watered anyway.

He poked the fork in her mouth before she had time to realize what was happening. And even though she'd just had that same dish at supper, prepared in exactly that same way, she'd never eaten food that tasted any better.

It sounded insane, but somehow having a fork in her mouth that had first been in his was almost like having his lips touch hers. She was already eying the next forkful when she took the time to consider how ridiculous she must have looked being fed, and how brazen she must have appeared to him.

"Open up," he said in a teasing tone of voice.

Her mouth was already partly open, anticipating the next bite. She pressed her lips together, glancing down at her hands. The game they were playing was dangerous, and she had no intention of opening her mouth again unless she had something important to say. In fact it was time to leave.

Maggie inched her chair back from the table and stood.

"I'm glad you're enjoying your meal," she said, "but I have to get back to the party. Roger and Miss Lucy must be wondering where I am."

She started to walk off.

"Now hold on there, Miss Maggie. I've got something I've been meaning to ask you for several days. I meant to mention it on the way here but never got around to it."

She paused. "And what would that be?"

"A couple of days ago I took a ride on the black stallion to try out that bridle you let me borrow. Remember?"

"Of course I remember. But what does that have to do with me?" she asked.

"I was up in the northeast pasture, the one you call the Santa Fe, after a rain, and I noticed tracks all around on both sides of that fence there—human tracks. The person walking around there wore sandals, not shoes or boots. I figure he or she must have come from the Rio Grande Valley or even Mexico. Nobody from around here wears sandals in deep sand." Alex cleared his throat. "Then Big Lupe told me one of your horses was missing."

ALEX THOUGHT Maggie looked surprised and a little upset by what he told her. If only she would share those concerns with him. Was she thinking about the man who shot him, wondering if he returned to finish what he started?

"Big Lupe told me about the missing horse, and I'm planning to hire another cowboy or two before spring roundup," Maggie said after a long pause. "But the stranger doesn't work for me. I wouldn't know who he is because we don't own the pasture on the other side of that fence. He might be one of Roger's men, but I'm surprised he was wearing sandals."

"Roger owns that land?"

"Yes. His ranch connects ours."

"That's right. I remember hearing that somewhere."

Her gaze drifted to the door leading to the hallway. "I must go before Miss Lucy comes looking for me. Do you have anything else you want to say before I leave?"

"Yes, ma'am. I want you to promise to go to Dr. Smyth's office with me in the morning."

"Why?"

He grinned. "I'm new in town, and I need you to show me around. By the way, how big is Bayview? It didn't look very big when we drove through it this evening."

Maggie rolled her eyes. "You need my help about as much as a coyote needs spectacles to find a helpless rabbit. Anyone could direct you to the doctor's office or anywhere else in town. The doctor's office is on the main street directly above the general store. We drove right by it earlier this evening."

"Please ma'am, say you'll go with me."

His voice had gentled to hardly more than a whisper. Perhaps she had gentled too. A hint of a smile formed on her lips of its own accord. She dismissed it immediately. "I'll be glad to ride over there with you," she said after a long pause. "But the population of Bayview is less than a hundred people."

"That's mighty kind of you. I appreciate it. I'd hate to get lost in a town as big as this one."

She laughed silently but looked away so he wouldn't see.

14

Alex watched Maggie stroll back down the long hall to the parlor. He loved the way she looked and especially the way she moved—so erect and graceful.

When he could no longer see her, he glanced down at his plate. A few of the pinto beans were left but not a bite of the fish. He wadded up his white napkin and put it to one side of his plate.

He'd leaned forward, preparing to get up out of his chair, when a flash of memory penetrated his conscious mind. He saw a line of cedar posts connected by a wire fence. The brief image was like a warning of bigger recollections to come.

Instead of getting up he sat back in his chair and closed his eyes. From recent experience he knew that memories flowed better when his eyes were shut. As these new memories surged through his brain, it was like scenes from the past that were happening right before his eyes.

In the vision Alex was horseback, reining his mount around a gathering of trees so thick he could barely see light between them. Yet he'd noticed something—a nearby fence looked as if the wires were broken, perhaps on purpose. He remembered thinking that even if it were true, what business was that of his? If he hoped to win favor with the people living in the big white house on the rise, he must focus on getting water for his horse, food and water for himself, and keep his nose out of matters that didn't concern him.

On the other hand, if the people in the big house were being robbed and he told them about the rip in the fence, he might gain their confidence.

Alex recalled dismounting and walking his horse over to the fence for a better look. But even before he got there, he could see the fence was cut, not broken as he first thought. Both human and animal tracks were all around the break. Somebody was stealing cattle from one side of the fence and driving them through the cut in the fence to the other side. From the look of the tracks and the direction they were headed, the folks in the big white house had a cattle rustler on their hands, and if he didn't warn them, they could lose even more cattle.

Alex sensed there was more to this vision than he was able to remember. But he did recall getting back on his horse and heading toward a plowed field. He tried to remember more —*really* tried—but nothing else surfaced.

Alex didn't want to believe the implications, yet it all fit. And then just days ago, the whole thing happened on the ranch again.

Cattle rustlers were stealing Maggie's cattle. The person or persons doing it must have seen Alex nosing around the cut in the fence. That was a good enough reason to take a shot at him. His first suspect was Roger because his ranch was next to Maggie's, giving Roger the perfect opportunity. But the outlaw didn't have to be Roger. Plenty of cattle rustlers were out there, and not all of them owned land across the wire fence from the Gallagher Ranch.

His brief memory put a new light on everything. In time

Alex must make Maggie aware of his suspicions. But would she listen?

It wouldn't be easy. Maggie was fond of Roger and his mother, and he'd have to be careful how he told her what he thought to be true. On second thought maybe he should keep his thoughts and opinions to himself until he knew more.

Alex got up from the table and was halfway down the stairs leading to the basement when laughter exploded from somewhere, maybe the parlor room. He climbed to the top of the stairs again and stopped briefly, hoping to see Maggie gliding toward him. All he saw was a maid carrying a tray of dirty dishes. Reluctantly he moved on down the stairs to his basement room and went to bed.

MAGGIE RETURNED to her room on the second floor not long after she left Alex in the kitchen. She wasn't enjoying Miss Lucy's fancy party. Most of the guests were old enough to be her parents, and Roger seemed to want all the guests to think that he and Maggie were practically engaged.

Roger was a childhood friend, and she would always have warm feelings for him and his mother. But she could never think of him romantically, no matter how many times he asked her to marry him.

Semi-darkness caused Maggie to pause in the doorway of the bedroom she was to share with Sarah. After a moment she tiptoed inside. One small candle guided her to the single bed under the window next to her sister's bed. Maggie undressed quickly and climbed under the covers. But even with the east windows open and salty air pouring through along with a healthy breeze, it was much too hot for a bed covering. She kicked off the sheet and the light blanket. The Gulf wind whipped at her hair, rumpling her soft undergarments.

Sleeping away from home was always a problem for Maggie, and she doubted she'd be able to catch more than an hour or two a night until she returned home. Her mind was too busy reviewing every single thing that had happened since they left the ranch, including how Alex looked, what he wore, and every word he said to her.

They had almost reached the Sunday house when she caught a good look at his profile, and it was already too dark to really see him. All she saw was an outline of his profile with his thick, curly hair blowing across his forehead. His straight nose and strong chin were silhouetted against a darkening sky.

Was she falling in love with Alexander Paul Lancaster? It was too soon to consider such a possibility. She decided to try and think of something else. Still she wondered, and it was likely she would keep on wondering in the days to come.

Though it was her custom to brush her hair 100 strokes every night and read one chapter from the Bible, that night she could do neither. She would never be able to find her Bible or her brush in such a dark room, and even if she found the Bible, the feeble glow coming from the lone candle would not provide enough light to read.

Sometimes when she had a hard time falling asleep, Maggie sang hymns—softly lest she wake other members of the household. But singing, even softly, would be impossible with Sarah's bed only two or three feet from hers. However she could sing mentally—inside her spirit. Often she prayed mentally rather than out aloud.

Prayers and songs played inside her head for several minutes. A sleepy feeling soon flooded her. Pleased that sleep was coming, she turned on her right side and closed her eyes.

LATER THAT NIGHT Alex climbed the stairs to the main floor of the mansion, needing a drink of water. Near the top of the stairs, he saw Roger and his mother bidding the last party guest goodbye. Quickly he hid behind a heavy tan drape separating the entry hall and a hallway the servants used. He should have hurried down the hall to the kitchen and poured himself a glass of water. Instead he stood there, listening to their private conversation and feeling guilty about doing it. Yet he wondered if they might know something that would help him find the answers to all his questions.

"Now Roger, dear," Miss Lucy said as if her son were ten years old and had just stolen a cookie from the cookie jar. "You can't embarrass a young woman you hope to make your wife by openly hinting that the two of you will soon marry—especially in front our guests, of all people—that is, if you hope that one day she will truly accept one of your proposals. Didn't you notice how she blushed when you talked that way?"

Roger didn't reply, and Alex didn't blame him. Young men didn't like being scolded by their mothers. Mother and son clearly loved and hated each other. Roger probably wished his mother would keep her mouth closed but knew better than to complain.

"Well, didn't you?"

"Didn't I what?" Roger mumbled.

"Didn't you notice how Maggie blushed when you told everyone there might soon be wedding bells here at the Sunday house? And then you looked over at Maggie and smiled so everyone would know she was the one."

"So what should I do about it now, Mama?"

"Do not go to the Happy Redfish and be with one of those women, that's for sure. A young woman like Maggie wants a man who will love her and only her forever. So if you expect to make her your wife before you're old and gray, you must pay close attention to what I'm telling you. A mother knows these things, Roger; you should listen. Now I'm going to stand here in front of the door until I see you go up those stairs and into your room. And remember, dear one, I'm doing this for your own good."

Roger turned and headed for the stairs. But if Roger had plans for the evening, Alex doubted he intended to change them to please his mother.

Miss Lucy went upstairs to her room. Alex was about to go into the kitchen when he saw Roger creep down the stairs and out the front door. Alex could either get his glass of water or follow Roger. Alex looked both ways and headed out the door.

MAGGIE HEARD A NOISE. She sat up in bed. Someone was outside her window. She didn't know how she knew; she just did. The white dressing gown that went over her sleeping dress was draped over the foot of the iron bed. She put it on and went down the stairs and out into the night. A full moon greeted her, casting its light across the landscape.

Someone whispered to her from the darkness. She couldn't make out all the words, but she distinctly heard someone say, "Maggie."

She turned. A man with a scar on his face glared at her in the moonlight. Her breath caught. It was the man she and Ana met the day they went to pick wildflowers.

"I've come for my revenge for what you did to my face."

Maggie took a step back, but she tripped and fell. She tried to get up but slipped down again. At last she got to her feet, but he was closing in. She screamed and tried to run, but no matter how fast she moved her legs, she stayed in the same spot.

It suddenly came to her that she was dreaming; she needed to wake up.

Maggie slowly opened her eyes, trembling. She was in a bed

at Miss Lucy's house in Bayview, and Sarah slept in the small bed beside hers.

She'd had another of those awful dreams like the ones she'd had off and on since she was fifteen. Before she fell asleep she'd been thinking about the tracks in the mud that Alex mentioned. He said the man that made those tracks was probably wearing sandals. The man in the pasture with Ana that day wore brown leather sandals, the kind you buy in Mexico.

Maybe thinking about what Alex told her caused the dream. What she didn't know was how to get the dreams to stop.

Big Lupe also saw a stranger on the ranch recently. He said he thought the man crossed over from Mexico, and he went on to say that one of her horses was missing. She knew it was silly to think the stranger Lupe saw was the same man she stabbed the day she and Ana went out to pick flowers. It was stranger still to assume he'd returned for revenge and took one of her horses to get even. She needed to put all such thoughts out of her mind, but somehow those very thoughts and memories kept creeping into her dreams.

Thunder boomed, and Maggie jumped. She turned quickly toward the windows. Lightning flashed, and the rapping sound of heavy rain pounded on the windowpane by her bed. Someone had closed the windows while she slept, likely Elena. And it was dark outside, not filled with moonlight like in the dream. In fact she couldn't see the moon at all. All she saw was blackness and flashes of light that cracked the sky.

She glanced at the small table between the beds. She'd forgotten to blow out the candle. It was still lighted but shorter than when she fell asleep. White candle-drippings gathered in the bottom of the small metal cup it stood in.

She should blow out the candle; candles cost money. Her late father reminded her of the importance of frugality often enough. But in her present state of mind, the thought of total darkness made her wish she could turn on every lamp she could find.

Maggie would have a hard time sleeping now. Nevertheless she blew out the candle, praying and then singing two hymns in her mind. She was about to sing a third when another sleepy feeling swept over her. She hadn't expected it, but she closed her eyes anyway.

ALEX GOT UP EARLY the next morning, mounted his black stallion, and went for a ride before breakfast. He was unable to follow Roger's fast carriage on the previous night, but maybe he would find someone in town or in the area that knew a young woman named Dee.

The heavy rains that pounded the Sunday house during the night disappeared before morning, but they left their mark. The land around Bayview was flat, but the soil was rich and darker than the sandy soil found on the ranch. That morning the ground was still damp from the recent rains. Mud covered the roads, and little puddles of water were scattered everywhere.

Alex asked several strangers along the road to town if they knew of a woman by the name of Dee, but nobody did. However an elderly farmer's wife stood just inside the white picket fence that circled her yard, and when Alex stopped in front of that fence, she made an interesting suggestion.

She said, "Maybe Dee is short for Doris or Delores."

Alex had never considered that possibility, and a wave of encouragement swept over him. The woman went on to say she didn't know anyone with either of those names, and after asking around again, he soon learned nobody else did either.

He'd hoped taking a tour of the area would answer some of his questions. After plowing down one muddy street after the other and riding by countless farm houses, he realized that so far nothing in Bayview produced any clues to Dee's identity or the identity of the gunman. It was becoming clearer that Dee lived on a ranch somewhere north of Bayview, and nothing Alex saw or heard caused more personal memories to surface.

A sign in the front of a shop on Main Street read *Nueces Barber Shop*. Alex could use a shave and a haircut, not to mention a decent bath. Somehow he knew men were often more willing to talk to their barber than to people in their own families. Maybe he could learn something if he went in and had his hair cut.

Alex had a shave and a haircut without learning anything that would help him find answers. Now he soaked in a bathtub in the back room of Nueces Barber Shop, apparently the only barber shop in Bayview. Mentally he complained about the fact that the barber, Wade Simpson, had left the door open a crack. He liked hearing what was being said in the shop, but he didn't like being able to see what was going on in the shop through the narrow opening because he figured if he could see them, they might be able to see him too.

He was about to get out of the tub and close the door when he heard the bell over the door of the shop ding three times. Another customer must have come in. Alex couldn't see the customer well from his location, but enough to realize the man was tall and well-built. He was wearing a hat, cowboy boots, and a green shirt.

Alex stayed put, crouching down in the tub and listening. Maybe one of these conversations would lead him to the man who shot him yet.

"Mr. Dawson," he heard Wade Simpson say. "Good morning, sir. Nice to see you again."

"Same to you."

So Roger Dawson had come in. His timing was perfect.

Roger nodded to the man in the chair. "Hardy." He looked back at the barber. "How soon can I get me a shave and a haircut around here? I'm kind of in a hurry with the all the doings in town today and all."

"Have a seat in the back," Wade said. "I'll get to you as soon as I get through with Hardy here."

Roger started toward the back of the shop without looking in Alex's direction. Alex was in the bathing room with a door between them, albeit a slightly open one. Alex was relatively sure Roger didn't see him, and now he couldn't see Roger either. Roger must be sitting on the bench against the back wall, waiting for a turn in the barber chair.

He'd only half-listened to the boring conversation between Wade Simpson and Mr. Hardy, the white-haired man now seated in the chair, but he'd perked up when Roger came in. Now he would soak in the tub a while longer.

Alex heard another dinging, meaning another man entered the shop.

"Morning, Slim," Wade said. "Good to see you up and around again. I hear you've been a little under the weather lately."

"Doc said I had a bad case of the croup is all, but I done whipped it." Slim must have spotted the man in the barber chair because he spoke to him next. "Mr. Hardy, good to see you again, sir."

"Same here."

"I noticed you've grown a beard since I saw you the last time," Wade said to Slim. "Guess you'll be wanting a shave *and* a haircut."

"Just trim the beard a little. I like this fuzzy thing now."

Wade laughed. "Well, you've got one man ahead of you besides Hardy here." The barber nodded toward the bench Roger sat on. "I'll get to you as soon as I can."

Slim smiled, moving to stand near Roger. Alex still couldn't see Roger, but he could see Slim just fine.

"Mr. Dawson," Slim said, "you can't guess who I done seen this mornin.'"

"Who was that, Slim?"

"That drifter that got himself shot up at the Gallagher place, the one with the fancy name—Alex Lancaster." Slim stood with his hands on his hips and a silly grin on his face. "You know, the cowboy what works for Miss Gallagher now."

"I know who you mean. So what's special about Lancaster?"

"According to what I've been hearing, you might have some competition."

Roger's voice took on a hard edge. "What do you mean?"

"As I hear it Miss Gallagher nursed him back to health—with tender loving care." His laugh had a mocking edge to it. "Maybe she's here in town so he can see the doctor now that he's back."

Slim scratched his scraggly beard. "The town was plum helpless with Doc and the sheriff both gone at the same time. Guess them no-account deputies did all right though."

"Where's Lancaster now?" Roger demanded.

Slim shrugged. "I don't know. Last I saw he was riding down the street early this morning on a nice-looking black stud. Likely Maggie's. He's a good-looking feller. Loco they say, but the women around here will swear he's handsome."

"Are you saying he's crazy in the head?"

"I 'spect so. And if I was a young feller like you, Mr. Dawson, I'd spruce up some."

"What do you mean, spruce up?"

"I'd buy me some new clothes and get me some of that new soap they sell over at the general store so I'd smell as good as I looked. Then I'd go after that Gallagher girl full speed. Least that's what I'd do in your boots."

There was a pause before Roger answered. "You could be right."

All at once Alex could see Roger again. He had risen from the bench and was standing next to Slim, holding his hat.

"Wade," Roger said to the barber, "I won't be wanting a shave and a haircut right now after all." He glanced at Slim. "Looks like you won't have to wait to get that beard of yours trimmed. I'm going to buy me a new suit of clothes." He turned back to the barber. "I'm going out for a while, Wade. Be back later for that shave and haircut."

Roger put on his hat, pulled the brim down a notch, and headed for the door.

Alex had a lot to think about as he dried off and dressed. *So Roger thinks I'm going to give him a run for his money.* Alex smiled to himself. The man just might be right.

He'd already started back to the Sunday house when sea-smells called. He reined his black stud down to the bay. Near the water's edge he saw a dark-haired couple, probably of Mexican descent, walking close together. The sun came out from behind the clouds, and their skin looked gold in the Texas sunshine.

At first he didn't think much about it, yet the more he looked, the more the woman reminded him of Maggie's maid, Elena.

But it couldn't be; Elena was looking after Jon Anthony. Still the resemblance was striking.

The woman turned, and he got a close look at her features. He knew at that moment his earlier assumptions were correct. Not wanting Elena and her companion to find him watching them, he reined the black stallion in behind a line of thick brush and scrubby trees to wait.

He wasn't able to get a good look at the man, but the skinny little brown-skinned man was not someone most women would look at twice. Alex never dreamed a middle-aged woman like Elena would have a lover, even one as unattractive as the man beside her. But now that he'd seen the two, Alex concluded that Elena hadn't volunteered to ride into Bayview and take care of the children for the weekend out of any kind of loyalty to her employer; she came to meet this man. He would have to decide the best way to tell Maggie about it.

Alex turned his horse back toward the Sunday house. If Elena disliked Alex before, she'd hate him if she knew he knew her secret, but it couldn't be helped. No sense telling the world about a private matter between Maggie and her maid. But out of respect for Maggie, he'd tell her what he knew as soon as they were alone.

He'd no sooner gotten back to the Sunday house than Miss Lucy sent word that she regretted Alex never received his invitation to the supper party. She asked that he please grant her the honor of his presence at a late breakfast in the family dining room.

Alex didn't believe for an instant his party invitation was lost or misplaced. Roger and his mother made it clear they didn't want him around. But knowing Maggie, she likely demanded Miss Lucy and Roger make things right.

He smiled. Why not accept the invitation? Who could say what he might learn over brunch? If late breakfasts at the Sunday house were as delicious as supper on the previous night, he would enjoy the meal, and it would also give him the chance to see Maggie again. Depending on who was there, he might even hear something that would clear up some of the mysteries surrounding the Gallagher ranch.

Maggie was serving herself when Alex came in. He moved in close beside her.

"This fancy buffet table is a far cry from the tin cups and plates at the camp house on the Gallagher ranch," he whispered. "Personally I like tin better."

She nodded and looked as if she were trying not to smile.

"How about those linen napkins and all that china?" he went on. "And silver serving dishes no less!"

She shrugged, and the smile emerged.

"Miss Lucy's kitchen staff prepared us a meal fit for royalty," he said. "But I'd rather eat out in the kitchen with my sleeves rolled up."

Maggie stabbed a piece of bacon and dropped it on her plate. Alex had probably said more than he should have, but at least he'd whispered so low nobody but Maggie could have heard.

She claimed her ranch was larger than the Dawson place, but the Dawsons had money. Where it all came from was a mystery to Alex.

Cattle rustling seemed likely. Or did Roger rob banks on the side? And why was Lucy Dawson so all-fired uppity? To be around her you might think she was the queen of Texas or something. But Roger was downright crude.

Maggie had let it slip that the Dawson family wealth came from Lucy's side of the family and that Roger's late father wasn't an educated man. Since Alex could see no refinement in Lucy's son, he assumed Roger favored his father in some ways and his mother in others.

Alex sidled up beside Maggie again. "Where's Elena this morning?" he whispered.

"In her room. Why?"

"Maybe she's there now, but I saw her down at the beach earlier."

"The beach?" She shook her head. "No. You must be mistaken. Elena wouldn't leave Jon Anthony alone. She's worked on our ranch since before he was born."

"Maybe so, but it was Elena all right. I saw her. And she was with a man."

15

"You're telling me Elena was at the beach with a man?" Maggie shook her head again, emphatically this time. "No. Elena doesn't know any men in Bayview other than Roger."

"I didn't get a good look at him, but it wasn't Roger." Alex had tried to make his voice sound gentle and kind, but it didn't seem to be helping. "The man I saw was of Mexican descent."

"You can't be saying Elena was with a man instead of caring for Jon Anthony because she wouldn't do something like that."

"That's exactly what I'm saying."

"You must be mistaken." Maggie took in a deep breath, releasing it slowly. "Elena has her faults, but she's devoted to Jon Anthony."

Alex was about to make another comment when he noticed Lucy Dawson staring at them from across the room.

"Watch out for Miss Lucy," Maggie whispered. "She has a good heart, but she can be difficult."

At least Maggie was looking out for his welfare, even if she didn't believe what he said about Elena. And yes, Miss Lucy could be difficult. However he doubted she had such a good heart.

"So, Miss Gallagher," he said, loud enough for those nearby to hear, "doesn't this food look delicious?"

"It certainly does."

Miss Lucy started toward them. Alex turned and flashed her the best smile he was capable of manufacturing. "I've been told you're the most gracious hostess in Texas," he said in a tone meant to flatter the woman. "Now I know it's true."

Lucy's facial expression changed from hostile to welcoming in what seemed an instant. A wide smile formed on her lips.

My plan is working. The woman is easier to read than the headlines of a weekly newspaper.

"Well, I wouldn't go so far as to say that my parties are the best in Texas." Miss Lucy's smile revealed every tooth she had, including the space in back where a jaw tooth must have been at one time. "But I've given quite a few parties in my day."

"You're being modest, ma'am," Alex replied. "I'm sure everything I've heard about you is true."

It amused Alex that while his comments about Miss Lucy were double-edged, she saw them as praise. Weren't there scriptures in the Bible about people who thought more of themselves than they should?

On the other hand there were also scriptures that warned against sarcastic tongues. He would need to think about that. According to that Bible he'd been reading and studying, everybody was guilty of wrongdoing at one time or another, but some folks took it to the extreme. Maybe Roger and his mother were examples of that.

"I understand you're staying at the Gallagher ranch now." Miss Lucy looked at him as though she was somehow able to see inside his head. "In the camp house, I assume."

"Oh, well...sure." Her comment surprised him for a moment.

"I've been sleeping in the camp house with the other single men."

"I'm glad to hear you say that, Mr. Lancaster," Lucy said. "You had us worried for a while. And there *was* talk." She hesitated, giving that phrase time to take root. "I'm glad to know it was untrue."

Maggie blinked and looked away. Alex could only imagine what she must be thinking. His mouth turned upward at the edges. "I'm sure a woman as upright and intelligent as you, Miss Lucy, would never listen to rumors and idle gossip."

The older woman glanced down and smiled even more. If Alex were guessing, he would say Lucy Dawson liked his newest appraisal of her character even better than the first.

Maggie wouldn't approve of lying in any form, and Alex had just told a lie—or perhaps a half-lie—on her behalf. He hoped she appreciated that he went out of his way to protect her reputation. If he'd let Lucy know he slept in the house before moving to the camp house, what was left of the Gallagher family's reputation might be lost forever. But lately he was beginning to wonder if what people thought really mattered. He and Maggie knew they hadn't done anything that should make them feel ashamed. In the long run of things, wasn't that what really mattered?

Miss Lucy glanced at Alex briefly, and then she looked away. "Roger was told by one of Maggie's cowboys that you were staying in…" She cleared her throat.

"The big house?" Alex said, hoping he looked absolutely stunned by the suggestion. "Oh, my."

Alex looked Miss Lucy straight in the eyes. "Would you mind telling Maggie the name of the cowboy who told him such a story? If I know Maggie she'll want to reprimand him, if not fire him on the spot."

Lucy's chin dropped down a notch. "Roger didn't—he didn't tell me his name."

"Maybe he'll tell me," Alex said a little louder than seemed necessary.

Miss Lucy shook her head. "No! No, please don't bring this up to Roger. I broke a confidence by telling you what I did."

"I can't promise I won't say something to Roger about it," he said. "But I won't reveal your name in any way, ma'am. You have my word on that."

Maggie hadn't said a thing during the exchange between Alex and Miss Lucy. She was possibly too astounded to utter a sound. Of course she wanted her reputation as safe and secure as possible, but not if it meant telling a lie.

Miss Lucy had calmed down a little when a young woman Alex didn't know came into the room. "Well, look who's here, Maggie," she said. "Roger's cousin Zoe."

Alex looked too, and from the way she paused before moving toward them, Zoe whatever-her-name-was must have thought she looked like a breath of spring. He had to admit she did look nice in her green dress with all those flowers in the material and a green straw bonnet. But she was not the Queen of England, and Alex disliked social climbers and those impressed by them.

Did Zoe think a photographer was taking her picture? Or did she simply enjoy being noticed?

Miss Lucy rushed to her niece's side, hugging her with a flair for the dramatic. Then Lucy took Zoe's hand and half dragged her to where Alex was standing.

Zoe was a pretty girl with those big gray eyes and brown, curly hair, and from the expression of excitement on her face when she looked at Alex, he thought she was interested in him as a man. But to flutter her eyes like that at a perfect stranger like Alex was downright silly. First impressions were important. His opinion of Zoe could be wrong, but if he were guessing, he'd say Zoe was a spoiled brat.

Maggie stepped back slightly as if she were keeping her

distance from the newcomer. But since Miss Lucy said Zoe was Roger's cousin, it seemed unlikely that Maggie could avoid her completely.

Maggie turned, carrying her plate of food with her, and headed for a table on the far side of the room while Miss Lucy introduced Alex to Miss Zoe Dawson. From what Alex had heard in the entry hall on the previous night, Roger's mother was a notorious matchmaker. Somehow and somewhere he'd seen that matchmaker's look in a woman's eyes before. If only he could remember when and where....

Maggie had described a Mr. and Mrs. Branley, and he thought he saw them seated at a table with a young girl. Maggie gazed at the vacant chair at their table.

Alex couldn't hear what they were saying, but when Maggie sat down in that extra chair, she must have known she was invited. Alex sat down at a table over by the kitchen door.

In a matter of moments, Zoe stood next to Alex's table, stopping near the vacant chair beside his as if she fully intended to sit down beside him. She might have if an elderly gentleman with cigar smoke on his breath wasn't also eying that chair. He probably didn't even notice Zoe when he pulled out the chair in question and settled onto it.

Alex held in a smile when Zoe's expression fell and she walked away and took a chair at Lucy's table. Then he just sat there listening to the conversations going on around him during the meal, but he didn't learn much of anything new. Everybody was either talking about the parade being canceled because of the weather or that the rain had passed on through and wasn't expected to return for a while.

Then Sarah walked up and stood behind his chair, chatting with Alex for a minute or two. He enjoyed her chatter about town life and how excited she was to be there and spent the remainder of the breakfast hour planning his day ahead.

Apparently Maggie didn't want to believe Elena did anything

wrong, and there was probably no point in mentioning it again. Elena was out of her element, and he considered that to be significant. Alex would continue to keep an eye on Elena because he didn't trust her any more than he trusted Roger. At the same time he would do all he could to protect Maggie and the children.

He'd fashioned a bridle and a set of reins from the rope he found attached to the back of his saddle. Now all he needed was a metal bit. He also intended to buy a saddle blanket, a few clothes, and a couple of other things. He'd find a way to pay back the money he found in the saddlebag if he learned it wasn't rightfully his.

He finished eating and stepped out onto the front porch. One of Miss Lucy's servants had already hitched up the wagon that would take them to the doctor's office. He had nothing to do but wait.

Maggie joined him a few minutes later. A small ladder leaned against the wagon, and he grinned when Maggie climbed the wooden steps and settled onto the hard seat. So she didn't want him to help her up, huh?

"Where'd the ladder come from, Miss Gallagher?"

"It's one Miss Lucy had in a storeroom out back."

"Is that a fact?" He was still grinning as he climbed up into the seat beside her.

The mules started off for Dr. Smyth's office at a slow pace. As Alex cracked the whip above the heads of the animals, he decided to break his own rule and ask about Elena.

"Why don't you believe me about Elena?"

"I told you before; it couldn't be her. Elena doesn't know any men in Bayview. She never leaves the ranch."

"Does she have a twin sister?"

"Not that I know of."

"Then it had to be her."

"You're mistaken, sir. It happens sometimes."

Alex knew what he'd seen. Not only that but Maggie's ranch cowboys were talking about a new curandero somewhere in the area. It crossed Alex's mind that maybe Elena was up to her old tricks again, and that it wasn't a curandero at all the men were telling about but a *curandera,* which was the female version of a Latin American witchdoctor.

He'd also planned to mention he thought Roger was up to no good. But after Maggie's negative response to his conclusions regarding Elena, he hesitated to bring up anything else.

The main street of Bayview was decorated with banners and flags to celebrate Founders Day. Maggie and Alex climbed the stairs attached to the outside of the Branley Building to the doctor's office on the second floor. At the landing Alex saw a sign on the door nearest the stairs stating that the office was closed for the local holiday.

Maggie moved ahead of Alex and went farther on down the deck-like landing. "I'll just knock on the door of his apartment. I've done that lots of times. He's nearly always home."

Alex wasn't convinced it was the right thing to do. "I wouldn't want to disturb the doctor on his day off."

"He won't mind." Maggie knocked at the door next to the one leading to the office. The old doctor, barefoot and wearing casual clothes, opened the door. Alex didn't have to be a mind reader to know Doc Smyth hadn't expected guests.

"Who's sick?" The doctor's eyes squinted as he studied Alex from head to toe. "You, or Miss Maggie here?"

"He is," Maggie said. "This is Mr. Alex Lancaster, Doc. He's the one Lupe told you about, the man I found shot on my ranch."

"Shot? Why, he looks all right to me." The doctor peered at Alex. "Step inside, son, and let me have a look at you. And I'm glad to see you are wearing that sling."

Maggie started forward, but the doctor waved her off. "You can wait outside, young lady."

157

Dr. Smyth shut the door. They were in a small sitting room. The doctor gestured for Alex to sit in an overstuffed brown chair by the entry door, and he didn't bother putting on his boots before starting the examination.

He cleaned the wounds and re-bandaged them then pulled off his spectacles and pinched the bridge of his nose. "Your wounds seem to be healing up fine. Maggie and Concha did a good job."

"Yes, they did. I already have pretty much full use of my left arm, but it still aches some. How long 'till the pain goes away? "

"I can't rightly say. I'd keep wearing that sling a while longer." Dr. Smyth wiped his glasses with the hem of his blue plaid shirt and put them back on. "Sometimes limbs come back real fast in cases like this. At other times it takes a while. Now I hear you can't remember things, even your own name. Is your memory coming back yet?"

"I can remember a few things. Not much though."

"Don't get yourself all worked up over it. These things take time. I broke my leg once when I was a kid. Darn near drove me crazy with the pain and the worrying. I didn't think I'd ever walk again, but I did. Ran, too, better than ever. I don't walk so good these days, but that's 'cause I'm getting on in years. When you're my age you might not remember things the way you did when you were a boy, but that won't have anything to do with my broken leg as a child or you getting shot. It's just the way things are in this world."

"Thank you, sir." Alex assumed the doctor had finished the examination, so he started to get up.

"Now hold your horses there a minute, young man. I'm not finished yet. I want to take another look at those blue eyes of yours." He grabbed a lamp from a nearby table and placed it close to Alex's right eye and then his left.

"How do they look, Doc?"

"Clear as a bell. Any idea who might have shot you?"

Alex shook his head. "No, but I do have some hunches."

"Sometimes hunches are better than anything else. Let me hear a couple."

"Well, I wasn't robbed and I don't have any enemies that I know of, so I figure maybe somebody thinks I saw something they wish I hadn't seen."

"If that's true you and Miss Maggie could be in a lot of trouble."

Alex nodded. "I know."

"Don't keep these hunches of yours to yourself, Mr. Lancaster. The sheriff needs to know everything you know if you want him to find out who did this."

MAGGIE WAS WAITING JUST outside the door. "What did the doctor say?" she asked with noticeable excitement. "Are you going to live?"

Alex grinned. "Sure hope so. He said I'm doing real good. And you know what? I like that old man."

"I knew you would. Everybody does."

Alex felt encouraged by the time he and Maggie went downstairs to the general store. But he wished the doctor could have told him a little more about his memory problem.

Bolts of dress material in a variety of colors were on display in the front window. Alex noticed when Maggie took a special interest in a bolt of pink material so thin you could look right through it.

"You'd look pretty in a dress made from that," he said. "It matches the roses in your cheeks. Why don't you go in and buy it?"

She shook her head. "I couldn't justify paying good money for something like that. It's too fancy. Where would a ranch-girl wear it?"

"After all you've done for me, I'd buy it for you if I thought you'd let me."

Her brown eyes widened. "I most certainly will not. It wouldn't be…"

"Proper." He grinned again and opened the door of the shop then motioned for her to go inside. "If you won't let me buy you anything, at least let me pay you for all that free nursing care you've been giving me."

"I won't hear of it," she whispered firmly. "And don't tell anyone I nursed you back to health—especially in public." She glanced around as if to see if anyone might be listening.

Alex followed her inside. While Maggie browsed, he bought himself a Bible. He'd borrowed Maggie's long enough. He was about to put all the items he'd collected on the counter near the main entrance when he noticed a tan brush-jacket all spread out on a table with a couple of nice dress shirts.

"Would you like to try on the jacket?" the woman behind the counter asked.

"Would it be all right to do that—just try on something?"

"Of course. Just slip it on over your shirt." The woman smiled. "Brush jackets are one of our most popular items. We always keep them in stock. They're made of tent material. Not only will they keep you warm in winter—if winter ever comes to South Texas—but it will also protect you from the wind and the rain."

Somehow Alex already knew what she'd just explained. Had he worked in a store at one time? Or were there other reasons he was aware of such information? He didn't know what was normal and what wasn't. Maybe knowledge of brush jackets was common knowledge to everyone.

With little money and no assurance he would be able to raise more, Alex decided not to buy the jacket. With summer coming soon it wasn't an essential. He paid for the bit, the saddle blanket, and the Bible, to be picked up later, and went outside to wait for Maggie.

She'd showed an interest in the pink material and several other items but still hadn't bought so much as a spool of thread. He wondered how long it would be before she finished her shopping.

A few minutes later he checked his pocket watch. It was almost ten o'clock, and he promised Maggie they would talk to the sheriff before the barbecue. At the rate Maggie was going, the sheriff's office could close before they got there.

Ten minutes later he was still standing in front of the store and no closer to speaking with the sheriff. He adjusted his sling and thumbed through his new Bible.

Seemingly from out of nowhere, Roger Dawson appeared. He must have come around the corner, but Alex hadn't noticed until he was standing right in front of him.

"Well, Lancaster." Roger chuckled under his breath. "What got you out of bed this morning and downtown? I saw you riding off with Maggie. Did she desert you or something?"

Alex released a deep breath of air. "Maggie's in Branley's store."

"Then that's where I'm going." Roger's smile was really more of a smirk. "See you around."

16

Alex wanted Maggie with him when he went in to talk to the sheriff, but he sure didn't want Roger tagging along. He glanced toward the door of the store, wishing Maggie would hurry up.

A woman came around the corner, and Alex recognized her as Matilda, the maid who served him supper the previous night. He smiled as an idea began to take shape. If she had a piece of writing paper and a pen so he could write Maggie a note, his idea just might work.

Two minutes later he handed his note to the middle-aged woman. It read, "Maggie, please meet me at the sheriff's office as soon as you finish shopping. You can leave your purchases at the store, and we'll pick them up later." He also added a line about getting rid of Roger before she came to the sheriff's office.

Once the maid had promised to deliver the note, Alex turned and walked away, rehearsing what he would say to the sheriff. But he was a stranger in town. Who would believe a stranger—especially one that got shot in what might look like a gunfight?

Maybe going on alone instead of waiting for Maggie was a

better idea after all. He was tired of waiting, and he could be more open if a woman wasn't around.

Alex moved on down the street toward the sheriff's office. Sheriff Ethridge was talking to another man when Alex entered the office. He sat down in the first chair he saw to wait, and it was near the door. The sheriff would have questions, of course, and there were plenty of things Alex wanted to know too. A lawman was bound to have the kind of information Alex needed to catch the man who shot him.

Seated there Alex had a perfect view of a line of "Wanted" posters on the opposite wall. A picture of a brown-skinned man with a black mustache caught his attention. He read that poster first: "Jose Garza alias Pastor Joe is wanted in Brownsville, Texas, for robbing the Rio Bank of $10,000. He served time in a Mexican prison for another crime and is believed to be back in Texas now. Jose/Joe Garza is possibly armed and should be considered dangerous."

Alex tensed. The names Jose Garza and Joe Garza meant nothing to him, yet he thought he knew the outlaw pictured on the poster. But how? As he continued to stare at the poster, he rubbed the ache in his shoulder and arm, finally concluding that his relationship with the outlaw was not a friendly one.

MAGGIE STOOD at the counter with Roger, waiting to pay for her purchases, when Miss Lucy's maid came in. Matilda persuaded Maggie to follow her to a secluded corner a few feet away so they could talk privately, and she gave Maggie the note. Roger and Mrs. Branley watched them with interested as if they were dying to know what Maggie and the maid were talking about. Maggie read the note, thanked Matilda, and sent her on her way.

Maggie knew it would be simple to leave her purchases at

the store and pick them up later, but getting rid of Roger wouldn't be so easy. If she left the store, he would follow her. If she told him where she was going, he would stick to her like that paste she made with flour and water. Roger liked to feel powerful. She needed to find a task that would make Roger feel special—but not just any task; it had to be important.

She hated to lie. But maybe this one time...

No, she wouldn't. Lying was a sin in God's eyes. She would have to find another way. She glanced out the show-window. Matilda had moved on down the street. Maggie noticed it was dark out. It looked like rain, and she'd forgotten to bring her umbrella.

"Roger," she said, smiling, "I have a big favor to ask of you."

"And what is that?"

"It looks like rain out there, and I forgot my umbrella. Would you be a darlin' and go back to the Sunday house to get mine? I'd go myself, but I have a list of things to do, and you know I don't come to town very often."

His smile seemed genuine and his eyes warm. "I'll be glad to help you out. Where would I find the umbrella?"

"Elena will find it for you." Maggie followed Roger out the door.

"All right, and if she can't I'll borrow one of Mama's. Where shall I meet you?"

"Either here at the store or next door at the hotel. I want to try out that new tearoom over at the hotel that I've been hearing so much about."

Maggie was thankful she hadn't lied. If it rained she really could use her umbrella, and she did want to see the tearoom Miss Lucy mentioned. Roger had already walked off, but he turned and waved. She waved back.

As she stood there, waiting until Roger was out of sight, her conscience chimed in. No, she hadn't outright lied, but she hadn't told the truth either. By avoiding the whole truth, she'd lied whether she chose to admit it or not.

A raindrop landed on her nose. She glanced up at a sky filled with dark clouds. The men she met at breakfast that morning had said the rain had passed through and likely wouldn't return, but they were wrong; it had already started to sprinkle. She went back inside.

Maggie shopped longer than she intended. Alex had probably finished talking to the sheriff and was no doubt wondering what had become of her. However it took time to make up her mind to buy the pink material in Branleys' window. She had nearly decided to do so when she learned from Mrs. Branley that a local dressmaker had already fashioned a dress in that same material; she suggested Maggie go to the dressing room and try it on.

She did as requested, and the dress fit as if the woman had Maggie in mind when she made it—ruffles, starched lace, and all. But questions remained. Would she have the nerve to put it on? And did she want it merely so Alex would see her wearing it?

"I can't tell you how lovely you look in that dress," Mrs. Branley said as Maggie stood in front of a big oval mirror.

"The dress is lovely, ma'am," Maggie said, walking away. "But it's so unlike me. I can't imagine where I would wear it."

"To the reception tonight after the barbecue of course. All the women of the community will be dressing up for the occasion, and this dress will be perfect for it. Now I want you to go back over to that mirror and look at yourself one more time. The dress was made for you."

Maggie shook her head, still not convinced. Nevertheless, she returned to the mirror, gazing at her reflection and pinching the puffed sleeves. Was that really Maggie Gallagher in the mirror?

After Sadie's scandalous return from Brownsville, pregnant

and unmarried, the people of Bayview probably expected Maggie to do something equally as outrageous sooner or later. But she had every intention of proving them wrong. She'd worn her "scarlet letter" long enough and was ready to start enjoying herself.

"I'll take it," Maggie finally said.

"Good. I'll put it in a box and wrap it for you."

"I have to run across the street for a minute. I shouldn't be too long. I'll pick up the dress on my way back to where I'm staying."

"You're here for Founders Day then."

"Yes."

Mrs. Branley snatched up a long piece of blue ribbon. "I'll have everything ready for you by the time you get back."

It wasn't sprinkling anymore, but a line of wet planks were set up on the street so the ladies of Bayview could cross without soiling their shoes and stockings. Maggie managed to get her stockings muddy anyway as well as the hem of her dress.

If she couldn't keep her green homespun clean and neat in the nasty weather, how could she hope to deal with silk under pink material so delicate she could see right through it?

There was a time she would never have considered buying a garment that couldn't be worn to the cow pen, but a lot had changed in a very short time.

As SOON AS she entered the sheriff's office, Maggie noticed the sheriff behind a desk, talking to a man she didn't know. Alex sat in a chair by the door, staring at a line of "Wanted" posters on the back wall. If her assumptions were right, Alex was either in pain or displeased in some way.

Maggie sat down in a chair next to his. "Did Sheriff Ethridge tell you anything helpful?"

"I haven't talked to him yet."

"Then what's wrong?"

"Wrong?" He shook his head. "Well, let me see. I was shot in the back, I lost my memory, and I have no idea who my enemies are. I guess that about sums it up."

"You knew that weeks ago. Tell me what happened before I came in here."

"Nothing happened." He glanced away.

"I don't believe you." She released an exaggerated sigh. "But for now I won't say more about it."

The stranger got up then, and Maggie hoped he was about to leave. He put out his hand and the sheriff shook it. Then the sheriff put his hand on the man's shoulder like they were old friends and walked him to the door. That seemed to be when Sheriff Ethridge first noticed Maggie.

"Miss Gallagher, what brings you in here when there's doings down at the fairground today?"

"Business," she said, tempering her abrupt answer with a smile. She prayed the sheriff would know she didn't want to state her business in front of the stranger. She offered the sheriff her hand and was introducing him to Alex when the other man finally went out the door.

"Now," the sheriff said, "let's go over to my desk and talk about this business of yours, shall we?"

She sat beside Alex on a bench in front of the big pine desk and related everything she could think of about what happened the day Alex was shot. The sheriff nodded several times but never said a word until she finished.

"That's the wildest story I ever heard tell of, Miss Gallagher. I could hardly believe it when I read your letter." The sheriff studied Alex closely. "I don't know who took a shot at you, Mr. Lancaster, but I'll sure try my best to come up with some answers."

Alex nodded.

Sheriff Ethridge looked down at a paper on his desk, appeared to read it, and then looked up at Alex again. "There've been scattered reports of cattle rustling the last couple of months. Would you know anything about that?"

Alex hesitated. "No, sir."

"Well, we don't have any outlaws around here. In fact you're the only stranger in these parts that I know of right now."

"What about the man you were just talking to?" Maggie put in. "I never saw him before."

"Old man Wilson? Why, he's lived around here for years. He works on one of the big ranches, though, and doesn't come to town very often. That's probably why you never met him." The sheriff rubbed his whiskered chin and looked back at Alex. "And you don't have any idea who might have done it—the cattle rustling that is?"

"I sure don't."

"Oh, I forgot. You said you lost your memory, didn't you?"

"Yes, sir."

Ethridge shook his head. "I hope you're who you say you are, Mr. Lancaster, 'cause folks around here don't take kindly to cattle rustlers."

"You're welcome to write my sister in San Antonio," Alex said, "and check my story out. At least I *think* she's my sister. Maggie found a letter from her in my pocket after I was shot."

"What's her name?"

"Mrs. Ruth Parson. Her husband's name is Will."

The sheriff sat back in his chair. "Well, you sure don't sound like a Texan, that's for sure." He studied Alex again. "I 'spect you're from up around the Carolinas somewhere. At least that'd be my guess."

"Yes, sir. You could be right."

"I gotta be honest with you, Mr. Lancaster. With cattle rustlers on the loose and you being a stranger in these parts and all, I'll be looking over your shoulder pretty regular from now on."

"I kind of figured that, sir."

The sheriff opened a drawer and retrieved a small book. "Now I got a sheriff friend who lives in San Antonio. Maybe I'll just write him and see if he's ever heard of you or your sister."

"I'd appreciate that," Alex said without expression.

Maggie had kept quiet during most of the questioning, but she longed to help Alex. She had no reason to trust him, but somehow she sensed that everything Alex had told the sheriff was absolutely true.

Alex rose from his chair, and then Maggie and the sheriff got up too.

Alex offered Sheriff Ethridge his hand. "I'm much obliged to you. You've been mighty fair."

"That's my job, Mr. Lancaster—being fair." The sheriff clasped Alex's hand. "But don't blame me if my friend writes and tells me something you don't want to hear."

"I fully understand that, sir."

Alex and Maggie bid the sheriff goodbye and left the office.

"So I guess we'll walk over to the general store, pick up the things you bought, and then I can drive you back to the Sunday house," Alex suggested. "The barbecue is coming up, and I know you don't want to miss that."

"We can't go to Branleys'," Maggie said. "Not yet anyway. I promised to meet Roger in the tearoom at the hotel."

"Tearoom? Why would you meet him there? In fact why do you have to meet Roger in the first place?"

"In your message you said to get rid of Roger. The only thing I could think to do was tell him to go back to the Sunday House, get my umbrella, and then meet me at the tearoom with it. It looked like rain when I sent him."

"Well, the sunshine's sure out now, so why don't you go on

over to the store, pick up your packages, and *I'll* meet Roger at the tearoom? I have a few things I want to say to him anyway."

She shook her head. "No, I'm going with you to make sure you two don't start arguing. Besides I'll need to thank him for fetching the umbrella—and if the expression on your face is an indication, you're ready for a fight."

"I wasn't thinking about Roger, not this time anyway," he said. "I think I might know one of the outlaws on the Wanted poster in the sheriff's office."

17

Maggie never expected Roger to miss their meeting in the tearoom, but after a lengthy wait, one of Miss Lucy's other maids came with the umbrella and handed it to Maggie. The maid didn't give any kind of explanation as to why Roger never arrived, and Maggie didn't request one. She was just glad they avoided a possible confrontation.

Maggie and Alex picked up the packages at Branleys'. A counter near the back served as the local post office, so Maggie mailed her letters, and Alex mailed one as well.

"Is that a letter to your sister in San Antonio?" Maggie asked.

"No, it's a letter to Mrs. Ruth Parson in San Antonio. She might or might not be my sister."

Maggie nodded her understanding, even as she wondered if perhaps Divine Providence hadn't stepped in to keep Roger from bringing the umbrella. If he had, a fight between Alex and Roger might have taken place. With that thought offering her some sense of relief, Maggie and Alex left Branleys' and returned to the Sunday house.

Alex stopped the wagon out front. As he tied up the reins, Maggie noticed Sarah sitting on the front lawn as if waiting for them. She was holding Jane, a rag doll with yarn hair in a bright shade of red.

Sarah jumped up when she spotted them. "Maggie!" She raced toward them, excitement bubbling in her enormous green eyes.

Maggie gazed at Sarah, trying to decide if worry clouded her little sister's face along with all the animation, or if she just imagined it. "Sarah, are you all right?"

"I'm fine, and I'm so glad you're back. I have things I want to tell you." She glanced at Alex. "Secret things."

Alex grinned at them. "I have to go now anyway. Guess I'll see both of you later."

Maggie nodded. "Yes. Thank you."

Maggie watched Alex unhitch the wagon. He put the animals away and then went inside the house through the front door. Maggie hoped Sarah's secret wasn't of a serious nature, sensing that was unlikely. According to Maggie's late mother, the blessings of childhood were simple. Most children seldom had real problems in life; they just thought they were serious.

Maggie led Sarah to a stone bench under a covered outdoor porch in the middle of the backyard. Miss Lucy's round porch with its rounded roof had always reminded Maggie of the bandstand in the town square where patriotic music played every Fourth of July. She patted the space on the bench beside her. Sarah sat down. Alex came out of the kitchen door, stood on the back porch watching them for a moment, and then went back inside.

"Well, Sarah, is there something you want to tell me?"

Sarah moistened her lips. "I saw Mr. McGregor today."

"The old man that wants to buy the Blevin place?"

"No. I'm talking about his son, young Mr. McGregor. He looks about my age, but he's very tall for ten or eleven."

"He is *not* about your age, Sarah. He's about my age. So what is it you want to tell me?"

Sarah looked off toward the pasture on the other side of the picket fence, hugging her rag doll close. "Do you think someone like me could already know who I will marry when I grow up?"

Maggie threw up her hands. "Heavens to Betsy, Sarah! Are you telling me you have a fella?"

"Maybe."

"Is it Noma Elaine's older brother? He's three years older than you are."

"It's not him."

"Who then?" Maggie asked.

"Someone very, very nice."

"Does the boy have a name?"

"I guess so. But I don't know what it is except McGregor."

Maggie froze. "Sarah! Did that young man hurt you in some way?"

Sarah appeared confused. "No."

"Did he...touch you in a way you didn't like?"

"He never touched me at all. I was sitting on the front lawn in front of the Sunday house playing with my doll, and he walked by. He wasn't looking at me; he was looking at the Sunday house. But he must have looked at me a little because he saw when I dropped the hard candy you gave me in the mud. I was really sad about the candy; it was the last stick I had. He must have seen me fretting about it because he came inside the yard and threw me a penny."

"He offered you money?"

"He gave me a penny to buy more candy was all."

"What exactly did he say to you?" Maggie demanded.

"He said, 'Sorry, little girl, about your candy. That happened to me once when I was several years younger than you must be.' Then he smiled and said, 'Here's a penny. Buy yourself another stick of candy the next time you're in town.'"

"And then what?"

"He said for me to tell Roger Dawson that he'd like to buy

the Sunday house if it was for sale. And then he went out the gate and walked on down the street. And Maggie, he was so nice. I think he's the nicest person in the whole wide world besides you. And someday I'm going to marry him."

Maggie put her arm around Sarah's shoulder. "No, Sarah, you're not going to marry him ever. He's way, way, way too old for you. In fact I hear he's sweet on Belinda Foster, that pretty girl with the dark brown hair we saw at church the last time we were here. Why, he'll be long married and have a couple of kids before you're ready to tie the knot."

Sarah shook her head emphatically. "Nope, that's not going to happen. I'm going to marry him someday. You just wait and see."

ALEX ASSUMED he would drive Maggie and the children to the barbecue since he drove them to town in the first place. He was waiting on the porch out front when Roger joined him. Alex immediately got the feeling that Roger might be waiting for someone too.

Neither spoke for several minutes. Alex pretended an interest in the cotton field across the road from the house. Roger just stood there, whistling off-key.

Alex could handle silence, but he couldn't abide Roger's rendition of a tune he'd probably heard in a saloon somewhere. If Alex hoped to shut him up, he'd have to initiate a conversation.

"Maggie said she's known you a long time," Alex said.

"Since we were babies."

"I guess you must like her a lot."

"Like her?" Roger's eyes narrowed. "I plan to make her my wife one day."

"Does Maggie know about this?"

Roger's mouth hardened.

Alex had questions he wanted to ask Roger, but he knew it wouldn't be smart to get Roger's dander up before he got some answers.

"Now if you were to marry Maggie," Alex said, using his friendliest tone, "that would about double the size of your ranch, wouldn't it?"

Roger nodded. "It sure would."

Alex smiled in hopes of putting Roger at ease. "Nice piece of land you've got there, Mr. Dawson. We saw part of your place when we were driving up from the ranch yesterday. And your grass is looking mighty good, too, since the rain."

Roger gave a surprised look that would almost pass for a smile. "Why, thank you, Mister."

"Let's see, your place is back a ways from the creek, isn't it?"

"Yeah, that's the only thing I don't like about it."

"That's too bad." Alex's voice practically rippled with friendship. "I know how important water is to a rancher, and Maggie told me you don't have much."

"You got that right on target."

Roger seemed to be warming to their conversation, so he decided to take it to the next step. "Had you ever thought that if you marry Maggie you could dam up the creek and get all the water you need?"

"Thought about it?" Roger gave a short laugh. "Why, that's exactly what I'm planning to do."

The muscles in Alex's jaw tightened, but he tried not to let it show. Now he knew for sure why Roger was so interested in Maggie. It wasn't just her land he wanted. Roger wanted the creek her land sat on in order to irrigate his own land. Loving Maggie probably didn't figure into it at all.

He could play his hand and let Roger know what he thought of him, or he could hold his cards a while longer. Alex chose to play his hand close to his chest.

Roger pulled out his pocket watch and checked the time.

"Going to the barbecue?" Alex asked.

"Sure." Roger studied his watch again, his brows drawing together in a scowl. "I'm going, all right, if Maggie and Jon Anthony ever get out here. Sarah went on ahead with that friend of hers, Noma Elaine."

Alex tried not to show his disappointment. "You driving them to the barbecue?"

"Of course I am." A sarcastic grin replaced Roger's scowl. "You didn't think *you* were taking 'em, did you?"

"I figured I might."

"Then you figured wrong."

Before the conversation could disintegrate further, Maggie stepped through the door, looking pretty and soft in a blue flowered dress. Roger turned and appraised her as if he thought she were a saloon girl or worked in a dance hall somewhere.

His hands at his sides, Alex clenched both fists. It was all he could do to keep from punching Roger in the nose for looking Maggie over the way he did.

Roger tipped his hat and smiled. "You're looking mighty good today, Miss Maggie."

"Thank you, Roger," she said without really noticing him. "Sarah went on ahead with her friend, and Elena will bring Jon Anthony out in a minute." She flashed Alex a quick glance. "You're still going to the barbecue, aren't you?"

"I reckon I will."

"Then why don't you ride along with us?" she suggested. "There'll be plenty of room."

Alex studied the two-seater buggy parked out front. There was enough room all right, but Roger would hate having Alex in the buggy as much as Alex would hate being there. But he considered taking Maggie up on her offer just to see Roger squirm.

"It was mighty kind of y'all to ask," Alex said as if he thought

Roger were in on the asking. "But I'll just ride over on my horse, maybe have another look around town and all."

Maggie tossed her head. "Then I suppose I'll...*we'll* see you there."

"I'm counting on it." Despite Roger's angry glare Alex flashed Maggie a grin that he hoped would melt her heart. Then he tipped his hat and stepped off the porch. If he was suspicious of Roger before their little talk, he was doubly so now. But without proof he didn't know what he could do about the situation.

***

THE BARBECUE WAS HELD on the county fairgrounds. Alex introduced himself to several people in hopes of learning more about Roger and his business ventures. One of the people he met was an attractive young schoolteacher who claimed to be new in town. It amused Alex when the schoolteacher also let him know right away that she wasn't married.

Smiling to himself, Alex moved over to the picnic area and sat down at a table under a shade tree. While pretending to enjoy the day's events, he watched Maggie and the children out of the corner of his eye. He never approached them, but he wanted to make sure they were all right.

Unconsciously Alex rubbed his left shoulder. The pain had decreased in intensity quite a bit, but the wound still troubled him some. Contrary to Dr. Smyth's orders, he'd discarded his sling shortly before he got to the fairgrounds. He knew Maggie would be upset when she found out, but he'd grown tired of wearing the thing. He didn't intend to put it on again.

At four o'clock that afternoon, Alex saw Roger drive Maggie and Jon Anthony back to the house. A few minutes later he heard Sarah tell another little girl that she was staying the night with Noma Elaine. Maybe he'd skip the shindig that night too and go back to the house, but not until he'd had a serving of pie.

Alex ambled over to the pie table. He was cutting himself a slice of apple pie when Sarah plowed right into him, almost causing him to drop his plate.

"Oh, I'm sorry," Sarah said in a breathless tone of voice. "We've been playing."

Alex chuckled. "I sorta figured that out."

She looked concerned. "I didn't bump your bad arm, did I?"

He shook his head. "It was my good arm."

Her face relaxed. "That's good."

She glanced over at a little girl standing a few feet away and motioned for the other child to wait. Then she peered back at Alex. "Why aren't you wearing your sling?"

"I want to impress the ladies," he whispered, leaning down a bit so she could hear him.

Sarah giggled, motioning for her friend to join them. The girl didn't budge.

"That's my friend Noma Elaine," Sarah explained. "She's a little shy."

"But you're not, are you?"

Sarah shrugged. "I don't know."

Alex decided to change direction. "Is Maggie going to the party tonight?"

Sarah had turned her back on Alex and was still trying to coax her friend to come a little closer. Noma Elaine merely shook her head.

Alex cleared his throat. "Sarah, are you listening to me?"

"Oh, I'm sorry. What did you say?"

"I want to know if Maggie's going to the shindig tonight."

"Well, of course she is. She wouldn't miss it, 'specially after she went and bought that new dress and all."

"Then where did she and Roger go just now?"

"To take Jon Anthony and Elena home. Jon Anthony got tired of being here and started fussing, and he's not going to the party tonight. He's staying with Elena at the Sunday house."

"I sort of figured that."

"But I'm going to the party tonight," Sarah reminded him. "For sure!"

Alex nodded. "I'm glad to hear that. So will Miss Maggie and Roger be back here after they take Jon Anthony and Elena to the Sunday house?"

She shrugged again. "I don't know exactly when they're coming back, but I know they'll be here in plenty of time for the party."

Sarah motioned for Noma Elaine to come on. When Noma shook her head again, Alex could almost see the word *no* float out from her.

"Well," Sarah said, shrugging in obvious resignation, "I have to go now since Noma Elaine won't come over here."

Alex flashed Noma Elaine a smile and then turned back to Sarah. "What do girls like you and Noma Elaine do at parties like this?"

"We hide from each other. Then we run around looking for each other so we can hide again."

Noma Elaine motioned for Sarah to come on.

Sarah nodded, still looking at her friend. "I have to go, Mr. Lancaster, and I hope you enjoy your pie."

Sarah chased after her friend, and Alex took his first bite of pie. As Sarah disappeared behind a display of cakes and pies, he realized that one day she would be as beautiful as her older sister.

With time to spare before the party, Alex explored more of the area in hopes of finding someone who knew Dee, but to no avail. When the sun dipped lower in the sky, he turned his horse toward the tent where the doings that night would be held.

As soon as he entered the party area, he spied Sarah and her friends. They were darting in and out between the groups of adults, playing tag. Maggie would be embarrassed if she knew, but it seemed Maggie hadn't arrived yet.

Alex saw Miss Yates, the schoolteacher he'd met earlier, standing with her back to him, talking to a group of young ladies. He was about to go over and speak to her when a young woman with brown curls appeared beside him.

"Hello again, Alex Lancaster," she said. "I'm Zoe Dawson. My aunt, Miss Lucy, introduced us this morning at breakfast at the Sunday house."

He hadn't recognized her, but when he realized who she was, he nodded. "Hello." She didn't seem as obnoxious as she had earlier, but she was much too bold to suit Alex. "I believe Miss Lucy said you're Roger's cousin."

"Guilty." Her giggle was loud and high pitched.

Alex had always disliked people that laughed at their own jokes, and her laugh sounded forced. But he did his best to be cordial. "Maggie and your cousin should be here soon," he said.

"Speaking of Maggie…" Zoe nodded toward the entry door. "…look who's here."

Alex hadn't needed Zoe to point out the young woman in the pink dress who glided into the room. He saw Maggie the moment she walked in. The only thing Alex disliked about the picture was that Maggie was holding Roger's arm as if their engagement were already announced.

18

Maggie hadn't minded riding in the buggy with Roger or allowing him to escort her to the party that evening. As far as she was concerned, sitting beside him in the buggy was no different than being seated next to Jon Anthony or Sarah or even Aunt Violet.

Yet in contrast she knew that being close to Alex evoked romantic feelings that nice girls didn't even think about. Even so she had to be honest and admit she wanted Alex to think she looked nice in her new dress.

She'd felt like a princess as she slipped into the tent on Roger's arm, closing her eyes and hoping that when she opened them again, Alex would be watching her. Now they were open, and she realized that he truly was watching her—but with Zoe Dawson standing right beside him.

Maggie tensed and shut her eyes again as if she thought shutting them would blot the image of Alex and Zoe from her brain. If seeing them together wasn't bad enough, Zoe's dress was as pink as primroses in a field of spring wildflowers. She could be wrong, but from where she was standing, Zoe's dress appeared to be made from the same kind of material as Maggie's—perhaps from the very same bolt.

If Maggie had her way, she and Roger would have turned around and marched right out of the tent. But before she could say or do anything, Roger grabbed hold of her elbow and dragged her forward.

"Hurry up, Maggie," he said. "I want to speak to Cousin Zoe."

The closer they got to Alex and Zoe, the clearer it became that Zoe's dress wasn't just pink—it was identical to Maggie's.

"So," Zoe said with a trace of sarcasm, "you bought one of the dresses Mrs. Branley had at the back of the store. I bought *my* dress a month ago."

Maggie blinked. "Mrs. Branley didn't tell me the seamstress made two pink dresses."

"Two?" Zoe laughed and motioned toward the room full of people. "Just look around you. There are a lot more than two."

With a sinking feeling Maggie discovered Zoe was right. Besides hers and Zoe's there were at least two other pink dresses—three unless she was seeing the same one twice.

Maggie bit her lower lip, hoping to swallow her disappointment. Why should she care that her dress wasn't unique? Christians shouldn't care about such girlish things.

Alex stepped into the conversation, grinning broadly. "For what it's worth, ladies, I think you two are the best looking women in pink dresses here tonight."

His words and the lighthearted way he said them set off a chain reaction in the area of Maggie's heart. Normally she would have thought what he said was funny, but not that night. She wanted to leave the party, to disappear as quickly as possible.

Alex's comment had reinforced what Maggie already knew —that she was placing too much importance in a dress she would seldom wear. And yet she wondered how Alex knew so much about women. Did he learn those things from his mother, his sister—or Dee? Maggie didn't want to think it was Dee.

Maggie had considered purchasing the pink parasol that went with the dress; she was glad she didn't. Zoe, she noticed, wasn't as wise. A matching parasol attached to a sort of bracelet dangled awkwardly from Zoe's left wrist.

You knew about the other dresses," Maggie commented.

Zoe nodded. "Yes, but I didn't expect anyone to buy one and wear it tonight. They weren't cheap, you know."

Alex elbowed Roger. "Why don't we head on over to the refreshment table and let the ladies figure this out?"

Roger looked a little surprised at Alex's suggestion, but he quickly recovered. Great idea, cowboy. I could really use something to drink." He turned to Maggie. "I'll bring you something cool."

Maggie smiled. "Thank you, Roger."

The men were barely out of earshot when Zoe said, "Two of the other girls are planning to demand that the Branleys give them back their money. I'm considering doing that myself."

"Mrs. Branley never said my dress was the only one."

"That's no excuse." Zoe lifted her head a little higher then looked down her nose at Maggie. "I should have had my daddy drive me up to Corpus to buy a dress, but at least mine was the smallest one in the store."

Sudden laughter bubbled up from inside, begging to come out, but Maggie refocused her gaze on a row of lace that edged the hem of her dress and forced her lips to behave. It looked as if Zoe might have had a hard time squeezing into her dress. But why did it matter? Maggie was a plain country girl, and she intended to have a good time, regardless of what other folks were wearing or what they thought. Yes, she'd wanted Alex to like her in the dress, but she wasn't going to let a dress issue rob her of a lovely evening.

A young man Maggie hadn't seen in years moved toward her

from the far side of the room, giving her a reason to drift away from Zoe and her ranting. "Excuse me, Zoe," she interrupted. "I see someone I need to speak to."

She'd always wondered what had become of Jasper Kingston but never expected to see him again. They visited for several minutes, filling in the missing years.

ALEX FROWNED but not so anyone could see. He knew Maggie didn't fancy Roger in a romantic way, but Alex wasn't so sure about the muscular young man talking to Maggie now.

He and Roger were still at the refreshment table, and Roger had told Alex more than once that he needed something stronger to drink than red punch. As Alex watched Maggie and her companion, Roger took a bottle of whiskey from the inside pocket of his jacket and poured some of it into his punch cup.

Alex turned toward Roger. "Hey, I'd go slow on that stuff if I were you. It'll make you crazy."

Roger smirked. "Do you think I care?"

"No, but Maggie might. You're driving her home tonight."

"Why would that matter?" Roger shrugged. "She's just a woman."

Just a woman? Alex's fists tightened. He wanted to hit Roger in that big nose of his. "Put that whiskey bottle away, Roger," Alex cautioned, keeping his voice low and steady.

"Put it away?" Roger laughed. "I like the taste of whiskey, and I like the way it makes me feel." He took a gulp straight from the bottle. "I'm gonna drink this whole thing tonight."

Alex blinked, shook his head, and walked away. It was clear to Alex that Roger was no good, through and through, but Maggie still thought of him as an old friend, a childhood playmate.

The lively tune the fiddler was playing came to an end.

When the music began again, Maggie was talking to still another young man, so Alex returned to the refreshment table. Roger was nowhere in sight.

The young cowboy Alex had seen Maggie talking with earlier was pouring punch into a crystal cup. Alex introduced himself and soon discovered the young cowboy's name was Jasper and he'd known Maggie for years.

"So you've known Maggie since y'all were children," Alex said after they had talked a while.

"My pa used to work on the ranch for Mr. Gallagher," Jasper said, "but we moved away when I was twelve."

"And now you're back looking for a ranch job."

Jasper nodded. "That's about it."

"Well, I'm new around here too, and I don't know of anyone hiring right now," Alex said. "If I hear of anything, I'll give you a holler."

"I'd appreciate that."

Alex put his empty punch cup on the serving table. He was about to go talk to Maggie when he noticed her near the square-dancing area. Maggie was surrounded by young men, and her obvious popularity was bound to displease the other young ladies in the community.

A square dance was forming in the middle of the room as Alex ambled back to the sidelines. He noticed Sarah standing with several of her friends. Wouldn't Sarah be surprised if he chose her as his partner?

Alex bowed at the waist and reached out for her hand. "May I have this dance, Miss Sarah?"

All the girls giggled. Alex had a difficult time swallowing a laugh of his own. Out of the corner of his eye, he caught Maggie watching them. And if he were reading her facial expression correctly, she was both amused and pleased that he'd taken such an interest in her little sister.

"I don't know how to square dance," Sarah said, her cheeks flushing slightly.

Alex winked. "Neither do I. But I understand there are people ready to teach us how to do it. Come on, Sarah. It'll be fun."

"Well, all right then." She took his hand.

After a little stumbling and a lot of laughs, the music ended, and Alex walked Sarah back to her friends. As he moved away from her, he noticed Zoe. How could he miss? She was peering right at him.

Obviously Zoe was interested in him, and she was headed straight for him. Now he knew how a bobcat must feel when its foot was caught in a trap. To avoid her now would be cruel and downright uncaring.

Zoe proved to be a poor square dancer, stomping all over the toes of his cowboy boots. At last the music stopped, but Zoe grabbed his arm, sticking to his side like they were nailed together. Then she half-dragged him as far from Maggie as she could get.

Zoe was some talker. She rattled on and on about first one thing and then another. He'd long since stopped listening. However, he did hear her say her father needed someone to work on their place. Then she invited Alex to apply for the job. He was about to tell her no when he had another idea.

Alex escorted Zoe over near the refreshment table and motioned for Jasper Kingston to join them. He pointed to Jasper as he moved toward them. "See that nice-looking young man coming this way?"

Zoe cocked her head. "Yes."

"Well, he needs a ranch job. Bad."

"So?"

"Maybe your daddy could use a man with his experience. Jasper told me he's been doing ranch work since he was a kid. I 'spect he knows just about all there is to know about cattle and horses."

She hesitated and shrugged. "Well, I don't know. Maybe..."

"How about if I introduce you? He might be just the man your daddy needs."

"Oh, all right."

He took Zoe by the hand and guided her to Jasper's side. Then he introduced them and promptly walked away.

Jasper was a nice fellow. Alex liked him, and he hated to banish him to the likes of Zoe Dawson. But maybe, for Jasper, finding a job made being with Zoe for the rest of the evening almost worth it.

Maggie stood a short distance away. With Jasper and Zoe out of the way, Alex joined her. "I see the caller is forming a new set. May I have this dance, Miss Maggie?"

She shook her head. "I wish I could, but I can't. I promised someone else."

Alex felt the muscles around his mouth tighten. "I see. Well, enjoy yourself." He forced a smile and walked away.

DURING THE EVENING Maggie caught bits of conversations among the young ladies, most openly admitting a deep desire to know Alex better. Maggie understood because she felt the same way. Quite obviously Zoe shared those feelings too, and Maggie still wrestled with the image of the two of them together.

When Alex headed for the door, she assumed he planned to leave the party. She wished he wouldn't. She had hoped to have a chance to explain to him that she wanted to be his partner in one of the squares now forming, but he dashed off before she had the chance. Now it was too late.

Occasionally she visually searched for Alex among the crush of men standing around the door of the tent. At last she saw him, though she hadn't wanted him to catch her staring at him. He did.

Briefly they shared a penetrating glance across the wide space that separated them. The connection might have gone on longer if Jed McGregor, the young man Sarah seemed to have a crush on, hadn't tapped her on the shoulder. Maggie forced a smile, but that didn't mean she trusted him.

"I believe you're my partner for the square dance," he said.

Maggie nodded and glanced back toward the spot she'd last seen Alex; he was gone.

19

Instead of joining in the square dancing, Maggie and Jed decided to get cups of punch and then find a place to sit and talk. Despite the candy incident with Sarah, Jed McGregor seemed like a nice person, though Maggie didn't really know him. Seated side-by-side with him in two of the straight-backed chairs that lined the back wall, she had the opportunity to get some answers.

"I understand you stopped by the Sunday house earlier today," Maggie said, getting right to the heart of the matter. "You gave my little sister a penny after she dropped her hard candy in the mud."

"Yes." Jed nodded. "But I didn't know she was your sister. I happened to be walking by when she dropped it, and when she started to cry, I knew I had to help."

"Why? You didn't even know her."

"I know I didn't, but tears get me—every single time. I knew I couldn't move on until I'd given the little girl money to buy more candy."

Jed McGregor was either one of the most compassionate men she'd ever met...or the biggest liar in the state of Texas.

Maggie hadn't quite decided which of those extremes fit him, but if nothing else he was certainly handsome and young looking.

He'd hesitated as if he expected her to reply to his last statement. When she didn't he continued. "You see, the same thing that happened to your sister happened to me when I was a little boy."

"You dropped hard candy?"

Jed nodded. "I was only about four or five at the time, and I didn't have enough money to buy more. I'd dropped my candy in front of the store right after I bought it, and my older cousin laughed. She laughed even harder when I cried."

Most men Maggie knew would take a whipping rather than admit he once cried, even if the crying took place when he was a young child. If Jed McGregor was who he claimed to be, he was truly an amazing young man.

"Do you live near the Sunday house?" Maggie asked, changing the subject. She took a sip of her punch, and when she'd swallowed a mouthful of the sweet liquid, she rested the cup and dainty saucer on her lap. "Or were you just out for a stroll?"

"My pa is hoping to buy the ranch-land that connects to the Sunday house, and he would like to buy the Sunday house too— if the Dawsons are willing to sell, that is. I decided to walk by and take a good look at the house just in case." He looked straight ahead, taking swallows of punch now and then, as if in deep thought. Then he turned and faced her. "You and your sister are staying at the Sunday house then?"

"We are guests of the Dawsons for the weekend, if that's what you mean."

"You wouldn't happen to know if they're willing to sell, would you?" He paused, clearing his throat. "No, of course you wouldn't. It was wrong of me to ask such a question."

"If I could give you an answer, I would, Mr. McGregor. But I have no idea what Roger and his mother are planning. I do know that Mrs. Lucy Dawson loves to entertain at the Sunday house."

"Oh yes," he said. "I've heard about Miss Lucy's parties. Have you known the Dawsons long?"

"Roger's a childhood friend, and Miss Lucy was always kind to me."

Maggie glanced toward the punch bowl. A familiar-looking young woman stood there, staring at them.

"Isn't that Belinda Foster in the green dress at the refreshment table?" Maggie asked. "I remember meeting her in church once."

"It's Miss Foster, all right. I've...I've been courting her for some months now. We'd planned to announce our engagement tonight, but we quarreled. She got so angry she went over and talked to another man we both know. So I—"

Maggie interrupted by completing his sentence. "Used me to make her jealous." She laughed. "Am I right?"

He sent her a sheepish grin. "I'm afraid you're right. Please forgive me for spitefully using you."

"Don't worry about it. And I hope your engagement goes off as you planned." She smiled, hoping he'd detect the conspiratorial twinkle she planted in her eyes. "And may I suggest you go over and make amends right this instant. My mother always said the best way to end a battle is to begin with 'I'm sorry' and take all the blame."

He shook his head. "I'm no good at making amends."

"You sell yourself short, Mr. McGregor. You just asked for my forgiveness, and I gave it. I'll bet it will work on your intended even quicker."

ALEX WENT OUTSIDE on the grounds in front of the tent. He considered getting on his horse and riding on back to the Sunday house, but Roger had been drinking since he arrived at the party. Alex wanted to make sure the man was sober enough to drive Maggie home. Until then he'd try to listen in on the various conversations going on among the men. He'd already learned a few things in the first minutes of standing around on the fairgrounds in front of the big tent. The most interesting bit of gossip he'd managed to uncover was the fact that "old man McGregor" and his son, Jed, were interested in buying the ranch-land connected to the Sunday house. Not only that but they also wanted to buy the Sunday house itself. He wondered what Roger and his mother thought about that bit of news, especially if it were true.

Alex noticed another group of men, huddled together, and he headed toward them. From the way they staggered around, he concluded that some if not all of them were drunk. Several of the men drank from small bottles of whiskey they held in their hands. Others poured the liquid into small cups. In their present condition they weren't likely to pay much attention to Alex. A fat man by the name of Skeeter was doing most of the talking. Alex moved over next to him.

"Did you hear about what happened to Gertrude Remmers?" Skeeter asked the group of men.

"No," a second man said. "What's she done now?"

Skeeter laughed under his breath and put his hand on the second man's shoulder. "Why, she went and got herself in the family way without getting married first—just like Sadie Gallagher did a while back."

"Well, I swan."

Alex could no longer keep silent. "You don't mean Maggie Gallagher's older sister, do you?"

All four men peered at Alex as if noticing him for the first time.

"I sure do, Mister," Skeeter said. "To put it bluntly Sadie Gallagher ain't never been married, but she had her a baby boy same as if she was."

All the other men roared with laughter.

"Sadie was living in Brownsville at the time," Skeeter went on. "She got herself all mixed up with some man down there. Then she just up and moved back home without no husband. Poor little Jon Anthony ain't got no daddy, much less a name."

Alex stiffened and clenched his fists. Whoever did that to Maggie's older sister ought to be ashamed. And now the drunks were acting like a bunch of hens, clucking and scratching in the henhouse, and he wanted to kick in Skeeter's front teeth for talking about Maggie's family in public. It was one thing to hear evil things about a woman he'd never met. It was another to speak against a child he was starting to care about.

Alex decided to walk away before he got himself in a fistfight and thrown out of town on a rail. However he had no intentions of leaving the fairgrounds, at least not until he was certain Maggie was safe and back at the Sunday house. A lot of drunks were on the prowl that night, and one of them went by the name of Roger Dawson.

A man like Roger might try anything with a beautiful woman like Maggie, especially when he'd been drinking. Alex intended to make sure nothing like that happened.

He moved toward the holding-pen to get his horse. He still couldn't believe what he'd heard about Sadie Gallagher and found himself feeling sorry for the woman.

What a terrible thing to happen to any woman, especially one from a family like Sadie's, and coming back to the ranch in her condition. She must have been extremely brave.

Toward the end of the evening Maggie picked her way across the crowded tent they called the county hall with its wooden floor for square dancing. She was ready to leave, but she wouldn't be riding home with Roger if it meant walking back to the Sunday house. Roger had filled his punch cup with something from a bottle all evening. By now he'd be disgusting.

Fortunately Sarah Ann was spending the weekend with Noma Elaine. Maggie only had herself to worry about. She'd just stepped outside the tent when Alex called to her from the darkness.

"And where do you think you're going?" he asked.

"Back to the Sunday house, thank you." Maggie turned and saw that he was alone and riding his horse. "Where's Zoe?"

"A cowboy is driving her home in her daddy's buggy, I think."

Maggie swallowed a smile. "How unfortunate for you."

He grinned. "Isn't it? And where's good old Roger? No, let me guess. He passed out."

She hesitated. "He just isn't ready to leave yet. But I am."

"Would you like to ride back with me? I'm here to rescue you."

"Rescue me?" She hadn't planned for the edges of her mouth to turn upward, but they did. "Thanks, but I don't need to be rescued."

Alex reined his black horse up close. She could have reached out and touched the animal if she'd wanted to.

"I'm taking you home, Maggie," he said.

"How? Wish me back to the house?"

"I thought a cowgirl like you would know something like that."

"I have no idea what you're talking about."

"Then let me show you." Alex tried to scoop her up with his good arm while holding the horse steady with the bad one. She saw the flash of pain in his eyes. Maggie grabbed hold of the saddle-horn, making his job a little easier and maybe saving him from a measure of embarrassment, if he failed to move her up and over the saddle.

Still, Maggie was caught by surprise. As she sat there squeezed between Alex and the saddle-horn with her feet dangling on one side like the queen of side-saddle riding, she could feel her hairpins slipping one-by-one out of the bun at the back of her head, but she was so astonished by what happened she was unable to speak or stop the pins from falling out.

"Put me down!" she said at last, though the protest was weak.

"Put you down?" Alex grinned down at her and situated her in the saddle in front of him. "Did you think I wouldn't notice when you grabbed that saddle-horn for dear life?"

"I did not."

"Did, too."

The skirt of her pink dress draped way down one side of the saddle; her long golden hair, now free of all restraints, cascaded across one shoulder and down to the third ruffle of her tiered evening gown. She wished for her divided riding skirt. Side-saddle riding was never for Maggie, and she wasn't exactly riding side-saddle now. But it was the closest thing to it.

Determined to be more forceful this time she declared, "I said, put me down!"

"No, Maggie, I'm not putting you down." His warm breath near her ear as he spoke sent shivers down her spine. "There are too many drunks out tonight. You need to be with me so you'll be safe."

"And who gave you the right to make that decision?"

"I did."

He placed one hand across her middle and squeezed her to him. "It's a good decision too, I think."

"I don't." But she knew she wasn't being truthful. She liked the safe, warm feeling that had swept over her when Alex lifted her onto his horse, like a princess in a fairytale when her prince rescued her. Despite what she'd just said, Maggie was so caught up in a sort of romantic fantasy that she almost forgot to be angry. When she realized she was in his arms, she stiffened. Thoughts of her older sister's tragedy filled her mind once more.

Loose women probably felt like this all the time. Wasn't that what her mama always said? But it was all so new to Maggie, not to mention downright confusing.

Well, she wouldn't blush if she could help it, not this time. But how could she stop her pulse from racing or save what was left of her family's reputation? Hadn't her mama also said men didn't respect worldly women? And hadn't romantic thoughts of a certain kind turned her own sister into "that kind" of woman?

Maggie stiffened and straightened her back. She and Alex were friends. She couldn't let him go on thinking she was another Sadie Jo. If nothing else she wanted his respect.

"It's all right for you to take me back to the Sunday house," she said, "because it's necessary. But being so close to you like this isn't something an unmarried lady should be doing. I won't let you hold me like this again. Ever."

"Ever's a long time," he said with amusement.

"It certainly is," she said, "and it could get even longer."

20

Alex rode his horse down a dark path some distance from the Sunday house. Maggie still sat in the saddle in front of him. All the cowboys she knew reined with their left hand, making the right available for roping. Alex had his good arm wrapped Maggie to keep her from falling off, and he had to admit that he liked holding her.

His memory seemed to be returning in bits and pieces, and he intended to share those memories with Maggie. Yet there was so much about his past that he didn't know, and he wondered if he ever would.

He might never have a better chance than now to talk to her about the things that troubled him, things he wanted Maggie to know before they left Bayview. He pulled back on the reins, easing his horse under an ancient live oak.

"Why are we stopping?" she asked.

"I want to talk to you about a few things before I take you back."

"Can't it wait?" She twisted around in the saddle. "It's dark out here. The chickens must have gone to roost hours ago. Only the night birds are still awake at this hour." An owl hooted as if to confirm her words. "See what I mean?"

Alex spoke low, his voice close to her ear. "I'm paying a visit to the sheriff's office again in the morning, Maggie, and I want you to hear what I plan to say before I talk to him."

"Tomorrow's Sunday. Everybody will be in church. I plan to go too."

"I'll meet with the sheriff early Monday morning then. I have a few more things to tell him. I'm leaving for good as soon as we get back to the ranch, and I want to talk to the sheriff again before we leave town. I figure it's the only honorable thing to do."

MAGGIE FELT herself begin to tremble on that warm night.

"Are you cold?" he asked.

"A little." She watched him remove his jacket.

"Here, wear this." He wrapped the jacket around her shoulders. "It's warm tonight, but maybe you're coming down with something."

"I'm not sick—just a little overwhelmed, I guess. A lot of things happened in a short period of time. I get this way when events I can't control grab hold of me."

"Another reason for me to leave. You need to return to the life you had before I got shot."

She turned as much as she could and spoke directly to him. "No, Mr. Lancaster, that's not what I need at all. What I need is someone to run my ranch."

Maggie paused. What had she been thinking? Was she waiting for him to volunteer for the job? He couldn't—wouldn't if he was truly intent on leaving.

When he didn't answer right away, she said, "Miss Lucy will worry if I stay gone too long. We'd better get back."

"All right, but…" He released a deep breath of air. "I'm remembering a few things now, nothing to write home about as they say, but now and then memories come to my mind. I'm hoping if I tell you what I remember, you can fill in some of the blanks."

"I'll try."

"I think I was looking for someone or some place when I ended up at your ranch."

"What do you mean by ended up?"

"I think I took a wrong turn."

"Meaning?"

"I think the place I was looking for is either way north of here or way to the south, not Bayview and not the Gallagher Ranch. Texas is a big place. It's not surprising I lost my way."

He cleared his throat. "Roger said I spent the night before I was shot at the hotel in Bayview, and I think he was right. The lobby of the hotel looked familiar when we went there today." He hesitated. "I reckon it might be best if you not tell anyone that I'm starting to remember things. Even folks you trust might repeat what you say in confidence, without meaning to of course." He sighed. "I really don't trust anyone—except you."

"Thank you," she said barely above a whisper.

"I need for you to tell me what happened before I got shot." Alex shook his head. "And you may not like what I have to say after that."

Maggie tightened her grip of the saddle-horn, remembering that the novel warned that giving a person with a memory loss too much information could be harmful. But she'd already told him more than she should have. She might as well tell him everything.

She sent a quick prayer to heaven and then began. "Before I heard gunfire on the day you were shot, I saw a dust cloud in the north pasture moving toward the house. I think your horse caused that dust cloud."

"Did you only see one dust cloud? Or were there more?"

"Sarah and I only saw one. We were on our way to the cemetery to put flowers on the graves. When I saw the cloud, I thought company was coming. But I also thought if we hurried we could leave our flowers and get right back to the house before our company settled in good."

"Couldn't that be a little dangerous if your company got there before you did? The cemetery is over a mile from the main house."

"Around here people think nothing of walking into a friend's empty house and making themselves at home until the family arrives."

Alex nodded. "So what happened next?"

"We heard gunfire."

"One shot or more?"

"One. We rode over to see what happened, and we found you in a plowed field, shot and bleeding on the ground. Your head was bleeding too. There was a lot of farm equipment where you fell, so I think you hit your head on the plow. I saw horse tracks all around you, but the horse must have run away. Finding your horse seemed to confirm that part of the events."

"Then what?"

"I bandaged you up, sent Sarah back to the house for help, and read your letter."

"Why? Why would you read that letter?"

"I wanted to know who you were and why you were on our land." She took hold of the horse's black mane and stroked it. "I wish we knew what happened just before you got shot. Do you remember anything at all?"

"My memory is still plenty fuzzy, but I think I remember a cabin out in the middle of nowhere. I guess I must have gone there before I got shot."

"That could be the old Ginner place, and it's not far from the ranch. Roger owns it now and uses it for a hunting lodge."

"I remember seeing a woman's dress hanging on the clothesline, and I think I've seen it before. The dress was blue with little pink and white flowers."

"I bought a whole bolt of material like that at Branleys' last summer. In fact half the women in Bayview bought bolts of material just like it. It was a very popular item because the cost was so low. I think Roger sometimes takes the wives of his hunting friends to the cabin to cook for the men. The dress you saw could belong to just about anyone."

"Then that explains it." He nodded. "But my memory doesn't end there. I remember walking up on the front porch of that cabin in the brush. I could hear people talking and laughing. But when I knocked, nobody answered."

Maggie shrugged. "What's so strange about that? Hunters go to Roger's cabin to hunt, not meet new and interesting people."

"One of those voices was female. Everything got quiet after I knocked, like something was going on in there."

"Maybe Roger has a girlfriend I don't know about. People have hinted that he does."

"They were talking in Spanish."

"Everybody talks Spanish around here." She peered directly into his eyes. "Is that all?"

He hesitated for a moment then continued. "No, that's not all. In order to reach the cabin, I walked my horse through a break in the fence. It was really more of a cut than a break. Cows and baby calves were crossing from one side of the fence into the other pasture. At the time it looked suspicious to me, and I don't think somebody was rotating the herd. Now that I know Roger owns the property on one side of the fence and you on the other—well, that changes everything. There's cattle-rustling going on, Maggie, and I have to tell the sheriff what I know. I just wish I'd remembered all this sooner."

Maggie's defensive mechanism kicked in then. "If you think

Roger is stealing my cattle, you're wrong. He has faults, but he would never do something like that."

"I'm not saying he did. But who else would profit from cutting a fence wire between your property and his?"

"I'm glad you're beginning to remember things, Alex," she said, taking a deep breath to settle her emotions, "but I don't want to talk about this anymore. All I want to do is go back to the Sunday house."

"All right." He touched the black stallion with the heels of his boots and it moved forward in a slow walk.

"Maybe later we can talk things over in a sensible manner," she said, facing forward again. "I do want you to share your memories with me, and you can be sure I will never repeat anything you tell me in confidence."

"I appreciate that."

Maggie glanced back at Alex. "And you're still driving us to church in the morning like you said?"

"That's my plan."

"Thank you."

Nobody spoke after that; they simply rode on through the darkness. All Maggie was able to hear was the wind and the squeak of leather stirrups that needed oiling.

She longed to break that silence, to make things right between them before she said goodnight. But she didn't know what to say or how to say it.

Lighted lamps hung from the ceiling of the long front porch of the Sunday house, from one end to the other, and Miss Lucy sat in the rocker right by the front door. She must have seen them as they approached the front steps. Instead of saying so much as a friendly hello, the woman kept rocking back and forth as if she intended to stay there forever.

21

Alex waited on the front porch of the mansion until Miss Lucy finally went inside and shut the door behind her. Maggie would be in her room on the second floor by now. Miss Lucy likely expected Alex to go inside too, but he had other plans.

After a few moments he mounted and turned his horse back toward the tent where the party was being held. He owed it to Maggie to make sure Roger made it back to the Sunday house alive. As drunk as he was when Alex left the Founders Day Party, it was doubtful. Roger could easily get into a fight or just fall right out of his carriage driving home.

Most of the partygoers were gone by the time he returned, but Roger's carriage was still parked where he'd left it.

Alex hurried to the door of the tent, offering his hand to the old man standing just inside. "Hello, sir." The men shook hands. "Would you know if Roger Dawson is still here?"

"Far as I know he is. Last I saw of him he was staggering pretty bad. By now he could have fallen on his face."

"Can you remember where he was the last time you saw him?"

He scratched his bald head then released a deep sigh. "Seems to me he was toward the back of the tent, up near the bandstand. The fiddlers were still on the stage then, but now they've done packed up and gone home."

Alex nodded. "Thank you, sir. I appreciate your help."

"Don't mention it."

Most of the men and women still in the tent were part of the clean-up crew. Alex headed for the back of the tent and found Roger, propped up with his head on the bandstand, his legs spread out in front of him and drinking straight from a glass bottle instead of the flask he had earlier. His hair was falling in his face, and his eyes were bloodshot.

Alex stood in front of him, his hands on his hips. "Don't you think you've had enough of that stuff for one night, Dawson?"

"Not as long as there's still whiskey in this bottle." He offered it to Alex. "Here, have a swig. I'm willing."

"Well, I'm not." Alex shook his head. "But I'll be glad to drive you back to the Sunday house."

"Nobody drives me anywhere. I've been driving buggies and riding horses since I was able to walk." Roger looked around. "Where's Maggie? As they say, I brung her to this shindig. I 'speck I have to drive her home too."

"You're too late. She's already back at the Sunday house."

"Well, that's good 'cause I don't want to go there anyhow."

"Where do you want to go, Roger?"

"To the Happy Redfish, where else? Ever been there, Lancaster?"

"No, can't say I have, not that I can remember."

Roger laughed. "That's right. You lost your memory." He sat up a little straighter and took another big swallow of whiskey. "Well, all I can say is, you better not find it."

"Find what?"

"Your memory, 'cause if you do you'll wish you hadn't."

Alex was about to question him further, but Roger fell back

against the stage again. Alex tried to rouse him but couldn't. He got two of the male workers to help him load Roger into his carriage. Then Alex tied his black stallion to the back of the carriage and drove Roger home.

———

EARLY SUNDAY MORNING Alex went out to hitch up the wagon. Guilt strangled him on the previous night, and he'd had a hard time falling asleep, tossing and turning in his bed in the basement of the Sunday house.

He should have told Maggie that he might be married when he had the chance. He wanted her to know he loved her. But it wouldn't be right to declare his love until he knew whether or not he was free to marry.

From the day Sarah first read to him from what some called the Good Book, Alex knew the Bible wasn't new to him. He'd read from it in the past and could recite verses from memory, and he knew he wanted to follow the Lord forever. If only his long-term memory were as clear as those verses. He was remembering things now but not enough to make a difference.

Every night Alex read at least one chapter from the Bible he'd borrowed from Maggie. But now that he had a Bible of his own, he planned to read two chapters or maybe three.

Maggie had conducted worship services in her home long before Alex came to the ranch, but he'd hesitated to attend. The other ranch cowboys avoided them, and he thought he might appear too ambitious if he went against the accepted norm by attending. But he looked forward to attending church that morning. His Bible reading caused questions to form in his mind, and he hoped today's Sunday sermon would answer some of them.

Later that morning he drove Maggie and the children to church. Maggie carried a big wicker basket that smelled like chicken and fixings, and she loaded it in the back of the wagon with Sarah and Jon Anthony. Clearly a picnic lunch was planned. Alex wondered if he was invited, but he wouldn't ask.

He never intended to ask Maggie to provide answers to some of his Bible questions, but as he sat there beside her with the reins in his hands, he thought, *Why not?* He had a feeling he'd once heard someone say, "Now's as good a time as any."

"I want to return that Bible I borrowed from you," he said, glancing at Maggie. "Guess you know I bought one of my own. I've been reading the Bible now for some time, and I wondered if I could ask you some questions before we get to the church. It's always good to be prepared."

"I'd be glad to help. What do you want to know?"

"The Good Book says that Christians are supposed to pray without stopping. I was wondering how to do that. Seems to me, ma'am, that if you prayed without stopping, you wouldn't have time to talk to anyone else, and I sure would miss talking to someone like you."

"I don't know the exact meaning of that scripture. But I can tell you what I think it means."

"Let's hear it."

"I think it means we are to include the Lord in our everyday thoughts."

"How would that work?"

"Well, let's say I was fixing to go out and feed the chickens, which is something I do every day unless I can talk Sarah into doing it. So instead of thinking, *I need to go out and feed the chickens*, I could make it a prayer by thanking the Lord for reminding me to feed the chickens. That way God would be a part of everything I do or say. I don't think there should ever be secrets between the Lord and me. When I pray like that, as often as I remember to do it, there aren't any secrets between us because He's a part of my thinking. See what I mean?"

"Yes." He nodded. "I think maybe I do."

But his answer wasn't completely true. He'd need time to think about what she said before he truly understood it.

The church was made of wooden planks and painted white. Maggie would probably call it quaint or charming. Alex liked the way it looked even before he slowed the mules and stopped the wagon.

"The church looks nice, Miss Maggie. Mighty fine."

"That's not the church, Mr. Lancaster. It's the church building. The church is the people—the body of believers who worship the Lord inside that building."

He was puzzled by her comment, and it likely showed on his face. "Are you saying then that you're the church?"

"I'm saying that I am a part of the Church of Jesus Christ, yes. It takes all believers to make up the whole thing—at least that's what my mama always said."

"I think I would have liked your mama."

"She would have liked you, too."

Everything about the worship service touched Alex in some way. He loved the prayers, the hymns, the sermon, and the smiles on all the faces of those who attended. He knew some of the hymns, and Maggie smiled up at him when he sang out as if he were a member of the congregation. His voice carried and might have sounded a little too loud for some of the church members, but Maggie appeared to like his thunderous singing.

Later as he stood in front of the church building and Maggie introduced him to just about every person there, he longed to read his Bible again. He'd heard scripture verses during the sermon and wanted to look them up and study them.

Alex loved country life, yet he almost wished he lived in town so he could attend services every week. He decided that if he stayed on at the ranch, he would attend the services Maggie held in her home, regardless of what the other cowboys thought.

The pastor had warned during the sermon that sometimes

wolves wore sheep's clothing, and Alex sensed that somehow he'd met such a person. He couldn't remember when or how, but he knew a wolf in sheep's clothing was part of his past.

Toward the end of the service that morning, the preacher gave what Maggie referred to as an altar call, inviting those who wanted to know the Lord to come to the front of the building. Alex had wanted to step forward and agree to be baptized that Sunday afternoon. He didn't because somehow he knew he was already a member of the family of God and had likely been baptized somewhere along the way. He just wished he knew more details before leaving the ranch and the people he had come to care about.

MAGGIE HAD INTENDED to invite Alex to the picnic lunch she'd planned for the children but never got around to it. Now that the service was over and they were back in the wagon and on their way to the Sunday house, it was time.

She cleared her throat. "Did you ever take off your shoes and wade in water up to your knees when you were a child, Mr. Lancaster?"

He chuckled softly. "Not that I can recall."

"Oh, I didn't mean…" She shook her head. "I've done it again, haven't I?"

"Don't worry. I'm not sensitive. And to answer you question, I have no memory of ever doing that. But it sure does sound like fun. I'll bet Jon Anthony and Sarah think so too."

"Oh, they do. They can hardly wait to get in the water. Anyway I'm sure you noticed the nice beach next to the Sunday house, and…" She blinked and shook her head. "That's right. You saw it when you think you saw Elena with that man."

"I don't think I saw her with a man, Miss Maggie. I know I did."

"Whatever you say." Maggie shrugged and swatted at a fly that had landed on her skirt. "I brought a picnic lunch today and thought we could go down to the beach and eat our lunch there. If you were of a mind to join us, we'd love to have you."

He grinned. "I accept. But don't expect me to take my boots and socks off and wade in the bay unless you're willing to do the same. Are you?"

Maggie looked away, hoping her cheeks hadn't turned pink.

"Well, are you?"

"I'd consider doing it if the children weren't around."

"Always the perfect lady, aren't you?"

She looked back at him, no longer concerned that her face might be flushed. "No, but I try. I wouldn't set a good example if I did something like that in front of the children."

He stopped in front of the Sunday house and tied up the reins. "I've decided to park the wagon here rather than risk getting stuck in the mud closer to the bay," he said. "We'll have to walk from here on." He saw her reach for the picnic basket. "I'll carry that, ma'am. Just let me help the children down from the wagon, and then we can go."

As soon as they arrived at the nearby beach, the children ran ahead. They stepped out of their shoes, pulled off their stockings, and went right into the shallow water, splashing and laughing and splashing some more.

"Try not to get your clothes wet," Maggie shouted.

But the only answer Alex heard was more laughter.

Maggie opened the picnic basket and took out a folded red and white polka-dot tablecloth. They spread it on the sandy beach, and when the children were dry and hungry, they all ate their meal.

But this time the chicken wasn't fried. It was part of a salad, served with shelled pecans, fresh oranges cut into slices—and fresh cornbread on the side. Alex thought it might be the most delicious lunch he'd ever tasted.

———————

MAGGIE WATCHED at a distance as the children made castles in the damp sand. Then Alex asked her to answer more of his Bible questions.

"You really know a lot about the Bible, Miss Maggie," he said after they'd talked for a while. "If I was gonna stay, I'd join that Bible study of yours, the one you have in your home. But of course I'll be moving on."

The smile she'd been wearing faded noticeably as he spoke, and the muscles around her mouth tightened. He looked away, pretending a sudden interest in the mounds of sand the children were forming.

"We've been here long enough," she said then. "Jon Anthony needs to take an afternoon nap, or he'll be hard to live with for the rest of the day." Without looking at Alex she turned around and started putting the rest of the food back in the wicker basket. "I'll need to wash our soiled things too, so they'll be ready when we leave in the morning. It would be easier to pack clean clothes than dirty ones."

"Need any help putting that stuff away?" Alex asked.

"No, thank you. I'm certainly able to clean up this mess by myself."

"All right." Alex got up then and stood with his hands on his hips. "Then if you don't need me, I guess I'll go over and see that castle the kids made."

"Tell them I said it was time to leave."

Maggie watched him walk away.

A few minutes later they all made their way back to the Sunday house. Maggie and Alex didn't talk with one another, but Alex got into a friendly conversation with Sarah and Jon Anthony about the art of sandcastle making.

Maggie wanted to be part of their fun, laughing together and talking, but had to accept the truth. Alex was leaving, and she couldn't stop him. She bit her bottom lip and moved on.

———

ALEX THOUGHT Maggie looked a little sad, and he longed to comfort her. He moved ahead, opening the front door of the Sunday house. At last he stood back, motioning for Maggie and the children to go in first.

"Thank you, Mr. Lancaster," Maggie said, her eyes downcast, "for driving us to church and everything."

"My pleasure."

"Sarah, Jon Anthony, don't forget your manners."

Sarah smiled. "Thank you, Mr. Lancaster."

"You are most welcome."

"Jon Anthony," Maggie said, looking down at the little boy. "What do you say to Mr. Lancaster?"

"Tank you."

Everybody laughed, including Maggie.

"You are welcome, Jon Anthony," Alex said.

It felt good to see Maggie's obvious change in attitude before his very eyes, but he wondered what caused it. Was she sad that he was leaving, or was it something else entirely?

After Maggie and the children had gone inside, Alex turned and headed for Roger's riding stable behind the Sunday house. His mother kept her team of town-horses there, and Roger kept the horses he brought with him from the Dawson ranch in Miss Lucy's stable when he was in town. Now Alex's black stallion was in a nice stall in that fancy horse barn as well. But Maggie's mules were banished to a small pen behind the stable.

Alex checked the mules first to see if they were being fed and watered. He was pleased to see their needs were being met. But when he arrived at the stable, those good feelings disappeared. A bit of oats was left in his horse's bucket, and there was plenty of hay, but not a drop of water in the animal's small watering trough.

Alex fumed. *Somebody here isn't doing his job.* He grabbed an empty bucket from a hook nearby and hurried to the hand-pump just outside the kitchen door. As he filled the bucket, he noticed Roger peering at him through the kitchen window.

After what happened on the previous night, Roger probably had a terrible headache or maybe an upset stomach. Alex hoped no serious harm had come to him. But if Roger got a headache or a belly-ache after getting drunk, it might teach him a lesson.

He hurried back to the stable and poured the bucket of water into the horse's trough. The animal drank immediately. As Alex stood there, eyeing the stallion, he felt someone watching him. Out of the corner of his eye, he saw a flash of blue. Roger, in a bright blue shirt, stood in the doorway of the horse barn.

Alex nodded a silent greeting, and Roger started toward him.

"Well, Lancaster." Roger came and rested his elbows on the top of the half-door of the stall and studied Alex and his horse. "I was standing at the kitchen window a while ago, drinking a cup of coffee and looking out, and there you were, filling a bucket with water. What happened?" Roger laughed. "Did you start a fire or something?"

"My stud was out of water. I had to fill his trough to keep him from dying of thirst."

"Sorry about that. The hands that work the stable were busy, I guess."

"No real harm was done. I have everything under control now."

Roger surveyed the black stallion carefully. "Nice looking stud you got there, Lancaster. I could use a stud like that. Are you interested in selling him? I could give you a fair price."

"I'm afraid not, but thanks for asking. I've grown attached to

Blackie here, since I came to realize he was mine. I think I'll keep him, but much obliged for the offer."

"Well, I sure to do like the looks of that stud. Good head and body formation. If you ever change your mind and want to sell him, let me know."

"I sure will."

Alex bit his lip. He hadn't said what he was thinking, and telling a lie—even a little white one—bothered him now. He would never tell Roger if he wanted to sell the black stallion and shouldn't have said that he would. Roger likely didn't treat animals any better than he treated women.

Roger didn't say anything more and neither did Alex, but he stood there watching Alex and his horse a little longer. Finally Roger said, "Well, Lancaster, I better go back inside. I guess I'll be seeing you."

"Goodbye, and thank your mother for me, will you? It was mighty nice of her to let me keep my horse here."

"I'll tell her. And I'd keep my eye on that stud if I was you. Horse stealing is a crime. But some folks would say it's worth it to get an animal like yours."

22

Early Monday morning Alex went out to the horse barn behind the Dawsons' house to check on Maggie's mules and his horse. Roger said his hands would hitch up the wagon for the trip back to the ranch, but Alex trusted Roger about as far as he could throw a thousand-pound weight. Before starting back to the ranch, he wanted to make sure the animals were fed and watered and the wagon was rigged as it should be.

The sun wasn't up yet, and the oil lamp he carried did little to light up the stable where his stud was being kept. He shined the light into the darkness. The stall was empty.

Empty? So where was the black stallion?

Alex rushed from stall to stall, hoping to find his horse, but the black stallion was in none of them.

One of Roger's men came in then and stood just inside the barn door.

"Come here," Alex called to him.

The large sandy-haired man still loomed in the doorway and didn't attempt to come any closer.

"Where's my horse?" Alex demanded.

The man shrugged. "Someone took him during the night, I guess. I told Mr. Dawson to tell you.

"Well, he didn't. And I need my horse right now. I'm leaving this morning."

The man shrugged and said nothing.

Alex grabbed his bridle from a hook by the empty stall and started toward one of Roger's horses. "Tell Mr. Dawson I'm borrowing one of his mares. I have things to do before I help you load the wagon."

Alex saddled a gray mare and raced off, hoping to pick up the trail of the person who stole his horse. He knew Roger wouldn't do anything to help him, but he doubted Roger took the stud. To steal an animal from his own stable wasn't logical, even for Roger. If Roger was going to steal an animal, he would do it away from the Sunday house so nobody would suspect him of the crime. Roger might not be the smartest man Alex ever met, but he had to have a measure of gumption even if it was so small nobody could see it.

Alex still planned to pay a visit to the sheriff's office before leaving town, but he wouldn't mention that he was starting to remember things because he had no way of knowing whether or not the things he now remembered were true. He would stop by the office again and file another report on their way out of Bayview to let the sheriff know about the missing horse. As crazy as it sounded, Roger could be the horse thief after all.

Horse stealing was a serious crime in Texas, and he couldn't stop thinking about how much Roger admired his black stud. Anyone with a brain in his head would think it strange that none of Roger's animals were missing. Alex intended to point that out to the sheriff.

An hour later Alex headed back to the Sunday house. He was unable to find his horse or the one who took him, and he couldn't afford to stay over an extra day in order to keep on looking. He would report the crime as best he could before he left town; the rest was up to the law.

On their way out of town Alex stopped by the sheriff's office and reported the theft and the other matters as planned. As he was getting back in the wagon, Zoe came running up, waving an envelope. One of the last people Alex expected to see was Zoe Dawson.

"I couldn't let you ride away without letting you know some things." Zoe handed Alex the envelope. "This will say it all a lot better than I can."

"Thank you kindly, Miss Dawson."

He wondered what Maggie was thinking as he reined the team on out of town. As they rolled along he opened the envelope and began reading. He expected to read something silly from someone like Zoe, a love note maybe. From the look of aggravation on Maggie's face, she did too. But the letter was quite different.

Zoe warned Alex to beware of her cousin Roger Dawson. Alex wondered if she knew about what happened to his horse, but there was no way to find out now.

If her eyes were an indication, Maggie was dying to know what was in the letter, but she would probably rather jump out of the back of the wagon and dive into a puddle of mud than ask him to read it aloud. She shut her mouth and didn't open it again for the next five miles.

"Why did you stop wearing your sling?" Maggie asked finally, changing the subject. "Didn't Doc Smyth say you were supposed to keep wearing it a while longer?"

"The thing bothered me. Besides, I don't need it anymore."

Maggie might have thought he was making a serious mistake, but if she had such notions, she kept them to herself.

THEY ARRIVED at the ranch earlier than Alex expected. About four hours of daylight remained. Elena and the children went inside, giving Maggie and Alex the opportunity to sit on the wooden bench near the yard gate and talk.

"You're really leaving, aren't you?" Maggie said.

Alex nodded. "It's time to get out of your way. I'll need to borrow a horse if I can, since mine was stolen. I'll return it when I can."

"Of course."

At the party on Saturday night, Alex heard enough to realize that many of the town-folk called Sadie Gallagher a fallen woman. He didn't want people to think Maggie was like her, and if he stayed much longer, they might.

Alex had to wonder if he was on some sort of quest when he ended up at the Gallagher Ranch. Was he looking for Dee, the woman mentioned in the letter, and ended up in the wrong place? As far as Alex knew, there were no women by that name anywhere around here. If there were, Maggie or someone would have told him.

"As you know," Alex said, "on the morning I was shot, I must have been on my way somewhere. I have to find out where that somewhere is."

"Wouldn't it be easier to find out where you came from if you were living here on the ranch where you have friends, rather than to go riding off to a place where nobody knows you?"

"I might have friends somewhere else that I know nothing about. How will I find out unless I leave?"

"You might have enemies, too, you know."

He nodded. "I've thought of that."

He looked away then, not wanting her to see the war of emotions he was sure was playing out on his face. He feigned a sudden interest in her hound playing with a small stick.

"Here, Ranger," he called. "Bring me that stick, boy."

The dog brought it, wagging his tail the whole time.

"Good boy." Alex threw the stick, and Ranger raced after it.

"Any idea when you'll be leaving?" she asked, pulling him back to their conversation. "I'd like to know."

He sighed. No sense putting it off. "As soon as I can get my gear together." The dog brought the stick back, placing it at Alex's feet. "But I hate to leave Blackie behind. I sure like that stallion, even if it turns out he isn't mine." He threw the stick again, and the dog chased it. Then he glanced back at Maggie.

Her face looked pained. "You don't mean you're leaving tonight do you?"

He hesitated. "No. I'll spend the night and then ride out before daylight. And maybe I should buy a horse instead of borrowing one. You will sell me a horse, won't you?"

Maggie nodded and swallowed. "Sure. I'll sell any horse you want."

THE MEN CAME HOME from cow-camp an hour later, leading about twenty wild horses they'd trapped in a pasture south of the creek. The animals weren't actually wild in the true sense, but Maggie's papa always called horses that weren't saddle-broken "wild." So did most of the other area ranchers she knew.

From the kitchen window Maggie watched Alex help the ranch hands pen the herd in a small pasture east of ranch headquarters. She'd invited him to supper but doubted he'd accept. Now that he was sleeping in the camp house, he ate there too. But after he finished working, Alex came to the house and washed up for supper. Maggie was pleasantly surprised, but still wishing he would change his mind about leaving.

She stood in front of the wood stove, stirring boiled rice and trying not to think about Alex being gone by morning.

He sat down at the table next to Jon Anthony's empty high chair. "Where are the children?"

"Playing. I sent Elena to tell them that supper is about ready."

"I guess your men'll be breaking those horses right away, won't they?"

Maggie nodded. "We do that every spring about this time."

"I saw some really fine-looking horses out there."

"My papa liked horses, and so do I."

She moved away from the stove and got the milk pitcher. Should she say what was on her mind? She hated to leave things the way they were and let him ride off.

Maggie got four glasses and poured fresh milk into them. "We sure could use some extra help. Big Lupe said two of our cowboys quit during the roundup, so we're kind of shorthanded right now." She set down one of the glasses in front of Alex's plate. "If you could see your way clear to stay a while longer, it sure would help."

She gazed at him. His face was stone serious. She tried to force a smile. "If you stayed I wouldn't expect you to do any bronco-riding or any heavy work with your shoulder and arm like it is. But there's still plenty to do if you're interested."

Alex still hadn't said anything. She wondered what was going through his mind.

"I could stay long enough to help you out," he said, breaking the silence at last. "I owe you that much, after all you've done for me."

She shook her head. "You don't owe me anything. I just wanted you to know you're welcome to stay—if you want to."

"Then it's settled." He scooped up a spoonful of pinto beans and put them on his plate. "I'll stay until you get that herd of wild horses topped off a little."

"And then you'll be leaving?"

"Yeah. And then I'll be leaving."

She didn't want him to stay merely out of some sense of

duty, but she could use an extra cowboy or two. What she really needed was a foreman to run the ranch full-time, but she knew he wouldn't consider that, at least not now, so she'd settle for what she could get. But deep down she knew hiring Alex to do ranch work wasn't the only reason she wanted him to stay. She honestly enjoyed his company, and she had never able to say that about any man before.

23

S pring roundup arrived before daylight the next morning. Even at that early hour, a feeling of excitement filled Maggie's heart. As the sun peeped over the horizon, she and Sarah hurried out the kitchen door and headed for the corral beyond the yard gate.

Sarah held two buttered biscuits, dripping with molasses. The biscuits were left over from breakfast and all wadded up and sticking to a cotton napkin.

"Want a biscuit?" Sarah asked. "I'll share."

Maggie shook her head. "Is that Spanish I hear coming out of your mouth, Sarah?"

She switched to English. "I keep forgetting."

Maggie smiled. "It's all right, but do try to remember. It's very important. You speak Spanish well, but you need to speak English well too. And thanks for the offer of a biscuit." Maggie patted Sarah lovingly on the shoulder. "But I've had enough to eat for one meal. I'm a stuffed turkey as it is."

Sarah opened the napkin, snagged one of the biscuits, and took a bite. Sticky molasses mixed with butter quickly covered her mouth and fingertips.

Maggie was looking off toward the herd of horses the men rounded up. The animals were racing around the big corral and kicking up their hind legs when she glanced over at her little sister again.

"For heaven's sake, Sarah, wipe your mouth. You've got food all over it."

Sarah took one end of the napkin and did a halfway acceptable job of wiping away the mess. It wasn't good enough for Maggie. Pulling a white handkerchief from her apron pocket, she wiped her sister's mouth and fingers as best she could. "That'll have to do, but you really need to wash your hands." She wadded up the soiled handkerchief and stuck it back in her pocket. "Now hurry up or we'll miss seeing the men rope the horses."

"Can we sit up on the top rail of the fence like we did last year?" Sarah asked.

"I plan to."

"Then I will too." She raced off to wash her hands.

The men were already swinging their ropes. None of the cowboys had successfully roped a horse, but Maggie thought they looked as if they were having a lot of fun trying.

Each cowboy would choose two wild horses from the herd, the two he thought he'd like to break and ride for the coming year. The trick was roping that particular horse or horses before somebody else did. All the cowboys hoped to claim the best horses, and there would be winners and losers.

After years of ranch life and a father who insisted she learn every aspect of ranching, Maggie had a good eye for horseflesh. She paid careful attention to the herd.

When Sarah returned Maggie said, "It's time you learned more about horses." Maggie pointed to a bay gelding over in one corner of the big corral. "See that bay over there? The one rubbing his nose on the fence?"

"Yes," Sarah said.

"Well, that's the best horse in the herd."

"How do you know that?"

"Papa taught me how to judge horses, and now I'm going to teach you—if you'll pay attention long enough."

"I will. I promise!"

"All right, now look at that bay real close. See if you can see any good thing about him that the other horses don't have."

"I'm looking, Maggie, but I don't see what you mean."

"Keep looking. You will. It takes time."

Alex threw his rope and looped the bay gelding in one try.

"Mr. Cowboy is a good roper," Sarah said in Spanish. "His arm must be a lot better."

"*Si*," Maggie replied. "It must be. And will you please speak to me in English?"

Maggie watched as the men helped Alex drive the bay horse into a holding pen. Fascinated by Alex's skill, she decided to put off the rest of what she intended to tell Sarah until another day.

Maggie had assumed Alex would merely assist the other cowboys in roping their horses. She hadn't expected him to do any actual roping, and she hoped it meant he planned to stay long after the horses were topped-off.

"Mr. Lancaster roped that horse before anybody, didn't he?" Sarah said. "Does that mean he's a good cowboy?"

"I would say so."

"I like Mr. Lancaster. Don't you, Maggie?"

"Yes, Sarah, I do."

"I like him almost as much as I like Mr. Jed McGregor."

"Don't start that again, Sarah Ann." Maggie gave her little sister a stern look. "He's my age. That makes him way too old for you. Jed is short for Jedediah, and that's a Bible name. It means loved by Jehovah."

"Who's Jehovah?"

"God the Father. I thought you knew that."

"I know his name is Jed and that I'm going to marry him someday."

"Sarah, you are never going to marry Jed. He's practically engaged. In the fall he's going back to college to become a lawyer. If he ever returns to Bayview, he'll probably have a wife and a couple of kids with him. So get this silliness about having a crush on Jed McGregor out of your mind right now. Hear?"

Sarah nodded, but Maggie didn't think she was convinced.

A few minutes later Alex selected a second horse from the herd, a mare, and roped her. Maggie was doubly confused. Was he still leaving? Or had he changed his mind? Cowboys didn't rope a horse from the herd just for the fun of it. They roped an animal they intended to saddle-break and ride during the coming year.

When every man on the ranch had roped and penned at least two animals, several cowboys went into the round pen to wait. The rest herded the first wild horse of the day into the round pen. The circular pen was built of sturdy wood planks. A big cedar fence post stood in the center of it.

Maggie and Sarah moved over to the round pen, climbing to the top rail of the wooden fence. At dawn the golden sun wasn't fully awake. Yet it was bright enough to make Maggie blink, and it lit up the pasture that surrounded the corral.

She shaded her eyes then noticed Sarah hadn't done so. "Don't ever look directly into the rising sun like that again, Sarah. It's bad for your eyes."

A rancher's wife and children knew not to go through the gate to the round pen in order to sit on the fence. To do so was dangerous. A wild horse could be in the pen, snorting and kicking up its hind legs. Maggie learned at a young age that ranch women and children did as they were told and stayed out of the way during spring roundup.

Alex roped the first horse. At the Gallagher ranch that meant that he would be the first cowboy to ride an unbroken horse.

Maggie worried about what might happen if he was crazy enough to do it in his weakened condition. She also knew better than to voice her concerns. Ranch women also kept those kinds of thoughts to themselves—at least in public.

If it wasn't enough that the sun was shining directly in her eyes, splinters coming from the rough cedar planks of the round fence poked painful holes in her thighs and back side through the soft material of her riding skirt. She readjusted herself, trying to find a more comfortable position and hoping one of the older hands would break the rule and be the first to ride. The first horse they brought out was the bay gelding Alex roped, and he followed the bay into the round pen.

The angry animal kicked and snorted as they tied him to the post in the center of the pen, and then they covered his eyes with a pair of leather leggings. It wasn't unusual for one of the cowboys to get kicked or seriously injured. It took all of the men working together to subdue the bay enough to get the saddle on.

With his wounds still not completely healed, surely Alex didn't intend to actually ride the big brown horse. It would be foolish to consider something like that.

The men finished saddling the animal, and Alex mounted. Maggie was trembling so hard she was afraid she was going to fall off the fence. Then she remembered to pray.

Prayer always comforted her, and this time was no exception. A kind of peace filled every part of her. She would continue praying until all the men were safe, and she was thankful that the worry and fear she had at first had already washed away.

Alex gripped the reins. The cowboys untied the rope that was tied to the center post and removed the leggings from in front of the animal's eyes. The bay gave a big leap forward. Alex's left leg slammed up against the center post, but he managed to stay on, using only his right hand instead of his reigning hand.

The men yelled and laughed, waving their arms in hopes of making the bay horse buck even more. Spring roundup and bronco-riding were what the cowboys lived for all year long. Nobody knew that better than Maggie. Building fences and repairing windmills was hard work. Apparently to the cowboys riding wild horses was play.

Maggie remembered seeing her mama cry when her papa broke wild horses in the round pen because she knew how dangerous it was. So did Maggie.

The bay kicked up his hind legs again, snorted, and attempted to bite one of the other cowboys standing nearby. Alex managed to hold on.

Maggie could tell by the way the other men behaved that they were impressed with Alex's riding ability. He'd already managed to stay on longer than most.

But sooner or later every cowboy was bucked off when riding a wild horse in the round pen during spring roundup. It was merely a matter of when. The men kept laughing and hollering and throwing the leather leggings in front of the horse again and again in order to make him buck.

The bay horse moved closer to their side of the fence. Maggie jumped down, pulling Sarah with her. "We'd better stand away from the fence for a while now until this horse settles down."

The bay horse banged the fence near where they'd been sitting, knocking a big hole in one of the cedar planks. Still kicking up his back legs, he jerked around to the left and bucked again. Alex lost his hat and his hold on the reins, tumbling to the ground.

He didn't move.

Maggie sent up another quick prayer, remembering the

other time she'd seen him stretched out on the ground and looking exactly like that.

The men secured the bay horse and helped Alex to his feet. He looked pretty weak, dusty, and dirty; other than that he survived the ordeal fairly well.

Alex waved at Maggie and Sarah. Maggie waved back, but a smile wasn't in her. She watched him help the other men remove the bay from the round pen. Maggie had seen enough of wild horses and the cowboys who rode them for one day, but she would have to stay or disappoint Sarah.

"Can we climb back on the fence now?" Sarah asked. "I can't see good from way down here."

"Sure." Maggie climbed back on the fence, motioning for her little sister to join her. "We have a lot more watching to do before the day's over, don't we?"

24

A lex filled in for Big Lupe that evening in the cow pen at milking time, volunteering to bring a bucket of warm milk up to the big house. He knocked at Maggie's kitchen door.

Ordinarily Big or Little Lupe delivered the milk, but the two of them and Concha went into town to get the mail and buy supplies and were late getting back. Alex was glad for the chance to personally deliver the milk to Maggie and the children.

While Alex waited for her to answer the door, he glanced down at the milk bucket. A soft bubbly foam covered the top of it exactly like the white bubbles around the calf's mouth when he sucked. Alex had tied the calf to a fence post until the bucket was full, causing the animal to bellow long and hard.

All at once Alex's memories of another place and another calf and cow came to him. He was but a boy then, seated on a stool and milking a cow on the family farm.

Alex recalled something else. He'd pretended life was good when it wasn't. On that morning he sat up straight and tall, but inside he shook with fear because he knew if he spilled any of the milk, his stepfather would beat him.

He was still remembering when Maggie came to the door, overwhelming him with a smile that soothed his soul. "Oh, you brought the milk," she said in a soft voice. "How thoughtful. Thank you. Would you like to come in?"

"Maybe for a minute."

He set the bucket on a small table just inside the door. Maggie covered the milk with a white straining cloth, and Alex followed her to the kitchen table.

She offered him a chair; he took it, tossing his hat on the back of Jon Anthony's high chair beside him. "Land of mercy, it's good to sit down."

He wished he had time to consider the memories of his stepfather's farm in depth to see if other memories followed, but in order to do that, he would need to share his thoughts with Maggie. Alex had more important things to discuss with her that evening.

"Care for something to eat or drink?" she asked.

When Alex shook his head, she took the chair beside him. He'd planned to chat with her for a minute or two before he told her what must be said, but now he thought he'd get right to the heart of the matter.

"How is your Bible reading going?" she asked before he could say what was on his mind.

"Fine." He removed a toy soldier from the seat of Jon Anthony's high chair, placing it on the kitchen table in front of him.

"Sarah and Jon Anthony are helping Elena gather the eggs for breakfast in the morning—in case you are wondering where they are. And do you have any more Bible questions you'd like to ask? I'm no expert, but I'll do my best."

He did have a question—maybe several. Since it appeared that he must put off what he wanted to talk about until later, now was as good a time as any to find answers to some of his Bible questions.

"I have a question all right," he said after a long and thoughtful pause. "It came from reading the Book of Ezekiel and chapter thirty-seven. In that chapter, it talks about the children of Israel as if they were divided into two different groups, the Kingdom of Judah and the Kingdom of Israel, and this got me all confused. If you could explain that, it would really help a lot."

"I'll do my best. But I've got a cake in the oven." She wiped her flour dusted hands on the hem of her apron. "I don't want to burn it. So if you smell anything odd, let me know."

"I'll do my best."

She sat back against the chair's wooden frame. "The Lord chose a man named Abram to be the father of a great nation, and God changed his name to Abraham. Then Abraham and his wife had a son named Isaac, and Isaac and his wife had twins, Esau and Jacob."

"Stop a minute," he insisted, "and give me time to think about what you just said. As I understand it we've got three generations here—Abraham, Isaac and the twins. Am I right?"

"Yes. But God chose Abraham, Isaac and Jacob to receive the blessing. And God changed Jacob's name to Israel. So Jacob's children were called the Children of Israel."

"That makes sense," he said. "I remember reading about Abraham, Isaac and Jacob in the very first book in the Bible."

"Yes, the Book of Genesis. The Children of Israel had what we might call a civil war."

"Like the war between the northern states and the southern states here in America?"

"I never thought of it that way, but yes." She smiled. "The actual separation took place after King Solomon's death which was many, many years after Jacob's time on earth and many years before the birth of Jesus that the Children of Israel were divided into two nations."

"And those two nations were the Kingdom of Judah and the Kingdom of Israel?"

She nodded.

"I thought so."

"But in some places in the Bible, Israel is also called Joseph or Ephraim, and that can be confusing."

"Confusing is right with Israel having three names while Judah only has one." He stopped speaking for a moment and then continued. "The word *Judah* sounds a lot like the word *Jew*. Do you think the word *Jew* could be a nickname for Judah?"

"Maybe." Her smile widened. "You are very insightful."

He grinned. "I'm not sure but I think I might have known a Jew once."

"Good, that's another memory," she said. "Can you remember anything about your Jewish friend?"

He paused and spent a long time doing it. At last he turned to Maggie, wondering if he should tell this very private memory. "I remember sitting on the front porch of our little house in South Carolina with my mother and my sister not long after our real father died in battle during the War Between the States, and it's like I was watching it as it was happening. I even remember what our mother said. She said, 'Children, your grandmother on your father's side was a Jew, and the Good Book says that it is an honor to be a Jew. But some people don't believe what is written in the Bible; so don't ever tell anyone that you have a Jewish ancestor. It could be dangerous for y'all, if you do.'"

"Now I feel honored," Maggie said, grabbing the toy soldier from the table where Alex put it and dropping it in the pocket of her white apron. "You were told never to tell anyone your secret. Yet you just told me, and that makes me feel special."

You are special to me, Alex wanted to say out loud, *and I'm glad I told you my secret.* Instead he said, "Who can tell how many family secrets I might reveal until I get my senses back?"

She laughed, but he thought she also looked a little disappointed. Maybe this was not a good time to discuss a new topic, but he might not have another opportunity any time soon.

He cleared his throat. "I saw Elena riding one of your horses last night, and I almost followed her. I will if I catch her riding out like that again."

"I thought I told you. Elena has my permission to ride my horses whenever she likes. So why would you want to follow her?"

"To find out where she goes and if she's meeting someone. Don't you think her actions are a little strange?"

"Maybe." Maggie shrugged. "I can agree that riding at night isn't something I'd care to do, but Elena likes it. And I need to make my help happy if I expect to keep them here."

"This business with Elena could be serious, Maggie. You could be in danger. Like I told you, I think Elena is meeting someone—a lover maybe. In fact I heard another horse neigh when she rode off into the darkness."

"You could have heard one of our horses."

"Maybe, maybe not. But I don't trust Elena. And I figured you should know what I plan to do."

"Well, go right ahead and follow her if it will make you happy."

He didn't think Maggie should allow her servant a clear rein to do whatever she wanted. However he'd said all he could say now.

"I'm planning to fry up some steaks on Saturday night when Roger comes, and this should interest you." Maggie smile held a hint of mockery. "I think he's bringing Zoe." She paused, grinning. "Roger loves steak and mashed potatoes. How about you?'

"I like steak—medium rare," he said, ignoring her reference to Zoe Dawson.

But steak and Zoe Dawson were the last things on his mind at the moment, and he felt that Maggie hadn't heard a thing he'd said.

All at once he smelled something. "Your cake," he shouted nodded toward the oven.

"Oh no. I forgot all about it." She jumped out of her chair.

Then Alex got up out of his chair and grabbed a thick towel from a hook by the stove. "Sorry but from the nasty odor, I think we might already be too late to save that cake."

JOE GARZA SAT on a cot in a small abandoned house in the middle of nowhere. With all the hunting rifles mounted on the wall next to the fireplace, he supposed the cabin could be a hunting lodge. It was late afternoon, milking time at the area ranches.

Elena showed him the way to the cabin and where to stake the horse he stole. He'd stayed in the cabin since then, feeling as comfortable and safe as a man on the run could.

He had left Mexico a free man—at least the Mexican government called him free. Nobody in Texas would be able to pin him to the bank robbery in Brownsville three years earlier except Alex Lancaster, and for a while it seemed he'd disappeared from the face of the earth. Things might have worked out for Joe if he'd stayed in Brownsville. His friend would have helped him get a ranch job, and he could have lived there for as long as the job held out. But he couldn't cowboy and look for Alex Lancaster at the same time. He also had to eat.

To solve his money problem, he robbed a store in a little town north of Brownsville, and on his way out of the store, he shot the woman behind the counter in the shoulder. Joe didn't think she was seriously injured, but the woman and owner of the general store could identify him. Then he stole another horse and headed north. By now drawings of his face could be on wanted posters from Brownsville to New Mexico.

Joe leaned over and took a sip of black coffee. The cot's springs squeaked. He breathed in slowly. He set the cup on the floor at his feet, studying the tin plate balanced on his knees. The beans and tortillas he cooked earlier were cold now, but he was too tired to warm them up. He dipped his spoon in the beans, scooping up a mouthful. Later today or tomorrow, he would see Elena again. Maybe he would also catch another glimpse of the beautiful *Señorita* Gallagher.

Bang!

Joe jumped. His plate fell on the floor. *What was that?*

The door was kicked open.

A tall, skinny Anglo man with slicked-down brown hair busted inside. He held a Henry Rifle pointed right at Joe. "What are you doing in my cabin?" the stranger demanded in clear Spanish.

Joe rose and raised his hands above his head. "Don't shoot, *Señor*." He glanced around the small cabin, looking for his hunting knife.

The man laughed, pulling Joe's knife from his gun belt. "Is this what you're looking for?"

Joe froze. Why had he left his hunting knife on the front porch of the cabin? He didn't know who the man was, but judging from the wild look in his eyes, Joe sensed danger.

"I didn't know this cabin belonged to anyone," Joe said.

"So you're the one who's been stealing my chewing tobacco and drinking up all the coffee and whiskey." The stranger cocked his rifle. "I own this land now, and I don't allow squatters."

"If you will put down the gun, I will leave and never return."

The man paused, spitting the chaw of tobacco in his mouth onto the bare floor. "Hey, low-life, aren't you the one what's been hanging around my ranch and over at the Gallagher place?

My men are calling you a prowler. But your back sure looks wet to me."

Joe gritted his teeth, but he could do nothing. His hands were still in the air, the gun still pointed at him.

The man continued. "Why, I'll bet you're the one who shot Alex Lancaster in the back." His eyes snapped with a sort of fiendish gleam, and he gave a short laugh. "What do you think the sheriff would do if I turned you in and told him I saw you do it?"

Joe tried to come up with a plan, some means of escape. But without his knife, he couldn't think of anything. "I have killed no one, *Señor*. I am a free man."

"And I'm George Washington."

Joe could have walked across the bridge, but his face was probably on wanted posters all over South Texas. He swam the Rio Grande River when he could have walked across the bridge because of the crimes he committed in Texas that the Mexican government didn't know about, and after walking across what some called the wild-horse desert, through prickly-pear cactus and rattlesnake infested brush, he didn't want to be captured now. It would be Joe's word against a gringo's, and it didn't take much of a brain to know who the sheriff would believe.

The gunman relaxed his grip on the gun, backed up, and straddled the straight-backed chair beside the bed. "If they don't hang you on the spot, they'll send you to a Mexican jail."

Joe knew he sounded like a weakling, but if he played along, pretending to be one, maybe later he would think of something that would get him out of this mess. He knew what a Mexican prison was like. Even an American jail would be better than that.

"By the way," the man said, "I'm Roger Dawson. You can call me Mr. Dawson." Roger grinned like a coyote licking his lips before an especially tasty meal. "Of course, there might be a way out of this for you."

"How, *Señor*? I will do anything."

"Well, now, if you came to work for me, I'd be obliged to keep you out of jail, wouldn't I?"

Joe forced a smile as anger welled inside him. "*Si, Señor.*"

"Now if you agree to work for me, you gotta do exactly what I say—no questions asked. Can you do that?"

Joe nodded. "Si."

Roger pointed the gun toward the floor, grinning as if he knew something Joe didn't. "All right then. Welcome to the Dawson Ranch."

Joe lowered his hands but kept a wary eye on Dawson. "I'll get my things and move to your camp house with your other men."

"No need for that. I need you to stay right here in this cabin where I can find you when I need you. Your job will be to keep an eye on Alex Lancaster and report back to me. He lives over at the Gallagher Ranch. Lancaster got hit on the head and can't remember much now. I want to know the minute he starts remembering things."

Thanks to Elena, Joe already knew this information, but he couldn't let on that he did. "You want me to live here? In this cabin?"

"Isn't that what I just told you to do?" Roger turned his head to one side. "You wouldn't happen to know anyone on that ranch, would you?"

"I know a maid who works at the big house."

Roger chuckled. "You know Elena?"

"*Si.*"

"I'll just bet you do," Roger said with a laugh. "How could I be so lucky? Now I want you to keep up your friendship with Elena. Find out all you can from her. Tell Elena if she'll spy for me, I'll make it worth her while. Elena knows everybody who works on the Gallagher Ranch, but I want you to keep away from the men who work there. Don't let them see you if you can help it. You haven't already met any of the ranch hands, have you?"

"No." Joe's jaw firmed. He'd talked to a ranch cowboy briefly, but he wasn't about to mention that. Besides, the cowboy hadn't been very friendly.

"And as for you…" Roger glared at Joe. "…I'm going to let you in on a secret you can't tell because nobody would believe you. I want Alex Lancaster dead, and there's a bonus in it for you if you pull the trigger."

If ever Roger Dawson had seen an evil eye, this man had one, and a mocking smile to go with it.

"By the way," Roger said, "what's your name?" His laugh was filled with mockery. "I'll need to know if I have to have you arrested."

Joe fumed. He felt like his insides were about to explode, but he managed to fake another weak smile. "My name is Jose Garza. My friends call me Joe."

"I'll call you Jose."

When Roger Dawson finally left, Joe sat on his cot, thinking about what he'd heard and wondering if it might be best to head on back across the border. But even as those thoughts raced through his mind, he knew he wouldn't leave until he discovered where the money he stole from the bank in Brownsville was hidden. Joe hid the money in the brush on the Mexican side of the river, and Alex had said something while they were in a truck headed for a Mexican jail that made him think Alex knew what happened to the money. It sure wasn't where Joe buried it because he checked as soon as he was released from jail. Maybe Alex saw him hide it; after Joe left, Alex dug it up and hid it or took it and kept it.

As for Roger Dawson, Joe didn't like the idea of working for him. He'd always been his own boss and preferred to keep it that way. It was obvious Roger Dawson didn't like Alex Lancaster any more than Joe did. Their goals were similar in some ways, but there was one big difference. Roger wanted Alex dead now. Joe wanted him dead too, but not until after Alex dug up the money. And Joe sure didn't want Roger to know there was any money.

He could be thankful he hid the stolen black stallion in the brush instead of putting him in the holding pen outside the cabin. If Roger saw the animal, he would have taken him in exchange for not turning Joe in to the sheriff.

He'd have to talk to Elena again very soon. Together they might find a way to satisfy Roger and at the same time keep Alex walking around a little longer.

SATURDAY NIGHT AT QUITTING TIME, Alex sat on a bench at the kitchen table in the bunkhouse, talking to Big Lupe and his son, Beto, and carving a wooden boat for Jon Anthony. As far as Alex knew, it wasn't the little boy's birthday, but he'd caught the child trying to build a sailboat with nothing but a leaf and a small twig. He'd promised then to build Jon Anthony a toy sailboat, and he'd almost finished.

Alex held up the boat so the other two men could see it better. "What do think?" he asked in Spanish.

"Very good," Lupe said. "You had a boat like that when you were a child, no?"

Alex shook his head. "I had no toys when I was a child after we moved to Texas, and I couldn't carve like this back then either. I learned to carve to make toys I didn't have. Now I make toys and things for other people."

I carve things for other people? Alex's mouth nearly dropped open. *Where did this information come from?*

"You are a good man, *Señor* Lancaster," Beto put in.

Besides being Big Lupe's son, Beto was the oldest of the single cowboys; he'd lived on the Gallagher Ranch all his life. To hear Big Lupe talk, Beto knew about everything there was to know about ranching.

After they talked for a while, Alex asked, "So what do you think of Roger Dawson?"

Beto stared down at his coffee cup. "*Señor* Dawson can be a tough *hombre*. But at others times, not so much. Some think *Señor* Dawson is two men in one body."

Two men in one body. Alex needed to think about that statement. Certainly Roger was somewhat unsure of himself while they were in Bayview, and that was very different from the outspoken cad Roger had appeared to be the day they met for the first time at the ranch.

"None of the cowboys here like *Señor* Dawson," Beto went on. "But *Señorita* Maggie sees with the eyes of a friend. She cannot see the kind of man *Señor* Dawson is because she is very loyal to her friends, and the *señor*ita has known him a long time."

Maggie wasn't blind, and she knew the Bible. At the least she knew Dawson was a drunk. Were there other reasons unknown to Alex that kept her loyal to the Dawsons?

Beto pulled out a knife and began cleaning under his fingernails with it. "My little sister, Ana, was also a childhood friend of *Señorita* Maggie Gallagher and her sister, Sadie."

Alex leaned forward. This was the first time anyone on the ranch but Maggie had referred to Sadie by name, and he wanted to hear more about her. For now, he would put away his other questions and listen to what Beto had to say.

Beto didn't mention Sadie again as Alex had hoped. He gave a detailed account of what happened to Maggie and Ana on the day the man from Mexico tried to attack them. Alex was sickened by what he heard. He was also full of sympathy for the girls and angry at the same time. How could any man be so uncaring and cruel to two defenseless young women?

"A few days ago," Lupe said in Spanish, "I saw a man here on the ranch that I think came from Mexico. I stopped and questioned him. The man said he was just walking through. Many good men and women from Mexico walk through this ranch each year, and most are the kindest and best people anywhere. The *señorita* always feeds them and gives them clothing. If they need rest, she let them sleep in the barn. But since the day *Señorita* Maggie and Ana were harmed, we look in the eyes of those who walk through this ranch to see if they have the evil eye. If they do we feed them and send them on their way."

Lupe paused for a moment before continuing. "There was something strange about the eyes of a man I found here the other day that was not good. So I fed him like I always do, and then I sent him away without offering him a place to sleep."

"Maybe we should watch out for him just to make sure," Alex suggested. "He could still be hiding out here on the ranch somewhere." Alex paused again before saying more in order to digest what he'd heard, and as he waited he smoothed off a sharp edge of the wooden boat with his knife. "How is Ana doing now?"

"Ana still has nightmares, and she never married. She is in the convent now." Lupe smiled and so did Beto. "One day she will be a nun."

"I'm glad she's doing so well."

Alex left the eating area, carrying the boat with him, and went to the big room where the men slept. He forgot to ask more about Sadie, but he'd have other chances.

He took the white pitcher from the bowl and went out back to the hand pump. He filled the pitcher with water, went back inside, and began shaving. When he'd finished, he dipped his razor in the bowl of water, wiping off the excess moisture with a clean rag.

To Alex Sadie Gallagher remained a mystery, but mysteries could be solved if the right person did the asking.

Alex patted his face dry with the rag. Then he put on the white dress shirt and a pair of tan trousers. He took extra care combing his hair, knowing full well he was doing it to impress Maggie.

He didn't need Little Lupe's help anymore getting dressed or for any other reason. But the boy seemed to like working for Alex. Maybe it made him feel needed, and Alex knew how important such feelings were to a boy his age. Alex would keep him on until he could find some special ranch chore for the child to do.

Five minutes later he arrived at the ranch house. The first thing Maggie said when he walked in the door was, "So you finally got here." Then she whispered, "But I knew you'd come because you knew Zoe was invited."

He frowned. Why did Maggie constantly assume that Alex was sweet on Zoe Dawson? For the life of him, he couldn't imagine.

25

A lex leaned against the wall of the covered back porch just off Maggie's kitchen. Without warning Zoe Dawson came around the corner of the house and stood before him, eyeing him up close. For an instant he thought she was about to lean in and kiss him. He had no romantic notions about Zoe, and it irritated him that Maggie thought he did.

Zoe didn't say a word but looked around as if to see if anyone was watching.

Alex decided to break the ice. "I heard from some of the ranch cowboys that your father hired Jasper Kingston as his new foreman. Mighty good choice, I'd say."

"We think Jas—" She blushed as she corrected herself. "We think Mr. Kingston was a good choice too."

Alex dared a grin. "Do I detect a certain fondness in your voice for Jasper Kingston?"

Her laugh held a ring of nervousness. "Maybe."

"Maybe?" He was feeling better about this situation already. "Now what does that mean?"

Zoe put a forefinger over her lips in a shushing gesture. "Jas and I fell in love the moment we met. I know it sounds crazy, but we knew immediately we were meant for each other." She leaned closer and whispered, "We're secretly engaged. Please promise you won't tell anyone. Daddy likes Jas, but he wouldn't like hearing we're engaged after such a short time."

Alex felt a huge weight lift off his shoulders; he was genuinely happy for them. "Your secret is safe with me. After all, I guess I'm partly responsible since I introduced the two of you."

"Yes," she said with girlish excitement in her voice. "And we will be eternally grateful."

Alex was about to question her regarding the note she sent to him before he left Bayview. He was anxious to learn as much as possible about Roger, but the kitchen door opened before he could say anything. Alex turned in time to see Maggie's expression go from surprise to something akin to anger.

"Oh, I didn't mean to intrude," she said quickly, her cheeks coloring as she slammed the door.

"Maggie," Alex called after her. "Wait!"

The door remained closed.

Alex glanced back to Zoe and shrugged.

"If I were you," Zoe said, "I'd go after her. I think Maggie is fond of you, and I should know. I was too until I met Jas."

Alex took Zoe's advice and went inside. Maggie stood at the stove, using a big wooden spoon to stir whatever was in a black pot.

"Maggie." He stood behind her. He wanted to put his hands on her shoulders, but decided it might not be a good idea. "I'd like to explain about Zoe."

She waved him off. "Not now. Can't you see I'm busy?"

Alex shook his head.

The scent of a Cuban cigar hinted that Roger was in the parlor puffing away. Alex wouldn't go in there, and he couldn't go back onto the porch. Zoe had gone inside, but Maggie might not know that.

He sat down in a kitchen chair and watched in silence as

Maggie puttered around the kitchen. At last they went into the dining room to eat.

During the evening meal Maggie was friendly to the rest of her guests, including Zoe, but she was coolly polite to Alex. He was certain Roger noticed, and good old Roger would no doubt try to take advantage of the situation.

Alex recalled the conversation he had with Roger in Bayview shortly before the barbecue. He all but admitted he wanted to marry Maggie because she owned a ranch with a creek running through it.

Roger gripped his water glass, and his jaw tightened. "So, Lancaster."

Alex blinked. *Here it comes.*

"Sure was sorry to hear your horse got stolen. Has that memory of yours come back yet?"

"Not yet, and I haven't found my horse either, not since I left him in that stable of yours. Funny that out of all those horses, only mine was taken."

"Isn't it?" Roger shook his head and laughed. "I'm just lucky I guess. But some in town told me you visited the sheriff's office while you were in Bayview for Founders Day Weekend. How come you went and talked to the sheriff? What was that about?"

Alex hurled what he hoped would be seen as a "this is none of your business" look at Roger. Then he lifted his glass and took a sip of water.

"Since Maggie and I were in town for the weekend," Alex explained, "I met with the sheriff and told him about the shooting and that somebody stole my horse. I couldn't tell him much, but Maggie filled him in on the things I couldn't remember."

Alex looked over at Maggie and smiled. When she sent back a cold glance, Roger's grin indicated he'd noticed and liked what he saw.

Alex raised his brows in cool appraisal of the man, sizing

him up inch by inch. Alex was sure he could give Roger a sound thrashing even with his arm only half recovered. "Then the sheriff told us about at least one cattle rustler in the area, maybe more." Alex's gaze still lingered on Roger. "Had you heard about that, Mr. Dawson?"

"No." Roger glanced down at his plate. "No, I hadn't."

Maggie hadn't defended him against Roger's attacks. But this time when she gazed at Alex, her eyes softened. The glimmer in her smile hinted that she'd warmed slightly in his favor.

"I have a friend who's a doctor in San Antonio," Roger said. "I mentioned your case to him, and he said your memory could return at any time, without warning. Did you know that?"

"I didn't know for sure, but I've been hoping. The doc in Bayview said more or less the same thing. He also said my memory might never return. So far it hasn't."

After supper Maggie announced she would be serving fruit punch on the covered back porch. Alex excused himself and paid a visit to the privy, so he was late getting to the porch. The only available chair was the one by Zoe. He sat down.

Zoe's punch glass was on the table in front of them. When Elena offered Alex a glass of punch, he took it from the tray she held and set his glass down on the table beside Zoe's.

The conversation turned to horses and cows. Alex leaned forward, clearly interested in what was being said. He felt comfortable enough to ask about the current price of cattle by the head, and he was so intrigued by the discussion, he didn't even taste his punch.

Fifteen minutes later Zoe became nauseated. Alex wondered if there was something wrong with the punch. But since everybody else seemed fine, he tried to disregard the possibility that the punch was flawed. Yet he couldn't help but wonder about the possibility, particularly when he discovered Zoe had drunk his punch rather than hers.

The nausea persisted for a short while. Then Zoe's physical

condition seemed to improve. Still Roger was forced to drive his cousin back to his ranch earlier than he'd planned. As Alex said his goodbyes to Roger and Zoe, her sudden nausea haunted him. If the punch caused her illness after all, Alex didn't think it was an accident, and he intended to share his conclusions with Maggie, whether she wanted to hear them or not.

After the Dawson carriage was out of sight, Alex glance over at Maggie, hoping to clear the air by explaining about his conversation with Zoe. He couldn't betray Zoe by mentioning her engagement to Jasper Kingston, but he did try to convince Maggie that he was merely being friendly to one of her guests.

His explanation sounded fishy, even to Alex. In hindsight he wished he'd said it in a different way.

Maggie turned away after he finished speaking. Plainly she hadn't approved of his explanation. She wandered through the house and out the front door to the wide porch, settling in the middle of the porch swing with no space left for Alex. He stood with his back against the wall of the house, arms crossed in front of him.

"By now I should know, Maggie, that you don't like it when we discuss certain things," he said in his slow southern drawl. "But it occurred to me that the glass of punch Zoe drank from tonight was the one Elena handed me. I set it down without tasting it. I think Zoe picked up my glass by mistake and drank from it. Didn't you say Elena made that punch?"

Maggie glared at Alex. "Are you saying Elena tried to kill you?"

"Not kill, but maybe she wanted to make me sick as a sort of warning."

She shook her head. "Mr. Lancaster, that makes no sense at all. What would she be warning you about?"

"Who knows what goes on inside that head of hers? We both know she doesn't like me. Maybe she was warning me to leave the ranch before something really bad happened. She might have considered it an evil omen or something. Bet she learned lots of tricks from her witch-doctor father."

"I wish I'd never told you her father was a *curandero* in the first place." Hands on her hips, Maggie rolled her eyes upward. "I know Elena's not perfect; she's made me angry more than once. But how can you believe I'd allow someone like that to work in my house—someone who wanted to make my guests sick? Why, she's worked for us here at the ranch since before Jon Anthony was born. And before that she worked for my sister and my aunt in Brownsville."

Alex perked up. "Elena lived in Brownsville?"

Maggie nodded. "For many years. But as you know Elena was born in Mexico where her father lived."

He chuckled. "The witch doctor?"

"Yes, but why did you have to go and mention that again?"

This new information about Elena astonished Alex. Though he didn't believe in witches, the thought of a witch serving as a family doctor amused him—until he remembered something he read in the Bible. In the Book of Deuteronomy, chapter 18, the Lord referred to witches as "abominations." On remembering he realized that being a witch doctor wasn't funny after all, but quite the contrary.

Alex wondered if he'd known Elena in Brownsville. It seemed unlikely that he did, but he didn't remember a thing about that border town. Mrs. Parson said in her letter that he visited there and that Dee lived there, so he supposed it was possible Elena knew more about his past than Alex did.

"Maggie," he said finally, "why didn't you tell me Elena lived in Brownsville?"

"It never occurred to me."

She got up out of the swing and moved over to the railing that skirted the front porch. Alex followed her to the rail, determined to explain himself before he turned in for the night. But maybe he should start off at a slower pace.

"One day I caught Jon Anthony trying to build a toy sailboat from only a twig and a leaf." Alex cleared his throat. "A creative idea but not very practical. So I carved him a sailboat. I want your permission to give it to him. What do you think? May I give him the toy?"

"Of course," Maggie said without looking at him. "I'm sure he'll be delighted."

From what he was learning from the Scriptures, the Lord cared about even the most mundane parts of a believer's life. Alex prayed the Lord would help Maggie become more open to what he was about to tell her.

"You're doing a wonderful job of raising Sarah and Jon Anthony, Maggie," he said in what he hoped was a gentle tone. "But there'll come a day when Jon Anthony will want to know about his real parents."

Maggie blinked. "I know."

"Have you given any thought to what you'll tell him when that day comes?"

Maggie spun around in order to face him. "Why do you keep asking me these questions? Can't you understand how hard this is on me?"

"I don't know how I know this," he said quietly, "but sometimes when we share our problems with others, it releases the pressure and makes us feel better."

"You spent an entire weekend in Bayview. You must know the trouble Sadie was in before she died."

"Yes, I know a few things."

"Sadie had Jon Anthony out of wedlock." Her voice cracked with emotion. "Satisfied?"

Maggie covered her mouth with the palms of her hands, as deep sobs poured out of her.

Reputations might not be important to some people, Alex reasoned, but Maggie was a lady. What people thought mattered to her.

Compassion engulfed him as he witnessed her in such distress. Alex put his arm around her, pulling her close. He wanted to cherish her—marry her. But until he knew his past, did he have a right to any of those thoughts and emotions?

Her shoulders shook with crying. Tears rolled down her cheeks.

"I'm here, Maggie. Don't hold it in anymore." Alex took a white handkerchief from the pocket of his trousers and handed it to her. "Let it out. It's time."

Even when the weeping stopped, she still trembled in his arms. Alex took her hand and led her to the porch swing. He sat down beside her and put his arm around her again.

At last she said, "I'm ready to tell you about Sadie now. As you said, it's time." Maggie coughed. "Sadie moved to Brownsville to teach school. She met a man there and fell in love with him, but she never mentioned his name in any of her letters. She called the man him, as if I already knew his name.

"Sadie liked to play guessing games when we were girls; she loved a mystery. When I was eight and she was ten, we both got puppies at Christmas time. I named mine Blackie, but she wouldn't tell anyone the name of her puppy. She made me try and guess. I never did guess that dog's name. Finally she said I could call him Skipper, but that wasn't his *real* name. Nobody but Sadie ever knew his real name."

She took a deep, shaky breath and continued. "When I asked her to tell me the name of the man she loved, she wrote back and said, 'Call him Skipper.' I came up with the names of several boys she liked when we were girls, but she said none of them were right and to keep guessing. So now you know how Sadie always was—a little silly in the head at times but a lot of fun to be around.

"I kept asking her to tell me his name after that. In one letter Sadie said she'd tell me his name when the time came. A few months later she quit her job and moved home."

Alex imagined how hard it must be for Maggie to tell him these things. He didn't make a comment, but he pulled her close and held her.

"Sadie was so unhappy." Maggie hesitated. "At night I could hear her crying, but she wouldn't tell me why. I didn't learn she was in a family way until two months after she came home. Elena came with her, but I never really knew Elena until after Jon Anthony was born and Sadie died."

Maggie still held his handkerchief. She wiped her eyes before going on. "Sadie was abandoned by Jon Anthony's father in Brownsville." Maggie swallowed as if it were an effort for her to speak. "I begged Sadie to tell me the man's name, but she wouldn't. Even when she was dying in childbirth, she wouldn't tell me."

"Do you think Elena knows who he is?"

"She says she doesn't, but sometimes I think she really does."

Alex shook his head. Waves of deep concern and empathy rippled through him. "It's hard for me to understand how any man could do what Jon Anthony's father did. But according to the Scriptures, we're to forgive others no matter what they do."

"I know that. But I just can't. Not him. Not Jon Anthony's father."

"It would really help if you did. It might not help him, but it would help you."

Maggie started sobbing again. Alex held her closer.

"I was holding Sadie in my arms, Alex, and then she just… she just…died." She buried her head in his shoulder, crying softly for what seemed like a very long time. Maggie finally lifted her head and said, "If I ever meet the man that destroyed my sister's life, I'll see he gets his just rewards."

THE NEXT EVENING Concha and some of the other wives from the ranch cleaned out the saddle room, so Alex was forced to unsaddle the bay gelding elsewhere. To get out of their way, he walked the bay up to the yard fence in front of the big house and started unsaddling him in the shade of a tree.

The yard gate faced the side of the house, making it possible to see the front and back porches at the same time. A few steps beyond the gate, the gravel path divided. The path to the left led to the front door; the one to the right swerved around to the back of the house.

Elena sat in a rocking chair on the back porch, and even from that distance, Alex could see she held a white bowl on her lap. He thought she might be snapping beans. He'd wanted to speak with Elena since he learned she once lived in Brownsville, and he planned to walk over and talk to her as soon as he finished grooming the horse.

He'd removed the saddle and was rubbing down his horse with a stiff brush when out of the corner of his eye, he saw Elena put down the pan and make her way to the yard fence. He turned and gazed at her as she moved through the yard gate in his direction, blinking at the tinny sound the gate made when the weights clanged together and wondering how his first real conversation with this woman would go.

Dispensing with formalities Elena dove right in, speaking in broken English. "Have you been to Brownsville, *Señor?*"

"Maybe," Alex answered. "I can't remember." Alex had expected to be the one asking Elena questions; somehow it got turned around, and she was interrogating him.

"Then your memory has not returned?"

"No. Why do you ask?"

"I think I know someone in Brownsville who knew you, *Señor.*"

"And who would that be? I have to know."

Elena looked away. "Maybe you are not that man after all."

She looked back toward the house. "I go now. I am wanted inside."

"Don't go," Alex said. "Not yet. Please. I want to ask you some questions about Brownsville."

"I must, *Señor*. Return to what you were doing before."

She opened the gate and let it slam behind her. Alex wasn't able to remember much, but he knew he'd long remember the metallic sound the weights made when they hit together as well as Elena's hurried steps as she moved toward the back door of the main house.

He'd felt as if he'd lost his only chance to learn his true identity, yet her questions stayed with him. Considering the way she treated him when he first arrived on the ranch, he doubted she'd ever tell him what he wanted to know.

That same evening Alex washed up in the camp house and strode up to the big house for supper. He'd promised himself he wouldn't eat in Maggie's kitchen every night like he once did. It simply wasn't fair to the other cowboys or good for her reputation. Tonight would be another of his rare exceptions, though there'd been too many to count. But he had to admit he missed Maggie and the children when he went without seeing them for more than twenty-four hours.

The small sailboat he'd carved for Jon Anthony now had a blue sail he'd fashioned from the oldest of the blue work shirts, the one with the rip down the back. Without wrapping paper or ribbons of any kind, Alex found an empty potato sack in one corner of the camp kitchen. He washed it and let it dry out. Finally he put the sailboat inside, curling a short rope around the top of the sack and tying it with a knot rather than any kind of fancy bow. A boy like Jon Anthony didn't need bows and ribbons to know his gift was worthwhile. Rope as rough as it comes symbolized the kind of man Alex expected the boy to become.

Now he stood just off the back porch, potato sack in hand,

while Maggie finished cooking the evening meal. He wished he had a gift for Sarah, but he would carve her something when he found the time.

Jon Anthony and Sarah were laughing and rolling around in the grass a short distance away and appeared to be having a lot of fun. But stickers and prickly pear thorns were as natural to South Texas as Spanish rice and Pinto beans. Alex had seen sticker-burs in that grass, though he didn't doubt Maggie would have alerted them of the danger. Yet he knew from experience how much it hurt to be punctured by one of those prickly plants. He hated to destroy their fun, but he wouldn't feel right if he didn't warn them before one of the children got hurt.

"Hey, Sarah, Jon Anthony," he shouted in a friendly tone. "There's stickers in that grass you're rolling around in— probably chiggers too. Are you doing all right?"

"We're having fun, Mr. Lancaster," Sarah called back. "Come play with us."

Before she'd hardly gotten the words out, Sarah yelled. "Ouch! I've got stickers all over me."

Jon Anthony was crying by then. "Hurt," he sobbed. Tears rolled down both his cheeks as he raced toward Alex. Alex dropped the sack, picked up the little boy, and grabbed Sarah's outstretched hand. "Come on in the house, kids, and let's get you fixed up."

It took half an hour to get all the stickers pulled out and the medicine administered, and then they had supper. At last Maggie said, "Elena, take the children upstairs and supervise their baths."

Elena picked up Jon Anthony and held him. Then in Spanish she told Sarah to follow her upstairs.

Maggie glanced at Alex. "Oh, I forgot to tell you. You have a letter from your sister, Ruth Parson."

"*If* she's my sister."

"She is. You also got a letter from Sheriff Ethridge." She

picked up the letters from the table by the kitchen door but didn't offer them to him. "I've had these letters for a day or two, and I keep forgetting to give them to you. But there's something I must tell you first."

"What's that?"

"Roger must have picked up our mail before Big Lupe did. Lupe said Roger gave him the mail when he was in town the last time, and your letters were opened." She shrugged. "I think maybe Roger might have read them."

"Might?" Alex knew he had.

"He sealed them back," Maggie went on, "but you can tell. I won't make excuses for Roger other than to say he's always been the curious type."

She sighed and shook her head. "Sadie was two years older than Roger and me, and she always taunted him. You know about Sadie's little guessing games, but Roger hated them. When I was ten, I caught Roger reading my diary. That's just the way he is." She paused. "Can you forgive him?"

"Maybe not at this instant, but I will in time. Now give me my letters." Instead of reaching for them, Alex pressed the palm of his hand to his forehead. "Oh my, I forgot to give Jon Anthony his sailboat."

26

Maggie glanced over at Alex. "Jon Anthony will love the toy sailboat you made for him, but I guess we should put off giving it to him. He and Sarah likely have their nightshirts on by now, and I really don't want to call them back downstairs. Is it all right if we give Jon Anthony his sailboat in the morning? I'll be sure to let him know it came from you."

Alex nodded. "Sure." He was disappointed but tried not to show it. "And please explain to Sarah that she'll be getting something from me too."

"I will." She hesitated. "Does this mean you plan to stay until after Sarah's birthday?"

He shook his head. "Frankly I don't know what I plan to do in the next five minutes." He looked out a nearby window. The outline of a horse standing in the corral could be seen in the dying light of sunset. "Is Sarah's horse ready for her to ride yet?"

"Not yet. You and I could ride the horse now, but Sarah needs a very gentle animal, what we call a plug."

He grinned. "I thought a plug was a really old horse."

"It is. But I wanted a fairly young horse for Sarah that she could ride for years but that acts like an old horse. I think the bay gelding she's getting for her birthday will do just fine. He had a gentle mother, and that's important if you want a gentle horse."

"You're a gentle mother to Sarah and Jon Anthony," he said.

Maggie's cheeks turned a flattering shade of pink.

He grinned. "You're blushing again." He'd noticed that compliments often made her blush.

"I know, but I'm trying not to. And I have to strain the milk. Then I need to do the dishes. It shouldn't take long. Why don't you go into the parlor and read your letters? I'll call you when I'm finished."

Alex stood in front of one of the north windows in the spacious parlor, gazing out and holding his letters. The breeze had picked up. A tiny whirlwind captured a leaf, spinning it around like a top. Alex couldn't remember ever seeing a tornado, but maybe it looked something like a whirlwind only bigger.

It was getting dark, but there was still enough daylight to see a dust cloud in the distance if someone was coming. Alex needed to make a dust cloud of his own because he must ride away—perhaps forever. Why did he keep putting it off? It wasn't a matter of wanting to leave. He would stay with Maggie and the children always if it were possible for him to do it. But what future would they have if his past remained a mystery? Unless he rode out, he would have no future at all.

Alex pushed the thoughts away and opened Ruth's letter.

Dear Alex,

It was so nice to hear from you again after all these years. For a while I worried that you might be dead, but as soon as I heard from Miss Gallagher, I knew you were my brother.

I have so many questions I want to ask as soon as your memory returns.

You asked about Dee, but I can tell you nothing more about her. I wish I could. You quoted Miss Gallagher as saying that nobody by that name lived in Bayview as far as she knew. You also said you thought you needed to go further north to find her. Well, San Antonio is north of where you are now. Why not pay us a long visit when you are well enough? You could look for Dee and visit us at the same time.

Our new baby should be here by then, and you could meet your nephew and the baby all in one visit. And if you need work, we know of several people needing a horse trainer. If you are as good as Miss Gallagher says you are, you should be able to get those jobs with no trouble at all.

I almost forgot to mention that I got a letter from the sheriff of Bayview. He asked a lot of questions as if you were in some kind of trouble. I hope everything is straightened out now. I told him I was your sister and you were the kindest and gentlest man I ever met other than my dear husband, Will. I said you would never steal anything, especially cattle and horses, because you are an honest man. I went on to say you were a baptized Christian, and I was there the day you were dunked, which was on your fourteenth birthday. I finally told him that I cannot imagine who would want to shoot you. You have no enemies, as far as I know. You and our stepfather never got along, but I saw no reason to mention that since he's been dead these seven years.

Our stepfather treated you badly, Alex. He beat you something awful for the slightest mistake. Mama and I never blamed you for leaving like you did. Mama always said the reason our stepfather hated you so much was because you look just like photos of our real pa. I don't guess you remember this yet, but our ma died of a fever two years after our stepfather died.

Well, I guess I'd better stop writing and fix supper for Will and the boy. But please come and see us. Even if you cannot come for a long visit, please come for a short one as soon as you are able. I miss you, Alex, and Will said he misses you too.

Your loving sister,

Ruth

Alex folded Ruth's letter and put it in his pocket. He had been baptized in a church and didn't even remember it, but the

Lord knew all along. After such an emotional moment, he wasn't ready to read the letter from the sheriff. He wanted to absorb Ruth's letter first to see if any fresh memories bubbled up.

At last he read the sheriff's letter, but didn't find it interesting. He would read it again later. For now, he wanted to read Ruth's letter a second time to see if he'd missed something.

June melted into July.

After an extremely hard working day, Alex sat down at the table with the other ranch hands, watching Big Lupe cook the evening meal. Conversations were going on all around him, but Alex wasn't listening. His arm was back to normal, but the guilt he felt at staying on at the Gallagher Ranch when he knew he should leave was like a pain that wouldn't go away.

All at once Lupe mentioned the word *prowler*. Alex started listening. Apparently the drifter that had been spotted off and on for some time was seen recently.

"Eggs are missing from the chicken house," Big Lupe said in Spanish, "and a laying hen disappeared too. I told *Señorita* Maggie about the prowler early this morning. Now I must also tell her about the chicken and the eggs."

"I'll tell her, Lupe," Alex put in. "No need for you to do it. I'll be seeing her in the morning anyway."

Maggie had asked Alex to ride out with her the next morning to help her check fences. Lupe was tied up with other ranch chores, and since she and Alex would be gone for most of the day, Maggie had promised to pack a picnic lunch with all the fixings.

But after Lupe mentioned seeing the prowler again, she seemed hesitant to leave the children alone with only Elena to care for them. She got Concha to step in and help keep an eye on Jon Anthony and Sarah.

Alex had her mare saddled and ready by the time she reached the corral. "Thank you, Alex." Her smile broadened as she climbed up onto the saddle. "When the men are busy, I saddle my own horse, and it takes time to do it. I love to go riding, but I feel guilty thinking of all the chores I normally do in a day and the chores I won't do because of the ride."

She patted the side of her horse's neck. "Sometimes I get to feeling sorry for myself, wishing I could let somebody else worry about the fences and the ranch. It would be wonderful if all I had to think about were the house and the kids. Wouldn't it be nice to just go back to sleep of a morning instead of getting up and doing chores? I'd do that once in a while if I had someone I could trust to run the ranch."

Alex knew she was offering him a job in a backhanded way —and in a backhanded way, he wished he could accept. But he was dreaming about Dee again, and it was time he went out and found her.

"According to Big Lupe," she went on, "more of my cattle are missing, and a prowler was seen near the house recently. I didn't want to believe it was happening, but now I must face the fact that it's true. A cattle rustler or rustlers are stealing my animals, and I have to do something about it. Lupe said I lost at least two more calves."

Alex cleared his throat. "Lupe also said eggs and a chicken were missing from the hen house. You need to get a good head count of all your animals."

"I agree." Maggie kicked her mare. The animal moved forward at a slow trot. "Lupe promised to do that."

"But Lupe is old and doesn't see too good. Is he the best man for the job?"

She fixed her eyes on him. "You're the best man for the job, Alex, but you're leaving."

Alex shook his head; he didn't feel up to discussing that now.

The rest of the morning was peppered with laughter and lighthearted banter. Alex thought the lunch of biscuits and fried chicken was delicious. Later they headed back to the house, checking fences along the way.

"I want to take a look at the fence I saw on the day I got shot," he said. "The one that was cut. It's in the north pasture, and I think I remember where it's located."

Alex hadn't expected to find that wire fence in the same condition he found it the first time, but that's exactly what they found when they arrived in the north pasture. The fence was clearly cut, and Maggie's cattle were still crossing over into the next pasture.

"Isn't that Dawson land?" he asked, pointing just beyond the fence line.

Maggie nodded. "Yes, but there must be some mistake. Roger would never cut a wire like that, especially one of mine." She pointed to a sagging wire farther on down the fence line. "See how the wire is sagging? Lupe probably cut the fence in order to repair it and then forgot about it. He's getting old, and his memory isn't what it once was."

"His eyesight may be failing, but his memory seems all right to me," Alex countered. "The Lupe I know would have fixed the fence before moving on."

"Maybe something came up. Lupe could have gotten distracted."

Alex frowned as his frustration mounted. "Why must you constantly defend Roger Dawson?"

"Because I know him—you don't—not really."

"This is the same fence I saw on the day I first arrived here, and the cut in that fence is one of the few things I actually remember. One of your men must have fixed it the first time, and Big Lupe would have known about it too. It's unlikely Lupe or one of your men would get distracted twice working on the same fence. I've never met a man who was kinder or more honest than Lupe. The same goes for his family, including Concha."

"Then who?" she asked.

"I think you know the answer to that." Alex dismounted. "I've got to fix this fence. Good thing I brought extra wire along."

Maggie kicked her mare, reining the animal on down the fence line without saying anything. Alex thought she knew Roger was the cattle rustler the sheriff was looking for and had known it for a long time, but he couldn't understand why she kept protecting him.

THE MEN WERE STILL EATING supper at the long table in the kitchen when Alex arrived at the camp house that evening. He wasn't hungry, but he thought he might sneak a biscuit later. Tired from the ride Alex went into the long bedroom and flopped down in his bed. Despite the heat, he fell asleep.

Almost immediately a dream took form. He was standing by Dee. She wore a beautiful white dress and carried a bouquet that smelled like roses. He looked down at her face, but she'd turned her head to one side. He saw only her profile.

A man with a Spanish accent said, "Do you, Alexander P. Lancaster, take this woman to be your lawful wedded wife?"

Alex woke with a start. He sat up in bed, thoroughly shaken. Normally he didn't remember dreams, but he knew he would remember this one forever.

He had no conscious memory of Dee, but if they really were married, he felt obligated to find her and make things right, despite his strong feelings for Maggie. Before he allowed himself to consider marrying Maggie or anyone, Alex must resolve this conflict and find out what happened to Dee once and for all. He'd waited too long as it was. But how would he ever find her?

Mrs. Parson, the woman claiming to be his sister, said in a letter that Alex was an honest man, and Sheriff Ethridge said in his letter that it was unlikely he'd be able to find Dee in a town the size of Brownsville unless Alex provided him with a full name and other information. But Alex had given the sheriff all the information he had.

Unless his full memory returned, he might *never* be able to find her. Regardless, he had to try. He'd put it off long enough.

27

M aggie suggested that she and Alex ride out the next morning to finish checking fences. Alex could think of few things he'd enjoy more than another entire day with her. However since dreaming that he and Dee were married, he hesitated to be alone with Maggie for fear he might do what he so longed to do—kiss her on the lips.

Alex wanted to marry Maggie. But suppose he was already married? Would a true Christian take a chance like that? The Bible taught the Temple of God was the body of the believer. God lived in him now. Would a true Christian marry when he might not be free to do so?

Nevertheless Alex promised Maggie he would ride out with her, rationalizing again that, after all, she was his boss. Checking fences was part of his job. But from now on he intended to keep Maggie at arm's length. He was a procrastinator, but today he would tell her he was leaving and exactly when he planned to ride out. He'd put it off long enough.

Big Lupe had said more cattle were missing from Maggie's herd, and Alex hoped to find proof of it during their ride.

Unfortunately they didn't know how many of Maggie's cattle were stolen before they started counting.

Alex never got around to telling Maggie what was in the letter he received from Sheriff Ethridge. Now that they had trotted side-by-side along the fence line for over an hour, maybe now was the time to do it. "Maggie, I've been meaning—"

His saddle squeaked, loud and clear, rudely interrupting his words.

Maggie giggled.

Then Alex laughed. It was a funny moment for both of them. What he intended to say was overshadowed by still more squeaks, coming from both saddles, as leather brushed against leather.

He reminded himself to oil those saddles or have Lupe do it. At last he turned to Maggie. "Remember that letter I got a letter from the sheriff? Well," he said—"

Squeak. Squeak, squeak, squeak.

He chuckled. "Have these saddles been oiled since you bought them?"

She let out another giggle that sounded high-pitched and girlish. "I'm not sure. I think maybe Papa bought them before I was born."

Alex shook his head. "I don't know about you, but I think it's time to have these saddles oiled before they get so old we have to shoot 'em."

She laughed again, louder this time.

Alex grinned, gazing out at his surroundings. "Can we see the sand hills from here?" Before she could answer, he said, "The cowboys down at the camp house told me they were something to see. Are you going to show them to me today?"

"As a matter of fact, we're on our way there now."

"That's good." Alex lifted his head and peered at Maggie. "You know, Beto said he was getting the same low cow count

Lupe's been getting." Alex studied her for a moment. "I thought you should know."

"And now I do."

"Yes, and now you do."

Conversation stopped. If it hadn't been for the squeaky saddles and a nest of locusts in the weeds nearby, the silence would have been all too obvious.

"I really am hungry," Alex finally said. "How about we eat?"

"I wouldn't mind eating a biscuit or two. I put sausages in them, and they're going to taste delicious."

The spicy scent of sausage filled the air as they spread their lunch under scrubby oaks. The dark colored trees grew close together in what Maggie had called a *mott*.

As they ate, they could discuss the drifter who prowled the countryside or debate the identity of the cattle rustlers stealing Maggie's cows—so long as he didn't mention Roger as a possible suspect. Or he could finally tell her what the sheriff said in his letter.

They could also talk on just about anything, including his plans to leave. Or he could forget all serious topics, and they could have fun. Alex chose fun.

"Maggie, please tell me about the sand hills."

She delivered a weak smile. "There's not much to tell. They're just white hills of sand that move when the wind blows, like during a hurricane. We're miles and miles from the bay, yet some of the land around here is as sandy as if we were living on a beach somewhere.

"Visitors always claim the sand hills are the most interesting place on the ranch to visit," Maggie went on. "I've been going there and making sand castles since Sadie and I were…since I was little."

Maggie's voice choked with emotion when she spoke her sister's name, and he glanced away, wishing he knew how to comfort her. "I'm looking forward to seeing those hills."

"And you will, as soon as we finish checking the fences you're so worried about."

After they finished eating they continued on toward the sand hills, checking wire fences as they rode. They found two wires that were broken or cut. While Alex repaired them, Maggie charted their location on a map she had made.

Farther on Alex noticed another fence, one Big Lupe had mentioned. He said several fence lines in that area of the ranch were broken. Alex wondered if they were cut. He got off his horse for a better look, examining the wires at close range. They looked shiny and new as if they were replaced fairly recently.

"Isn't that Dawson land on the other side of the fence here?" he asked.

Her answer was short and her expression unreadable. "Yes."

He wanted to say more, but it seemed pointless. Maggie knew what he was thinking without his saying a word.

She hesitated and then announced, "Roger asked me to marry him."

"When?"

"A long time ago. And again the last time I saw him. But Roger is always asking me to marry him. It doesn't mean anything. It's just something he does."

Again Alex recalled the conversation he had with Roger in front of the Sunday house in Bayview. Roger made it clear he would like to gain control of Maggie's land and the creek that ran through it, but he never once said he loved her.

On the wings of a soft breeze, Maggie's flowery perfume floated over to Alex. As he breathed in its sweet aroma, he realized his mother had worn that same fragrance, and a wave of childhood memories coursed through him.

Like a thick veil concealing his past, a curtain opened. Events once hidden became clear. His recollections weren't restored completely, but he knew he'd had a breakthrough.

Alex recalled his mother's shy grin and the fact she didn't

smile very often. He remembered his sister, Ruth, and parts of his childhood home in South Carolina. He also remembered that as an adult he followed a brown-skinned man into Mexico to bring him to justice. If only he had time to take it all in. He sensed if he ever did, clearer recollections would surface.

Maggie continued to watch him as if she expected him to say something. "I know what you're thinking, Alex Lancaster," she said at last.

"All right, Maggie, what am I thinking?"

"That Roger Dawson is a thief, but he isn't. Roger is one of the richest men in Texas; he doesn't need me or my land. Yes, he has problems, but he and his mother were kind to me when I needed kindness the most. I'll always respect them for it."

"I wasn't thinking about Roger Dawson—not this time anyway."

The heat stifled him, but in the distance Alex spotted a windmill. Beyond the windmill he saw the outline of a shack of some kind. He pulled his canteen from his saddlebag and drank. Wiping his mouth with the back of his hand, he offered the canteen to Maggie. "Thirsty?"

She nodded, took the canteen from him, and lifted it to her mouth.

"If we're thirsty," Alex said, "the horses probably are too. I think we should ride over to that windmill and give them a drink before going on. You said it's still at least a five-mile ride to the sand hills, and they'll need water long before we get there."

Alex turned the bay toward the windmill and coaxed him into a brisk walk. Maggie kicked her sorrel mare and pulled up beside him.

The soft breeze he'd felt earlier had evaporated. There was barely enough wind to turn the crank on the windmill. The big wheel groaned and squeaked in tune with dozens of crickets chirping in the tall grass nearby. Water dripped slowly from a metal pipe into a round wooden watering trough.

Maggie dismounted and led her mare to the windmill. Holding her hair back with one hand, she leaned over, taking a drink of cool water before it hit the trough. Then she coaxed her mare up to the tank. She threw the reins over the horse's head and let the animal drink. The ends of the leather reins tumbled into the trough.

Alex had dismounted too. The trough looked cleaner than most he'd seen on the ranch; the cows must not have visited there lately. He sat down on the edge of the tank to cool off, motioning for Maggie to join him.

Maggie took off her boots, dangling her feet in the cooling water, stockings and all.

"I thought you said it would set a bad example if you waded in water."

"I'm not wading. I'm soaking my feet, and it feels wonderful. Why don't you give it a try?"

"No thanks." He grinned. "You won't catch me getting my feet all wet. I hate wet stockings and boots."

"Coward."

He laughed. Alex considered pushing Maggie into the water. She accepted his jokes now, but he doubted she would see the humor in being soaked to the skin. But it sure would be a good way to cool off in the heat of the day.

"Maggie, I've been meaning to tell you what the sheriff said in his letter."

"Let me guess. He said that he and his men would be camping at the ranch in early July and might stay a while if the hunting and fishing was good."

"Then you knew?"

"The sheriff and some of his men come here every year to hunt and fish in the big lake near the sand hills, and of course, I knew. I got a letter from the sheriff at the same time you did.

Oh, and did I tell you my Aunt Violet from Brownsville is coming for a visit?"

"No, I don't think you did."

"She could be here as soon as tomorrow. Sarah's birthday is next week. She's staying for it. I want you to meet her—or rather, I want her to meet you."

Alex realized then he wouldn't be around for Sarah's birthday, but he didn't want to tell Maggie when they were having such a pleasant day.

The horses still had their heads down, drinking from the other side of the tank. All at once his bay perked up his ears as if aware of an unknown presence. Then Maggie's mare did the same.

Somehow Alex knew animals heard sounds humans couldn't, and he watched the horses, listening. After a moment the animals began drinking again.

"Is anything wrong?" Maggie asked.

"I'm not sure. But why don't you go ahead and put your boots back on? I think we should get on with our ride."

The windmill hadn't turned for what seemed like several minutes, and Alex heard a strange noise that almost sounded like a cough followed by silence. The horses had settled down again, drinking water from the trough and causing small ripples in the small pool. A bee buzzed around his head, and he swatted it away with his hand. It was too quiet. Something was wrong.

The wind picked up, and a strand of Maggie's hair blew across her face. She brushed it away. The windmill squeaked when it started turning, but he also heard that other unnamed sound again. Was someone watching them from the underbrush? Without proof he wouldn't mention it to Maggie, but he was glad he brought his pistol.

He went around to the other side of the trough. "Hurry up, Maggie. We need to ride."

A horse snorted, and it wasn't one of theirs. Both their

horses perked up their ears again. His horse lifted his head from the water-trough.

Alex grabbed the reins, swinging into the saddle.

Maggie still sat on the edge of the water trough, slowly pulling on her boots. Big Lupe had said that there weren't any wild horses in this pasture, but Maggie might not know that. She could presume the snort came from one of her horses, and he didn't want to alarm her. But they could be in trouble.

"Could you hurry up, Maggie?" He checked his pocket watch as if the time mattered. "We need to be on our way."

"I *am* hurrying." She paused. "See? I'm finished now."

Maggie got up, moving around to her mare. She retrieved her reins from the water trough, pulling the wet, leather strips over her mare's head. At last she mounted.

A twig snapped nearby, and then a branch moved despite the lack of wind.

"What was that?" she asked.

"Probably an animal of some kind."

Alex knew if it was an animal, it was the two-legged kind, and the two-legged variety was known to carry guns. He pulled his pistol from the holster. If he were alone he'd find out who was following them and do whatever was necessary. But Maggie's safety came before anything else.

A gunshot boomed just above their heads. Another boom sounded an instant later.

"Let's get out of here, Maggie," he said just above a whisper. "And don't look back. Understand?"

He saw her lips tremble. "Yes, I—I understand perfectly."

28

Sheriff Ethridge couldn't have picked a better time to pay Maggie a visit. He stood in the middle of the corral as if he'd been planted there, straight yet stout, like a spreading live oak. Just seeing him made Maggie feel safer. Though she was breathless and tired from such a long ride, she told him everything that happened since they left Bayview.

"Have you found the man who shot me?" Alex finally asked.

"Not yet, but we're still looking into the case."

"What about my horse? Found him yet?"

"We're still working on that too."

"How about the cattle-rustling problem we discussed in Bayview?" Alex asked. "Does this mean I'm no longer a suspect?"

The sheriff grinned. "We're all suspects, Mr. Lancaster, but I can pretty well say you're no longer at the top of the list."

"That's good to hear."

The sheriff turned to Maggie. "I'm going to need to maybe stay here longer than we planned, Miss Maggie. It's good that my deputies and I already planned a hunting trip here on your land. Is there room for me and two of my men at the bunkhouse?"

"You're welcome to stay in the big house."

"No, I wouldn't want to put you out, ma'am. In fact I'd like it better if we stayed anyway from ranch headquarters. The less folks know we're staying here, the better."

"I noticed a shack near that water well on the way to the sand hills, close to where we got shot at," Alex said. "Maybe you could hole up there."

"What shack would that be?" the sheriff asked Maggie. "Is that where those trappers lived when they worked for your pa?"

"Yes, that's the one. And that pasture is real big and a long way from headquarters. But Papa turned it into a camp house so the men would have a place to sleep when they worked cattle in that area of the ranch."

"Then that's where we'll stay." The sheriff nodded. "I'll go tell my men. We need to saddle up anyway. We have to find out who's been shooting near that windmill even if all they did was fire bullets in the air."

At last the sheriff and his men rode off, and Maggie and Alex went inside.

FOR WEEKS ALEX'S mind played games with his better judgment on the subject of wedlock. He loved Maggie and knew he'd never forget her. But he had to face the fact that he might be married and stop hoping for a different conclusion.

He was a Christian. Maybe he was also the pastor of a church, and he could be married. Alex knew he should tell Maggie about his wedding dream with Dee beside him, but he felt embarrassed actually doing it. However he knew she'd be pleased to hear how much closer he was drawing to the Lord now.

Maggie sat on the leather settee in her late father's study. Alex stood before her, thinking exactly how he would finally tell her what was on his mind. Before he could say a word, she opened the subject for him.

"I'm not surprised to hear you're a devout Christian, Alex. You might even be married."

He lifted his eyebrows. "What makes you think that?"

"I've considered the possibility since you said the name Dee the first time."

"You have?"

"Yes." She cleared her throat. "So what will you do now?"

Alex paused, hoping Maggie would provide an answer he could live with. When she looked down, Alex did the same, casually brushing a speck of something from the right knee of his tan trousers.

Somehow, perhaps in childhood, he'd learned to present a calm demeanor, even when his inner thoughts and emotions were in turmoil. He felt fortunate to have that ability, especially now.

"I reckon I should leave for Brownsville as soon as possible," he said. "I've put it off long enough. I need to start looking for Dee. As you said, I might be married."

He saw the look of disappointment in her face, and he wished he could say something to change the way things were. But of course, he couldn't.

"With the sheriff here to look after you," he went on, "this is probably a good time."

"I suppose so. But I wish you'd at least stay until tomorrow. Remember, Aunt Violet is coming for a visit."

"That's right. She is, isn't she? And I do want to meet her. So I reckon I'll wait and leave the day after she arrives. But I can't stay until after Sarah's birthday, as much as I'd like to. I'll stay in Elena's little house out back tonight in case that drifter comes back and you need me. Elena can move into the big house with you and the children."

He delivered a prolonged and soulful gaze, allowing his

whole heart to join with hers without having to say anything. Alex hoped Maggie somehow knew that though he hadn't declared himself, he wanted to be with her. Always.

"The sheriff and his men could be camping here for as long as two weeks," she reminded him, "maybe longer."

The steady tone of her voice couldn't hide the blush in her cheeks and the shy smile that formed on her soft lips. He hoped the tender look in Maggie's eyes meant she cared for him as much as he cared for her, but he might never know for sure.

"That should give me plenty of time to ride to Brownsville," he replied in a calm tone as if nothing was happening between them. "I'll see what I can find out about Dee and be back at the ranch in plenty of time before the sheriff leaves."

"And if you are married, will you write and tell me?"

"I'll come back and tell you myself. I don't want to quit my job here until you can find someone to take my place, and that shouldn't be too hard. There are plenty of cowboys who would love to work for an outfit like yours."

IT RAINED HARD THAT NIGHT. Maggie wondered if a storm brewed somewhere in the Gulf of Mexico. If so she doubted her aunt would pay them a visit, and that meant Alex would be leaving sooner than planned. The rains had disappeared by the next morning; sunny skies reigned. Still Maggie worried that muddy roads and water-drenched crossings could become a serious problem for her aunt if she drove her wagon up from Brownsville after all.

Maggie went out on the front porch for a breath of air. She'd always loved the fresh odor of soil after a rain, and the new-green look of the trees and grasses motivated her to continue on, no matter what.

A few minutes later Alex joined her there, and they sat, side by side, in the porch swing. Maggie hoped they would discuss exactly when Alex planned to return to the ranch so she would have a date to hang onto. As it turned out they didn't talk about any of the things that mattered to her. They were addressing the merits of wire fences and modern agriculture when Sarah and Jon Anthony came out on the porch.

Jon held the sailboat Alex made up above his head.

"Jon," Maggie said. "Remember when I told you that Mr. Lancaster made that sailboat for you with his own hands. Now, wasn't that nice?"

Jon nodded. "Nice."

"I'm not sure you ever thanked him. So what do you say when someone gives you something nice?"

"Tank you, Mr. Lan-castle."

"You are welcome, Jon Anthony."

"Now go and give him a hug, Jon."

Alex knelt down, and Jon Anthony ran into Alex's outstretched arms. The hug was big and warm. Alex looked over Jon's head and smiled at Sarah.

"I'm carving something nice for you too, Sarah, but I'm not telling what it is yet."

"You're carving something for me? Really?"

"Really."

At noon Elena brought sandwiches and lemonade on a tray. Alex refused to touch his. Maggie didn't want to believe Elena tried to poison him, but she had to consider the possibility.

"Since this is your last day," Maggie said, "what would you like to do?"

He grew thoughtful, rubbing the dimple in his chin. "Well, you never did show me the sand hills. How 'bout if we pack us a lunch and ride on up there?"

"I'd love to. But what if my aunt comes while we're gone?"

The disappointment showed on his face. "I hadn't thought about that."

Maggie tried to think of something else, something they could do together. But nothing sounded as exciting as a trip to the sand hills.

"Why don't we go down to the creek instead," Maggie suggested. "We can watch for my aunt from there."

"All right, let's go."

"Can we go too?" Sarah asked.

"No, I want you and Jon Anthony to stay here with Elena. You have some pages to do in your workbook, and I want you to read the next chapter in the Bible. I probably won't ask you to do schoolwork while Aunt Violet is here, and you need to work ahead so you won't get behind."

Sarah looked disappointed, but she didn't say anything.

"Now..." Maggie gazed at Sarah and smiled. "Take Jon Anthony to Elena. Then go sit at the kitchen table and get started."

"Yes, Maggie," Sarah said in a sad little voice.

Sarah took Jon Anthony by the hand and led him inside. Then Alex and Maggie headed for the creek on foot.

Maggie found herself noticing the smallest details about that special day alone with Alex. It was windy, and the air felt cool and damp on her face. Alex had tucked tan trousers into his cowboy boots and wore a blue shirt. It seemed only natural that he took her hand in his as they stepped across a wide puddle of muddy water. After today Maggie might never see him again, but she tried not to think on those things. Rainwater soaked the ground for miles around. She got her shoes and stockings wet, plowing through the tall, moist grass. Alex wore cowboy boots, and Maggie wished she'd worn hers.

"Normally at this time of year, Gallagher Creek only has a trickle of water in it," Maggie said, "but look at it now."

The rains had swelled it to overflowing, and a crisp breeze sent Maggie's thick mane flying about her shoulders. The cooling wind rushed on and on amid the roar of waves. The expanding banks climbed closer to where they stood, and brush and soggy logs swept by.

She pushed long strands of golden hair behind her ears, but it didn't do much to smooth back her disheveled locks. She didn't know when they stopped surveying their surroundings and started gazing at each other in that warm and special way.

"I have no right to say this, Maggie," Alex began tenderly. "In fact I promised myself I never would. But I can't leave in the morning without telling you how I feel."

Tingles shot through her—tingles and a painful hope. She could scarcely breath, waiting to hear what he would say next. Alex put his arm around her shoulders and held her close. She'd dreamed of this moment, but she never expected it to actually come. Now that it had her heart did flip-flops, exactly as she read about in novels from her father's study.

"I could be married," he said in a deep, throaty voice.

Her eyes burned with unshed tears. But she'd known all along this was coming; she just didn't want to admit it.

"And if I am," he went on, "I can never hold you like this again. But until I know for sure, I wanted you to know how much these weeks here on the ranch with you have meant to me. I've fallen in love with you, Maggie, and I can't imagine life without you." He squeezed her hand. "I long to kiss you—right here, right now. I've dreamed of kissing you for a long time. But I'm sure you can understand that it wouldn't be right until I know I'm free."

Tears she'd been holding inside now dampened the corners of her eyes. "I know, Alex. I do."

"Is it possible you might love me too?"

"Of course I love you." Maggie hesitated before continuing. "Surely you must know how I feel by now. Why do you think I've been trying so hard to keep you here? But a lot of good that's going to do if you're already married."

"That's why I have to leave—to find out, one way or the

other. Until I do we'll never be able to make plans for the future."

The future, she thought. What if there wasn't going to be one for them as a couple?

The sweet emotions she felt on hearing that he loved her and perhaps wanted to marry her made saying anything almost impossible. She wanted to capture the moment and stay in it forever. But there were things she needed to tell him, important things like, *I want you to stay, but I know you have to go*. Yet she felt too glorious, knowing he loved her, to say anything at all.

When she finally did look up, she noticed a wagon in the distance. Alex followed her gaze.

"Could that be your aunt?" he asked.

Maggie smiled. "I think so. At least, I hope so. I'd hate to think of Aunt Violet stranded in the mud somewhere. I'm glad she made it across the bridge before the water got too high. I guess when you leave in the morning, you'll have to go around the creek, and that'll mean going through Dawson land. The gates will be locked, but I have an extra key I can give you."

"Thanks."

Maggie loved her aunt, but she knew she should have prepared Alex for her aunt's bold, rather opinionated outlook on life. As her late father often said, "There's your Aunt Violet's way, and there's the wrong way."

Alex didn't have any idea what he might be in for if her aunt set him down for one of her discussions. The folks in Bayview called Aunt Violet an odd duck, but they didn't know the half of it. Neither did Alex. But it was too late to educate him now.

The wagon moved closer, and Maggie found she couldn't manage to keep still. She had to go out and meet the wagon.

"Why don't we go back to the corral gate and wait for my aunt? I want to be there to welcome her."

Alex grinned and offered her his arm. "Let's go."

Maggie smiled long before the wagon moved close enough

for them to actually see the older woman's face. But even at a distance, she could clearly see her aunt's flaming red hair.

"Another redhead," Alex observed. "Is that a family trait?"

She nodded. "It sure is."

Aunt Violet's hair was streaked with gray now, but her back looked as straight and stiff against the hard seat of the wagon as ever. Her brown-skinned carriage driver from Mexico sat in the seat beside her, but as usual her aunt was doing the driving.

"Your aunt looks like a determined sort of lady," Alex said, his voice low. "Is she?"

"Oh yes, she is, but in a good way." Maggie cocked her head to one side. "I'll admit at times she can be a bit idealistic, even bold, but I just know you're gonna love her."

Alex opened the wooden corral gate. As he swung it wide, the old metal hinges creaked like an ominous warning, perhaps a reminder that he was leaving soon. Maggie was happier than she'd ever been, and he looked happy too. If only he could stay forever.

Maggie turned to Alex and smiled, hoping she'd managed to pour all her love for him and her dreams for their future into that smile. "I'm so happy, Alex. I don't want anything to spoil it. Let's not discuss the fact that you're leaving tomorrow—at least not now."

"All right then. We'll talk about it in the morning, just before I leave."

When Aunt Violet wrote to say she was coming for a visit, Maggie had written back and finally told her about Alex. She'd wanted to prepare Aunt Violet for their first meeting, but Maggie wasn't sure her aunt received the letter before she left Brownsville.

Maggie wanted her aunt to like Alex as much as she did. Yet she'd never seen Aunt Violet look as grim and out of sorts as when she stepped down from the wagon. Maggie couldn't imagine what might have caused it.

"What's wrong, Aunty?" Maggie asked before she'd even had time to hug her. "You're not ill, are you?"

"Not ill, dear. Just heartsick." Aunt Violet put down the small carpetbag she held and glared at Alex. "And it's all *his* fault. Alexander Lancaster is a cad."

29

Maggie's entire body stiffened. She tried to swallow the nasty taste in her mouth. What bitter pill was her aunt attempting to serve here? And who gave Aunt Violet the right to say such terrible things about Alex? She dared not glance at him for fear he would see the doubts now forming in her mind.

"The man is heartless," Aunt Violet said in a loud voice.

Maggie touched her throat, urging it to allow her to speak. "Alex is…heartless?"

"You heard me." Aunt Violet Gallagher looked over her shoulder at her servant, still in the wagon. "Bring my bags up to the house, Hector. Then take your bags to the bunkhouse where you stayed the last time we were here."

"*Si*, Miss Violet."

"I'm going to forget what you said about Alex," Maggie said in a calm voice. "I'm sure you're tired from your trip. But you shouldn't be saying such awful things." Reluctantly Maggie gave her aunt a brief hug. "You must have Alex mixed up with someone else. Now come on up to the house and let me fix you something cool to drink."

"I'm only doing what your mama would do if she were alive,

Maggie Sue." Aunt Violet's face seethed with anger, and it was all focused on Alex. "So get off this ranch, Alexander Lancaster, and never come back. Do you hear?"

"Have you lost your senses, Aunty?" Maggie cleared her throat, stalling for time to compose herself before saying anything more. "This is the man I...the man I love."

"Over my dead body!" Aunt Violet threw up her hands. "And don't expect him to marry you because he isn't the marrying kind. Are you, Alexander?"

Alex gazed at Maggie and shook his head as if he had no idea what her aunt was talking about.

"I utterly despise you, sir," Aunt Violet said, "and I always will. Will you be so kind as to get out of my sight?"

Alex looked flabbergasted, and he'd turned his full attention on Aunt Violet. Obviously her aunt hated him, but Maggie still didn't know why.

"What has Alex ever done to you, Aunty?" Maggie asked as sedately as she possibly could. "Why, he can't even remember where he came from, much less anything else."

"Oh, he remembers all right, and he's done plenty to harm me. And this...and this..." Her voice trailed off, she turned pale and her muscles went slack. Maggie thought she might be about to faint. Sure enough Aunt Violet fell backward, but Alex managed to reach out and catch her before she hit the ground.

"Let's get her inside," Alex suggested. "Your aunt needs to be where she can put her feet up."

"Yes, of course."

Maggie led the way into the house. They took Aunt Violet into the parlor, placing her on the over-stuffed brown divan.

"I'll go and get a damp cloth," Maggie said.

Maggie headed for a connecting door that led to the long hall. In the doorway she paused and looked back. Alex held Aunt Violet's hand in his and appeared to be praying. If only she could hear that prayer. The Lord knew why her aunt was upset, but she and Alex had no idea.

When Maggie returned with the cloth, Alex was kneeling beside her aunt. Was he still praying? She took another step. A wooden plank under her feet squeaked.

Aunt Violet's blue-violet eyes popped open. She sat up, trembling with a kind of senseless fury and pointing her forefinger at Alex.

He stepped back from her. Maggie wondered if he feared his presence might cause yet another of her spells. "Have we met, ma'am?" he asked. "I can't rightly recall ever seeing you before."

"Don't play that 'loss of memory game' with me, Alexander Lancaster. I'm well aware of all your tricks. And if it hadn't rained, I'd have arrived even sooner and tried to stop whatever is going on here. We got stuck in the mud last night and had to wait until morning to continue on."

"Aunt Violet," Maggie pleaded, "you're going to make yourself sick if you don't calm down. Will you please explain yourself?" Maggie placed a pillow behind her aunt's head and put the damp cloth on her forehead. "Now doesn't that make you feel a lot better?"

"Better?" Aunt Violet's angry eyes widened. "I won't feel better until Alexander Lancaster is out of this house and off this ranch forever."

Maggie put her hands on her hips. "I've had just about enough of this, Aunt Violet. What in tarnation are you talking about?"

"If Sadie was still alive, she'd tell you," Aunt Violet exclaimed. "But since she isn't, I guess I'll have to."

"Tell me what?" Maggie asked. "And what does Sadie have to do with Alex and me?"

"What does Sadie...?" Aunt Violet shook with rage as she spoke. "Why, everything, that's what." Aunt Violet glanced around as if looking for something. "Find me that carpetbag I had when I arrived, and I'll show you what I'm talking about."

"I think she left it on the ground outside," Alex said. "I'll just go and fetch it."

"Yes," Maggie replied, "please do that."

Maggie poured three cups of black coffee and set them on the table beside her aunt. When Alex returned with the carpetbag, he put it on the floor alongside Aunt Violet's coffee cup. Then he found a chair and sat down—as far from Maggie and her aunt as possible.

"All right, Aunt Violet," Maggie said, "let's hear what it is you have to say, and you better have good evidence to back it up."

"If you want evidence, Maggie, I have plenty." Aunt Violet sat up and opened the carpetbag. Balancing it on her lap, she pulled out a photograph and handed it to Maggie. "Just look at this, and see what you think."

Maggie didn't expect the photograph to prove anything, but out of respect for her aunt, she looked at it anyway.

"Oh," she said, "it's a picture of Sadie, and— Why, she's wearing a wedding dress!" Maggie smiled. "So she got married after all."

"Not exactly. Now look at the groom."

Maggie was so pleased to see Sadie in a white wedding gown and veil that she hadn't noticed the man beside her in the picture. She looked down at the photograph again, and a silent scream slowly formed in the depths of her soul. Alex Lancaster stood beside her late sister, and he was holding Sadie just he'd held Maggie only a short time before.

"What is this?" Maggie stared at her aunt. "Some kind of a joke?"

"It's no joke, Maggie dear. Sadie and Alexander were sweethearts. In fact, I introduced them."

"You didn't."

"Yes, I did," the older woman insisted. "He visited our church once, but I should never have played the matchmaker and introduced him to Sadie. But at the time I thought he seemed nice. And then they had that fake wedding."

"Fake wedding?"

"Oh, yes."

Maggie handed the photograph to Alex, hoping for an explanation. He studied the picture and shook his head as if he didn't know what to make of it.

"I'm sorry, dear," Aunt Violet put in, "but it's true, all of it."

"Then who is Dee?" Maggie asked, staring at Alex.

Alex shrugged as if he still had no idea how to answer.

"I'll tell you who Dee is," Aunt Violet volunteered. "Dee was Alexander's pet name for *Sa-die* Gallagher."

"No." Alex looked astonished. "That can't be right."

"Oh, but it is." Aunt Violet's accusing frown centered on Alex. "And these pictures tell even more." Violet Gallagher leaned forward and handed Maggie another photograph.

In this one a pastor in a long white robe stood between Sadie and Alex with the rest of what appeared to be the wedding party lined up beside them.

"Pastor Joe is in the middle," the aunt said. "The fake preacher who married them."

"Fake?" Maggie released a deep breath. She'd scarcely recovered from her aunt's shocking news when she noticed something else. Elena was in that line of well-wishers, smiling from ear to ear and wearing a blue-flowered dress Maggie had seen her wear many times. Maggie covered her mouth with one hand, afraid to speak, and handed the photo to Alex. He held the photograph in both hands, appearing to study it carefully.

"That's Elena," he said in a loud voice. "I've seen her wear that dress before. And I've seen the man too—the one you call Pastor Joe. His face was on a Wanted poster in the sheriff's office back in Bayview."

Maggie gazed at her aunt. "Then Sadie was—was married after all?"

"No." Aunt Violet shook her head. "Sadie only *thought* they were married. The minister wasn't a man of the cloth as she believed. He was nothing but a common criminal. In fact the day after the fake wedding ceremony, he robbed a bank in Brownsville of ten thousand dollars. Then he ran off to Mexico to hide."

Maggie felt woozy, as if she were about to faint. She took a deep breath. "Then what happened?"

Aunt Violet glared at Alex. "And then Alexander disappeared the day after the ceremony, leaving poor Sadie alone, unmarried, and in the family way."

"No!" Trembling Maggie shook her head again and again. "No, no, no."

"Oh, yes, Maggie," Aunt Violet insisted. "Alexander just took off. We never heard from him again. I didn't know where he was until you finally wrote me just before I came here, saying he was working here on the ranch. I wish you'd told me sooner."

"I wish you'd sent me those pictures and told me about the wedding. Why didn't you?"

"Sadie made me promise never to tell anyone she was deceived by the man she loved and he deserted her. She made Elena promise never to tell either. But how could I keep that secret after you finally wrote and told me he was here on this ranch and working for you?"

"There has to be a reason for all this." Maggie gazed at Alex, hoping he would provide one. But he just sat there, staring at them as if he was as overwhelmed as Maggie.

"I still don't remember much," Alex said with deep emotion. "But I'm sure there must be a logical explanation."

"And what about little Jon Anthony?" Aunt Violet said. "Has it entered your head, Alexander, that you're the boy's father?"

Alex looked dumbfounded. "Me?"

"Yes, you." Aunt Violet pointed her forefinger at him, and her violet eyes became enormous. "And you're also the man who destroyed our Sadie's life."

Maggie pulled a white handkerchief from the cuff of her dress and wept into it.

"See what you've done?" Aunt Violet pulled Maggie into her arms, patting the back of her head and comforting her in a motherly way. "I came as soon as I could, Maggie dear, as soon as I possibly could."

ALEX ROSE FROM HIS CHAIR. Standing in front of Maggie and her aunt, his hands outstretched and elbows to his sides, he tried to think of something to say. He hadn't said much so far because Aunt Violet's revelations stunned him to the core. But surely Maggie knew him well enough to know he would never abandon his wife the way her aunt said he did.

"Well, Alexander," Aunt Violet exclaimed, "don't you have anything to say for yourself?"

"I knew there was a Dee in my life, but I didn't know Dee and Sadie were the same person. I can't remember either one of them. Could it be I was looking for Sadie when I came here, the day I got shot?"

"Who shot you?" Aunt Violet demanded. "The father of some other unfortunate girl?"

"I don't know who shot me, ma'am. I can't remember my past. But I sure intend to find out."

He studied the expression on the older woman's face. When he met Roger's mother for the first time, he saw a look like that, and he'd called it the look of a matchmaker—cold, then warm, and then cold again. Now he knew Aunt Violet was the matchmaker who introduced him to a woman he couldn't even remember.

Maggie's sobs had grown louder and more intense. Alex longed to reach out and comfort her, but he knew he didn't have the right to do that, at least not now.

"Haven't you done enough to this family?" Aunt Violet shouted. "Why don't you leave here and never come back?"

Alex swallowed. "Is that what you want me to do, Maggie?" Alex asked. "Ride away and never come back?"

Without looking up she shouted a muffled, "Yes!"

An invisible knife penetrated his chest, slicing through to his heart. He'd expected Maggie to believe him, defend him against her aunt's insults, but she refused to listen. And Alex had no proof of his innocence. He just knew, deep down, he hadn't done the things Aunt Violet said he did.

"Maggie," Alex began softly, "you can't mean what you just said."

Her shoulders still shook with her sobs, and she wouldn't look at him. Still he wanted to hold her, comfort her, and tell her everything would be all right. But the truth was he didn't know for sure how things would turn out.

He tried again. "Maggie?"

"Just go away, Alex. I never want to see you again."

"Never?" Alex forced calmness into his tone. "All right, I'll go. Since my horse was stolen, I'll need to borrow one of yours. The bay I've been riding suits me if you would be so kind as to loan him out. Of course I'll return the horse as soon as I can."

"Take him. Take any horse you want," Maggie said between sobs. "Just go."

"As you wish." Anger edged his normally gentle voice. "But I'll be back. In the meantime keep an eye on Elena. I have a feeling she's back to her old tricks again. If I were you I'd look under all the beds. Check for eggs."

"Will you just go, Alex?"

"I'm going, but I'll be back—for my son. I'll return the horse, get Jon Anthony, and you will never see me again."

30

Maggie hadn't believed him. Why was he surprised at that outcome? Hadn't he believed from the first time he met her that she was a hardheaded woman?

A cold empty feeling started in the middle of his heart and spread. The weight of what had been said—the harsh words, the accusations—all shouted at Alex from inside his brain.

No, no, no. Alex shook his head with his hands on his ears, hoping to shut out what Maggie and her aunt had said, but the detestable thoughts wouldn't stop. If anything they increased.

Maggie's aunt had called him a heartless cad. Then she demanded he get off the Gallagher ranch and never return. He could hear her saying it inside his head at that very moment. He heard Maggie's voice too, telling him to "just go."

"Pray and praise the Lord in the midst of your trouble," the pastor at the church in Bayview had said on that Sunday morning in town. "And do not fear. God looks at the heart, and He knows whether or not a person is guilty or innocent."

Alex *was* innocent. But why had he recalled the pastor's words just when he needed to remember them the most? Yet for an instant the words spoken from the pulpit blocked out his memory of the harsh ones.

He thanked God he knew how to pray. Maybe now was the time to do so.

He bowed his head and began to speak to the Father. When the prayer ended, he knew without a doubt the Lord was with him, just as the pastor had said He would be. Alex straightened his shoulders and headed for the horse barn.

As he saddled the animal, his thoughts turned to Sadie. Was she hardheaded too? Now he might never know because he still couldn't remember her. Nevertheless, he felt a sense of deep loss. Too much happened in a short period. It appeared that until two and a half months ago, he'd never laid his eyes on Maggie Gallagher.

Alex needed to put his thoughts in neat stacks so he could understand them, and he wanted time to think. Later he stood by his bed in the bunkhouse, thinking as he packed his belongings for a move to...to nowhere.

At last he rode through the corral gate on Maggie's bay gelding. Ranger bounded up to him, wagging his tail in a playful manner. "Good-bye, Watchdog," Alex said to Maggie's hound. "Take care of 'em for me, will ya?"

As soon as he said it, he questioned his decision to leave. Yes, he and Maggie had a terrible fight, but he still loved her. And that would never change. He glanced back toward the big white house. Were Maggie and the children safe in there? That prowler could be hiding in the brush somewhere right now, waiting to attack—not to mention the person or persons who took a shot at them. Maybe the prowler and the shooter were one and the same.

The sheriff and his men were staying in a cabin miles from ranch headquarters, and the camp house was a good ways from the main house as well. If Maggie needed help would she have time to ring the bell? Would Lupe, Beto, and the other cowboys arrive in time?

The grave took Sadie, the woman he apparently called Dee, and she was lost to him forever. Was he expected to lose Maggie and Jon Anthony and Sarah, too?

———

As soon as ALEX LEFT, Maggie had hurried up the stairs to her bedroom, sobbing every step of the way. Now spread across her bed, the crying slowly faded. New thoughts filtered into her brain.

Maggie shook her head. She hated Alex and loved him all at the same time. She even found herself wondering if Alex might have been right. She thought of his warning about Elena. Was it possible she put eggs under the beds?

She got off the bed and was on her knees in seconds, looking under her bed. But all she saw was darkness. She reached under the bed, feeling around for foreign objects. She found nothing more than a pair of dirty stockings. She gazed at the stockings, took in the sweaty odor, and let them drop.

So Alex was wrong about Elena too. But Maggie didn't feel victorious. Another thought found its way into her mind.

On the day Elena put an egg under Jon Anthony's bed and lighted candles around it, Maggie had taken charge of the matter. She'd thrown away the evil egg and hidden all the candles. She would have thrown them away, but Elena said the candles were dear to her. Maybe the reason she was so fond of them was because they were a gift from Elena's curandero-witchdoctor father.

But were those candles still in the place Maggie had stored them? Elena *was* acting strangely, borrowing horses at night and riding out alone. In fact she'd requested permission to use one of Maggie's horses yet again, and it was still daylight out.

To prove Alex wrong, she would check the box where the candles were kept. She gazed at the door that opened into a much smaller room. Maggie's clothes and other belongings were kept in that little room. She moved to the door and opened it.

Hooks lined the walls on each side of the little room, and Maggie's clothes hung on those hooks. The back wall was filled with shelves. The children's outgrown clothes, which she planned to give to the poor, were packed in a box on the bottom shelf. The candles were at the bottom of the box.

It occurred to her then that this might not be a safe place to hide things you didn't want others to find. Her little clothes room would be the first place a criminal would look, but it was too late to worry about that now.

Elena had the entire run of the house, but she'd promised never again to use the candles as long as she lived on the Gallagher Ranch; Maggie believed her. But what could be wrong with checking to make certain the servant was telling the truth?

She pulled out the box, opened it, and removed all the clothes. Then she felt around with her hands in search of the candles and found—nothing. With the clothes out of the box, the box was now empty. She released a deep breath. It was dark in the little room even with the door open. Maybe the candles were hidden in the clothes. Where else could they be?

She snatched up the clothes, pushing the box with her feet as she went back to the bedroom. She grabbed one of Sarah's outgrown dresses and felt around for something round and thin and shaped like a pipe. Nothing. She continued her search, but no foreign object was found in any of the garments.

Elena must have taken them. What other of Maggie's rules had she broken?

ALEX TOUCHED THE REINS. The bay horse moved forward. The photographs Aunt Violet showed them flashed across his mind. At first they were merely images, but as he continued to think about them, they became something more, evolving slowly into pictures that moved inside his brain.

All at once Alex remembered incidents long forgotten, causing him to feel transported, as if those events were happening before his eyes. Memories once locked were now opened.

When he looked inside, a heavy sadness swept over him. Clear recollections of Sadie stirred his conscious mind, and guilt mixed with a deep sense of loss left him emotionally drained. He knew now that he'd loved the woman he called Dee —very much. *Oh, Dee*, he thought, *how I wish I could have come back to you and explained.*

But he loved Maggie too. With all these conflicting emotions piling in on him, he was glad he knew how to pray. Deep sorrow squeezed his insides. After a moment his shoulders shook and tears moistened his eyes. He sniffed.

He now remembered everything, or as much as his mind could hold in one lump of memories. His body trembled as wave after wave of recollections sent his heart spinning. His throat felt tight, but his tears were dwindling.

Sorrow engulfed him, but at least he knew he never willingly deserted Sadie Gallagher. That fact gave him a measure of peace, energizing him and providing him with the courage to move on. He nudged the bay with a light kick. Alex and his horse could move on.

He would give Maggie time to cool down, and then he would go back to the house and try to explain. Even if on hearing what he had to say she still turned him away, he would have tried.

Alex reined the bay down the road. It looked like rain, and he would need to find shelter for the night. The cabin Maggie referred to as Roger's hunting lodge loomed in the brush ahead. If the cabin was vacant, Alex would hole up there for the night.

A half-hour later he found it. The cabin was located in a low place near Gallagher Creek as well as the property line that divided Maggie's land and Roger's, but Gallagher Creek was on her land. Alex found it interesting that Roger built the cabin as near the water's edge as possible. What a convenient location for a man who hoped to one day control that creek.

Six steps led to a rustic porch across the front of the cabin. Roger had positioned two old rickety rockers by the door. The structure stood on elevated posts, and to Alex this made sense. The creek overflowed its banks after a big rain. If Roger hadn't built his cabin high off the ground, it could be under water if the rains continued.

Alex tied his horse behind the house, out of sight. Should the hunters return he would simply get on the bay and ride away.

As soon as he stepped inside, he knew someone was staying there. The wood stove smelled of smoke and ashes, and a tin coffee mug and a plate filled with yesterday's pinto beans still sat on the table. Flies swarmed all around; several rested on the beans.

Alex took the mug and the plate outside, scraped them off with a stick, and dipped them in the water trough. It wasn't the best way to wash dishes, but it would have to do. He brewed himself a pot of coffee then found another mug on a shelf. He set the mug at the far end of the table, away from the annoying buzz of the flies.

When the coffee was ready, he poured himself a cup and went out onto the front porch to think. He remembered another rocking chair that had belonged to his mother, and he recalled that when she wasn't sitting in it, he sometimes did. If his recollections were correct, he did his best thinking when he rested quietly and rocked.

He'd taken his first sip of coffee when he saw two riders in the distance. Alex sat up straight in his chair, peering out at the approaching riders. If he could see them, they could see him—if they were looking toward the house.

He hopped out of his chair, dashed inside, and cleaned up his mess as fast as he could. Then he ran out the back door.

His horse must have wandered off. By now the gelding was likely in the brush somewhere, eating that green grass the rains produced. With no chance to ride away now, he looked around.

A picket fence about three feet high ran from the floor to the ground, providing a skirt for the cabin and making it difficult to see anyone if they hid under the floor. Alex managed to crawl through one of two holes in the cabin's skirt.

It would be difficult for anyone to see him while he hid under the floor, and he planned to stay there until he decided what to do next. In the dark crawlspace Alex had a perfect view of the riders without fear of being seen.

A brown-skinned man rode up on...on Alex's black stallion! *What the...?*

His eyes widened in disbelief, and a blast of scorching rage filled every part of him. Alex had never expected to see his stud again. For a moment he sat there staring, unable to think or move.A gentle tug from the Lord reminded him of the Savior's love and sacrifice for sin. The wrath and vengeance inside him slowly faded, and he sat back against a wooden post, his heart pounding. He pulled his hat back from his brow and wiped his damp forehead with the back of his hand. It took a moment before his breathing returned to normal.

A woman rode one of Maggie's horses, and Alex realized it was Elena.

Alex swallowed. He wasn't surprised. Elena's nightly horseback rides made sense now. Was she meeting the lover she met at the water's edge in Bayview? And had Elena told that man where to find his black horse? Alex had followed Elena several times when she went riding at night, but until now he was never able to catch her.

The man shouted something to the woman, but Alex couldn't hear what was being said. Did the man and Elena have a quarrel?

Alex reached for his pistol but came up empty-handed. He'd left his pistol behind, probably in the camp house. What happened earlier with Maggie and her aunt must have made him careless and kind of crazy in the head. Without a gun he would have no protection if they fired on him.

Alex moved farther back into the shadows and prepared to wait, praying the bay horse wouldn't make any kind of a sound that might make Elena and the man suspicious. Oh, he intended to go inside the cabin and confront them, all right, but not just yet. When he did go in, he would be fully armed—with his pistol and the protection of God.

"See about the horses, Joe," he heard Elena say in Spanish, "and I'll cook us something to eat."

Joe? Didn't Aunt Violet call the preacher that married Alex and Sadie Pastor Joe?

"I want beans and fresh tortillas, my dear sweet sister, and hot coffee."

Sister? Was Elena Joe's sister? He'd assumed they were lovers.

"You'll eat whatever I can find, my not-so-sweet brother," Elena said with sarcasm. "And tonight when I light the candles with the curandero, all the evil spirits will fly away. But if I catch you looking at the *Señorita* Gallagher again with the eyes of lust, I will turn you in to the sheriff."

Alex's jaws hardened, and anger poured over him again. The man with Elena was Pastor Joe, and not only was he Elena's brother but he'd been watching Maggie with what Lupe called the evil eye. The realization that someone deceived him and stole his horse was bad enough. To know that person was also responsible for destroying his entire life infuriated him, and seeing that person face-to-face, knowing he also wanted to harm Maggie, made it worse. Alex's hands became fists, and the word *revenge* burst to the forefront of his mind.

He would like to punch Joe in that big mouth of his for all the things he'd done to Alex and to the Gallagher family. He had to force himself not to climb out from under that cabin and do what he had a mind to do right then. A man like Joe should be behind bars, and he intended to make sure he ended up there.

"And what will you tell the sheriff, Elena?" Joe asked with a sneer in his voice. Elena had climbed the steps to the front porch with Joe Garza right behind her.

Alex heard her say in Spanish, "I'll tell him about the bank you robbed. And don't forget the promise you made to me when we were living in Brownsville. If I got Alex and Miss Sadie to let you marry them, you'd share the money you got from the bank with me. No?"

At the sound of a door closing, Alex felt more secure, but his anger was growing. His whole body felt rigid. It was only when he reminded himself of his Savior that he was able to take control of his thoughts and emotions.

All sorts of memories filled his mind. At first they were jumbled together, but the longer he thought, the clearer they became.

He recalled his wedding to Sadie and the bank robbery the day afterward. He also remembered the pain and embarrassment he felt when he realized Joe was not an ordained minister as he'd claimed, meaning Alex's marriage to Sadie wasn't valid.

Alex might never know all the reasons Joe pretended to be a minister or why he performed an illegal marriage ceremony the day before he robbed a Brownsville bank. Maybe Joe thought joining Dee and Alex in matrimony in her home and in front of witnesses would make him appear legitimate to the local community and therefore harmless. Who would suspect a trusted minister of such a crime? The robber was an outlaw with a bandana over his face. Who would guess Pastor Joe was under that mask?

At the time Alex was furious. Now as he remembered the wrath he felt then, Alex recalled following Joe across the border into Mexico and then hiding behind a clump of trees while Joe hid the loot he'd stolen from the bank. Alex took special notice of exactly where the money was hidden, and after Joe had gone, he dug it up and buried it at another location not far away.

Alex had a vivid memory of the root of a tree, sticking partly out of the ground. He dug the hole under the root so that perhaps nobody would notice the ground was disturbed as the result of his digging, and he carved a small A for Alex on the trunk of the tree as a marker. Nobody would find the A unless they knew it was there.

He must have intended to return the money, but before he had the opportunity, he was arrested for having a fistfight with Joe. Alex and Joe both wound up in a Mexican jail. Three years later he was finally released. Frustrated and anxious to find the woman he still considered his wife, Alex went looking for Dee. When he found her, he'd planned to marry her in a church and then go back to Mexico, dig up the money, and return it to the bank in Brownsville.

Yet his memory still wasn't completely restored. Was it possible he dug up the loot before he came to the Gallagher Ranch and didn't remember? Could he have put part of it in his saddlebag, planning to return it later? If so where was the rest of the money? Had he hidden it somewhere else?

Alex felt heartsick for more reasons than one. His thoughts turned to Elena. She'd attended his wedding to Sadie in Brownsville and so had Maggie's aunt—and Aunt Violet had photographs to prove it.

There were things Maggie still didn't know, and Alex

intended to tell her what he'd learned and what he now remembered. Elena's lies needed to be exposed, and now that Alex recognized the man in the cabin as Pastor Joe, he must be exposed, too.

Could Joe Garza be the man who shot him? Was it Roger or someone else? If Joe was the one who took a shot at him, he must have arrived at the ranch before Alex did.

Curses rang out from the cabin above his head. Pots and pans banged and rattled against the wooden wall. Joe and his sister were having a huge fight. It was time for Alex to go back to the Gallagher Ranch and change things, but not without his black stallion.

It rained earlier, but it had stopped. He found the bay gelding in the brush not far from the cabin—saddled, ready, and eating grass.

Alex led the animal to the holding pen. The stallion snorted as he opened the gate. He glanced back to see if those in the cabin had heard. Fortunately Joe and Elena were so involved in their argument they likely couldn't hear a thing.

Alex looped his rope around the stallion's neck and led him out of the holding pen. Then he mounted the bay and rode away, pulling his stallion behind him. Despite a light rain he headed back to the ranch to talk to Maggie. But would she be willing to listen?

MAGGIE STOOD AT A PARLOR WINDOW, chewing her bottom lip and thinking. She'd paced back and forth from the kitchen to the north windows of the parlor dozens of times, looking outside for some indication Alex was coming. Would he come? Had he crossed the bridge at Gallagher Creek? She felt uneasy and discouraged, and it was all Alex's fault.

She secretly hoped that he would come back, and she knew

she still loved him and always would. But there was too much anger between them, anger that might never be resolved. Maggie turned away from the window, unwilling to dwell on that possibility.

Aunt Violet said terrible things about Alex, but her ravings evoked more questions than answers. Yet one fact remained: Alex had married her late sister, but the marriage wasn't a real one. She couldn't help but wonder if Alex knew who Dee really was all along.

Her aunt said Alex deserved to suffer for what he'd done to the Gallagher family, no matter how Maggie felt about him. Maggie didn't agree. She was angry with him, but that didn't mean she wanted him to suffer. But however confused she might be in her feelings toward Alex, one thing was certain: she would never surrender Jon Anthony regardless of the fact Alex was his father.

Sarah came in and joined Maggie at the north windows. "Mr. Lancaster is waiting for you on the back porch. He wants to talk to you."

"Do you mean he's here?" Maggie asked, feeling her eyes widen and her heart begin to race. "Now?"

Sarah nodded.

"He must have looped around and come by the back way," Maggie said more to herself than to Sarah. "Otherwise I would have seen him when he rode up."

But it didn't matter how he got there. Alex was waiting for her on the back porch.

Her insides fluttered just thinking about it. Her breath came in short gasps, and Maggie struggled with the desire to run, perhaps even hide in a bedroom until he left. But she needed to face him if only for a short time.

"All right," Maggie said after a moment. "Tell Mr. Lancaster I'll talk to him in the kitchen, but just for a minute. Make sure he knows that."

"Knows what?"

"Never mind. Just send him on in here. And as for you, Sarah, go to your room."

Maggie sat down in a kitchen chair, hoping she'd set her mouth in an uncompromising line. If she and Alex were to discuss Jon Anthony's future, it would not be with Sarah near enough to hear.

Sarah paused in the doorway as if she expected Maggie to explain herself. At last she went on. Moments later Alex appeared in the same doorway.

Maggie noticed worry lines on his handsome face. Concern and compassion crept over her as she watched him take a seat at the table. He probably noticed her brief smile when he sent her that half grin, but later she managed to put him in his place by refusing to return his full-blown smile.

"Would you like to go into the parlor to talk?" she asked.

"No, the kitchen's fine." He sat stiffly in a chair near hers. "My memory returned, Maggie, almost all of it. I can remember the important things now."

"Do you remember marrying my sister?"

He glanced down at his boots. "Yes."

"And?"

Alex shook his head as if he wanted to put off saying anything more.

"Well, if you came for Jon Anthony, you can forget it. I'll never give him up—not ever."

He lifted his head, and her heart squeezed at the sadness she saw in his eyes. "I would never ask you to do that. I shouldn't have said what I did. I know how much that boy means to you and that you'll teach him about the Lord. Homes are important, Maggie, and I'd never take him away from his."

Maggie swallowed. She felt better but not much.

"I knew Elena in Brownsville," Alex said. "She must have known everything that took place there with your sister. She could have explained everything. I don't know why she didn't. But it was Elena who introduced Dee and me to a fake minister by the name of Pastor Joe Garza. Now I know that Joe Garza is Elena's brother."

"Brother? The fake pastor is Elena's brother?"

"Yes. Pastor Joe could be a charming fellow when he wanted to be. In fact, he was so personable and charming I introduced him to some of my friends at the bank in Brownsville as the new minister in town. Joe needed a job, and they hired him at the bank to do the cleaning—because of me. Then he robbed that bank of ten thousand dollars."

He sighed as if the weight of his words took a toll on his strength. But he continued. "Joe became a close friend of Dee and me—I mean Sadie and me. Pastor Joe wanted to perform our wedding ceremony, and we agreed. He was our pastor after all. At the time his sermons seemed sound, but looking back I now think otherwise. Still we had no reason to think Joe wasn't who he said he was. But Elena knew the truth and wouldn't tell us."

"He really is her brother then?"

Alex nodded. "Elena knew I'd lost my memory. She could have cleared all this up the day I was shot. I'll bet even your aunt wonders why she didn't."

Maggie had no intentions of telling him that her aunt had indeed wondered and wanted Maggie to fire Elena at once. Alex was right about Elena. Was he right about Roger too?

If she told him what Aunt Violet had said, Alex could remind her that he was suspicious of Elena all along. Maggie would defend her earlier position, and another argument would be well on its way again. She decided not to pursue it.

Alex told Maggie all he could remember about his past and everything he saw and heard at the cabin earlier, including getting his black stud back. When he finished he got up, went to the kitchen door, and then stopped and looked back at Maggie.

Maybe he expected her to ask him to stay. When she didn't say another word, he walked slowly out the door. Maggie assumed he left because he thought she wanted him to go, and considering all that had happened, she couldn't afford to let Alex know she wanted him to stay—at least until she'd had time to think.

Was Alex telling the truth when he said he never intended to abandon Sadie and he really was in a Mexican jail for the last three years? She wanted to believe everything Alex told her, but she couldn't, not yet anyway. Too much depended on her actions. She needed to be sure she was right before she did anything.

Besides the candles Maggie thought of the lies Elena told the Gallagher family by simply not telling them anything. Her late father had called that the sin of omission. Alex said Elena and her brother were staying in Roger's cabin near the creek. Maybe Maggie would ride out there and take a look for herself.

31

A lex rode out to the cabin that night and hid under the floor again; only this time he carried a gun. It was a long night. He stayed awake as long as he could then dozed a little, off and on. Elena and Joe arrived early the next morning. Now he felt stiff from being crouched in the same position for so long.

Alex wondered where Elena and Joe had gone. What mischief were they involved in? He might never know.

He heard a thump, thump as feet hit the steps leading to the front porch. Alex inched his gun from its holster.

"What's the matter with you, Elena?" Joe said in Spanish. "We went to the house of what you say is the new curandero from Mexico. We stayed for the ceremony, using the candles our papa gave you, and you walked away. The curandero healed many. Why did you insult the grave of our late father by not staying to hear what the curandero had to say?"

"I've been attending meetings with Miss Gallagher and her little sister, Sarah, where we pray and study the Bible." Elena's voice had sounded hesitant at first, but it gained strength as she spoke. "Miss Gallagher says only God heals. That's why I left. What business is it of yours what I do, Jose?"

"You dishonored the memory of our papa."

Elena's tone changed instantly. "Hush! Someone's coming. We must go inside."

Alex heard hoof beats and the patter of shoes on the front porch. He crawled to the edge of the house, peering out through the second hole in the floor's picket skirting.

It was Roger. He dismounted, carrying a rifle. The front door banged shut.

Alex pointed his gun at Roger, watching as Roger hitched his gray horse to the hitching post to the right of the steps. He sucked in his breath. Roger stood only a few feet away. In addition to the rifle, Alex noticed six shooters attached to Roger's gun-belt, one on each side.

Alex's gun was cocked and ready. Earlier he'd noticed a crack in the floor where light came through, making it possible to see inside of the cabin. He crawled to the crack and peered upward. All he saw was the leg of a chair, but he could also hear every word they said.

"I stopped by the Gallagher ranch early this morning," Roger said in a loud voice, "and little Sarah let it slip that Alex is beginning to remember his past. It's time for Alex to die." His laugh sounded almost demonic. "I told you to kill him weeks ago. Which one of you snakes is willing to pull the trigger?"

Something bright blue caught Alex's attention. He glanced away from the crack for a moment. Maggie, wearing a pretty blue riding skirt, appeared in the clearing not thirty feet from the cabin. She'd tied her horse to a tree and was walking straight toward the house.

Alex tensed. No telling what Roger and his crew would do if they saw her there. Somehow he must warn her. He aborted his plan to draw on them.

He crawled back to the edge of the floor near the porch

where the second hole was located. He knew better than to say anything to Maggie. Any strange sounds might alert the ones inside. He took out a white handkerchief, fastened it to a stick he found, and poked it through the hole, waving it like a flag of surrender. He could only pray Maggie would notice and retreat before it was too late.

She stopped in time to keep from scaring off a reddish hen or stepping on one of her chicks, parading in front of her. Alex saw her glance in the direction of the handkerchief. She frowned, looking puzzled.

Alex dropped the flag and crawled partway out from under the flooring. Her eyes widened as she peered at him. Alex put his forefinger over his mouth, motioning for her to backtrack.

Hands on her hips Maggie didn't speak or move, but the hen clucked to her baby chicks, and the yellow chicks peeped in reply. A cow mooed in the distance, and soon angry voices shouted from inside the cabin.

Maggie paused an instant longer while Alex crawled all the way out from under the house. Then he followed her into the underbrush. The shouting coming from inside the cabin blocked other sounds. Had God provided yet another distraction?

"What's going on?" Maggie demanded.

"Speak softly, please," he whispered. "And I might ask you the same thing. What are you doing here?"

"I stayed up all night, waiting for Elena to come back. She never did. Early this morning I tracked her here."

Alex shook his head. "Was that wise, Maggie? Roger's inside and well armed. I heard Roger tell Elena and her brother to kill me."

"Kill you?"

"Yes. Roger wants me dead. I was about to draw on them when I saw you. I think Roger's the one who shot me, and Elena and Joe Garza are working for him. Now that you're here, I'll have to protect you, making it twice as hard for me to capture them. You should have stayed at the ranch where you belong."

"Maybe. Maybe not." Maggie gestured toward the field behind her. "See those clumps of weeds there? One of my men is behind every one of them, and they're armed. If that's not good enough for you, I also sent Lupe to bring the sheriff and his men. They should be here any minute. I'd say Roger and the other two inside are outnumbered, wouldn't you?"

Alex grinned. "If you say so, boss lady. But right now I have serious business to attend to. Would you be so kind as to stand behind that tree there and out of sight while I—"

Before he could finish his sentence, the sheriff and two of his men appeared in the distance. Those inside must have seen them too because someone fired at them through a window.

Alex pulled Maggie to the ground. Another shot rang out. Sheriff Ethridge didn't seem intimidated by the shots. He and his men galloped on toward the cabin.

Standing up, Alex shouted, "Come out of there, Dawson, and the rest of you outlaws. You're surrounded." He turned to Maggie's men. "Show 'em your rifles, cowboys. Hold 'em up high so these outlaws can see 'em. Let's put this bunch of crooks behind bars."

Maggie's men held their rifles above their heads.

Someone from inside fired again, and the bullet hit a fencepost not far from Beto's head.

"All right, Dawson!" Alex shouted. "Now come out with your hands up before we blast you out."

The door to the cabin opened a crack. A stick with a woman's white petticoat hanging from it was waved out the doorway. But Alex was unable to see the hand holding the makeshift flag.

"You're more of a coward than I thought, Dawson," Alex said in a loud voice, "hiding behind a woman's clothes. Now come out of there with your hands up like a man."

Hands above her head, Elena was the first to come out on the porch.

"So it's ladies first, huh?" Alex pointed his gun toward the door, waiting for the other two to join her. "You heard what I said, Dawson. You two no-goods, come out and join Elena, or you'll wish you had."

Joe came out, followed by Roger, just as the sheriff and his men rode up.

Maggie stood; without warning she burst into tears.

"What's wrong, Maggie?" Alex asked, reaching out to steady her.

"The...the man on the porch with... Roger," she said in a shaky voice. "At first I thought he was the man who attacked us that day when I...when I was fifteen."

"Is he?" Alex put his arms around Maggie as the sheriff tied up the three criminals. "Is that the man who harmed you?"

She shook her head. "No. I can see him better now, and I was wrong. It isn't him."

Alex held Maggie close. At last she stopped shaking. Maggie felt soft and warm in his arms, reminding him of—of Dee.

His chest tightened. Delayed sadness and grief invaded his mind, and Alex realized he needed time to mourn for his late wife. But would Maggie be willing to wait until he was ready?

"I still care for you, Maggie." His voice choked with pent-up emotion. "And I know when this is all over you're the one I want to spend the rest of my life with. But I remember Dee now. And I need—"

"Time to grieve." She spoke the words for him, with passion and deep understanding. "Oh, Alex, of course you need time. Anyone would in your situation."

She put one hand on the back of his head and the other on his shoulder. Nobody appeared to notice when they embraced.

MAGGIE HAD NEVER LOVED Alex more, and she'd promised to wait for him. But people change. Would he come back to her one day? Would she ever see him again?

Shortly before the sheriff and his men left to take the criminals to jail, Lupe arrived with the wagon. Maggie suggested Lupe and Beto ride their horses back to ranch headquarters while she and Alex rode back together in the wagon Lupe brought from the ranch. There were things she wanted to say to Alex, and she might never have another chance.

"All right, Maggie," Alex agreed. "We'll go back in the wagon."

Almost as soon as the wheels began to turn, Maggie's good intentions disappeared along with all the meaningful discussions she'd hoped they would share. Instead of words spoken, her mind exploded with scattered thoughts and worries.

She was glad Alex cared enough for her late sister to grieve for her. But she hoped and prayed the mourning process would be shortened and Alex would turn to her again very soon.

As the wagon bumped and squeaked through the tall grass, Maggie gazed at his mouth, and a feeling of shyness crept over her. It embarrassed her to realize she still wanted him to kiss her. Quickly she glanced ahead so he wouldn't catch her blushing. She couldn't let Alex know what she was thinking or how lonesome and vulnerable she felt.

At last she turned and asked, "Are you all right, Alex?"

"As right as I'm going to be for a while."

"Don't feel guilty because of what happened to Sadie. I know now it wasn't your fault."

"Wasn't it?"

Maggie wanted to say more, but the words stuck in her throat. At last she said, "You're leaving for sure now, aren't you?"

"Yes, I am. I have to."

She pressed her lips together in a fine line, considering whether to ask when he would return. She still wanted a date to dream on. The thought of him leaving, perhaps forever, made it impossible for her to say anything.

Alex looked straight down the road as she'd done earlier. She wondered what he was thinking. It was five miles back to the big house, but she didn't say another word.

When they got to the corral gate, Alex put down the reins as if he intended to get out.

"No," Maggie insisted, "let me open the gate."

"I'll have to get out anyway to help you down."

"Not this time, you won't."

Maggie grabbed hold of her skirt, preparing to leap to the ground. Out of the corner of her eye, she saw Little Lupe, standing at the gate beside his grandmother, Concha. They waved, and Maggie waved back.

"Well, bless his heart," Maggie said. "Little Lupe's going to open the gate for us."

A smile curved the boy's wide mouth as Alex guided the mules through to the other side.

"Nice young man," Alex commented.

"Yes, he is. Concha is nice too."

Alex appeared to feign a painful scowl. "Are you sure?" A grin replaced his fake frown, warming his handsome face. "Concha's a fine lady, Maggie. I've known that for a long time."

Gloom covered her, but she tried to hide it.

A group of people had gathered in the center of the corral. Now she'd have to share him with others. She studied an unfamiliar wagon. A man she didn't know stood with Aunt Violet, Sarah, Jon Anthony, and the sheriff. The sheriff's men and some of her cowboys waited off to the side.

Maggie squinted for a better look. "Alex, who's the stranger in the sombrero?"

"Why, it's Juan Villa. He was my boss when I worked at his

ranch in Mexico." A hint of expectation freshened his smile. "I
didn't know I remembered him until I saw him just now."

As they moved in closer, the sheriff trotted his gray horse to
the wagon and gestured for them to stop. "Ma'am." The sheriff
tipped his hat at Maggie. "We'll be taking my prisoners to
Bayview now. I was kinda wondering, Miss Maggie, if I could
borrow your extra wagon."

"Of course."

"That's mighty neighborly of you. Thank you kindly."

"I'm glad I can help. And Sheriff, what's to become of my
maid, Elena? She's a mischief-maker for sure, and I will never
allow her in my house again. But she's been studying the Bible
and praying with Sarah and me pretty often lately. Despite all
she's done to me and my family, maybe there's good in her after
all. Is she going to jail?"

"I'm taking her in partly because she's a witness to several
crimes. But we'll see what happens. And of course I'll let you
know what we find out." He turned his attention to Alex. "And
what are you going to do, Mr. Lancaster, now that you're free of
all those charges against you?"

"I'll be looking for a home. I never really had one after my pa
died in the war."

"Well, don't spend too much time looking," the sheriff said
with a grin. "You might find one right under your nose."

As ALEX TIED up the reins, he couldn't stop looking at Maggie
and thinking about her. All at once the story of Jacob and
Rachel and a Bible verse from the Book of Genesis popped into
his mind.

*And Laban had two daughters: the name of the elder was Leah and
the name of the younger was Rachel.*

Maggie's father had three daughters, and Alex loved all

three. He even fell in love with two of them. The name of the oldest was Sadie, and the name of the younger was Maggie.

Still perched beside Maggie on the wagon seat and thinking about how he loved two women at the same time, another scripture came to him. But it wasn't about a man's love for a woman; it was about God's love for the world and all mankind.

For God so love the world, that he gave his only begotten Son, that whosoever believeth in him should not perish, but have everlasting life.

He heard that scripture verse for the first time when he was a young child attending a church service with his mother. After the pastor read that scripture to the congregation, he said, "If you believe in the Lord, you must also follow Him."

When they got home that day, Alex had asked his mother what *believe* and *follow* meant.

"Believe means to surrender, Alex," he remembered her saying. "Give up doing things your way and live your life as the Bible says. Your earthly father is stronger and wiser than you are, and even though he's away fighting a war, you must do what he told you to do before he left. In the same way Christians believe the Lord is wiser than we are, and we must surrender our lives to Him and do things *His* way."

He had listened intently as his mother continued. "Remember that time you got a bad belly ache, and Doctor Billings gave me some medicine to make you all better? Well, if I hadn't believed it would work, I would have thrown away that nasty-tasting medicine. But I *did* believe it would work, so I made you hold your nose and take it." His mother had looked down at him and patted him on the shoulder.

"And remember that picnic Grandma had at the beach when you and your cousins played follow-the-leader? Your cousin Wyatt was the leader. Everybody there knew who the leader was. But only you kids did what Wyatt did. According to the rules of the game, knowing who the leader is isn't enough. You must also do what the leader does.

"The same is true when following the Lord. Jesus is our leader. Jesus follows God the Father, and we follow Jesus. It's not enough to know who Jesus is. You must do what Jesus does, and the only way you can do that is to repent of your sins, read and study the Bible, and pray. As I said, Jesus is our leader, and we must follow Him."

"Is something wrong?" Maggie asked, cutting into his reflections. "You've been sitting there, staring."

"I've been remembering." Alex smiled. "It's nice I'm able to do that now." He went around and lifted Maggie down from the wagon for maybe the last time.

Nobody seemed to notice because everybody was standing in the middle of the corral, all talking at once. Then as if reminded they hurried toward Maggie.

Everybody hugged her except the ranch hands and Mr. Villa. Alex was still lost in his thoughts and memories until he noticed that Mr. Villa, the man Maggie called the stranger, stood apart from the others. He should go over, speak to him, and introduce Maggie to him.

"Maggie." Alex reached out and gently touched her arm. "I'd like you to know Juan Villa."

Maggie looked at Juan. "I'm glad to meet you, *Señor*. I've heard of you. In fact I wrote you a letter once."

"I know, *Señorita*," Juan said. "And I would have answered it, but I've been in Central America buying cattle for my ranch. I read your letter for the first time a week ago when I returned."

"Thank you for telling us," Maggie said. "That explains a lot of things."

"Yes." Alex nodded. "It does."

Juan turned to Alex. "I talked to you, *Señor* Alex, right after you were released from jail. I gave you the money I owed you, and I gave you a letter from your sister. Do you remember that now?"

"Yes, I think I do. That was thirty dollars you gave me, wasn't it?"

"Si."

More memories from his past tumbled into his conscious mind like water from a windmill flowing into a wooden tank.

"I gave you the back pay I owed you the day you were released from jail," Juan explained.

Alex smiled. *The money was mine, after all.*

"I lost my memory for a while," Alex explained. "Got hit on the head. So when I found money in my saddlebag, I wondered where it came from. Thanks for telling me."

"You told me about your marriage to Dee," Juan added, "and about the fight you had with the robber in order to get back the stolen money. And you said you buried the money in Mexico and planned to return it after you found your wife." Juan hesitated. "You are a good man, Alex Lancaster—always reading your Bible. Because of you, I read my Bible too now."

Alex smiled as more memories filled his mind to overflowing.

"You will collect a big reward, *Señor* Alex," Juan continued, "when you return the money Joe Garza stole from the bank in Brownsville."

Alex swallowed. He had no interest in any kind of a reward, but Juan's words confirmed what he thought the Lord was telling him. He would go back to Mexico, dig up the money, and return it. In the process he would have time to heal, to think about everything that happened and decide what to do next.

On the drive back to ranch headquarters earlier, Alex had allowed his gaze to rove longingly over the vast acres of the Gallagher lands. He hadn't realized how much he'd come to love the place and especially the people who lived there. Still he knew in his bones he must leave now. Alex had to believe the Lord had a purpose for calling him to leave Maggie and his son behind, or he would never have found the strength to do it.

After he returned the money, he would pay a visit to his sister in San Antonio, and then he would see where the Lord led him after that.

Before he left the ranch, Alex rode the black stallion out to the ranch cemetery and put flowers on Dee's grave. Her name was written there—Sadie Gallagher. A lump formed deep in his throat. *It should read Sadie Gallagher Lancaster.*

He'd loved Sadie deeply, and he still did. But he loved Maggie too. It would be hard to ride away, leaving Maggie and the children behind, but he really had no choice.

32

Maggie stood on the front porch of the big house, thinking about the day she found Alex all bloody and covered with dirt. He left six months ago, and she hadn't seen him since. As she stood there remembering and contemplating, a cloud of dust appeared in the distance. Someone was coming.

She'd only received two short letters from Alex since he rode off into the sunset, and she doubted he'd show up at the ranch without writing first. By now Alex would have completed his visit with his sister in San Antonio. Who knew where he would go next?

The approaching rider was probably Lupe. She had sent him to town to check the mail in case she received a letter from Alex. On the other hand, if her dreams were about to come true, the rider was Alex.

She prayed then. By the time she finished, Sarah, Jon Anthony, and Aunt Violet had joined her on the porch. Maggie and Aunt Violet and the children had recently returned from Bayview where they attended Zoe Dawson's wedding.

On the very next evening, they witnessed a second wedding, the marriage of Jed McGregor and Belinda Foster, the young woman Jed had loved for so long. Once during Jed's ceremony Maggie thought she saw tears in Sarah's eyes, and she didn't think it had anything to do with Sarah's good hopes for Jed and Belinda as a couple. Maggie could only hope it was the end of her sister's girlhood fondness for Jed McGregor, a man much too old for her. And now he had a wife.

On the drive back to the ranch, her aunt had spent an enormous amount of time discussing the outcome of Roger's and Joe's trials in Brownsville. Maggie was glad both men were behind bars and Elena had gone back to Mexico, but she was tired of hearing about it.

Aunt Violet had packed her bags and would be leaving the next morning after another of her extended visits, and Maggie couldn't say she was sorry to see her go. Though her aunt wasn't talking against Alex anymore, she wasn't singing his praises either, and Maggie refused to hear or think anything unkind about Alex Lancaster.

Maggie peered at the north pasture again. She could almost see the rider now. He was mounted on a black horse.

A black horse?

Her breath caught. Maggie shut her eyes, praying in earnest.

"Why, it's Mr. Lancaster!" Sarah pointed toward the rider. "I'd know that black horse anywhere."

Joy bubbled up from deep inside Maggie's heart. She'd allowed herself to hope and pray the rider would be Alex; now she knew for certain he had returned.

Aunt Violet's sigh was long and deep. "Yes, it's Alexander all right." She turned to Maggie. "So what are you going to do now? Forgive him?"

"I already have."

It was another few minutes before he arrived at the yard gate. Maggie stood, waiting, along with the rest of her family. Alex dismounted, tipped his hat, and tied his stud to the yard fence.

Juan Villa had said that Alex would receive a reward when he returned the stolen money, but the only reward Maggie wanted was Alex and the children. She simply wasn't sure he still cared. He could have come to tell her he would never see her again.

Alex stopped a few feet from her, pulling something small from the pocket of his trousers. When he held it up, Maggie could see it was a carved whistle like the one he used to call her with when he was too ill to get out of bed.

She'd thought he was probably so broken by Sadie's death he was unable to care for her anymore. So why had Alex returned? And what was he doing with that wooden whistle of all things?

He'd held in his true feelings before they declared their love for each other. Was he doing it again?

Alex's smile rippled across the space that separated them, and then he put the whistle to his lips. Slowly he blew. The sound appeared to go on and on.

Aunt Violet eyed Maggie as if she were accusing her of a crime. "Maggie, why is Alexander blowing that silly whistle?"

"I'm not sure."

As soon as she said it, Maggie sensed Alex needed her and was calling her to his side again. She rushed toward him and threw her arms around him in front of God, her nephew, her sister, and her aunt.

"I love you, Alex Lancaster, and I always will."

His eyes danced as he looked down at her. "I love you too, Miss Maggie Gallagher."

Jon Anthony broke loose from Aunt Violet's hand and slipped between Alex and Maggie.

Aunt Violet frowned. "Come back here, Jon Anthony."

He shook his head, craning his neck and looking upward. "I need a hug, too."

Alex laughed and so did Maggie.

Slowly the edges of Aunt Violet's lips turned up, giving her wrinkled face a pleasant expression. It wasn't a true smile, but it was one Maggie hoped Alex could accept.

He gazed down at Maggie again, with love and joy and a promise of the future wrapped in the tender gleam in his blue eyes. "Will you marry me, Maggie?"

She nodded without hesitation. "Yes. Oh yes, Alex, I will."

Hearing Alex say he still loved her and wanted to marry her wiped away all her doubts, sealing Maggie's heart forever and allowing love and happiness to burst forth. Alex continued to smile as he motioned for Sarah to join them, and the four of them embraced as a family for the first time.

"Sorry I couldn't make it back in time for your birthday, Sarah," Alex said, winking at her. "Did you have a happy birthday?"

"Yes, but it would have been better if you had been here." She grinned.

"I appreciate that. So how do you like riding a full-grown horse?" He returned her grin. "Pretty special, isn't it?"

"It's wonderful, and I named him Brown-Boy. I gave Short Legs to Jon Anthony."

"That's good. He'll need a horse, same as I did when I was his age. And Sarah, I carved something especially for your birthday, late as it is. It's a jewelry box, and it's in my saddlebag."

"Thank you, Mr. Cowboy." Her smile widened and she ducked her head. "I mean, Mr. Lancaster."

"You're welcome. And Maggie, I have something in that saddlebag for you too."

Maggie gazed up at him and smiled, but she couldn't find the words to speak.

"It's a wedding ring," he said. "I never had a real home as a child, and all my life I've wanted one. It wasn't until I left here that it dawned on me that my true home is where God is, and where you and the children are."

"Yes," Maggie said softly. "I agree completely."

His gaze gentled even more. "I felt guilty for loving you, Maggie, because of what happened to Dee. But I want you at my side, and I'm not taking no for an answer."

"You won't have to because I need you at my side too."

Alex kissed her for the first time. When he finally pulled back, love seemed to flow from her heart to his.

"By having the three of you," he said, "God has given me the desires of my heart." He leaned over and kissed her lightly on the cheek. "As I said, I'm home, Maggie. It's time. And no matter where God leads us, we'll always be together."

"Forever and ever?" Maggie whispered.

"Yes, forever and ever, amen."

AUTHOR'S HISTORICAL NOTES:

When the Cowboy Rides Away is a western romance novel set in the ranching country of South Texas near the Gulf coast. This area of Texas was once called the Nueces Strip, named for the Nueces River. It was also called the Wild Horse Desert, and the entire area has a hot and humid semi-tropical climate. Yet some of the largest ranches in the country, if not the world, are located in the area of Southern Texas where this story takes place.

The Famous King Ranch is said to be larger than the state of Rhode Island, and today it is headquartered in the town of Kingsville or about forty-five miles southwest of Corpus Christi. Twenty-five or so miles farther south from Kingsville is the headquarters of the huge Kenedy Ranch.

Many of the cowhands on these ranches came from Mexico. Even today, some of them and their families practice a kind of religion that combines Christianity and witchcraft known as the curandero or the *curandera*.

When the Cowboy Rides Away is a work of fiction, and it is set on a South Texas Ranch in 1880. At that time and even later, it was possible to travel on horseback or on foot from the area where the King Ranch is located all the way to the Rio Grande River without seeing a town of any kind, simply by journeying from one ranch to the next.

The cowboy is fading into American history, along with the frontier spirit that made that time and place so special. However, those that visit South Texas can find it again—if they know where to look.

STUDY/DISCUSSION QUESTIONS

1. What is the significance of the title, When the Cowboy Rides Away?

2. What is the book's major theme?

3. Where does the dark moment occur in the novel?

4. At what point does the climax occur?

5. In what way is the black stallion a symbol in the novel?

6. Name some characters' actions that come full circle during the course of the novel.

7. Identify some conflicts that were resolved by the end of the story.

8. How did the inspirational aspects of this novel affect you with regard to your enjoyment of the novel as a whole?

ABOUT MOLLY NOBLE BULL

I am a wife, a mother of three sons, a grandmother, and the daughter and granddaughter of ranch managers, real Texas cowboys. I spent part of my growing up years on a 60,000-acre cattle ranch in South Texas where *When the Cowboy Rides Away* is set. I know cowboys, and many of my ranch scenes were written from first-hand experience. A popular country song warns mamas not to let their babies grow up to be cowboys, but all three of our sons did just that.

MORE HISTORICAL ROMANCE FROM SCRIVENINGS PRESS

Books Afloat

Columbia River Undercurrents

Book One

Blaming herself for her childhood role in the Oklahoma farm truck accident that cost her grandfather's life, Anne Mettles is determined to make her life count. She wants to do it all–captain her library boat and resist Japanese attacks to keep America safe. But failing her pilot's exam requires her to bring others onboard.

Will she go it alone? Or will she team with the unlikely but (mostly) lovable characters? One is a saboteur, one an unlikely hero, and one, she discovers, is the man of her dreams.

The Rancher's Legacy

Homeward Trails

Book One - Coming February 23, 2021

Available for pre-order now!

Matthew Anderson and his father try to help neighbor Bill Maxwell when his ranch is attacked. On the day his daughter Rachel is to return from school back East, outlaws target the Maxwell ranch. After Rachel's world is shattered, she won't even consider the plan her father and Matt's cooked up—to see their two children marry and combine the ranches.

Meanwhile in Maine, sea captain's widow Edith Rose hires a private investigator to locate her three missing grandchildren. The children were abandoned by their father nearly twenty years ago. They've been adopted into very different families, and they're scattered across the country. Can investigator Ryland Atkins find them all while the elderly woman still lives? His first attempt is to find the boy now called Matthew Anderson. Can Ryland survive his trip into the wild Colorado Territory and find Matt before the outlaws finish destroying a legacy?

Ring of Death

Cozy Mystery

Dorey Cameron just wants to do her job. But that's nearly impossible when her dental patients don't show up for appointments. The bizarre accidents causing them not to appear can't be a coincidence. Someone is sabotaging her. But why?

Things take a terrible turn when vandalism, mugging and murder have the police pointing the finger at Dorey. Something in her possession must be worth killing for. If Dorey can't figure out the mystery in time, will she be the next victim?

September Shadows

Book One - Justice, Montana Series

A mystery

After the sudden death of their parents, Jess Thomas and her sisters, Sly and Maggie, start creating a new life for themselves. But when Sly is accused of a crime she didn't commit, the young sisters are threatened with separation through foster care. Jess is determined to prove Sly's innocence, even at the cost of her own life.

Cole McBride has been Jess's best friend since they were children. Now his feelings are deepening, just as Jess takes risks to protect her family. Can Cole convince Jess to trust him–and God–to help her?

Scrivenings
PRESS
Quench your thirst for story.
www.ScriveningsPress.com

Stay up-to-date on your favorite books and authors with our free e-newsletters.

ScriveningsPress.com

,

www.ingramcontent.com/pod-product-compliance
Lightning Source LLC
Chambersburg PA
CBHW060620100726
47907CB00006B/1706